RPS / 2044

RPS / 2044

An Oral History of the next American Revolution

Miguel Guevara & Michael Albert

Interviewees: Lydia Luxemburg, Bertrand Dellinger, Juliet Berkman, Andrej Goldman, Senator Malcolm King, Governor Celia Curie, Harriet Lennon, Rev. Stephen Du Bois, Cynthia Parks, Mayor Bill Hampton, Barbara Bethune, Mark Feynman, Anton Rocker, Peter Cabral, Robin Kuntsler, Leslie Zinn, Noam Carmichael, & Dylan Cohen

Copyright © 2017 by Michael Albert

A Z Communications Book, First Edition
Z Communications
215 Atlantic Avenue
Hull, Mass 02045

https://zcomm.org/znet/

Library of Congress Cataloging in Publication Data
Albert, Michael, 1947- RPS / 2044: An Oral History of the Next American Revolution
ISBN-13: 9781975772437
All rights reserved.
ISBN: 1975772431

Oh, the fishes will laugh
As they swim out of the path
And the seagulls they'll be smiling
And the rocks on the sand
Will proudly stand
The hour that the ship comes in

And the words that are used
For to get the ship confused
Will not be understood as they're spoken
For the chains of the sea
Will have busted in the night
And will be buried at the bottom of the ocean

- Bob Dylan

TABLE OF CONTENTS

Foreword ································· xi
In his own United States, in his own 2040, Miguel Guevara began questioning eighteen prominent revolutionaries...
Video Playlist ···························· xv
Can a music playlist usefully accompany an oral history?
Introduction ····························· xxi
From 2030 to 2036 I wrote over 500 topical essays.
Selected Timeline ······················· xxiii
Selected RPS events, project's, and campaigns by year.

CHAPTER 1 **First Steps** ························· 1
Juliet Berkman and Andrej Goldman discuss the first major march and boycotts.

CHAPTER 2 **Overcoming Cynicism** ················ 15
Juliet Berkman, Senator Malcolm King, and Andrej Goldman discuss overcoming resistance, and early momentum.

CHAPTER 3 **Getting Started** ···················· 23
Andrej Goldman and Bill Hampton discuss hope, activism, and program.

CHAPTER 4 **2016** ······························ 39
Senator Malcolm King discusses the 2016 Election.

CHAPTER 5 **Reacting to Trump** ·················· 49
Andrej Goldman and Senator Malcolm King discuss Trump winning.

Chapter 6	**The First Convention** ·······················58
	Andrej Goldman, Senator Malcolm King, and Cynthia Parks, recall the first convention and its immediate aftermath.
Chapter 7	**Initial Commitments** ······················69
	Cynthia Parks and Andrej Goldman discuss vision, structure, and program.
Chapter 8	**Forming Chapters** ························82
	Cynthia Parks and Andrej Goldman discuss building RPS chapters.
Chapter 9	**Housing and Rights to the City** ···············90
	Bill Hampton, Cynthia Parks, and Harriet Lennon discuss transportation, housing, and rights to the city.
Chapter 10	**Actor's Activism** ························101
	Celia Curie discusses Hollywood activism.
Chapter 11	**Health and Class** ························113
	Barbara Bethune and Mark Feynman discuss the initial emergence of the health front and class conceptions.
Chapter 12	**Athletics and Religion** ····················132
	Peter Cabral and Stephen Du Bois discuss athletic and religious renovation.
Chapter 13	**Courageous Courtrooms** ···················145
	Robin Kunstler and Peter Cabral discuss legal upheaval.
Chapter 14	**Media Makeovers** ························153
	Leslie Zinn discusses media makeovers.
Chapter 15	**Economic Campaigns** ·····················162
	Anton Rocker discusses minimum wage and workplace organizing.
Chapter 16	**Concepts** ······························170
	Lydia Luxemburg discusses ideas at the heart of RPS.
Chapter 17	**Values** ·······························184
	Bertrand Dellinger and Lydia Luxembourg discuss values at the heart of RPS.

CHAPTER 18 **Defining Ourselves** · 197
Dylan Cohen, Malcom King, Lydia Luxemburg, Bill Hampton, and Barbara Bethune discuss shadow government.

CHAPTER 19 **Gender and Race** · 211
Juliet Berkman, Bill Hampton, Lydia Luxemburg, Cynthia Parks, Noam Carmichael, and Peter Cabral discuss gender and race.

CHAPTER 20 **Class** · 228
Mark Feynman, Lydia Luxemburg, and Juliet Berkman discuss class.

CHAPTER 21 **Leadership, Pace, Solidarity** · · · · · · · · · · · · · · · · 240
Robin Kunstler, Celia Curie, and Noam Carmichael, address leadership, pace, and solidarity.

CHAPTER 22 **Reforms, Revolution, Violence** · · · · · · · · · · · · · · 250
Lydia Luxemburg, Andrej Goldman, Peter Cabral, and Juliet Berkman discuss reforms, revolution, and violence.

CHAPTER 23 **Elections** · 259
Mayor Bill Hampton, Celia Curie, Lydia Luxemburg, Bertrand Dellinger, and Malcolm King discuss electoral participation.

CHAPTER 24 **Political and Kinship Vision** · · · · · · · · · · · · · · · · · 271
Bertrand Dellinger and Lydia Luxemburg discuss Political and Kinship Vision.

CHAPTER 25 **Economic and Cultural Vision** · · · · · · · · · · · · · · · 283
Andrej Goldman, Peter Cabral, Lydia Luxemburg, and Bertrand Dellinger discuss economic and cultural vision.

CHAPTER 26 **Media Seeds** · 297
Bertrand Dellinger, Mark Feynman, and Leslie Zinn discuss media future.

CHAPTER 27 **Health and Justice Seeds** · · · · · · · · · · · · · · · · · · · 306
Barbara Bethune, Mark Feynman, and Robin Kunstler, discuss health and justice future.

Chapter 28 **Education and Economy Seeds** · · · · · · · · · · · · · · · 315
Bertrand Dellinger, Anton Rocker, and Harriet Lennon discuss education and economy future.

Chapter 29 **World and Planet** · 330
Bertrand Dellinger, Dylan Cohen, and Stephen Du Bois discuss international relations and ecology.

Chapter 30 **Ship Ahoy** · 337
Miguel Guevara has a few final words.

Afterword · 339
Did our oral history move you? Did its participants make useful observations?

Postscript · 341
In November 2044, Senator Malcolm King interviewed after being elected President of the U.S. with his running mate, Governor Celia Curie.

Addendum · 349
Excerpt from Miguel Guevara's Press Briefing, April 9, 2045.

The Interviewees · 351
A brief biographic list of this oral history's eighteen interviewees in the order they first appear in the book.

FOREWORD
By Michael Albert

In his own United States, in his own 2040, Miguel Guevara began questioning eighteen prominent revolutionaries about their Revolution for a Participatory Society (RPS). From the resulting interviews, Guevara stitched together an oral history, *RPS/2044*.

Guevara lives on an "alt earth" whose initial divergence from our earth shuffled people, morphed names, tweaked events, and shifted time 28 years. Alt earth's 2016 closely resembled our 2016, but when we endured 2016, alt earth enjoyed 2044. Our future won't mimic their past, but could their experience inform ours? Could their commitment inspire and incite ours?

An eye blink ago, in our own 2016, 52 activists and 2,000 additional advocates signed a statement titled, "We Stand for Peace and Justice."

> "We stand for peace and justice. We see an organized anti worker, anti minority, anti immigrant, anti woman, anti LGBTQ, anti ecological, pro imperial, incarceration minded, surveillance employing, authoritarian reaction proliferating around the world. It calls itself right wing populist but is arguably more accurately termed neofascist. It preys on fear as well as often warranted anger. It manipulates and misleads with false promises and outright lies. It is trying to create an international alliance. Courageous responses are emerging and will proliferate around issue after issue, and in country after country. These responses will challenge the unworthy emotions, the vicious lies, and the vile policies. They will reject right wing rollback and repression. But to ward off an international,

multi issue, reactionary assault shouldn't we be internationalist and multi issue? Shouldn't we reject reaction but also seek positive, forward looking, inspiring progress? To those ends:

"We stand for the growing activism on behalf of progressive change around the world, and their positive campaigns for a better world, and we stand against the rising reactionary usurpers of power around the world and their lies, manipulations, and policies.

"We stand for peace, human rights, and international law against the conditions, mentalities, institutions, weapons and dissemination of weapons that breed and nurture war and injustice.

"We stand for healthcare, education, housing, and jobs against war and military spending. We stand for internationalism, indigenous, and native rights, and a democratic foreign policy against empire, dictatorship, and political and religious fundamentalism.

"We stand for justice against economic, political, and cultural institutions that promote huge economic and power inequalities, corporate domination, privatization, wage slavery, racism, gender and sexual hierarchy, and the devolution of human kindness and wisdom under assault by celebrated authority and enforced passivity.

"We stand for democracy and autonomy against authoritarianism and subjugation. We stand for prisoner rights against prison profiteering. We stand for participation against surveillance. We stand for freedom and equity against repression and control.

"We stand for national sovereignty against occupation and apartheid. We oppose overtly brutal regimes everywhere. We oppose less overtly brutal but still horribly constricting electoral subversion, government and corporate surveillance, and mass media manipulation.

"We stand for equity against exploitation by corporations of their workers and consumers and by empires of subordinated countries. We stand for solidarity of and with the poor and the excluded everywhere.

"We stand for diversity against homogeneity and for dignity against racism. We stand for multi-cultural, internationalist, community rights, against cultural, economic, and social repression of immigrants and other subordinated communities in our own countries and around the world.

"We stand for gender equality against misogyny and machismo. We stand for sexual freedom against sexual repression, homogenization, homophobia, and transphobia.

"We stand for ecological wisdom against the destruction of forests, soil, water, environmental resources, and the biodiversity on which all life depends. We stand for ecological sanity against ecological suicide.

"We stand for a world whose political, economic, and social institutions foster solidarity, promote equity, maximize participation, celebrate diversity, and encourage full democracy.

"We will not be a least common denominator single issue or single focus coalition. We will be a massive movement of movements with a huge range of concerns, ideas, and aims, united by what we stand for and against.

"We will enjoy and be strengthened by shared respect and mutual aid while we together reject sectarian hostilities and posturing.

"We stand for and pledge to work for peace and justice."

Here is a list of the *We Stand* Statement's Initial Signers:

M. Adams U.S., Ezequiel Adamovsky Argentina, Michael Albert U.S., Vilma Almendra Colombia, Bridget Anderson UK, Omar Barghouti Palestine, Walden Bello Philippines, Medea Benjamin U.S., Peter Bohmer U.S., Leah Bolger U.S., Patrick Bond South Africa, Jeremy Brecher U.S., Leslie Cagan U.S., Adam Carpinelli U.S., Avi Chomsky U.S., Noam Chomsky U.S., Marjorie Cohn U.S., Steve Early U.S., Mark Evans UK, Bill Fletcher U.S., Lindsey German UK, Angela M. Gilliam U.S., Linda Gordon U.S., Andrej Grubacic, U.S., David Hartsough U.S., Chaia Heller U.S., Pervez Hoodbhoy Pakistan, Kathy Kelly U.S., Joanne Landy U.S., Dan Leahy U.S., Rabbi Michael Lerner U.S., Mairead Maguire Ireland, Ben Manski U.S., Robert McChesney U.S., Miranda Mellis U.S., Leo Panitch Canada, Cynthia Peters U.S., Francis Fox Piven U.S., Justin Podur Canada, C J Polychroniou U.S., Milan Rai UK, Manuel Rozental Colombia, Boaventura Santos Portugal, Irene Ramalho Santos Portugal, Lydia Sargent U.S.,

Kim Scipes U.S., Marina Sitrin U.S., Norman Solomon U.S., Verena Stresing France, David Swanson U.S., Rudolfo Torres U.S., Tom Vouloumanos Canada, Bob Wing, U.S.

The *We Stand* statement didn't yield a broad U.S. project, but Black Lives Matter, the earlier Occupy Movement, the Sanders campaign, the Women's March, on-going anti-war resistance, persistent Sanctuary organizing, and vigorous anti-Trump resistance broached the likelihood of more to come.

Interviewed at a People's Summit in Chicago, heading into summer of 2017, the noted actor, producer, and activist Danny Glover voiced widespread activist sentiments: Develop clear vision. Seek fundamental change. Transcend being peripheral to power. Avoid circling wagons.

Guevara's *RPS/2044* takes Glover's advice. Can an oral history from a revolutionary alternative future inspire advance in our world? Time waits for no one, and time will answer.

- Michael Albert, 2017

VIDEO PLAYLIST

As I prepared channeled *RPS/2044's* many eloquent voices for release in 2017, I turned seventy. In my years of journeying from under-aged neophyte to over-aged veteran, people, events, books, talks, and beats, melodies, riffs, and lyrics led the way. The people, events, books, and talks informed *RPS/2044*'s interviewees' words. What about songs?

The playlist below reveals my limited tastes, but for me each song's message, sound, and original context augment RPS history. Perhaps it needs additional entries. Perhaps we can together add some in later editions of *RPS/2044*, in print and/or online. In any event, the playlist like *RPS/2044* are a work in progress.

The site RPS2044.org includes links to video performances of each entry.

Chapter One: First Breaths
Chuck Berry: Roll Over Beethoven
Elvis Presley: Jailhouse Rock
Billy Holliday: God Bless the Child
Impressions: People Get Ready

Chapter Two: Overcoming Cynicism
Rolling Stones: Satisfaction
Otis Redding: The Dock of the Bay
Jackson Brown: The Pretender
Lorde: We'll Never Be Royals
Sam Cooke: A Change Is Gonna Come

Chapter Three: Getting Started
Woody Guthrie: I Ain't Got No Home
Nina Simone: Mississippi Goddam
The Beatles: Here Comes the Sun
Bruce Springsteen: The Rising

Chapter Four: The 2016 Election
Woody Guthrie/Pete Seeger: Deportees
Odetta: Jim Crow Blues
Richard and Mimi Farina: Bold Marauder
Buffalo Springfield: For What It's Worth

Chapter Five: Reacting to Trump
Creedence Clearwater Revival: Bad Moon Rising
Bob Dylan: A Hard Rain's Gonna Fall
Iris Dement: Wasteland of the Free
Rhiannon Giddens: Freedom Highway

Chapter Six: The First Convention
Mavis Staples: You Are Not Alone
Ben E King: Stand By Me
Tom Morello: Let Freedom Ring
Bob Dylan: It's All Over Now Baby Blue

Chapter Seven: Initial Commitments
Lead Belly: Bourgeois Blues
Alejandro Escovedo: Wave
Laura Nyro: Save the Country
Chrissie Hynde: Revolution

Chapter Eight: Forming Chapters
The Tokens: The Lion Sleeps Tonight
Marvin Gaye: What's Going On
Odetta: This Little Light of Mine
Bob Marley: Get Up Stand Up

Chapter Nine: Housing and Rights to the City
Billie Holiday: Strange Fruit
Bruce Springsteen: Youngstown
Amy Ray: Laramie
The Clash: London Calling

Chapter Ten: Actor's Activism
Donovan: Catch the Wind
The Neville Brothers: Sister Rosa
Gil Scott Heron: The Revolution Will Not Be Televised
Bob Dylan: It's Alright Ma

Chapter Eleven: Health and Class
Jim Carroll Band: People Who Died
Paul Simon: The Boxer
Bob Dylan: Maggie's Farm
Drive By Truckers: Once They Banned Imagine

Chapter Twelve: Athletics and Religion
Jimi Hendrix: The Star Spangled Banner
Donovan: To Try for the Sun
Bob Marley: Redemption Song
Joan Baez: Blowing in the Wind

Chapter Thirteen: Courageous Courtrooms
Bob Dylan: Hurricane
Bruce Springsteen: 41 Shots
Ruthie Foster: Lord Remember Me
Rage Against the Machine: Killing in the Name

Chapter Fourteen: Media Makeovers
Simon and Garfunkle: Sounds of Silence
Jimmie Cliff: Sitting Here in Limbo
Leonard Cohen: Everybody Knows
John Lennon: Imagine

Chapter Fifteen: Early Economic Campaigns
Jim Page: I'd Rather Be Dancing
John Lennon: Power to the People
The Clash, Revolution Rock
Leonard Cohen: Democracy

Chapter Sixteen: Concepts
Buffy St. Marie: Now That The Buffalo's Gone
Shannon Labrie: It's Political
Randy Newman: Political Science
Public Enemy: Fight the Power

Chapter Seventeen: Values
Lucinda Williams: Soldiers Song
Neil Young: After The Gold Rush
The Clash: The Call Up
Louis Armstrong: What A Wonderful World

Chapter Eighteen: Defining Ourselves
Neil Young, Rockin' In The Free World
Indigo Girls: Go Go Go
Jimmy Cliff: The Harder They Come
Bruce Springsteen: Born in the USA

Chapter Nineteen: Gender and Race
Aretha Franklin: Respect
Indigo Girls: Closer to Fine
Nina Simone: I Wish I Knew How It Would Feel to Be Free
Laura Marline: Next Time
Ani Difranco: I Am Not A Pretty Girl

Chapter Twenty: Class
Hooray for the Riff Raff: La Pa'lante
Drive By Truckers: What It Means
Valerie June: Workin' Woman Blues
John Lennon: Working Class Hero

Chapter Twenty One: Leadership, Pace, Solidarity
Maryanne Faithful: Broken English
Patti Smith: People Have the Power
Jimmy Cliff: You Can Get It If You Really Want
The Clash: Spanish Bombs

Chapter Twenty Two: Reforms, Revolution, Violence
Tracy Chapman: Talkin' 'bout a Revolution
Thunderclapp Newman: Something in the Air
Rolling Stones: Street Fighting Man
Joan Baez: Farewell Angelina

Chapter Twenty Three: Elections
Creedance Clearwater Revival: Fortunate Son
Paul Robeson: No More Auction Block
Rolling Stones: Brown Sugar
Run for the Jewels: "A Report To The Shareholders / Kill Your Masters"

Chapter Twenty Four: Political and Kinship Vision
Sharon Jones: This Land Is Your Land
Nina Simone: I Wish I Knew How It Would Feel to Be Free
Beatles: Dear Prudence
Lady Ga Ga: Born This Way
Joan Baez: We Shall Overcome

Chapter Twenty Five: Economic and Cultural Vision
Peter Gabriel: Biko
Los Lobos: Revolution
The Roots: Next Movement
Kendrick Lamar: How Much A Dollar Cost

Chapter Twenty Six: Media Future
David Bowie: All The Young Dudes
Lucinda Williams: Born to Be Loved
Tom Morello: Which Side Are You On
Public Enemy: Get Up Stand Up

Chapter Twenty Seven: Health and Justice Future
Johnny Cash: Man in Black
Bruce Springsteen: Badlands
Prince: Sign O the Times
Bob Dylan: Chimes of Freedom

Chapter Twenty Eight: Education and Economy Future
Pink Floyd: Another Brick in the Wall
Mavis Staples: Wrote a Song for Everyone
Jackson Browne: Lives in the Balance
Jefferson Airplane: Crown of Creation
Bob Dylan: Times They Are A Changin

Chapter Twenty Nine: World and Planet
Marianne Faithful: Broken English
Buffy St. Marie: Universal Soldier
Phil Ochs: Cops of the World
Shannon Labrie: War and Peace
Bob Dylan: Masters of War

Chapter Thirty: Ship Ahoy
Phil Ochs: Ringing of Revolution
Leonard Cohen: Hallelujah
Los Lobos: Will The Wolf Survive
Chambers Brothers: Time Has Come Today
Bob Dylan: When the Ship Comes In

On RPS.org the above references appear as links to YouTube videos. Enjoy!

INTRODUCTION

From 2030 to 2036 I wrote over 500 topical essays for a Latin American media project. They required immediacy, preferred facts to lessons, and welcomed names, dates, and happenstances but not whys, from wheres, and to wheres. I obeyed, but I also griped. In early 2037, I happened to read an oral history of social media. By late 2039 I began interviewing 18 participants in the on-going U.S. Revolution for a Participatory Society (RPS). From 2039 into 2041, I heard about initial aims, early activities, and the birth, maturation, and success of seeking a better world.

My interviewees evaluated RPS's early efforts in health, housing, urban relations, economics, entertainment, sports, religion, law, and media. They recounted RPS's gender, race, and class policies, and its approach to solidarity, leadership, and correcting its own inadequacies. They explored RPS's shadow government and shadow society programs, and described RPS's social vision. They addressed ecology, health, legality, education, media, economy, city life, family life, elections, international relations, and prospects for final victory.

But, my questions had an intent that left much out. I asked about events, programs, ideas, and feelings but always and only seeking to understand the emergence and success of RPS. I asked questions that ignored the mindsets and history of the twenty five years' opponents of change, fascist or liberal, of new technologies, of economic, social, and cultural trends, of fashion and sports, of cultural creations, scientific and, medical, of natural and even global warming caused storms, and even of wars and near wars and interventions and near interventions, if at all, only to illuminate the forward motion of RPS. Of course what I didn't ask about is important, it just wasn't part of my limited agenda.

In 2041, I excerpted their interviews into topical chapters and prepared a website (available at http://rps2044.org) to display testimonials, reviews, related essays, and comments. At that site you can add, comments, complaints, suggestions, and explorations, and send questions to myself or to any interviewee. The website includes YouTube links for all items in the Playlist.

Everything worthwhile about *RPS/2044* is due to the interviewees. The flaws are mine.

Miguel Guevara, 2041

SELECTED TIMELINE

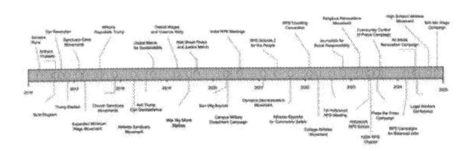

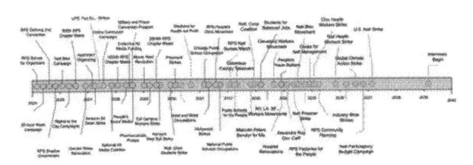

2015 Sanders Runs
2016 Black Lives Matter Program
2016 NFL Anthem Protests
2016 Sanders' Our Revolution Founded
2016 Trump Elected
2017 Immigrant Sanctuary Movements
2017 Expanded Minimum Wage Movement
2017 Women's March Repudiates Trump

2017 Church Sanctuary Movements
2018 Athletes Sanctuary Movement
2018 Anti Trump Civil Disobedience
2018 Global March for Sustainability
2019 Detroit Wages and Anti Violence Rally
2019 War No More Rallies
2019 Wall Street Peace and Justice March
2020 Firearms Manufacturers Boycott
2020 Campus Military Divestment
2020 Initial RPS Meetings/Groups
2021 Public Schools for the People
2021 Olympics Decentralization Movement
2021 Athletes for Community Safety
2022 RPS Founding Convention
2022 College Athletes Movement
2022 First Hollywood RPS meeting
2022 Journalists for Social Responsibility
2023 Religious Renovations Movement
2023 Hollywood RPS School
2023 One Hundredth RPS Chapter Meets
2023 Press the Press Campaign
2023 Community Control of Police
2024 RPS Campaigns for Balanced Jobs
2024 Alternative Media Renovation Campaign
2024 Legal Workers Conference
2024 High School Athletes Movement
2024 $25 Hr. Minimum Wages Campaign
2025 RPS Schools for Organizers
2025 30 Hour Work Week
2025 RPS Defining Second Convention
2025 RPS Shadow Government
2026 National Bike Campaigns
2026 Rights to the City expansion

2026 Five Hundredth RPS Chapter Meets
2026 Gender Roles Renovation
2027 Apartment Organizing
2027 Amazon Sit-down Strike
2027 UPS, Fed Ex…Strikes
2027 Online Curriculum Campaign
2027 National Alternative Media Coalition
2028 1000th RPS Chapter Meets
2028 Collective Alt Media Funding
2028 Military and Prison Conversion
2028 People's Social Media
2028 Pharmaceuticals' Protests
2029 Movie: Next American Revolution
2029 2500th RPS Chapter Meets
2029 California Campus Workers Strike
2029 Harvard Med School Strike
2029 National Grad Students Strike
2030 Prisoners Strikes
2030 Hotel and Motel Occupations
2030 Medicine for Health not Profit
2031 Chicago Public School Occupation
2031 Hollywood Strikes
2031 RPS People's Clinics Movement
2031 National Public Schools Occupations
2032 RPS National Nurses March
2032 Colombus Factory Takeovers
2032 Public Schools for the People
2032 Malcolm King Senator of Ma
2032 National Coop Coalition
2033 Students for Balanced Jobs
2033 Cleveland Workers Movement
2033 People's Prison Reform
2033 NY, LA, Chic., SF Worker Movements

2033 Hospital Renovations Movement
2034 Celia Lopez, Gov. Cal.
2034 National Bloc Movement
2034 National Prisoners Strike
2034 Coops for Self Management
2034 RPS Factories for the People
2035 Chicago Health Workers Strike
2035 RPS Community Planning Movement
2035 National Health Workers Strike
2035 Coops for RPS Economy
2036 Industry Wide Strikes
2036 Global Climate Action Strike
2036 Participatory Budgeting Campaign
2037 Week Long U.S. National Strike
2039 Interviews Begin
2041 Interviews End
2042 Published
2044 President Malcolm King
2045 RPS Construction Proceeds

CHAPTER 1

FIRST STEPS

*Juliet Berkman & Andrej Goldman
discuss the first major march, and boycotts.*

Juliet Berkman, a militant feminist, born in 1993, you are a workplace and union organizer, who advocates nonviolence and emphasizes organizing people holding contrary views. You have been shadow Secretary of Labor. Do you remember how you first became radical?

My parents were radical in the 1960s so when I entered college, I already had radical beliefs though I hadn't taken any actions. Trump's election deeply upset me, but so did many radicals who seemed more bent on preserving their radical credentials than on preventing Trump from winning. Within hours of the election, I got deathly drunk and my dissolution lasted many weeks.

Literally?

Yes, I drank away days on end. I felt, if society was a mess, why not me too? Trump was off the charts uncouth and extreme. Neo-Nazis rejoiced and rallied. His rootedness in where society appeared to be going scared the hell out of me. Thankfully, a friend intervened and she and the anti-Trump resistance restored my focus.

Can you tell us a few RPS formative events for you?

The first two conventions and the campaign for balanced jobs in 2024, and for the 30-hour work week in 2025. But I also experienced two especially formative personal events not on any map of RPS history.

At a meeting RPS arranged with workers in a defense plant connected with a university where students were opposing military research, I spoke to an assembly of protesting students and defense-oriented employees. I called for closing the offending workplace but didn't mention the employees' future livelihoods. I had warfare on my mind, and I called the employees "peace killers" for not joining student protests that sought to terminate their jobs.

I was militantly confident offering my suicidal notion of how workers should express solidarity with students, but by the next day I was depressed and angry at myself for having adopted a stance that ignored the conditions and feelings of those I was trying to reach. Of course the workers dismissed my rhetoric for disdaining their reality. They found me obnoxious. I had to change.

So you turned the bad moment into a good path. What was the second highpoint?

I attended a memorial service for civil rights activists from past years. The music and solidarity transported me until I felt I was in Birmingham. I saw activists risk life and limb. It was a waking dream, I guess, but no less powerful for that. I still wonder how common experiences like that are. The next day I re-read Martin Luther King Jr.'s letter from a Birmingham Jail and his more famous Mountaintop speech. King's words powerfully moved me. I memorized the letter and talk, and later, in jail or choosing to avoid jail, I repeated his words to myself.

What can you tell us about the first signs of RPS?

I had my first RPS feelings at a Detroit rally for a higher minimum wage and reduced police violence. It was a nice day and the rally appeared typical, but I felt something beyond the event's stated priorities.

Speakers linked class, race, gender, and sexuality to low wages and police violence and vice versa. I had heard those connections before, but the Detroit speakers urged that we had to renovate everything to comprehensively change anything. They sought new organization to raise wages, reduce violence, gain peace, and win new social relations.

But surely those weren't new thoughts…

At prior rallies and demonstrations and at home with my parents, too, I had often heard similar powerful, inspiring rhetoric, but when sobriety returned, I noticed little follow-up substance. Past events sought short-run gains. Detroit sought more. It said what it wanted, and it meant what it said, and I wanted in.

Many pinpoint the 2020 March on Wall Street as their RPS start. Were you there?

Yes, and the 300,000 strong March on Wall Street addressed income distribution and corporations. It revealed an emergent community defining our local, national and international connections. It delivered focused dissent and excellent demands. A rousing speech called "We Are the Future," was given. Have you heard it?

"We are a movement for dignity and justice. We support one another. We seek change for all. We are no longer content to operate on the periphery of power, complaining about its abuses. Beyond curtailing evils, we favor returning power to the people in pursuit of new fulfillment.

We do not solely oppose impoverished budgets, escalating inequality, resurgent racism, sexual predation, assembly line schools, pharmaceutical drug dealing, corporate profiteering, divisive classism, heinous war, hideous repression, OR planetary climate catastrophe. No. We oppose them all.

We don't demand racial solidarity, cultural integrity, gender equity, sexual diversity, life style liberation, political freedom, collective self management, OR economic equity and classlessness. No. We demand it all."

The speech continued but even those few words reveal where we were headed. Still, if you had told me that thirteen years later I would be Secretary of Labor in a Shadow Government and twelve years thereafter we would celebrate transforming society, I would have laughed. A hundred years, okay. Fifty years, maybe. Twenty five years? Absurd.

My initial RPS sentiment was simple. When someone points a gun at your head and demands your money or your life, you hand him your wallet because his gun makes lone dissent suicide. Similarly, when your capitalist employer demands that you give him your subservience or you get no income, you obey because his power makes lone dissent suicide. I knew that to escape our plight we had to overcome our loneliness and isolation, but I had no inkling how fast collectivity would spread.

Andrej Goldman, born in 1987, you have held various movement jobs and taught in various institutions while writing numerous books and articles. From its start, you have helped author RPS program and vision. Do you remember your radicalization?

In college, I saw economics as a good career choice. I did the discipline's relatively simple equations, recited its rote answers about supply and demand, and repeated its advisories about government spending and private investment, and after three years of that, I got bored.

I had taken course after course. I had learned to recite acceptable answers to sterile questions. I was a happy idiot masquerading as an informed scholar. But I learned nothing about how corporations really functioned much less about their impact on life. I wasn't political, much less radical. Just bored.

As a junior, a friend took me to my first demonstration. I wasn't even curious but then I was surprised to find that I agreed with various speakers and admired their willingness to take a stand. At the same time, taking a stand certainly wasn't on my agenda. I just watched. Weeks later, and I can't even tell you why, I wondered why I had watched, admired, and respected, but had not joined the events. That wondering changed my life.

How?

I decided I ought to at least have an informed opinion of the activists and their agendas. I expected I would appreciate their courage and drive, but feel they were confused and wasting their time. I began looking into it, wanting to be fair about it. I started to read - and I guess some would say that that was my undoing. By the time I graduated I had taken some critical courses and read a few books, but it was still only ideas. After graduating, I visited some workplaces and asked people doing rote jobs, and managers too, what their jobs did to them. Their answers propelled my permanent radicalization.

Can you tell us what RPS events most affected you?

I was hugely inspired by the 2021 Schools for the People campaign and, much later, by the 2027 Amazon sit-down strike. During the Schools for the People campaign, I heard parent after parent demand a community center where they could learn and socialize. I heard them demand roses on their tables, not diamonds on their necks.

During the Amazon strike, I lent support and saw the strikers sit down and tell the owners and state that they would not be moved short of their winning dignity and income. I watched the strikers sparkle with energy, compassion, and militancy. I watched them dance and demand. Their passion inspired everyone and I was irretrievably moved.

Returning to the origins of RPS, what role did the early boycotts play?

I was in college, near Boston, still studying abysmal economics, when a Wall Street March speech had called for all those present, their families, their friends, and everyone they could reach out to, to stop buying products from producers of the automatic high velocity weapons prevalent in public mass shootings. The call reverberated across society and sparked activism.

I didn't own a gun and was never going to buy one. It would be pushing an open door for organizers to talk to me or to anyone I was in school with about not buying from Remington or Glock. People who wanted to work on the gun boycott had to talk to people who owned, or who might soon own, a product from the gun manufacturers. Indeed, it was a wonderful benefit of the campaign that boycott organizers had to bring to gun owners precisely the message gun owners most rejected. Nonetheless, activists started doing just that and, in hindsight, it was a major turning point toward RPS.

How?

Activists had always sought gains for their own constituencies, but allotting energies to those who strongly disagreed started in the early boycott and probably in earlier work battling Trump, too. At any rate, campus boycott activism started when a bunch of students went to Wall Street and heard the call for a boycott of arms dealers and started talking about how to relate to it. We could organize students to boycott producers of automatic weapons, but doing so would be silly. We were not prospective buyers of M-16s and Sig Sauers.

I was at MIT and we wondered why confine ourselves to boycotting manufacturers of hand-held weapons? Individual students didn't buy tanks or missile systems but MIT has contracts with tank and missile builders. Why not organize students to resist militarizing local and campus police and to resist all campus complicity with war? We consulted organizers of the BDS boycott to aid Palestinians, and also the earlier boycott around South African Apartheid, and we even studied the still earlier grape boycott in the U.S. We demanded that MIT not seek war profits for investors, but social justice for humanity. We urged fellow students to agree that war and war complicity were wrong.

Success can't have been easy. What were the main obstacles?

Some students believed that there were just wars and that U.S. interventions were selfless. To counter that we offered well known evidence showing the economic and geopolitical motivations and cruel callousness of war.

Other students noted that for MIT to end war research would mean budgetary suicide and neither they nor faculty wanted MIT closed. We saw that to grow, we had to show the moral failings of militarism but also propose how to survive without it. We proposed transition to climate and peace research paid for by revised government budgets and punitive taxes on arms producers.

I remember endlessly discussing how to win over hesitant students. We made it hard for administrators to oppose our calls for greater attention to global warming. We made it hard for them to reject focusing research on new energy sources and on various health campaigns and social innovations. We left them no way to refute our rejection of weapons research.

What was your personal experience of the boycott?

I worked a lot on social media and also helped arrange face-to-face dorm meetings. I worked on teach-ins, organized rallies, and helped occupy labs. I also researched similar efforts during the late 1960s because I knew that that tumultuous period did not prevent, decades later, Trumpism, and I worried that our effort might also grow large only to later dissipate. One of our priorities became trying to clarify past errors so we could do better.

How did your boycott differ from earlier efforts?

We faced some difficult periods but our campaign grew and soon we had a national boycott of manufacturers selling assault rifles and also our campus boycott of war research and military relations that spread from MIT to Johns Hopkins, to Stanford, to Cal Tech, as the first few military-connected schools involved.

What did the boycott's growth feel like?

Schools with fewer Pentagon ties had smaller battles, but the overall campaign kept spreading and growing. I knew we were winning when to support the boycott indicated student responsibility. We didn't shame people who disagreed with us, we celebrated whoever joined us. Before long, cross-campus solidarity provoked citywide demonstrations. Movements on different campuses shared lessons and lent each other support. After two years we held a rally culminating in a sit-in at MIT that attracted over 50,000 students from all over the Boston area. When even more attended a subsequent rally and sit-in at Harvard, and when Northeastern and Boston University then held simultaneous campus-wide strikes, we realized we were not going to be stopped unless we undermined ourselves, and we were steadfastly committed to avoiding that.

Our movement went from opposing war research, to opposing war per se and U.S. Foreign policy. We went from railing against drone policy and drone manufacture and research as murderous immorality, to railing against all wars as outgrowths of imperial profit seeking and geopolitical coercion.

Can you tell us about some of the "difficult moments"?

One hard step was to discover and reveal the research. Students had tough class schedules and few resources and each research project was isolated from the rest and from general visibility.

In that context, a few daring students snuck into a secret site, took pictures, and stole revealing documents. They proved MIT was a big corporation loyally and greedily designing drone, surveillance, and missile technology for repressing domestic and foreign populations. Students elsewhere adopted similar tactics. Once we had incriminating information, we escalated our activism.

Have you read the Whitman poem that references seeing the universe in a grain of sand? I read something like that from a famous scientist, Richard Feynman, who said nature uses only the longest threads, so each small piece reveals the organization of the entire tapestry. In the same way, each radical campaign taught a remarkable amount relevant to all radical campaigns.

For example, I remember how knowledgeable, highly logical, and even socially concerned liberal officials, swept aside contrary evidence so they could admire themselves in their mirrors, oblivious to their own murderous culpability.

But not all administrators were liberal, were they?

Mostly they were, but a significant minority of right-wing officials openly celebrated their militarism and a few caring officials allied with us. I remember finding the staunch right wingers' absence of hypocrisy easier to stand than the more prevalent liberals' self delusions. At least with the right-wingers, what you got was what they said, albeit what they said was vile.

What key lessons did you take from the boycotts?

I mainly learned a lot about the mindset of students who balked at joining the effort. Discussions would last hours, as students offered first one rationale for not joining, then another. The weapons weren't really offensive, they would say. Or they won't be used. Or we need them to preserve peace. Or, most strange, when used they will provoke dissent.

Did you keep your temper facing those responses?

Sadly, I often got prickly hearing self-serving rationalizations about death-dealing weaponry, but as we overcame each rationale with evidence, we got closer and closer to the heart of the matter with each student we talked to. From campaign to campaign, in one dorm and then the next, on one campus and then the next, students resisting boycott appeals would ultimately tell us, "Okay, you are right about the facts. You are right about the ethics. But resisting will achieve nothing." We heard it over and over. "You are right, but you will fail, and failing isn't worth my time."

How did you deal with that?

We would patiently explain how attracting enough informed and committed support could win until we convinced students it would be senseless for administrators to preserve war research for "patriotic," greed, or budgetary reasons when doing so would cause students and faculty to permanently close their institutions. But even then most students resisted our call. "I am still not going to join you, because even if you eliminate war research here, it will be done elsewhere. Even if you have lots and lots of people in many places, it will still come back somewhere and eventually everywhere. People are greedy. People are violent. There is no stopping war. There is no reversing injustice."

Looking back, it seems as if young folks were jaded and beaten old folks...

Yes, back then sometimes college did feel like an old folks home. At bottom, hopelessness fueled almost all student reticence though students admitted it only after we overcame other rationales. Only then, when all else was rebutted, students would finally say, "Human nature sucks. We are all fucked. You should make the best of it. Play along. Change is impossible."

I looked into past movements to find this was nothing new. Deep-rooted despair had impeded earlier change too. For example, sixties cynicism, though it was severely challenged and shaken, had ultimately retained command. Fifty years later we had to do better.

Where does such cynical despair come from?

Upbringing and schooling tenaciously drum in defeatist attitudes and society's roles reinforce them. Defeatism and greed become attractive short-term responses to inequalities. Being cynical about winning change not only bolsters people who think they are going to be well off, it also colonizes people destined for low income, low status, and debilitating circumstances. From our campus experiences, we soon realized that in communities, workplaces, and everywhere else, people considered suffering inevitable. I began to see escaping cynicism as essential to becoming radical.

Juliet earlier told me how the anti-Trump resistance helped her escape her demons, Was that more generally true, too?

For some people, yes, but writ large - I don't think so. Anti Trumpism sought to remove an aberration not challenge people's deeper cynicism. It spurred great motion. It was a rip in the tide of hopelessness. It had moments of elation, hope, and fierce struggle, but it provided no glue to hold it all together. Its moments didn't persist. Each rip was too partial. Its activism sought small gains against deviant horrors, not huge gains against the whole social order.

Many of us saw we had to go beyond warding off reactionary evils and even during anti-Trump resistance, we sought to create hope for a new society, but it took years for such sentiments to define what most activists daily did. The anti Trump resistance way more often elevated liberal than radical views.

> *Did you take other lessons from the boycott? Did anything surprise you?*

We fought to get our universities to stop supporting military agendas but we knew victory wouldn't end murderous research. Schools would spin off labs by making them private corporate firms. We called that trend a massive version of "not in my backyard" you don't put that crap - but, okay, you can keep it in its current building as long as you legally disown it while it keeps right on operating as in the past.

> *Aren't you being a bit hard on students trying to move the tools of war off their campuses? Wasn't it good they did so?*

Yes, because rather than settling for cosmetic changes, we realized our movements had to transcend campuses and take on private corporations. Today MIT, Stanford, and Cal Tech. Tomorrow, not only the spinoffs, but also the NSA and Boeing. Instead of confining our experience to campuses, we talked with workers at war-connected companies. Instead of trying to get war-involved firms to stop cold and therefore go out of business, we confronted war firms with demands to do socially desirable work in place of war work, and simultaneously demanded that Congress re-assign funds from military to social use.

Thinking deeper, we began to realize resistance to our anti-militarist demands reflected factors beyond war fighting. Would our economy produce tanks or quality affordable housing? Drones or ecologically sound infrastructure? Aircraft carriers or renewable energy sources? Missiles or efficient public transport? Would government spend on war or on education, housing, infrastructure, and health?

We wondered why society pursued militarist production over humanist production and concluded that preserving military spending must ward off a threat. We knew the threat wasn't an external enemy, that was nonsense. We realized that redistributing wealth from military to social use must be way worse for those in power than producing weapons that benefitted only those who directly profited off their production.

Did you determine why spending on public well being was more dangerous to elites than spending on weapons?

We assumed that those who favored war production didn't build tanks rather than schools because they literally preferred killing to learning. We knew that shifting war-related firms to socially valuable production could enlarge their workforces and even their revenues. The government could pay for a transit system, schools, and hospitals just like it could pay for a missile system. Private firms could receive payments in either case.

Sherlock Holmes advises detectives to rule out all but one explanation, and settle on what is left. We settled on the idea that war production reduces the government acting on behalf of the population and that that curbs two effects elites desperately feared. First, enlarged government social spending reduces conditions of instability and poverty. That, in turn empowers workers and insures them against threats of firing. And that increases workers' ability to win greater gains. Second, social spending establishes the anti-elite idea that the government ought to benefit the whole population. With that established, people start demanding what they want. I remember how seeing these two points made capitalism's disgusting logic more real to me.

Did you take any more personal lessons?

I gave a public talk at a university in Florida about the boycott of military work and people asked lots of questions about private guns. I remember, after the talk, on the way out, being accosted by a charismatic student advocate of open carry who wanted students freed to bring handguns to classes. We argued and before long twenty people were listening and tossing in comments.

After awhile, I realized that at bottom, the gun advocate took for granted permanently abysmal societal conditions. He felt that at any moment some maniac could unholster a gun and start shooting people. Having this view, the gun advocate believed in a miniature version of the old notion of mutually assured destruction in which gargantuan stores of nuclear weaponry on both sides meant neither Russia nor the U.S. could use what they had without being annihilated. Similarly, my gun advocating adversary believed that if most students carried hand guns, no bully could impose his will. Even a crazy student hell bent on murder couldn't do much harm before succumbing. For me to point out that he was ignoring that open carry would unleash crazy fear often escalating what would otherwise be moderate disputes into violent catastrophes missed his point. The gun advocate took violent catastrophe as his baseline. In his view, that was unavoidable. He thought he was reducing the fallout.

I realized then that gun advocates believed society was headed to hell in a hand cart with no significant renovation possible. They weren't being academic. They weren't posing a hypothetical. They felt social corruption couldn't be averted and reversed, and they thus favored a mutual assured destruction logic.

I couldn't win a trivially simple and limited issue - students carrying guns in classes would be horrible for everyone - without first winning a bigger issue, that society did not have to keep devolving into a kill or be killed danger land.

Leaving Florida to return home, I replayed the confrontation in my mind and realized the lesson was general. When people expect horrible circumstances to only get worse, things that are insane when considered in light of positive social prospects can seem perfectly sensible and even necessary for self defense. If you believe social sanity is unattainable, you sensibly adopt the most effective "insane approach" you can find.

Often, people took that path based on flawed assumptions, not evil intent. Learning this stood me in good stead when I would later try to communicate past gigantic chasms of programmatic difference.

CHAPTER 2

OVERCOMING CYNICISM

Juliet Berkman, Senator Malcolm King, and Andrej Goldman discuss overcoming cynicism and early momentum.

Juliet, when organizing, did you encounter cynicism? How did you reply?

We all encountered it, including in ourselves. Trump becoming President depressed us, and while resistance to Trump grew quickly, going further nearly always encountered cynicism. I usually replied indirectly. I would ask, can you think of even one person who is not evil? Perhaps your grandmother, a famous person, yourself? Everyone would answer, "Yes, I have someone in mind."

I would say place that person on the social side of a ledger. Now list as many folks as you want on the anti-social side. Hitler, Trump, the Clintons, the rest of your friends, your family, yourself, whoever you like.

Now notice that if evil was inevitably wired into human nature, everyone would appear on the evil side of the ledger. If you didn't list everyone there, you know evil isn't inevitable. It isn't like having a stomach. On the other hand, you also know human nature doesn't preclude people becoming evil. Evil routinely lies, manipulates, and fear mongers its way into our lives. For me to deny that would be ridiculous. Evil happens, so it is possible. But if evil isn't wired in, why does it happen and. why is it so prevalent?

To answer, I would say look around and notice how our society rewards greed, violence, and callousness and how it punishes more caring inclinations. I would urge that our better traits must be in our nature, albeit able to be muted. They have nowhere else to come from since institutions don't foster them. But our anti-social aspects can be produced by circumstances that impose them.

Sometimes it would have to end there. I would give a talk, offer the above arguments, and move on. Other times, discussions would continue, and we would consider how our existing roles mute social inclinations and impose anti-social ones. Though the reasoning is obvious, people often found the claims opaque. But it wasn't a communications problem. They resisted accepting that they had taken false things for granted.

So, the approach didn't work?

You rarely know for sure whether you efforts work. If you are pessimistic, you often walk away thinking not. If you are optimistic, you often walk away thinking you have succeeded. At the extremes, my efforts likely had no lasting impact. But with most folks, they likely lodged in peoples' memory, set to join other factors later to cumulatively reverse cynicism.

Did you have other ways to address cynicism?

Sometimes I borrowed an approach from Noam Chomsky. Imagine you are looking out a window on a really hot summer day. You see a child with an ice cream cone. Along comes a big adult who takes the cone, swats the kid into the gutter, and walks on.

Watching from a window above, do you think, there goes a fine specimen of humanity? Do you think, that guy's human nature is freely expressing itself? Do you think "gimme that ice cream and get out of my way" is in our genes like having a liver is in our genes? Or do you think, there goes a pathological deviant who was warped by his past or born messed up?

Chomsky had another approach that I did not like as much and that he eventually stopped using, as well. He would say, look, I know that if we do nothing, the result will be dismal or worse. If we work hard to win change, the result may be better. Clearly, we should try.

The reasoning was valid, but I had little success using the approach. People have personal lives, jobs, overtime, and families. To give time, energy, and emotional focus to fighting for change incurs emotional, social, and sometimes material costs. People hearing that to not fight for change is suicide but to do so may accomplish good tended to ask themselves, "But will my personally fighting for social change benefit those I care about better than my working to directly benefit them?" To answer yes required having informed hope and a broad sense of solidarity. To inspire participation required more than arguing that activism might thwart disaster.

So it required more than listing all the disasters befalling us?

Yes, I first saw that with my parents and some close friends. I was on my activist path. They were liberal, progressive, and even radical about issues, but they did not seek change. A significant shift in my parents' and most other peoples' choices had to wait for them to gain a sense of efficacy and hope, and it often took years. We suffered plenty of familial tension along the way to unity.

I saw how many resisted activism due to hopelessness. Events that spontaneously generated hope - such as massive outpourings of dissent that betokened more outpourings to come - were, to an extent, kryptonite for cynicism. But I couldn't provide that kind of jolt in a one-on-one discussion. Operating one-to-one, I had to resort to thought experiments about a loving grandma or an ice cream grabbing brute. Even socially sparked involvement needed something more to help it persist beyond initial outrage. Cynicism could defuse spontaneous activism. Writ larger, encountering cynicism made me see that accurately criticizing unjust relations and showing their catastrophic implications would rarely alone generate sustainable forward-looking activism.

What more did you need to provide?

We had to address people's emotional resistance to becoming active. We had to overcome people's view that we cannot win a better world because the enemy is too powerful or because our internal natures are so anti social that any victory will eventually become oppressive. We had to provide hope that each person could meaningfully advance lasting change. We had to reorient our intellectual and organizing efforts from overwhelmingly emphasizing what was wrong to clarifying how a good society would look and how we might win it.

I went from repeatedly saying war kills, poverty starves, diminishment stifles, racism subjugates, bad is bad, to showing the shape of new fulfilling institutions and showing new ways of organizing and struggling. But I don't want to make it sound easier than it was. Turning myself around was hard enough. Communicating vision that could sustain hope to someone skeptical about a good society even being possible and who because of that had avoided involvement and who had the added factor of not wanting to admit that they had been wrong, was very daunting. After all, if bridging that set of obstacles took forever with a sibling, parent, or child, it was going to be hard with others too.

Senator King, born in 1985, you were an avid student of history but initially an assembly worker and cook. You were attracted to RPS and became a member and not long thereafter ran for office within the Ohio Democratic Party and became the first highly placed national elected office holder to use your position to propel the RPS platform. You became a U.S. Senator, and many, myself included, think you will be President in a few years. Can you remember what precipitated your becoming radical?

I was fascinated by history and it gave me great sympathy for those fighting against oppression as well as considerable understanding of the institutions that create oppression. When I left school I couldn't get a history-related job, so I worked as an assembler and then a short-order cook.

Suddenly, I wasn't looking at working class conditions as subject matter. I was living them. I like to think that had I gotten a teaching job at some elite institution, my life would have been like it has been, but I know the odds are slim so I now celebrate what I horribly resented at the time - that I had to enter working class life and endure its injuries. Doing so ensured my radicalization.

Can you tell us some events, campaigns, or moments in RPS history that were personally most moving for you?

Being a short order cook taught me a whole lot about work, economy, and class attitudes, but two other moments jump out in my memory. First was when Bernie Sanders died. I know, he wasn't in RPS and his politics, at least publicly, never rose to RPS allegiance. But his life, and particularly his Presidential campaign, greatly influenced me. His way of engaging, his sense of proportion, his compassion for working people, greatly inspired me. The slogan, "Don't mourn, organize" is fine for a dying revolutionary to intone as advice to others. But for those still around who really cared, while it may be good advice, it denies reality. So when Sanders died, I mourned.

Second, during the Campaign for Military and Prison Conversion in 2028, I happened to give a speech at a U.S. military base in Oklahoma. After that session, I sat around with some soldiers at Fort Sill and we talked about their experiences, motives, and what the campaign might mean for them. I was greatly impressed by their thoughtful concerns for the country, themselves, and their families.

The proximity of change for their military base and thus for their lives, and the sober calm of our conversion campaign caused our exchanges to be heartfelt. We talked for hours covering incredible ground. The lessons I took about the need to hear people's actual beliefs, not those imputed to them from a distance, and to relate to those beliefs in ways that could create solidarity rather than fear and antipathy, made my interactions not only with those soldiers, but with lots of different constituencies, much wiser.

Looking back, what do you think spurred the early boycotts and other campaigns emerging when they did?

I think the proximate cause was energy from the March on Wall Street. But I also know the importance of the earlier Occupy movement, the Black Lives Matter movement, and, still more broadly, the Sanders campaign and the stupendous turn out of women to kick off sustained resistance to Trump. I guess we were all realizing if we didn't stand for what's right then we would likely fall for what's wrong.

I began to realize that a lone effort at change rarely wins much, but carried through well, a collective effort can provide lessons and sentiments that lead to another effort, and then another. We never get a continuous, uninterrupted piling on of desires, capacities, and gains. We win some, lose some. Our task is to learn from the losses so the gains accumulate and feed off each other.

Some say, just pick a target, commit, and do the hard work. But what target, commit on what basis, do what hard work? How?

The person saying "just do it" is right, but you are right, too. Saying activism is easy, so just do it, is technically valid but flippant about or ignorant of the obstacles people feel. Many pre-RPS efforts aroused peoples' worthy desires. Many taught useful skills. Many conveyed needed confidence and overcame harmful biases. But not everyone involved at each stage experienced lasting changes. Many participants would gain new inclinations for a time and then lose those attributes due to the pressures of returning to daily roles to survive. Their activism would decline when they had to refocus on restrictive jobs. Other participants would retain lessons, skills, feelings, and hope, and bring their energies to a next round of activity. Their forward trajectory of lasting involvement was crucial. To be effective, organizing had to generate that.

For example, for the immediately pre-RPS arms boycotts, we had campuses where twenty or thirty percent of students and faculty were vigorously active and eighty percent agreed with ending war research. Yet, as the dust temporarily settled, sometimes with total divestment, sometimes partial, most participants returned to attending classes and getting along. Getting such folks back into activism was a recurring priority. Having them never leave would be even better.

Andrej, you were intimately involved at the outset, too. Was your experience similar?

Yes, I also saw people leave after the boycott. And I too was saddened by that, but, overall, I also saw some people keep on keeping on. I saw even those who returned to their prior ways retain a residue of the boycott experience, able to resurface. We who remained active just had to do good work.

What characterized those who did remain active?

We were changed and retained the changes. We no longer fit our past patterns. A few of us became social misfits when our outrage toward all injustice blocked our engaging thoughtfully in anything. Others of us designed new slots for ourselves. We knew society had to fundamentally change and we resolved to help make it happen. Perhaps most important, activists who stayed began to realize that the right norm for judging events, meetings, and campaigns wasn't did our effort win what was directly demanded or cause the disruption that was directly sought. The real criteria was did our effort increase consciousness, organization, and commitment in the people it communicated with? Did "movement first" replace "me and mine first."

What makes you think that happened?

A lot of things, not least my experiencing it myself. But for an outward indicator, imagine a major demonstration called to shut down some elite meeting. In earlier periods, in the initial organizing activists would emphasize what the meeting was for, why we considered it a heinous gathering, why we opposed it, and what we wanted beyond merely shutting it down. When the new criterion gained sway those focuses would persist right through when the meeting occurred and into its aftermath. But before the new criterion gained sway, pretty early on and steadily more so as the meeting neared, organizers and left media would shift from focusing on the goals of the meeting and on the movement's reasons for opposing those goals, to the technical details of blocking the meeting and dealing with police. Our message would become stop the meeting, we win. Fail to stop the meeting, police win. Focusing on tactical success would cause radical insights to fade from discussion. Police would only have to coerce us into tactical retreat and we would feel defeated. But with the new norm, our priority became how today's choices impact tomorrow, not whether today's action accomplishes some short-term tactical aim. When we organized to stop some meeting or to win some campaign, with the new norm we understood our demands and actions mattered for the immediate benefits they could deliver to worthy recipients, but also for how they facilitated winning more gains in the future.

Why was that recognition such a big deal?

It informed how we chose targets and our words and methods. It caused us to realize that being a revolutionary wasn't mainly about supporting particular ideas or even advocating a transformative vision. It wasn't mainly about courage or even about being in some organization. Being a revolutionary required life reorienting from being about one's job or even an immediate radical agenda, to being about winning a changed society. "I am a revolutionary" came to mean that the organizing principle guiding my life is to win a new society.

CHAPTER 3

GETTING STARTED

*Andrej Goldman and Bill Hampton
discuss hope, activism, and program.*

Andrej, what was most critical for activism to successfully build a lasting, growing, revolutionary movement like RPS?

I remember a talk I heard years back that focused on a case study. The speaker told us that in April of 1968, France had considerable activism but also a vast sea of passivity. Then some modest campus disputes over male and female hours of dorm access erupted. In days the country exploded and for weeks was a revolutionary cauldron of creative energy. The great Paris upheaval. Everyone began delineating the horrors of modern life and fighting for comprehensive change. People rallied, marched, occupied, and fought on a huge scale. France tottered. Yet, in a few months, quiet returned. Unprecedented rebellion succumbed to resurgent passivity.

The speaker asked how we might best explain such sudden turning on and off of gigantic social upheaval? He said one possibility was that ideas about how society works were suddenly widely conveyed, and fueled the uprisings. A bit later the insights melted away and upheaval subsided back into life as usual. The speaker then wondered, however, how a whole society could become suddenly enlightened and then just as suddenly apocalyptically dis-enlightened? Did mass lobotomy eradicate massively injected wisdom?

Rejecting that explanation, the speaker proposed that before May 1968 France's population had had no hope for a transformed future. During May they had hope. Later, hope dissipated and hope's exit terminated turmoil. I thought claiming aroused hope was paramount was astute. I agreed pinpointing suddenly learned and equally suddenly forgotten ideas was ridiculous.

But that was then, what about now?

My understanding of then explains why, when you ask what ideas I think aided RPS emerging, I emphasize RPS offering compelling, desirable vision that aroused informed hope.

Suppose we compare the half century extending from 1965 to 2015, to the quarter century extending from 2015 to 2040. What changed so that in the earlier period, despite that at many moments large numbers of people understood or were only a hair away from understanding society's ills, nonetheless that period never generated sustainable projects for winning a new society - yet now such projects are nearing full success?

Many say it was a recent brilliant insight we didn't have earlier, or a recent event they didn't experience earlier. And while I don't deny the importance of ideas or events, I think RPS activism has been at least as much caused by other factors as by brilliant insights or specific events.

What other factors?

First, hope replaced absence of hope. We went from believing that "there is no attainable alternative," to believing "there is an attainable alternative."

Second, we stopped mainly criticizing, rejecting, and denigrating one another and old social relations, and started celebrating, advocating, and supporting one another while proposing new social relations.

Third, we recognized that "united we stand, divided we fall" is not just a catchy slogan but a powerful insight we had to embrace to succeed. One person can have impact. Many people can have more impact. But many people won't cooperate unless they acknowledge each other's diverse desires.

Another factor was style versus substance. The former is the clever, emotive impact of words. The latter is the meaning of sentences in paragraphs and arguments. In the half century to 2015, style exceeded substance. The climax was Trump, who paid zero attention to evidence, logic, and even truth, and instead used catch words and slick phrases to stoke passions. But Trump was more culmination than cause. Before Trump, Twitter and Facebook distorted communication into short nuggets that precluded presenting serious evidence and argument. Narcissistic selfie culture bent priorities. Clickbait titles deceived readers. Fake news became policy. Toxicity spread, and finally Trump emerged. So, this change was that, fourth, we tried to reverse the imbalance between style and substance, and that too helped birth RPS.

In sum, enlarged hope, mutual aid-oriented insights, unyielding commitments to develop and share vision, growing desire for organization, and increased emphasis on substance all aided RPS in the last quarter century, where these factors had been far less present in the prior half century.

But that's all in people's heads. What about material conditions?

Yes, it's in people's heads. Where else should we look for what causes persistent changes to people's behavior? For centuries material conditions have warranted sustained, revolutionary activism. So why did it recently emerge? Some look toward material conditions. I instead highlight changes in our views and choices. Changes which others can enact as well.

Bill Hampton, born in 1997, you became highly active in anti-racist politics and then in RPS. You focused on city life, transportation, and urban planning and became an inner city activist, a Mayoral candidate, and finally Mayor of New York City. Do you remember first becoming radical?

Under Obama, I had grown horrified at the racist resurgence that birthed Black Lives Matter and sensitized many to Islamaphobia and immigration. Joining the campaign for sanctuary in my local church greatly affected me. Feeling the need to connect with other emerging struggles primed me for RPS. I never said I want to be radical. I want to be revolutionary. Instead, something inside took over, and that was that.

Can you tell us what about RPS most personally moved you?

The first thing that comes to mind was when I was at a sanctuary for immigrants slated to be deported. The site was a church in Texas, with an incredibly courageous pastor, choir, and congregation. Police came and announced they were going to take the immigrant families for deportation. They had their vans and were set to do their duty. They lined up in three rows, ten abreast, facing the church entrance. The Pastor stood atop the Church steps, with maybe 50 congregants, and the full choir. He told the sheriff that to take the immigrant families, the police would have to go through the church's extended family. He said, and I will never forget, "You will have to assault us. You may even have to kill us. We will not be moved in our minds. We will only be moved in our bodies and only then if you brutalize our limbs into physical silence and shove our trembling husks aside. If you feel that is warranted, come ahead."

We all simultaneously locked arms and before the police could even process that, the doors of the Church opened to reveal rows and rows of congregants, also with locked arms. You could see the families, in the distance at the pulpit.

This was Selma, the Pettus bridge. It was Birmingham. The sheriff may as well have been Bull Connor reincarnated. Likely most or perhaps all the officers who accompanied the sheriff hoped they would get some action. But two sat down with us. Welcomed, crying, they must have thought they would be unemployed by days' end, but they sat.

The sheriff knew that breaching our human barrier would only succeed if we crumbled and ran. The Pastor said, no, we won't run. But the sheriff had so little regard for anyone who could side with immigrants that he felt, of course we would fold. A few big swings of their overlong batons and we would scurry off leaving a clear path to the deportees. So the sheriff gave a two minute warning. The choir began singing. "We shall not be moved, we shall not be moved…" The two minutes passed. The sheriff and his deputies marched into our human barrier. They struck viciously with their long, scary batons. Our singing continued. "Deep in our hearts we know…" As the officers tromped and battered us, we grunted and moaned, but few screamed.

With the choir singing, with more folks from within the church coming out, and with onlookers clearly horrified, incredibly, the defenders, including myself, reached up and embraced our tormentors. Our hugs diminished their capacity for brutal swings. There was an intimacy about it. We weren't begging. We were understanding. We weren't fighting fire with fire, but with water. We weren't fighting racism with racism, but with solidarity.

After a moment, some deputies relented. Then the sheriff did too. He had to. They certainly could have physically demolished us, leaving a battlefield of blasted souls in their wake, but nothing less would take the families, and scorched earth was too much.

At first indication of retreat, the Pastor, bloodied and bent, invited the sheriff and his closest deputies to enter the church. I can still hear him. "You just have to leave your batons and guns with your fellow officers outside. If you will do that, you are welcome to talk to the immigrant families, myself, and others in our space of peace and worship within."

Tears flowed. Medics aided congregants. Calmly, respectfully, after what seemed like an eternity of just standing there staring at the bloodied Pastor, and in what I will never know but suspect was a shock for the Pastor like for the rest of us, the Sheriff took off his gun, and walked with the Pastor into the Church.

I don't know what they talked about, but the next day the Sheriff held a brief press conference. "I will no longer recognize federal orders, or any orders at all, to deport immigrants."

That was the whole thing. It was the shortest, longest, press conference ever. It was also the beginning of the end, not just in Texas and the U.S., but around the world, of the blame the immigrant, beat the immigrant, expel the immigrant, mindset. When those who are paid to impose rule break bread with presumed violators, rule succumbs to resistance. This was such an incredible sight, such an incredible event, so meaningful an occurrence in so many ways, that, I have to name it in answer to your question.

I should add the event changed me in another major way. Before, I had always been afraid of and hated cops. I knew their worst side firsthand. To me, my family, my friends, cops spelled danger and even death. I used the epithet "pig" more than "officer." I saw only one way to deal with them: fight fire with fire, eye to eye, toe to toe.

The sanctuary didn't make me a pacifist, but it did make me reassess defaming people and reconsider what made tactical sense. The sheriff was an archetype cop, but we disarmed him. Non violence plus compassion beat what would have totally demolished any attempt by us to fight back. I learned that instead of violence being first resort, it had to be last. I learned there was a huge burden of proof on being violent and even on creating conditions leading to violence. I learned police could be turned our way. Indeed, they had to be.

With such powerful events happening, how did RPS program emerge?

I think program became a natural focus to expand events like the above. It emerged against the backdrop of the Sanders campaign and the Occupy and Black Lives Matter movements, as well as related efforts in Greece, Spain, Turkey, Portugal, South Africa, and the Corbyn experience in the UK and the huge women's demonstrations against Trump. I had myself been hugely affected by Occupy and very involved in it, and also by the Venezuelan experience, and Greek and Spanish uprisings.

Trump's victory was traumatic. Before long, he was appointing climate deniers, vicious racists and misogynists, and even overt fascists. His administration propelled an orgy of right-wing excess made even worse by fears the country wanted it, or would at least accept it, though we soon saw the country did not want it and would not accept it, when millions rebelled against austerity, racism, war, and global warming. Still, the anti Trump surge could either fizzle back into business as usual pre Trump for lacking positive focus and wide solidarity, or it could move toward encompassing program and organization. The latter happened, though it wasn't an easy path.

How did program emerge and why was it hard to achieve?

First, there was already program proposed by the Sanders campaign and almost simultaneously Black Lives Matter rebounded from largely ignoring program to seriously and excellently offering it. But if you look back, you will see that most people, even on the left, were still unimpressed with program. The same thing was evidenced when the massive women's marches offered program. Dozens of essays addressing Trump's tweeter insanities appeared for every one that addressed the BLM or Women's program or any positive program at all.

That must have been extremely frustrating...

Yes, but it wasn't new. It continued a long-time failing into our new context. At any rate, the resistance to Trump clearly needed a more substantive, forward looking orientation. It wasn't that people weren't asking what's next and how do we persist. It was that even that discussion rarely included positive program, visionary substance, and encompassing organization. People regularly addressed important immediate details, but rarely longer run aims and methods.

In response to Trump trying to hugely escalate deportation, activists organized sanctuaries. Even earlier were the airport demonstrations. Then I remember a mosque burning in Texas followed by a temple handing over its keys to the Moslems left without their place of worship. Incredible things like that happened over and over, but tying together the disparate sentiments and actions into lasting positive program was difficult.

To expand the reaction to Trumps' anti immigrant efforts, activists created local sanctuaries in churches and universities and even in some private homes where people offered to harbor deportees to protect them. One solidarity slogan was, "If you take our friends, you have to take us, and neither they nor we are going without a fight."

Venues like churches and campus centers provided housing and protection and when deportation authorities even sneezed at such venues, masses of supporters situated themselves to block police entry. During the days and nights of the sanctuaries, we held teach ins and cultural events to build support and develop trust. This activism kept spreading until groups of major athletes welcomed immigrants into sports arenas the same way the New Orleans Saints arena had been used to house Hurricane Katrina victims, years before. This, unsurprisingly, stopped Trump's deportation schemes cold and also created a mutual aid mindset that had been absent in some other anti-Trump activism.

Another effective choice was our response to white supremacist, war mongering, climate denying, Cabinet members. We first exposed their views, then proposed progressives for their posts, and explained clearly how they would be better. We even rallied where the appointees worked, lived, and worshipped. I remember the shock to us and them of our going into their rich neighborhoods and demonstrating at their homes. First we did it in groups of thirty to forty and cops quickly cleared us out. Then we got smarter and held rallies in poor neighborhoods and city centers in their towns. From the rallies we collectively marched to their homes. We were peaceful, but there were often hundreds or even thousands of us. The cabinet members wanted us driven off, but imagine the impact of doing so on their neighbors. Just telling us to leave wouldn't work. What next. Gas suburbia? Then we started inviting kids from nearby homes to join us, and in a few cases even kids of the cabinet members we were confronting. Imagine their subsequent family dinners.

Perhaps our most effective anti-Trump project was responding to enlarged military and police budgets by positively pointing out better ways to spend the funds and demanding changes in police structure, policy, and community oversight and control, all echoing earlier BLM efforts, and in using military bases to build low income housing funded by military budgets. Fighting to earmark the first houses to soldiers who built them did wonders for outreach.

We also invited and welcomed police into neighborhood and even household meetings to discuss how to create safer communities and avoid racist policing. We went to military bases and police stations and organized. Of course, it all took time and we had to overcome a lot of our own fear and very real and aggressive anger, but I think these endeavors helped the anti-Trump resistance not just restrain Trump, but also move toward RPS activism.

We understood that we had to find worthy things to demand and effective ways to fight which appealed to every crucial constituency and polarized no worthy constituency away from progressive participation. Of course, after Trump was beaten by Warren in 2020, and once momentum had grown and a degree of coherence and clarity had emerged, we began to build grassroots neighborhood and workplace assemblies. Warren may well have been not only our first woman president but our first honest President. She wasn't RPS born, but nor was she aggressively anti RPS.

But pre- and post-Warren, we also needed organization. I remember when Trump won I wondered, for the next four years should we only have disparate, disconnected movements about all manner of separate issues, overwhelmingly aimed only at preventing reaction? Or should we have at least one overarching, multi-issue, multi-tactic organization emphasizing proposing, organizing for, and trying to win wide ranging elements of positive program and vision?

I remember debating whether a new visionary organization should look like those we had seen in the past, or if we needed to conceive and implement powerful new ways to welcome and enhance diversity, celebrate and practice collective self management, and chastise and structurally guard against arrogant, sectarian, apocalyptic, and especially too narrow, in-grown organizing. Our answers fed the momentum that created RPS. But it wasn't simple or quick. There was so much passionate anger, so much defensiveness, so much chaos, and so much skepticism, that at first it was very hard to get coherent results.

One striking aspect of those times was that many activists opposed having any program at all. They didn't resist specifics of program, rather they feared that highlighting program or anything intellectually substantive would lead to the most verbal, confident, least time pressured, and best educated activists dominating discussions and governing outcomes.

People didn't want program to protect participation? Please explain.

Activists intuitively understood the negative implications of elevating what we later called the coordinator class of managers, doctors, lawyers, et. al., but back then resistance to coordinator elitism often deteriorated into resisting thought itself. Distancing from evaluation and exploration obstructed dealing with the substance of movement goals and structure, but the sentiment driving it was not anti-intellectualism. Rather, we resisted leaders monopolizing decision making, and our resistance, even if not how we expressed it, was warranted.

I remember heated arguments where the polished "advocates of reason" would encounter opposition that for all the world looked to be rejecting reason itself, and even rejecting thinking, rather than only rejecting perverse thinking that advanced narrow interests.

What finally made the underlying truth pretty clear was to see who lined up where. The battle wasn't pretty, and it didn't resolve quickly, but, over a period of years we made major progress, though even now the issues are still resolving. The gain for RPS's future from analyzing this phenomenon was RPS deciding early on that our sometimes seemingly "anti intellectual" dynamic was mainly about or could be made to be mainly about class interests, not rejecting thought.

And what became of seeking program?

As calls for program grew, we built momentum to reduce inequality by raising the minimum wage. We sought increased taxes on the rich, a program that had become real, earlier, in Seattle. We sought to shorten the work week to attain full employment and generate more leisure.

We sought free health care for all, desirable housing for all, and enriched schooling for all, including cancelling student debt and making higher education free. We sought free day care for all. We sought to reorient government spending from war and social control to housing, health care, education, infrastructure, and vastly expanded social services. We didn't have demands for new underlying institutions, but our pursuits fostered discussions that propelled such desires.

Still, most people's responses to queries about program remained disjointed. We would discuss one programmatic idea or another. Do we like this or that. One project or organization would latch onto one aim with gusto. Another project or organization would latch onto a different aim with equal gusto. No one strayed far from prior priorities. Few adopted broad program.

Trump's victory stalled positive program by causing most activists to focus on fighting reaction, but it didn't end program. An example was the massive women's rallies during Trump's inauguration. Left Liberals and even more mainstream democrats were prominent, which they needed to be. The danger was that they alone would define directions. But lots of women not only wanted massive participation but also understood the need to develop broad and deep program, and their efforts in seeking both scale and substance were exemplary.

At any rate, that was the state of dissent when some people began to pursue what would become RPS. We proposed shared program and shared vision. We proposed an organization able to flexibly pursue and refine its commitments. We hoped that while single issue movements and highly focussed organizations would each and all persist and retain their priorities, they would also sign on to an overarching agenda and lend their support to all its components.

It wasn't just that we wanted good programmatic ideas or demands. Those existed. It was that we needed to meaningfully share good program so we all supported campaigns not only for the one or two aspects that were immediately most meaningful to us due to our own past priorities or current ties, but supported all aspects to foster real mutual aid and solidarity and to make each aspect stronger than it would be without partnerships. Those who focused most on war would aid those who focused most on immigration would aid those who focused most on global warming, and so on, in a web of emerging mutual aid.

Bill, I wonder if you could tell us what were the obstacles to successful organizing before RPS. What failings did RPS have to correct to succeed?

A lot of factors had been interfering with movements succeeding. For example, society debilitates us and most people didn't have sufficient mental or other health support to participate well. Oppression even harms our ability to cooperate and think clearly, which makes it difficult to work collectively and be strategic, and, sadly, makes it all too easy to lash out at one another. Many people would use left spaces - meetings, forums, and workshops - to "act out" their issues and feelings of desperation. RPS needed to help members reduce and eliminate those difficulties.

Racism, sexism, and classism in our operations was another obstacle. We grow up in society and are schooled by it, not just in schools, but in all the roles we occupy each day. It isn't our fault, but we pick up many habits that destroy unity and clarity. Sometimes we do oppressive things, sometimes we are too passive. Before RPS, we had few non-shaming ways to learn new behaviors. People felt their choice to be 1) feel constantly ashamed and scared that you might behave badly and be attacked for it, or 2) quit. RPS needed to dismantle oppressive systems in society while it simultaneously provided ways for movement members to feel safe from attack and able to change.

Defeatism was rampant and severely debilitating to activism in a host of ways. If we think at some deep level there is no alternative, we have no motivation to be serious and careful in addressing events. We may try to please friends, or maybe to win something short term while ignoring long term prospects. We may try to punish opponents, or to prove our worth more than to win a new system. We may posture to appear radical. Similarly, since it is easier and more pleasurable to talk to people who like us than to reach out to those who disagree with us - we might become insular. RPS needed to generate and share vision and strategy able to sustain hope and ward off such habits.

Another problem was that while people realized it was important to organize and be democratic, we didn't understand what either required. Too often we didn't create channels for new recruits to participate in theory and strategy. We wrote for graduate students or for people who already knew what "the left" was and knew its jargon. Left writers wrote for other (highly educated) leftists. Why didn't we write for working people? It was because we got no recognition for that. And why didn't we write in a way that showed we actually wanted to be understood? Perhaps it was because we didn't want to be understood?

I'm not suggesting dumbing down. I'm suggesting not making our work less accessible than it could be, which was what we very often did. More, too much of our writing, and speaking, even when it was accessible, just railed against society or even against other leftists, rather than advocating anything positive. When non leftists read us, they typically didn't know what we were talking about or did know and wondered why we were bothering to say the same negative things over and over. Hell, I often wondered whether most of the people writing knew what they were talking about other than when it was just obscurely enumerating the ills of society which their readers knew too. RPS had to get positive and get accessible.

A related issue was the left being anti-religious, anti-country, and anti- most everything else working class people liked, like religion, race car driving, country music, and fast food. This was a big issue, of course, and extended right into left organization and program reflecting academic and professional values and aims far more than working class values and aims. RPS had to reverse all that.

Still another problem was that we operated in what some called "isolated silos." Organizations wasted lots of time and money by not coordinating and collectivizing. It was like suburbs where everyone had their own washer-dryer, sit-down lawn mower, and two-car garage. Each movement had its own separate promotion, bookkeeping, communications, data base manager, fundraising, residence, etc. So movement budgets replicated purchasing all that stuff, leaving less for actual work. And then, in silo mode, each acted without coordinating with the rest, severely diminishing overall impact. RPS needed to find ways to bring issues and campaigns into mutual support.

Infatuation with violence was another problem as was susceptibility to liberalism, hostility to reforms, and denigration of folks who weren't yet as wise as oneself. RPS had to turn all that around, too.

You get the idea. There was plenty to fix. But that was good news. If everything before RPS had been fine, RPS couldn't have done better than those who preceded it, and wouldn't have had any more success than them.

We will see about these various issues and how RPS related to them as we go along, I am sure, but I would like to ask you a little more about one, even now, to avoid it leaving a wrong impression. When you describe the difficulty of organizing given people's emotional and behavioral baggage getting in the way, it almost sounds like you think the left needed to have lots of psychiatrists on board...

Not shrinks, more like collective supportive attention to all the baggage we drag around. Here are some steps I saw taken by RPS.

People were given a chance to tell their story. Everyone listened. Tears happened. People got heard. Perhaps people got a hug but the point was we all saw the full person. We could remember that the person had all that going on. It generated new levels of respect and connection, and not just a utilitarian connection based on what a person "will get done." People felt less needy and more present, more able to think and engage because they got seen and heard. It took time to hear a story, and you had to develop some trust first - a good thing - but it ultimately saved time because the person would then be more functional. Over time, everyone got a turn, but it wasn't forced. People told their stories when ready. Relationships got built. People felt more compassion for each other which prompted sticking to the tasks at hand and showing up for each other.

Another version of addressing this issue was that at the beginning of a meeting, there would be time for people, if they wanted, to do one-on-ones or "pair shares," where they just said how they were doing, or they said something was going well or something was not going well. Or they said what they hoped to get out of the meeting. One person listened and perhaps asked questions to prompt the other person to say more. Of course it was possible to turn these approaches into shaming or make them intrusive. Smash or be smashed. But more often I saw it be hugely beneficial.

People got their feelings out in the pair share and then didn't have to take up the time of everyone in the meeting to air them. When it worked, it was win win. Healing took place and people and meetings became more effective.

> *One more question before moving on, if you would. You described that pre-RPS many leftists wrote and spoke in unnecessarily obscure ways. It is so obvious why that would fail, I wonder, why did it exist at all? Why would anyone communicate in ways that alienated essential constituencies?*

My reaction was like yours. This was suicidal. Why do it? I asked some writers and while a few said it was the only way to deal with intrinsically complex matters - which was self-serving nonsense - most said, roughly, "if I don't dress up my writing like that I will be ignored. Faculty, publishers, and even certain audiences consider it mandatory to use that language to demonstrate preparedness and competence. Write or even speak plainly and you appear unprepared, unversed, unprofessional, and even ignorant. The people who buy, review, and publish books expect obtuseness. They talk up ideas or they dismiss them. I have to impress those people to reach anyone else."

In context, it therefore made personal and even social sense to be intentionally obscure, just like passively working as a wage slave makes perfect sense as long as you believe replacing wage slavery is impossible and you need to eat. Writing and speaking in obscurantist jargon at the expense of comprehensibility and even coherence made sense as long as you believed it was the only way to be graduated with honors, published, celebrated, or even to be heard at all. And if you did it a lot, it became a kind of reflex. And you would not just do it, but defend doing it and see criticisms as ignorant or even anti-knowledge.

CHAPTER 4

2016

Senator Malcolm King discusses the 2016 Election.

Malcolm, I know it was a quarter century ago, but it was right before RPS got going so before we address RPS history, can we consider the 2016 Elections? For example, what role did they play in RPS emerging?

Twenty five years ago Bernie Sanders ran for President as a Democrat. His speeches, writing, and platform leaned toward what would become RPS positions. He got tens of millions of voters to hope more ambitiously than in the past and his campaign gave tens of thousands confidence defending dissident views. It taught going door to door, phone banking, raising funds, conducting meetings, and working together.

During the campaign, Sanders' team turned out huge, passionate crowds. Clinton's machine used rules that had earlier been added to U.S. election law precisely to marginalize dissidents.

Getting the nomination was supposed to be a Clinton cakewalk but Sanders so bested her among young voters and independents that he won many primaries. Clinton won overall because the Democratic Party stacked everything in her favor, as well as because minority, and especially Black voters supported her, a strange dynamic that befuddled many.

I have wondered about that. Can you explain it?

The Clintons had a reputation for personally treating Blacks as equals, Hillary was rhetorically good at addressing personal race relations, and the Democratic party apparatus, with all its benefits to hand out, played a big role. Grassroots ignorance of Sanders, largely due to media mendacity, also contributed. Still, Sanders' positions were clearly better for Black and Latino advancement, and lots of young Black and Latino voters knew it, and some older folks did too. Yet Clinton won and I suspect the Black community voted for her over Sanders mainly fearing that in a general election Sanders would suffer media assault plus red baiting defection by Democratic Party elites allowing Trump and other extremist Republicans to win.

At any rate, with Black support in hand, and the media and Democratic Party torpedoing Sanders at every turn, Clinton got the nomination. Should a serious person who viewed Clinton as a war mongering corporate shill vote for her anyway to ensure that Trump didn't win the election? Doing so was called voting for the lesser evil and was applicable only to contested states. Alternatively, should a Clinton critic, even in a contested state, abstain or vote for a third party candidate to be true to self, to show the scale of dissent, and to build a third party, believing that Trump would lose anyhow or wasn't worse, or that opposition would keep Trump in line?

Why did that choice matter for RPS emerging?

For decades few activists had taken seriously winning a new society. We gave nearly zero time to thinking about what a good society's institutions should look like. Some said thinking about vision would distract from more immediate concerns. Others said vision was beyond us, or vision wasn't our responsibility. But I think we mainly avoided vision because we didn't believe winning was possible. If a new society was impossible, thinking about the features of a new society or about how to reach a new society, would be like thinking about a round square. If you can't win, why try? But in that case, why are you radical?

We weren't radical for income, since income for activism was low or nonexistent. We weren't radical for fun, since activism had too much tedium, trouble, and sacrifice, to be fun. For decades I think we had been radical to be right, to be moral, to be able to look at ourselves in the mirror. We were radical as a moral high ground lifestyle. We were radical to express rather than bottle up outrage. We sniped at power never even thinking about taking power.

For decades angry, frustrated people had become active for short upsurges seeking quick victories. Or patient people became active for longer durations, to "be on the side of the angels." For them, "Be radical" meant "be virtuous, despite that you aren't going to win." Do it to respect yourself. They weren't trying to enhance prospects of winning unattainable fundamental change.

And Sanders awakened hope?

Yes, Sanders' accomplishments legitimated reaching a large audience and galvanizing lasting support. Sanders also revealed the Democratic Party's fragility. He amassed huge support while talking about revolution.

But then why did many people on the far left, as compared to folks then just getting involved, dismiss and disparage Sanders?

In just a few months Sanders and his supporters arguably did more to move the national psyche than radical activists had done in the prior twenty years. Of course, Sanders built on what went before, but people who had been active for a long time had difficulty acknowledging just how much Sanders accomplished. It was less painful to one's self image to dismiss him than to acknowledge his achievements and what they implied about our prior activity.

The second factor was when Clinton sewed up the nomination Sanders supported her, albeit unenthusiastically. He emphasized stopping Trump. He also kept highlighting the need to organize on behalf of a political revolution, and he even worked toward building an organization called Our Revolution. Yet to many of his supporters - spurred on by some writers who should have known better - it smelled like a sellout. These folks didn't contemplate that maybe the guy they had loved yesterday hadn't changed. Maybe beating Trump was necessary to further an agenda they all believed in. Maybe if the left did other than vote against Trump in contested states, Trump would win.

Okay, but what was the impact for RPS?

Heading into the 2016 election, if you were fatalistic about winning more than modest gains you were accustomed to ask, what is the moral thing to do? What is the radical thing to do? What fits my radical identity?

Many answered, "even in my contested state I want to vote for a third party candidate or for no one at all, and I will not vote for a war criminal like Clinton." This was called voting your conscience. Its advocates said it was true to themselves, whereas voting for the lesser evil would deny themselves.

But why did that matter for the initial stages of RPS.

First we reassessed what being true to yourself meant. Why was it more true to yourself to say "I hate both Trump and Clinton so I won't vote for either one," than it was to say, "I hate both Trump and Clinton, but I believe Trump would be way worse, so I will vote for Clinton wherever it is close enough that Trump might win, to stop him, not out of any belief in her"?

Second, we wondered why downplaying the importance of the effects on others and emphasizing attention to expressing "self" was admirable at all? Why was being driven by one's personal hate for Clinton more moral than addressing the plight of those who would suffer greatly under Trump?

Other factors also played a role, for example, assessing the impact of different approaches on prospects for later organizing. Opponents of voting the lesser evil in contested states emphasized, accurately, that a Trump win would accelerate immediate activism. Proponents of lesser evil voting replied, accurately, that anti-Trump activism would focus on preventing rollback and ignore winning new gains. With Clinton as President, we would have to work harder to generate activism, but it would be forward seeking.

In the earliest days of RPS, heading toward Trump's defeat in 2020, future RPSers managed to help the anti-Trump opposition become more than a temporary upsurge. We took resistance beyond the social democratic rhetoric of progressive Democrats. We ratified the idea that politics required moral choices, but also that morality required paying attention to more than one's own personal feelings. This pushed us to highlight long-term effects over short-term feelings. We had to assess beyond ourselves. We had to take responsibility for our choices rather than striking a pose.

What did thinking about what was good for future organizing involve?

First, we saw it was possible to finance a campaign from the grassroots, to win the Democratic Party nomination, and even to win the Presidency. After all, had Sanders won the nomination, and we all saw quite plausible ways that could have happened, we all thought he would have trumped Trump. So, the idea of running for President to win was back on the table as a conceivable, and even promising, future possibility. This lesson was imbibed by RPS, which became positive about people running to win, and I think it is fair to say Sanders is as much responsible for my now being a Senator as I am responsible for it.

Second, in the debates about voting for Clinton versus voting for Trump, the point was repeatedly made that having a Democrat rather than a Republican as President was better for organizing. A Democrat would be more hampered in repressing opposition. Also, dissent against a Democrat would pursue positive aspirations and seek new institutions in a new society, whereas dissent against a reactionary would be about rebutting insanity to prevent going backwards. Dissent against Clinton would be against Democrats whereas dissent against Trump would be led by Democrats.

Railing against Clinton reduced opposing Democrats?

Those who didn't vote for Clinton even in contested states like Ohio, Pennsylvania, and Florida, where 70,000 votes gave Trump the presidency, understandably wanted to avoid ratifying the Democratic Party as a vehicle of social change. They wanted to avoid movement energy being co-opted to Democratic Party agendas. Trump's election, however, elevated Democrats to militant guidance of the opposition, whereas Clinton's election would have galvanized movement energy against Democrats and toward more basic change.

Ironic...

Yes, but I remember how evident it was, how unavoidably obvious, though it took a long time to get across. What made it so evident was that it was happening even while people were discussing it, even before Trump won. Not only was mainstream media constantly crowded with articles about Trump, so was left media. You could cull from the latter ten, fifteen, and sometimes even twenty different articles a day about what was wrong with Trump. On the other hand, the number of articles about systemic problems was modest and the number of articles that even alluded to, much less emphasized, seeking new defining institutions was nearly none. When activists stared into the Trumpist abyss, we rightly tried to toe the line against going backward. Some of us also saw the need to go forward and saw the obstacles and started to agitate to overcome them. That fledgling dynamic became RPS.

A more complex matter was the efficacy of developing a third party approach to electoral politics. Of course it would make sense to have a third, fourth, and fifth party after a switch in the electoral system away from winner take all voting toward proportional power sharing. But before attaining proportional representation and related innovations, a third party unable to fully win, could, in closely contested states, cause the worser of two main candidates to win. This was evident well before 2016, of course, but was made blatantly obvious in 2016.

Some said, let's not bother with third party politics at all. We should contest only within the Democratic Party. Others said, we have to build a third party because the Democratic Party is a graveyard for radical aspirations. We need to survive the period during which we can't win by growing our alternative so in time we can win. A compromise position was to support third party development whenever one could do so without ushering in a grossly more evil candidate.

Running for office is complicated. You try to speak to hearts and mind. You try to avoid bad side effects. You try to support other activist efforts. But the pressures on candidates to minimize everything other than their own campaign and to focus only on winning votes and raising money become enormous. RPS learned to welcome third party activism and also sincere activism inside the Democratic Party, but to avoid the distorting effects of itself fielding candidates.

> *Why did so many people support Trump before and even after his sexual braggadocio meltdown? What was the nature of Trump's initial support - was it not support for his racist misogyny?*

Many looked at the situation as you say. But others looked and said, hold on a minute, what about the massive support for Sanders, just months back? And while Trump's support is partly about race and gender, isn't it also about working people suffering immeasurably and trying to get change?

Trump was buffoonish and grossly racist and sexist. Trump's utterances were not only disgusting but also well beyond familiar, sugarcoated support for injustice of the sort that Clinton and all past presidents routinely delivered. And, yes, virtually every racist, neo-Nazi group in the country supported Trump. And so did many besieged men who felt women's gains imposed unjust losses on them. So that was one part of Trump's support. But what mattered more for what happened later came from economically disaffected workers. So the important question was why did so many economically disaffected workers vote for Trump? Saying he had more upper income support was true, but it was his worker support we had to understand.

Trump was a billionaire. He was known for his horrible treatment of workers. But, he was also the opposite of a typical calculating politician. Many of his votes came from people who felt that Trump turning everything topsy turvy offered more hope than Clinton preserving what they found horrifying. Working people hated their declining circumstances. They hated feeling denigrated and denied. They hated joblessness and drug-ravaged neighborhoods. And Trump managed to attract a lot of justifiably angry workers even though he was, in fact, no working class hero but exactly the opposite.

Okay, but how?

Partly he scapegoated others. Partly he lied and manipulated. Partly he benefitted from mainstream media trying to profit by keeping him a big story. Partly he benefitted from some leftists and Greens saying voting for Clinton was a sellout and voting for Stein or not voting at all, even in contested states, was wise. But I think a different factor was decisive.

Decades earlier, Spiro Agnew had also tapped into class anger to galvanize support for the right. He did it by ridiculing and distancing himself from what he called bullet-headed liberal intellectuals - and the key word was not "liberal," but "intellectual."

Agnew tapped into justified anger at what were then called professionals but what RPS later called the coordinator class, and Trump did the same thing. Working people felt Trump was one of them rather than establishment. When he got into office, they thought he wouldn't ignore them and might even be their tribune.

This perception of Trump overlooked reality, but voters' desperate desires to reverse working class decline were real. And that was why the working class support that Trump surfaced, once radical organizers got over their tendency to look down on working people and instead listened to them and learned from their desires regarding their deteriorating circumstances, pushed RPS from being isolated from working people to expressing working class desires.

Did Sanders' campaign impact your later becoming a candidate?

After college, I was very radical and not interested in pursuing a lucrative career disconnected from people's needs. I got an assembly job and then worked as a short order cook. My focus was organizing my workmates and trying to get involved in worker-based community organizing. I was very anti war and very angered by ecological concerns. I detested electoral politics but Sanders got me to see that as rigged, alienated, corrupt, and mindless as the electoral system was, it had room to fight, and even to win. Sanders got me thinking about elections being part of winning major change.

I saw that among many routes to contributing to change, due to my history and circumstances, I was most likely to have electoral impact. I think many folks came away from 2016 with that thought, and while our hope was temporarily obliterated in a haze of recriminations and fears when Trump won, it quickly resurfaced. Of course not all who were inspired to run for office succeeded, but many are now in office, doing excellent work. If Sanders were here, I would thank him profusely.

There was another factor for me. My working class background and especially my time as an assembly worker and short order cook taught me just how hard it was to not explode at customers in suits and ties using erudite language who so clearly looked down on you, or who didn't even do that since, to them you were less consequential than a five minute delayed dinner.

Agnew had exploited justified working class anger long before, and now Trump did the same thing. The anger often embraced racism, sexism, and a kind of macho defense of an impoverished situation, but I avoided that path, though I understood it and I could empathize with it enough to talk to folks without being hostile. I could hear their misery and frustration and convey to them meaningful hope and program.

I took workers' views and desires seriously because I felt much of what they felt. I could also talk to coordinator class types. I didn't pretend to like where they were coming from. I didn't condescend to, suck up to, or manipulate them. I challenged their harmful views even while clearly understanding their motives and rationales.

I wonder whether Obama' victory affected you.

Of course, though neither he, his program, or his administration informed my beliefs based on anything they said or did. Quite the opposite. I was a harsh critic. But in 2008 I was 23, black, working class, just out of college and working on an assembly line. My politics were instinctual, not RPSish. I did not become liberal due to being ecstatic to see Obama win, but his victory did show me the country could rally around a black man. I think it is possible that had Obama lost, I would never have become a candidate. Sanders' affect on me may have been less than enough, had not Obama earlier affected me.

Did any technical, organizing-related issues emerge?

Yes. In Massachusetts, Sanders had roughly 120,000 people volunteering. He got about 600,000 votes. How many of the 600,000 would have voted for Sanders if he had had no one making phone calls and going door to door? 400,000? 500,000? Let's suppose only 300,000. If so, then 120,000 volunteers contributing many hundreds of thousands of hours of effort, attracted 300,000 votes. In this generous accounting, on average, each volunteer added 2.5 votes.

The question arose, was their time well spent? Were they talking to prospective voters in the most useful ways? Couldn't a volunteer, in ten, twenty, or more hours over a few months enlist more voters than that? We are talking about Sanders volunteers talking to future Trump or Clinton voters and winning them over. The time Sanders volunteers spent chatting with people who were already going to vote for Sanders because of his talks, views, ads, or whatever, wouldn't win new converts, though it might certainly have other virtues. There was a lot to think about in all this for future campaigns. How could we more effectively address confusion among potential voters, and, even more, how could we better address doubt and despair.

CHAPTER 5

REACTING TO TRUMP

Andrej Goldman and Senator Malcolm King discuss Trump winning.

Andrej, at the risk of focusing too much on one event and its aftermath, I wonder if you could tell us a bit about your reaction to Trump winning?

Lots of people wondered why Trump became President. My first reaction was to wonder, why ask why? Were we morbidly curious? Were we seeking someone to blame? Were we looking to escape blame ourselves? Or did we hope to find a workable path for the future? I opted for that last motive.

I knew mainstream media coddled Trump throughout the primaries and well into the national campaign. I knew it delivered eyes to advertisers, not truth to the public. I knew that even when relatively more enlightened media moguls finally saw a disaster brewing, they continued to prioritize short term profits.

What I took from this was that if all the largest megaphones were operated by profit-seeking elites and if our smaller megaphones were operated as a discordant cacophony, we would continue to face insurmountable odds. We had to carve our own communication paths. We had to "press the press" and also build alternative print, radio, video, and social media.

I knew the DNC torpedoed Sanders' campaign and if the Democrats had not squandered grassroots white working class support in prior decades, Trump would not have won no matter who he ran against. I knew it was accurate to blame the Democratic Party but that the

Democratic Party did what it does, which was to protect privilege. I took from this that progressives could benefit from a reconstructed Democratic Party and radicals could benefit from new parties plus major election reform.

I also knew if the Republican base had decided to forego their party to block Trump on grounds of his incredible debits, Trump would have lost. But other than pointing to the obvious need to "organize, organize," did that observation lead anywhere new? I took from these thoughts that we shouldn't ignore allies but we also shouldn't spend all our energy organizing only allies. We ought to solidify existing support but also grow new support.

Malcolm, didn't blaming white workers happen a lot?

It was certainly true that had fewer white male and female workers voted for Trump, he would have lost. Even just voting for Clinton at the same level that white voters had supported Obama over Romney would have sunk Trump. So the choice of a great many white workers to vote Trump abetted Trump's victory. Deciding why they voted Trump is where heated controversy arose.

Some argued voting for Trump meant you didn't care about his misogyny and racism or you even desired misogyny and racism. You were a little Trump. Most who said this totally dismissed Trump voters as lost to reason. Others agreed that while Trump voters were horrible, we must still reach out to them. However this seemed to mean we should shame them, "call them out," confront them, label them backward, ignorant, or worse, and demand that they repent. No point discussing, debating, or organizing. Repent, and we will like you. Don't repent, and we will hate you.

Some replied, "do you really believe Latinos who voted for Trump are little Trumps? Do you really believe women who voted for Trump, which is most white women, are little Trumps? If you don't, then presumably you think that these groups saw reasons to vote for Trump that not only weren't racist and sexist, but that overrode their distaste for Trump's racism and sexism. But if you see that this could be true for Latino and female Trump voters, then why assume that most white male working class Trump voters weren't moved by the same non racist and non sexist feelings as some Latino voters and the majority of white women voters? If white workers who voted for Obama had voted for Clinton, Trump loses. Did many white workers vote for Obama but not Clinton because they were racist? Did they vote for Obama but not Clinton because they - and remember, this includes more than half of white women - were sexist? Why isn't it possible that many white working class Trump voters from devastated communities who were suffering drug-invaded and unemployment-saddled neighborhoods and bombarded with horribly faulty media misinformation, were mainly voting against the status quo and not for racism and misogyny"?

Similarly, couldn't even better-off, white, working class Trump voters fearing job loss, suffering indignity, hating doctors, lawyers, managers, and coordinator class elites, and inundated with confusing and contradictory information, have been voting against the status quo and not for racism and misogyny? Wasn't fear of working class decline that great?

Andrej, many interviews done with Trump voters pointed toward better, albeit confused, motives. So why did so many upset anti-Trump commentators and even left activists assume worse motives?

Perhaps one reason was they lacked knowledge of the pain, suffering, and daily fear contemporary working class Trump voters felt. If you didn't see that, you wouldn't deem it an important motive. But I didn't think ignorance much less dispassion for working class suffering was a major reason why so many progressives castigated white workers as irretrievably racist and sexist.

So what else might have caused it?

Imagine you thought that more people believing rampant racism and misogyny motivated Trump voters would lead to more effective follow-up activity to reduce racism and misogyny. Imagine you also thought that more people believing that most Trump voters were attracted to Trump's claim that he would aid the "working class," would reduce effective anti racist and anti sexist follow-up activity. You might label racism and sexism paramount not because you had compelling evidence it was so, but because you felt convincing folks it was so would best counter racism and sexism.

Those who said racist and sexist motivations were paramount seemed to feel that to deal seriously with racism and sexism those phenomena had to be aggressively "called out," shamed, and even punished. In this view, asserting that other factors played a significant role would lead to less calling out and shaming of Trump voters. It would in this view cater to them, coddle them, and reduce prospects for improvement.

In contrast, some felt Trump voters were largely motivated by anti establishment anger funneled into a candidate who appeared to acknowledge them, hear their grievances, and say relevant (albeit, lying and manipulative) things. They felt activists needed to avoid adding to Trump's voters' feelings that liberals, progressives, and radicals reflexively dismiss white working class concerns as stupid or vile. They felt we needed to show what action on behalf of working class gains should include. We needed to explain, without denigration and dismissal, why Trump wasn't an avatar of desirable change. We needed to point out the incredible injustice and harm racist and sexist policies did without pointing our fingers at the people we were talking with. We needed to address that economic and social support for workers faced opposition not only from owners, but also from managers, doctors, lawyers, and the top-level union bureaucrats who the Democratic Party catered to. We needed to talk not at Trump voters but with Trump voters. We needed to hear their valid insights and debate important differences. So for me the big divide was should we we try to shame Trump's voters, call them out, and label them racist and sexist, somehow thinking that doing that would cause them to side with us? Or should we try to reach out, listen, hear, and strongly address the class issues that both white and non white and male and female Trump supporters powerfully felt, but also not yield an inch regarding racist or sexist beliefs? More introspectively, should organizers working with white workers assess our efforts to see if anything we had been doing may have contributed to workers willingly voting for Trump?

Didn't some feel black voters deserved a share of the blame?

Blacks voted only marginally less for Clinton than for Obama. How could they have been even partly at fault for Trump's victory? The answer was, a few months earlier blacks voting for Clinton against Sanders in the primaries ended Sanders' chances of winning the nomination. There were various reasons, such as Sanders starting out little known, initially emphasizing economics to the near exclusion of race, and especially fear that Sanders might do worse against a Republican, as well as, less compellingly, Clinton's undeserved reputation as a friend of the Black community. Still, if black communities, particularly in the south, had voted more for Sanders, he would have easily won the nomination.

A lesson this implied was that while attention to race, gender, and sexuality was critically important, insular identity politics bred confusion and hostility. Just as organizers of white workers needed to assess if aspects of their work were partly responsible for many white workers holding views that allowed voting for Trump over Clinton, so too organizers in Black communities should assess if aspects of their work were partly responsible for many Blacks holding views that allowed voting for Clinton over Sanders.

What about blaming women, and especially white working class women?

Women certainly voted way less for Clinton than she needed if she was to win. Women who voted for Trump were in some cases branded racist or even misogynist. The formulation came not only from antifeminists trying to parlay it into feminist division, but from some feminists, too.

It seemed to me that this almost exactly paralleled the class and race issues we just addressed. I thought in this case, too, organizers of women should assess if aspects of their past work were in part responsible for so many women (and men) holding views that allowed voting for Trump against Clinton (or for Clinton against Sanders in the primaries). Had feminists too often organized women in ways that unnecessarily polarized men and neglected other important aspects of women's lives?

Malcolm, what about blaming young Sanders supporters?

This view accurately claimed that by abstaining, many young Sanders supporters helped raise Trump over the bar. But why did it happen?

Suppose you thought Trump and Clinton were terrible, and you didn't see much difference. Or maybe you thought Trump winning would be good due to the resistance it would provoke. Having those views, you might abstain. Then, once the election was over, you would protest and organize as best you could, and since Trump won, that would mean going into the streets.

One lesson was it is possible for caring, courageous people to have temporarily highly distorted perceptions, which we already knew from all of history. What I found especially striking, however, was that Sanders had no such confusion. Nor did at least some radicals who urged strategic lesser evil voting even while holding firm to their radical views on all issues. And because such clarity did exist, including coming from Sanders, it took strong feelings, I think, for Sanders supporters to abstain in contested states. I thought that however painful to dwell on, this was worth understanding and that some additional lessons lurked in the experience.

Both Trump's voters and Sanders voters who abstained seem to have acted on feelings of anger and fear. For the Trump voters it was anger at their life situation and fear of Clinton. For the Sanders abstainers it was anger at their electoral mistreatment during the primaries and fear of cooptation. I felt both groups allowed their fully warranted anger and fear to wrongfully overcome other factors. I took from that that organizing needed to become considerably more compassionate, subtle, and persistent to overcome this tendency.

> *Even now, I find it hard to hear blame going toward those who were surely among the best and most committed to change at the time. What about the role of the Green candidate Jill Stein and her advocates?*

Stein's voters, Stein herself, and various left pundits disseminated a steady stream of messages claiming there was no major difference between Trump and Clinton, that Clinton was absolutely going to win, and that votes for Stein were wise because Stein could do quite well. But votes for Stein certainly took votes from Clinton in contested states. And it wasn't just that if Stein's voters had all voted for Clinton in those states it would have stopped Trump. It was also that abstentions generated by Stein disparaging voting for Clinton as shilling for the Democrats also reduced Clinton's votes in those states.

It was one thing for a constituency that was quite reasonably fearful, suffering, and subject to poor information to make desperation-motivated electoral mistakes, as did Blacks voting for Clinton over Sanders or white workers voting for Trump over Clinton. It was another thing for people with lots of political experience who enjoyed relative safety and maximal information access to not only make a mistake, but to then adamantly and aggressively urge it on others and to even castigate those who were rightly trying to point out the error.

I don't want to belabor this twenty-five years later, but one lesson it conveyed to me was that strategic lesser evil voting makes sense whenever the gap between evils is large enough and no other use of one's vote offers greater benefit. Of course, assessing the size of the gap between evils and the merits of other choices can and should be debated - but in 2016 there was no debate but only baiting, disparagement, and dismissal. Yet the gap was so wide, and the benefit of voting for Stein or abstaining in contested states was so minor, that it was hard not to be incredulous at those who doubled down after Trump was elected by celebrating Clinton losing or even celebrating Trump winning as a prod to resistance.

Another lesson was that having an astute analysis of the ills of elections but applying it only to mainstream participants is self defeating. Stein understood elections and was sincerely radical, but nonetheless let her desire for votes overwhelm her desires to achieve good or ward off bad. Likewise, many radical writers who became caught up in Stein's campaign urged that people saying we should vote for Clinton in contested states were, on that account - and sometimes despite decades of evidence otherwise - shills for Clinton, a label that caused many to want to avoid that false stigma. People who earlier gloried in his work even labelled Noam Chomsky that way, which was incredibly striking.

I took from all that, that radicals needed a far more nuanced approach to elections and, when we managed to win, also to holding office, than we had ever before had. We needed to not only have good programmatic aims but also to not get sucked into the vote-emphasizing and audience-manipulating we rightly decried in the mainstream.

Andrej, was there tension between Sanders' Our Revolution and early RPS?

The Sanders-spawned project, Our Revolution, sought to raise money, galvanize volunteers, and provide grassroots organizing for candidates and some policy campaigns. The danger was that it would become so enmeshed in electoral pitfalls that its value would dissipate.

There was a moment when Our Revolution may have become what RPS later became, but no one in Our Revolution's leadership displayed that inclination, though many of its energetic local organizers did. While some efforts were made to galvanize its more radical elements to radicalize Our Revolution, mistrust of the dangers of cooptation kept away folks who might have helped that happen. Nonetheless, Our Revolution helped RPS in three ways. First, it helped elect RPS candidates, and helped aid their efforts in office to win new policies. Second, people working with Our Revolution often joined grassroots campaigns, including RPS. And third, with Our Revolution in place, RPS didn't have to angst over its choice to ignore electoral intervention. Our Revolution took care of that, even if not always precisely as RPS favored.

Reciprocally, if RPS hadn't become so effective - including greatly strengthening the more radical members of Our Revolution - my guess is Our Revolution would have devolved into a Democratic Party booster club.

CHAPTER 6

THE FIRST CONVENTION

*Andrej Goldman, Senator Malcolm King, and Cynthia Parks
recall the first RPS convention and its immediate aftermath.*

So, Andrej, we come to the founding convention. Did it matter? How did it emerge? What conflicts occurred?

I think having the founding convention was fundamentally important, although at the time we had doubts. Would enough people attend? Would attendees split over minor differences? Would we ignore others' views and fail to compromise? Would we implode and do more harm than good?

One aspect of having the convention was its mechanics. We didn't want fifty people, or a hundred, but thousands. We already had two or three dozen local groups who hoped to become part of a national organization. It was a good start, but none of our groups had an agreed structure or membership criteria. We lacked sufficient coherence to have delegated representatives.

A bunch of us took initiative. Luckily, we had considerable credibility because of our participation in past collective efforts, and we proved able to mediate and organize. Most of the work was familiar. We had to get a space, put out a call, arrange housing, and develop an agenda.

What was the initial plan?

We sought to create an organizational bridge to a workable future but we were nervous that if our effort failed, it would delay arriving at a multi-issue, multi-tactic, vision-oriented organization. I lost sleep worrying about that.

Was your worry warranted?

Certainly. A storm might have curtailed attendance. People might have come ill-prepared and wasted the available time. People might have feuded. Arrangements might have collapsed. We knew attendees needed to arrive having understood diverse proposals for program and structure including bringing their own views, so we disseminated proposals months before the convention and urged people to bring their concerns, amendments, and extensions.

We knew bitterly settling on perfect demands would be significantly worse than collaboratively celebrating a "less perfect" agreement. We agreed decisions would be provisional until the fledgling organization could attract more members into local chapters, meet again, and solidify. We didn't seek immediate perfection. We sought good results able to inspire later better results. To that end, we consulted many activists about initial program and internal structure. We proposed that RPS should centrally address economics/class, politics, culture/race, kinship/gender, ecology, and international relations without privileging any above the rest. We proposed it should reject capitalism, racism, sexism, and authoritarianism, and explore and advocate long term vision to inspire effective current activity.

We left plenty of leeway for insights that might emerge at the convention, and for what we would learn later. That mindset was arguably the organizers' key contribution. Instead of establishing an identity to defend, we adopted shared agreements for adapting to new circumstances and refining our views as needed. Each new day, we sought to prepare ourselves for the next day, not to prove we had been right the prior day.

Malcolm, though you weren't an organizer you attended the convention. Were you confident it would succeed?

When I got the pre-convention package, I liked the contents, but I feared too few people would attend. I also worried that those who did attend would agree on nothing. I feared we would squander potential. I remember arriving and being impressed with the crowd, but once the convention got going, I was still more impressed that people hadn't come just to have their own way. Everyone sought real solidarity. Everyone sought positive results. You know how sometimes people discuss possible wording of a document and each person fights for their own words paying no attention to what others want. We avoided that.

How?

People had paid attention to proposals before arriving at the conference. They had added refinements beforehand, which were also circulated. As a result, often there was no dissent and an item would pass immediately. Other times, someone would propose an amendment or replacement and we would hear a case for it, but rather than asking for an immediate rebuttal, the chair would ask for a straw vote. If there was only minimal support for the amendment, she would ask to have a second advocate speak, and then ask if anyone wanted to speak against. She would next ask if the proposer had any questions. Generally not. Did anyone want to add an additional case for the proposal. Sometimes someone would, but mostly not. A vote would occur, and the item would typically fail as it simply didn't have support. No rancor and no time wasted.

On the other hand, if a straw vote showed a considerable majority or overwhelming support for a change, the chair would ask if anyone supporting the unchanged version wanted to reply. Sometimes yes, sometimes no. If no, the change would quickly win. If yes, the person would present, and there would be some discussion. Mainly, no one wanted to win just for the sake of winning. We weren't parading our egos. We all wanted decisions that would be worthy and universally respected. For decisions that had close straw ballots after a few arguments were offered, debate continued or the decision was delayed so people could think on it overnight. As a result, at least two-thirds preferred every ratified decision, and often far more than that.

I don't think we avoided contending egos because we were better people than past groups, or more mature, or anything like that. Rather, I think our advance preparation, the methods we employed, and especially that we believed what we were doing was going to really matter helped with the ego problem.

We all thought, we have a responsibility. Forget about seeking phony perfection. Instead of each person acting as a kind of primadonna competing to have more of his or her own words adopted, each person sought lasting unity and a flexible readiness to innovate regardless of the source of each idea or phrase. I repeat this point because activists often minimize these type issues and instead emphasize arcane details of economy or subtle interpolations of identity. We focused on what mattered using plain language and transparent motives.

Do you remember the initial activist program?

We didn't want a laundry list, though it was hard to prevent. Remember we were just getting started. Nearly 3,000 people wanted plans that met the convention's programmatic guidelines and which we could immediately strongly support. It was a bit of a miracle that we limited our first campaigns to seeking:

- 30 hours of work for 40 hours pay
- Sharply progressive property, asset, and income taxes, with no loopholes
- A dramatically-increased minimum wage of $20 an hour
- A comprehensive full employment policy
- Curriculum reform, improved teaching methods, enriched teacher-student relations, and reduced average class size to a maximum of 20 students per teacher in all schools.

- Guaranteed free education for anyone who wanted it - plus debt forgiveness.
- Amnesty for immigrants and regulated but ultimately open borders for refugees.
- Community control of police, an end to mass incarceration, and reassessment of current prison terms and policy.
- Protecting the rights of women to control their own bodies and to enjoy equal benefits and responsibilities throughout all parts of society, including abortion rights, public day care, and equal payment requirements.
- Improved preventive medicine, increased public education about health-care risks and prevention, a massive campaign around diet, and penalties for corporate activity that subverts health in employees or consumers.
- Universal health care for all, including a single-payer system with the government providing comprehensive and equal coverage for all.
- Civilian review of drug company policies including price controls and severe penalties for profit seeking at the expense of public health up to nationalization of offending companies under the auspices of Congress and an expanded Center for Disease Control.
- A truly massive national and international campaign to turn the tide against global warming, water depletion, and other life threatening environmental trends.
- Nuclear disarmament, massive military cutbacks, cessation of arms shipments abroad and elimination or conversion of overseas military bases to peaceful purposes such as natural crisis assistance.

Do you have any special personal memories of the convention?

A speaker recounted her trajectory from student organizing, to community organizing, to becoming a revolutionary. She spoke eloquently of being sick of hearing activists complain about how bad things are while blaming everyone but themselves for their lack of success. She told how she had recently been moved by a report that instead pinpointed failings radicals themselves had with the intent of correcting their own faults. Her talk pursued that same theme and was immediately memorable. That we later became partners made it all the more so.

Another thing I remember, was the downtime when people would congregate, meet, and share experiences. We would convene groups by job, locale, or whatever, and those sessions may have been the birthplace of RPS, even more than the general assemblies where decisions were made, because the informal meetings led to local chapters and to work groups in fields like health care, law, and sports.

Cynthia Parks, born in 1992, you watched your family lose their modest home in 1998 due to unemployment. Years later you advocated inexpensive quality public housing and championed rights for the city. A militant activist, a tireless organizer, you were secretary of housing in the second RPS shadow government. Do you remember first becoming radical?

When I was six, as you researched, my family lost its home. I remember my mom explaining that the economy was in trouble so we didn't have money to pay bills. The banks took our home and I asked how that helped the economy. My mother told me it helped the bankers. It helped the rich.

I watched my father sink into alcohol-enhanced depression. I watched my mother protecting the family from poverty and from my father's illness as well. I remember ice claiming the insides of our windows. By age seven, my life was mapped out, though years passed before I knew what I had become.

Can you tell us your most personally inspiring RPS events or campaigns?

Two things are when I first used People's Social Media and when I attended the first talk by Edward Snowden after he was pardoned and welcomed back to the U.S. Using our new social media moved me because I was doing something natural by way of an institution conceived and built by RPS people that I knew was going to last all the way into a new society. I think it was the first time I felt that level of confidence in our future. And the Snowden talk wasn't memorable so much for his talk - though it was good - as because his return felt like a milestone of progress and potential. It made me feel that our destructive divisions were going to be bridged by understanding that moved everyone forward. Those two events bolstered my hope, something I needed at the time and without which I may have fallen by the wayside.

Once the first convention was over what do you think kept things going?

In any social project, the hardest part is nearly always when one has no evidence one's actions will succeed and when mistakes can devastate prospects. First starting out, RPS lacked certainty. Nights of sleepless doubt followed days of wandering focus. Once we were well underway, we knew our bad choices would be less destructive. We knew the more we embraced diversity, the more we would have flexible insurance against sudden collapse. When one path didn't work, we would have others we could pursue. But when we first came out of the convention fear of failure thrived and caused many people to think each choice was paramount. We vested each choice with too much weight. We defended positions too inflexibly.

Imagine meeting with ten or fifteen folks to form a chapter. You discuss how often to have meetings, or how to conduct them, or who to invite to the next one. It feels like survival depends on every choice. It feels like you have to get everything perfect, or fail. In that situation, we often fought tooth and nail over modest differences we wrongly saw as monumental.

Three thousand people attended the convention and then returned to their jobs and homes. We estimated that 500 attendees immediately became committed full time revolutionaries. For those, and I was one, our criterion for decisions was first to contribute to creating the organization and movement and second to live our lives with family and do our day jobs. Another 500 attendees became revolutionaries, eager to help, but with less time to allot. And the remaining 2,000 became supporters with varying commitments. They often called themselves revolutionary, but few had changed to a point where winning a new world had become the center of their way of thinking and acting.

Okay, but why did RPS persist?

Persisting meant creating many chapters which could work on campaigns, attract new support, further define the organization, and help other organizations and movements. But a Catch 22 blocked our way. The 500 most committed participants were central. We would call meetings in our locales for friends, neighbors, or workmates who hadn't yet connected with RPS. We would do the needed work, but where we were absent, nothing happened. If that had been everywhere, the whole undertaking would have fizzled.

What was the Catch 22?

It was that we who were most intent on success, and most essential to keep things moving, were for those reasons also most susceptible to being afraid of failing, and thus most prone to fighting over details.

So at the beginning we really had two obstacles to surmount. First, we had to depend on relatively few people to carry too much of the initial workload and responsibility. This might entrench them with too much relative power and contacts or it might induce exhaustion and burn out. Second, RPS depending so much on only about 500 people caused the 500 of us to be so averse to failing, that we often wouldn't listen and hear others.

We made it past those difficulties, but we certainly could have failed. The enormous project that is RPS two decades later, now well on the road to complete success and with nary a chance of unraveling, could have died at many points. Dissident outcomes are never preordained.

Revolution is never inevitable. If you want to sing the praises of anyone for RPS succeeding, I would nominate the subset of 500 who brought to the early efforts not just great energy, but, also, despite the pressures, enough sensitivity and flexibility to cool down themselves and the hot tempers of others. To me, that may have been the most basic RPS achievement on which everything else depended, and the achievement that was absent in earlier attempts.

Was it personally difficult for people?

Absolutely. The convention was over. Now let's say you are one of the 500. Evened out, that was only ten per state which meant you maybe knew one or two other people near you who were as energetically committed as yourself. So now you are working yourself toward exhaustion. You believe in RPS and its potentials and you fear that the relative lack of effort by others will torpedo it. You believe errors could be fatal. You believe your commitment and growing experience make your views better informed than the views of others. Do you see how you could become inflexible and even sectarian? Do you see how you could become hostile toward less active members?

How did RPS ward off those possibilities?

We pushed ourselves to understand that progress and success depended easily as much on how patiently we interacted with folks and on how willing we were to abide what we thought were poor or even wrong choices, as it depended on getting some arcane decisions made precisely as we desired while having steadily fewer people committed to those decisions. For most of us, and this was true for me, finding one or two people who would keep our priorities in order was critical. I think some of us prioritized avoiding these ills as our own special contribution. I remember myself pledging that.

> *I would like to ask a tangentially related question. In those times there was tension over how to weigh family as compared to movement responsibilities. Post convention, you had a young child. How did you think about the choice between family and movement?*

It isn't tangential. Rather it is pivotal to success, but rarely explicitly addressed. I first focused on the family/activism question at the time Trump was elected, and then after I had my first child. Honestly, I felt strange even having a child with Trump's malevolence lurking over society and I started to think about what it means to serve loved ones. I didn't think the best one could do for one's kids was to earn as much as possible, or to maximally shield them from worrying about the direction of society. That struck me as a kind of magical thinking. Instead, for one's kids, as well as for society, I thought we had to seek change.

I later read a decades old interview with David Dellinger, the foremost American civil disobedience revolutionary of his time. He was asked whether he ever had misgivings about having spent considerable time in jail, away from his kids, and about his having not accumulated nearly the wealth he could have earned for them during their childhood and to pass on to them after he died. His reply was that he had no such misgivings, though he did feel endless sorrow about it. He felt it was his duty to provide an image of socially responsible behavior and he felt he had done what he considered right, and from there on it would be up to his kids what road they took. He was sorrowful, however, that the world was so perverse that being responsible for his kids and others required him to devote less time to engaging directly with them than he would have otherwise preferred. I was moved by that, and encountering his response pretty much completed my thinking about the topic.

As to others' views, I think there have been over the past quarter century many pressures on parents, siblings, daughters, and sons, vis a vis life choices. Should I shield my kids, keep my home a sanctuary of fun, and not address society and the responsibilities it raises? Should I pay peripheral attention to social turmoil, but overwhelmingly address my family's immediate well being? Should I give more time and focus to concerns about society, and bring concerns about society home, share them, and hope the whole family will address them?

Different strokes for different folks. And many regrets along the way, no doubt. But over time, if the trajectory hadn't been toward the more participatory perspective, there would now be no RPS, and I think there would be no worthy future, either, for the families in question, and our whole species.

As you went down your trajectory toward greater involvement, were you hostile toward those who didn't?

Sometimes, yes, but mostly no. I thought that to prioritize self and family and to deny the need to change our choices as Trump took office would be objectively harmful to future prospects. I thought if that behavior was dominant, it would totally swamp future prospects. So I tried to change such views.

How?

Well, how would you react if someone replied to your suggestion that they might demonstrate, or study up, or join a chapter, or whatever, by saying - "why should I? I don't think you stand a chance. Injustice will prevail. More, what can I contribute? What can I do that would matter? I know I can work with considerable chance of success to make my family more healthy and fulfilled, but the whole country? The whole world? I can't affect that. To deny my kids, my spouse, my family, my friends, to pursue that dream. Not me."

It wasn't easy to answer even knowing that for everyone or even just for most people to adopt that stance would be a self fulfilling recipe for civilizational disaster. But for one person to think that way - whose fault was that? Was it really that person? Or was it we who for whatever reasons better understood social potentials, needs, and possibilities, but had not, as yet, made activist insights compelling and believable? And for that matter, was the lone person making that assessment even wrong? If so, in what way? It took a leap of faith to commit to the needed tasks. We had to facilitate people leaping.

CHAPTER 7

INITIAL COMMITMENTS

Cynthia Parks and Andrej Goldman discuss convention vision, structure, and program.

Cynthia, can you summarize the first RPS convention's initial vision?

Our visionary proposal for politics was that the organization should seek new government that facilitates all citizens participating in decision-making. Choices should be transparent. Roles should convey to all citizens a self managing say proportionate to decisions' effects on them. New government should utilize grassroots assemblies, councils, and communes of the sort forming around the country. It should include direct participation by plebiscite, representation, or delegation, case by case, whichever would better implement self management. It should utilize majority rule, two-thirds, or consensus as means to further self management, case by case, whichever would be better.

We advocated freedom of speech, press, religion, assembly, and organizing political parties. But we added that new government should facilitate dissent and promote diversity so individuals and groups could freely pursue their own goals while not interfering with the same rights for others. It should fairly, peacefully, and constructively adjudicate disputes seeking justice and rehabilitation.

The whole commitment was to a few basic values and some broad thoughts about how social institutions could further those values while incorporating lessons from past movements in the U.S. and around that world. We said this is for a new society, but to reach that society, it is also for us, now, in our own organization.

It has few details, arguably none...

The then recent Sanders campaign had legitimated the idea of having a revolution in how politics was conducted. We gave its vague rhetoric more reach by proposing values plus a loose scaffolding of means. The aim was to ensure that new government would support community members contributing to solving problems while also ensuring that no political hierarchies would privilege some citizens over others.

What about initial vision for economy?

We wanted no individuals or groups to own resources, workplaces, or workplace infrastructure. We wanted no ownership to distort decision-making or determine income. But we knew that beyond that we needed to say what would positively replace capitalistic means of distributing income, organizing work, and allocating inputs and outputs.

We proposed that workers who work longer or harder or at more onerous conditions doing socially valued labor should earn proportionately more, but that no one should earn payment for property, bargaining power, or the value of their personal output.

We proposed that councils of workers should self manage workplaces and guarantee workers and consumers a say in decisions proportionate to effects on them, using majority rule, consensus, or other arrangements as appropriate.

We knew each worker needed to be sufficiently confident, informed, and knowledgeable to participate effectively in decision making, so we proposed that all workers do a socially average share of empowering tasks. We explicitly rejected about a fifth of workers doing predominantly empowering tasks and four-fifths doing mainly rote, repetitive, and obedient tasks.

Finally, for those choices to succeed we knew we needed allocation that would enhance all the above, and for that we proposed decentralized participatory negotiation of inputs and outputs by workers and consumers councils...

You are remembering almost verbatim, yet this was twenty years ago. How do you explain that?

I figured it would come up in the interview, so for accuracy I went back and re-familiarized myself with how it was stated then. But in any case, our economic aims sought to implement our values. We never had to memorize our aims, because we could always argue their logic.

Surely some of your economic vision was contentious even in the group working on the proposal. How did you resolve differences before sending out proposals?

Most of what we proposed had been previously enunciated by people who had earlier had limited organizational success. We adapted from them in the same way we hoped that RPS's convention would adapt and refine what we offered. Nonetheless, we struggled to agree on the parts where our wording slid from broad guidelines into statements about specific ways to accomplish those guidelines. For example, we easily agreed on wanting classlessness, but we contentiously debated equitable remuneration, balanced job complexes and participatory allocation.

What was in dispute?

The biggest controversy was should we institutionally outline preferred features of envisioned division of labor and allocation, or should we only indicate what good labor organization and allocation should achieve in broad value terms, without saying how? If you look, we mostly did the latter for visionary details and even for much that was broad and general. But for division of labor and allocation some of us, myself included, favored being more specific.

Why?

Largely due to fear...

Fear? Fear of what?

For almost all aspects of vision we thought details could be added at the convention or later within the organization, rather than settling them right off as a kind of precondition for the organization getting started. But after much discussion we agreed that division of labor and allocation weren't only important to broadly address, as so many issues were, but were also more subject to biases from old unexamined habits. We thought if we left it for later to arrive at certain basic institutional details for division of labor and allocation, the whole project could be sidetracked by contending class interests even within an emerging RPS. We didn't want to establish an organization whose initial clarity was insufficient to prevent it from getting hijacked.

You stacked the deck?

We created a foundation for what we sought. Suppose we wanted an antiracist organization but had no clear initial commitments preventing people with serious racial biases from joining, and also had no procedures or mechanisms preventing their democratically twisting the organization away from its intended aims. We wanted self management built on an initial definition that ensured that whatever else members freely developed or altered, their residual biases wouldn't distort basic priority commitments.

And you feared potential members' economic views?

We feared that if we required no prior agreement about division of labor and allocation, people who initially joined might not be well steeped in and might even resist really understanding how coordinator class interests could silence working class needs and potentials. We thought that for race, gender, and other aspects of focus, attendees would have differences, of course, but given the strength of anti racist and feminist organizing, if we agreed on good broad values in those realms we thought none of our operational differences would be so severe as to subvert potentials for worthy unity and clarity. However, around issues related to class hierarchy, we felt getting a result able to ward off tendencies toward coordinator class rule depended on our being more explicit about institutional solutions for division of labor and allocation.

What about gender vision?

We wanted new gender and kin relations that would not privilege certain types of family formation over others, but instead actively support all types of families consistent with society's other broad norms and practices.

We proposed that living units should promote children's well-being and affirm society's responsibility for all its children, including affirming the right of diverse types of families to have children and to provide them with love and a sense of rootedness and belonging.

We proposed to minimize or even eliminate age-based permissions, preferring non-arbitrary means for determining when an individual is ready to participate in economic, political or other activities, as well as to receive benefits or shoulder responsibilities.

We proposed to respect marriage and other lasting relations among adults as religious, cultural, or social practices, but to reject them as means to gain material or social benefits.

We proposed to respect caregiving as a valuable function and to utilize diverse means to ensure equitable burdens and benefits.

We proposed our kinship vision should affirm diverse expressions of sexual pleasure, personal identity, and mutual intimacy while ensuring that each person honor the autonomy, humanity, and rights of others. We favored diverse, empowering sex education, including legal prohibition against all non-consensual sex.

Our initial kinship vision was mostly guidelines and values, not specifics. We left precision - much less perfection - for after chapter members had better means to participate and own the vision, and after we all had more experience with the issues. Our main kinship innovation wasn't our vision's substance, which had all existed before. Rather we brought the many facets together and urged that we needed to relate to the whole picture, not just one or another part.

What about culture vision?

We wanted new cultural and community relations to provide the space and resources necessary for people to freely have multiple cultural and social identities and positively express their cultural beliefs and habits. We urged recognizing that which commitments any particular person at any particular time finds most important depends on that person's situation and assessments.

We knew that all people deserve self management, equity, solidarity, and liberty, so that while society should protect all people's right to affiliate freely and enjoy cultural diversity, society should also affirm that its core values, if not their exact means of implementation, are universal.

We proposed that new cultural relations guarantee free entry and exit to and from all cultural communities, including affirming that communities that have free entry and exit can be under the complete self determination of their members so long as their policies don't subvert society's basic values.

Overall, it seems insular...

Yes, and so we proposed that international relations extend societal commitments beyond national borders. Internationalism should replace colonialism and neo-colonialism. New internationalist relations should steadily diminish economic disparities in countries' relative wealth and protect cultural and social patterns interior to each country from external violation. Nations should facilitate internationalist globalization in place of corporate globalization.

And the ecology...

We proposed that new ecological relations account for the full ecological (and social/personal) costs and benefits of both short and long term economic and social choices. That would allow future populations to make informed choices about levels of production and consumption, duration of work, energy use, husbandry, pollution, climate policies, conservation, and consumption as part of their freely made policy decisions. But we also wanted new environmental relations to foster ecological connection and responsibility consistent with ecological preferences, so future citizens could freely decide their policies regarding animal rights, vegetarianism, or other matters that transcend sustainability and even husbandry. Remember, Trumpism had at that time charted an ecological path denying climate change. It may as well have been a suicide note to the planet, and as you know a big part of RPS's emergence was fueled by horror at world-threatening ecological insanity.

The convention message was so much. Even today, despite decades of familiarity, it still weighs heavy. Was that a problem?

Yes, I think it was, and as you say, I bet it will be a problem for some who read this interview. But concision and simplification aren't the only virtues when communicating. You have to convey important subject matter and it takes time and effort to minimize misinterpretation.

I could describe glorious moments, evoke related emotions, paint a picture of high points vibrating with personal pathos, all without conveying underlying thoughts, but for an oral history that wouldn't be enough. Someone could do that, a better story teller or writer than I, in a novel, and it could be useful. Protagonist, conflicts, surprises, resolutions, drama. But in an oral history, such dramatic answers might sound more exciting, but they would not be better.

RPS history should feature ideas, lessons, and vision, not people or even events. It should show people engaged, but it should't become a story built around a protagonist overcoming personal flaws or evil agents. It shouldn't be a tale of technologies. It should include feelings, but not become a tale of feelings.

Asked about RPS, I and I bet all your interviewees, want most to convey insights, aims, and lessons. If doing that to provide source material for informed inspiration is less lively than a good thriller novel, or less emotive than a person-centered novel brilliantly conveying human pathos, so be it.

What were some complexities of filling out and advocating RPS vision?

It was hard arriving at good ideas without subverting others doing likewise. It was hard having good ideas persist. It was hard understanding when and how this or that good idea would be helpful.

How did you hold a view and not become sectarian about it? How did you hold a view that typically percolated into existence via a long path, and not treat anyone who didn't immediately agree with you as either a moron or an enemy? How did you not forget that maybe a month or a year earlier, we who now held new views didn't hold them? How did you passionately advocate vision but remember that dismissing partial gains in the present because we want all or nothing was a surefire way to get nothing?

These questions were hard because we lived in contexts that nurtured flawed judgements. I always found it strange when a revolutionary bemoaned how harsh social relations and institutions were, but then acted as though that didn't affect the probability that his or her own views, influenced by those harsh social relations, were sound or sympathetic and not flawed or biased.

All radicals rightly realized that racism distorted the views of racists but back than few radicals admitted racism also distorted the views of those who suffered the indignities and violence of racial denigration. All radicals knew sexism and classism imprinted all kinds of harmful beliefs and habits on the personalities, values, and ideas of sexist men and on owners or coordinators, but back then few radicals admitted sexism and classism also distorted women's and workers' inclinations and habits.

RPS admirably emphasized that we ought to continually re-assess our views and choices, rather than reflexively assuming their wisdom. But walking a fine line between being over-confident and over-diffident was difficult and made the RPS journey far from smooth.

I remember being gently, but also forcefully, chastised about inclinations of my own to judge people as if they had to immediately know what it took me years to learn. I remember having to overcome my unwillingness to welcome refinements of views I held. I remember discussing such issues when I was one of those doing the intervening, and also when the intervening was aimed at me. None of that was easy. I remember sometimes - actually all too often - lying in bed at night wondering, had I been unfair to others? Had I been inflexible? Or were others avoiding responsibility and clinging to past identities? Each was possible. Each could be the case. Each did occur. It wasn't easy.

Andrej, what about proposals for the organization itself?

As much as personal choices influenced outcomes, we knew we would fail to enact exemplary policies if our organizational context propelled harmful ends. For example, we wanted no minority to form even an informal decision-making hierarchy. We didn't want less experienced members to merely follow orders and perform rote tasks. To avoid that, we proposed that RPS structure and policy be regularly adapted to always be internally classless and to implement the norm that "each member has decision-making say proportional to the degree they are affected." We wanted to protect members' rights to organize dissenting "currents" so we proposed that RPS guarantee those "currents" full rights of democratic debate plus resources to develop and present their dissenting views. We proposed RPS celebrate internal debate and test contrary views alongside preferred views.

Wanting collective self management, we proposed that national, regional, city, and local chapters respond to their own circumstances and implement their own programs, but not interfere with the shared goals and principles of the organization or with other chapters addressing their own situations.

Wanting participation, we proposed RPS provide extensive opportunities for members to influence organizational decisions including deliberating with others to arrive at the most well-considered decisions. We also proposed RPS provide transparency regarding elected or delegated leaders and impose a high burden of proof for secreting any agenda whether to avoid repression or for any other reason. We required ways to recall leaders who members believed inadequately represented them...

This is getting long winded...

I know. I feel it too. But building a new organization to revolutionize society is complicated. More than high points mattered. Making a revolution is not a pile of Tweets. So, seeking to model and pursue classlessness, we proposed that RPS apportion empowering and disempowering tasks to participants to ensure that no individuals control the organization by having a relative monopoly on critical information or levers of daily decision making. We wanted members to actively participate in the life of the organization including taking collective responsibility for its policies, so we proposed that RPS structurally involve its members in developing, debating, and deciding on proposals and that it treat lack of participation as a problem to address whenever it surfaced. We also proposed internal structures to facilitate participation including offering childcare at meetings and otherwise aiding those with busy work schedules.

We knew we were not remotely perfect people. We knew we couldn't escape centuries of mutilation in minutes of celebration. We knew RPS had to monitor and respond to sexism, racism, classism, and homophobia internally, including having diverse roles suitable to people with different backgrounds and priorities. But we also knew we shouldn't let seeking unattainable immediate perfection erase seeking immediately attainable excellence. We had to know where we were going. We had to want to get there as expeditiously as possible. We also had to realize it was not a day's, a week's, or a month's journey. We had to always be being born into our preferred aims, never dying away from them.

Cynthia, I see how what you proposed was geared to guide an interim period without deciding too much at the outset. But what about program?

The proposal for consideration leading to the founding convention added to the above visionary and structural aspects, that the organization's broad program should be regularly updated and adapted and should always incorporate seeds of the future in its present, both in how members act and by building liberating alternatives to the status quo.

We proposed that RPS's program constantly seek to grow its membership among class, cultural, and gender constituencies. It should learn from and seek unity with audiences far wider than the organization's own membership. It should attract and empower young members and help build diverse social movements and struggles.

It should seek changes in society for citizens to enjoy immediately and also should help establish a likelihood that citizens would pursue and win more change in the future. It should connect efforts, resources, and lessons from place to place, even as it recognized that strategies suitable to different places often differ.

We favored flexibility, feared sectarianism, and sought to win reforms in non reformist ways. These were the three foundational programmatic desires most critical, I think, to RPS being a project with staying power. And while no one would have explicitly argued that instead we should be inflexible, sectarian, or reject reforms, these matters were sometimes given only lip service whereas we prioritized them.

How?

We proposed that RPS program seek short term changes by its actions and by its support of larger movements and projects, including addressing global warming, arms control, war and peace, the level and composition of economic output, agricultural relations, education, health care, income distribution, duration of work, gender roles, racial relations, media, law, legislation, etc.

But that was guidelines, not specifics…

Yes, and that was intentional. First, we wanted the proposal to be timeless and we knew that as context changes, priorities and circumstances change. Second, we felt specific program should emerge from discussion and debate and we didn't want to prejudge that occurring.

We also proposed that RPS program should provide financial, legal, employment, and emotional support to RPS members so they could most easily negotiate the challenges and difficulties of participating in radical actions.

Similarly, we proposed RPS Program should seek to substantially improve the life situations of members. It should enlarge our feelings of self worth, our knowledge, skills, and confidence, our mental, physical, sexual, and spiritual health, our social ties and our leisure enjoyments. Being part of seeking a new world would take sacrifice and involve boredom and risk, but it didn't have to require foregoing well being. In a new world we should not only fulfill our potentials, we should also enjoy life...

It seems awfully broad...

We wanted our guidelines, however people might later refine them, to provide a framework for deciding specific shared program but not to predetermine program. We also proposed that RPS program develop, debate, disseminate, and advocate contentious news, analysis, vision, and strategy among its members and in the wider society. We proposed RPS develop and sustain needed media and personal communication. We wanted educational efforts, rallies, marches, demonstrations, boycotts, strikes, and direct actions to win gains and build movements.

We also proposed putting a high burden of proof on utilizing even purely defensive violence, including cultivating a decidedly non violent attitude and we proposed, as well, that RPS assess electoral participation case by case, including cultivating a cautious electoral attitude.

In sum, we proposed a kind of meta program that specified the kind of things specific campaigns in different places and times ought to accomplish and therefore the kinds of demands and practices program should include, but we didn't overextend by explicitly specifying universal demands and practices.

Did those who prepared the proposals have differences?

Yes, even after weeks of collective interactions and even as the convention approached, we especially differed on what the convention should do. Some of us thought the convention should just ratify the advance proposals with some modifications. Others thought the convention should ratify with modifications, but also apply the proposals in the current moment to decide some specific campaigns for people to pursue back in their home regions.

I leaned toward the latter view and expected that settling on some shared campaigns would be a significant contribution of the convention and that specifics would emerge from meshing the specific programmatic aims that had emerged earlier during the Sanders campaign and its aftermath, and the program that Black Lives Matter had settled on, as well as what flowed from other efforts, with our own guidelines leading us to add some features, so the whole would better fulfill the emerging RPS norms.

Were you confident after preparing your various proposals?

We looked at the pile we had generated and envisioned people hearing that to usefully attend they should read the proposals, discuss them with others, and decide their attitude toward them. We were far from confident. Some who we consulted called us crazy to ask so much from people. But there was motive in our madness.

We knew someone first hearing all this, I guess like someone first reading this interview, couldn't possibly quickly process it. We knew it would require time to read so many proposals much less have opinions of them. But we felt that was okay. We weren't gathering people just to celebrate one another. We didn't want people to attend just to say they had been at the convention, or they supported it, without participating and knowing what they were supporting. We wanted attendees who would make serious choices based on carefully addressing the issues.

CHAPTER 8

FORMING CHAPTERS

*Cynthia Parks and Andrej Goldman
discuss building RPS chapters.*

Cynthia, returning to early RPS, I assume as people left the initial convention they prioritized forming chapters. Was that so?

Yes, when we left the convention we all knew that RPS's success was going to depend on it having reliable, informed chapters in communities, on campuses, and in workplaces. We felt a chapter with ten members would be okay, but one with forty or fifty members would be much better. When a chapter reached the larger scale it would divide in two, not a nasty split, but a friendly break so each half could grow and divide again. In that way, on a campus, in a workplace, or a community, we would have steadily more chapters, each representing a steadily more focussed venue, with all tied to the rest.

You might start with a few people constituting a chapter for a community, workplace, or college. You might reach forty or fifty members and divide in two. Then it would happen again. As more chapters formed, we hoped each would remain entwined with its sibling chapters, so the many chapters in a community, workplace, or on a campus, would constitute an assembly for the larger unit - and so, as time went on, we could form federations of those assemblies.

It was an ambitious picture, but that was the whole point. RPS wasn't asking what modest task can we perhaps accomplish to then go home. We were asking what big tasks must we accomplish to win a whole new society. We knew without chapters RPS would be a cyber organization with tenuous connections. Chapters could make it personal, direct, and participatory.

What were the chapter building steps? What difficulties occurred?

I left the convention and within a week hosted a group of friends. I was still in college and I spoke about the convention, handed out materials summarizing the nature of RPS, and urged those who were interested to return for another session a week later. In the meantime, I urged people to discuss the ideas and read the materials, and offered to answer questions.

It was pretty easy where I was, but imagine trying to assemble meetings of white Mississippians in Oxford Town in 2020. RPS chapter building depended on overcoming fear among people receptive to your message, plus overcoming militant opposition from people you eventually wanted to welcome.

At any rate, twelve people attended our second session. We met twice a week for dinner and rotated responsibility for bringing food. We held a cultural/entertainment gathering each week, and at each Sunday meeting someone would propose the coming week's movie, picnic, or whatever.

Beyond getting to trust each other, we started discussing what more we could do. Some members thought we should practice presenting RPS views and vision and reach out more widely. Others thought we should join an already developed activist campaign or initiate a new one. Instead of endlessly burning ourselves out arguing the difference, we compromised. We would continue recruiting but as soon as we had twenty people we would establish our own campaign to pursue.

In three weeks we assembled twenty members. We reached forty amidst considerable campus turmoil from our first two campaigns, and at that point we split into two chapters and kept growing. In places where fear of relating or hostility were ubiquitous, progress was slower, but more exemplary.

What campaigns did you pursue? How did you get people to work together?

Our first campaigns were a campus anti-war version of the national arms manufacturers boycott, plus a campaign to end campus violence against women and racist attacks on minorities. To develop trust, we paid close attention to getting to know one another. Our chapters became not only the locus of our political hopes and activism, but a main site of our social lives. Once we had more chapters, we created intramural sports leagues, hosted regular parties, and sponsored classes taught by members with special skills or knowledge. People taught everything from learning to crochet to becoming a photographer or learning computer skills. We developed painting classes and assemblies of chapters sponsored stage plays and street theatre. Whenever we branched out, took up a cause, or developed anything new, we wrote it up and sent it to folks on other campuses, who did likewise. All this occurred with little opposition - what was there to oppose? - yet before long it provided a foundation for powerful campaigns.

I should note, our extensive socializing could have become insular. We could have become content in our own virtues, happy in our own social life, unwilling to address those disagreeing with us. It was undeniably more pleasurable to revel in each other's support than to go out and talk to people hostile to our beliefs, but we knew we had to avoid becoming too comfortable in our own little universe. We committed most time to reaching out. We insured that even our social events were always looking to get non RPS participants involved.

We, approached groups and individuals able to broaden our potentials. We made lists of people popular in various constituencies on campus - including big living groups, sports teams, and influential fraternities - and we assigned people to reach out to each such person until successful. We celebrated getting our first chapter inside a fraternity, and then our first on a campus sports team, and we grew from there.

Andrej, did you help get a chapter going after the convention?

Not at first. I was deeply into RPS, but my history made me quite shy once the discussion turned from politics to daily life. I didn't jump into forming a chapter, but I was recruited by others to a chapter they were trying to create.

I was an older graduate student at the time, and I felt I couldn't give time to a chapter, but how could I write up ideas for RPS yet ignore chapter building? I reluctantly signed on, and to my surprise I not only benefitted and hopefully contributed, I enjoyed it.

My chapter progressed and I was assigned to reach out to the president of our campus inter fraternity conference - and surprisingly we got on great and he joined leading to connections in every fraternity.

RPS chapter building didn't succumb like most prior campus organizing to constant tension, overwork, and alienation. Perhaps the main factor that led to our continued success was the way chapters developed healthy habits.

Once you were chapter building, what was your personal involvement like?

I prioritized improving internal education and external outreach to help overcome people's lack of confidence and develop ability to non-defensively interact with students who didn't already agree with us. We needed to hear them, relate to them, and hopefully welcome them. But to do that, we needed to prepare ourselves. So I focused on establishing a mini school to prepare folks to organize effectively on campus and before long our internal education efforts developed into an activist curriculum which then spread not only to chapters on many other campuses, but also to fledgling chapters in communities and workplaces.

It seems like there was no one right approach to getting a chapter going. Was that true? Did you require attendance? Did you have dues?

You are right that there was no single approach. In fact, even when we had hundreds and then thousands of chapters, there was still no one right way to operate. Chapters differed in different places and changed over time.

Daycare, for example, came later for most chapters than for ours. So did collecting dues to help pay costs of preparing documents and hosting events. Our chapter recorded attendance at the two meetings we held weekly, and also at one group cultural event a week. I am sure many others didn't.

One problem we all faced was member resistance to breaking up chapters. Members spent a lot of time relating to chapters. We became good friends. So when we reached forty members, and it was time to break in two, we wanted to stick with our friends but we knew growth was essential. To proceed, we conceived an arbitrary line through the campus and moved it around until we had 20 on each side. East and west chapters were born. Before long, we had a few chapters in each dorm. Similar developments occurred in communities and workplaces, albeit more slowly than in colleges.

One of the best aspects of frequent diversification, beyond that it led to rapid growth, was on our personalities. It used to be that when a left group formed, it would grow for a time and then turn inward. Members would even start to dress and talk alike. Membership would reach a workable size and then become more intent on maintaining itself as a community than on growing as a movement. We countered that tendency by regularly dealing with new folks. To us, growth, not mere survival, indicated success.

What about people disliking each other or even feuding?

Some people like to think that if you are on the side of justice and you are courageous, all will be absolutely wonderful. Not true. We still had disputes, jealousies, and tensions.

Small chapters suffered most. Suppose you had five members and two disliked each other. That would not only affect how the two members felt, but all five. Whose side am I on? Whose side are you on? What did you say? When a chapter reached twenty members, it became easier for everyone to do their thing and for those at odds to avoid conflict. Finally, when chapters broke up to form two out of one, we would separate those at odds.

The question became what could we do while two feuding members couldn't separate or accommodate? We had no perfect answer. Different choices would solve different cases. The contending parties might just back off until there were more members. Or they might accept demands for restraint coming from friends. They might avoid attending the same sessions. Whatever. But it wasn't pleasant and it could literally derail a group.

Were you ever personally in a harmful conflict?

Yes, twice. Once, distance solved it, at least as much as possible. The other time we both had to control ourselves for quite awhile, which was no fun but better than the alternative. As bad as it could get when friends fell into dispute, or lovers - it was worse when parents, or parents and their children, or two siblings became hostile. After all, being part of the same lineage doesn't mean people are never going to disagree. On the contrary, family incompatibilities happened often. In an ongoing situation like RPS, the most troubling, depressing, and often disruptive situation was when the difference causing people to fight was over how much time should be given to RPS, or being positive about it at all.

Twenty years into the experience, I still don't think anyone can sensibly say, here is how to deal with a child, sibling, parent, or spouse who disagrees with your involvement so the situation inevitably turns out well. RPS created a strong community of support, but when a family member ridiculed your choices, it was hard to navigate no matter what support you had.

What other chapter priorities contributed to success?

After Trump's election we all finger pointed, emphasizing flaws in everyone but ourselves and our closest allies. But then some of us looked in the mirror, and though I am not sure it was your intent with this question, I remember when I examined my mirror, four areas of concern greatly troubled me.

First, as an anti-sexist feminist I looked at Trump's female vote and wondered why five decades of feminist effort left so many women and men who did not rebel against Trump's misogyny. Clearly our being right about society's gender injustices hadn't created an unstoppable tide against sexism. Did we say too little about medium and long run goals? Did we alienate potential allies?

Second, as an anti-racist internationalist I looked at the admittedly small numbers of low or modest income blacks and Latinos confused about Trump and while I was happy about that, I also wondered how any could exist. And while I certainly understood some racism still existing in various white constituencies, I looked and saw the relative lack of white fury at Trump's racism, Islamophobia, and immigrant bashing, and I wondered, again, how could that still exist?

Had five decades of anti-racist organizing not tried often or energetically enough to reach resistant whites? Had our movements preached overwhelmingly only where we already had a receptive audience? Had our tone or substance unnecessarily alienated many who we needed to reach? Had our anti-racist values, aims, or methods been flawed? Should we have said more about medium and long run goals? Could we have put off fewer potential allies and pulled others more sustainably into anti-racist commitment?

Third, as an anti capitalist I looked at a narcissistic billionaire bully attracting tens of millions of working class votes and I wondered how that could happen. How could five decades of anti capitalist organizing leave so many workers susceptible to Trump's posturing? Did we not sufficiently address what working people feel and experience in ways they relate to? Did we give off hostility toward working people mirroring what they daily encountered from authority figures in hospitals, courts, and workplaces?

Being right for five decades about capitalism's horrors hadn't created an unstoppable tide against class oppression. Should we have said more about medium and long run goals? Could we make uncompromising, comprehensive demands about economy in ways that didn't polarize away workers and didn't ignore other social phenomena affecting workers like gender and race? Were we too dismissive of workers? Did we even aspire to be above workers, both in the movement and in a new economy?

Finally, fourth, as an activist, I looked at progressive and left writing over election year 2016, and I saw a lot of people saying that Trump had a silver lining. Trump will galvanize us. Trump is just another ruling class lackey so that not voting in contested states or voting for Stein in contested states was a wise choice. I wondered how such seeming callousness toward the plight of those who would most suffer Trump's fascistic inclinations and ecological madness could exist among people who were generally the opposite of callous.

How could such views arise among radicals immersed in left literature and activism? What had those of us who knew better done wrong that had caused us to fail to reach the commentators who offered such suicidal views? How could months much less years or even decades of involvement in radicalism have yielded such results? I wondered what had been wrong with the accumulated literature and practice of all the left's many parts, taken in sum, such that a good many left commentators and incredibly many young radicals could be highly versed in all that radical output, yet nonetheless hold the views many had been propounding.

CHAPTER 9

HOUSING AND RIGHTS TO THE CITY

Bill Hampton, Cynthia Parks, and Harriet Lennon discuss transportation, housing, and rights to the city.

Bill Hampton, one thing that emerged early in RPS was attention to urban transportation. How did that occur, and what were its early features?

Even before RPS, I visited various European countries where the use of bicycles dwarfed that in the U.S. The benefits were exercise, clean air, a more social experience, cost effectiveness, and even reduced time of transit due to the inner city crowding that so delayed fueled vehicles. The obvious question was, why was bike transport almost completely absent in the U.S.? The answer was that fossil traffic was immensely profitable and therefore hard to jettison even after becoming disastrous for society.

When we asked whether long run health provided sufficient reason to accept some short run disruption, peoples' reasons to resist declined until all that remained was that less cars would hurt some who didn't deserve losses. This didn't mean rich elites becoming less rich, which was just another virtue of bike campaigns. It meant auto workers and some travelers.

An interesting aspect was the interface with the "rights to the city" consciousness that had arisen long before in the developing world. "Rights to the city" advocated cities and regions designed for citizens to enjoy. It was not only about bikers, and clean air, but also food and housing, migration, education, a healthy environment, public space, non discrimination, and venues for popular political participation. "Rights to the city" became RPS program applied to urban areas, while RPS program became "rights to the city" applied universally.

Cynthia Parks, can you tell us what drew you to RPS?

My family lost its home when I was ten years old. Many people we knew lost their's too. I was young, but I saw families of four, five, and more living in one or two room ramshackle apartments or two or more families living together in a space too small for any one family. I saw families living in cars, as my family did for two years. I saw families plunged into anger, despair, alcohol, and opioid addiction. I saw incredible tension and violence. I had rats for roommates. But as I got older I met folks who devoted themselves to preventing evictions or to helping those who were evicted find new homes.

The contrast between housing activists who sought just results and real estate developers, bankers, and police who callously carried out evictions and arrests, decided my life. Within a short time of joining with housing activists my understanding broadened even while my passion remained housing.

I learned that the movers putting families onto the street weren't the core problem. Nor were the bankers foreclosing on mortgages, or the cops, legislators, or real estate developers. They were each part of the problem, of course. And while some showed remorse, most acclimated themselves to their roles making it hard to empathize with them. But the core problem was a system of requirements that pushed people into these behaviors. That system was our enemy. I was already revolutionary because I not only despised that system, I also felt that despite all the deprivation and depravity, we could do better.

As a result, when I first met various RPS organizers, it was a perfect fit. I didn't have to change my agenda. I only had to welcome their support others and lend my support to them. I realized I was more prepared to contribute to RPS than many of the people already in it. Housing organizing required listening, hearing, and empathizing. It involved consciousness raising, skills development, and confidence building. It needed informed, tireless solidarity from everyone involved. Housing organizing required collectively conceiving and sharing creative solutions. You had to pay close attention to the means at hand and attainable ends. You had to be patient with people but impatient with institutions. Housing organizing involved a type of activism RPS needed. And what we housing organizers needed back from RPS was a large organization's support. We were a round peg fitting a round hole.

Could tell us about your difficulties first becoming radical?

The difficulties were more cultural than ideological. My up bringing made the ideas of the left familiar and welcome. The style of the left was a different matter.

Activists I first encountered still had the manners, words, and style of people who I had always despised. They had lots of education, and it showed. They were comfortable and confident, and it showed. Their habits included expecting people who looked, dressed, and talked like me to defer to them, almost as second nature. They didn't revel in their class position. They might get defensive about it, but they also tried to be welcoming.

The hard part of my becoming radical was deciding how to hang out with this crowd but keep my working class identity and connection. Luckily for my prospects, some of the folks I was relating to were already aware of these issues and trying to not just welcome workers but to hear and learn from workers' ways of interrelating and living.

My ties to self proclaimed Redneck lefties who used gun culture to reach into rural communities with anti-racist and anti-capitalist commitments horrified some radicals I met, though others realized this work was so far beyond what we were achieving in those locales that we needed to listen and learn. Redneck organizers showed how to move beyond passively enduring class oppression without becoming academicized. Wealthier organizers being willing to reject monopolizing confidence and influence helped. Before long I realized that our stylistic differences were rooted in worker/coordinator conditions and commitments.

Cynthia, you worked with Bill Hampton on transportation issues, right?

Yes, the campaign for "bicycles not cars" sought ecological benefit, safety, and improved urban social relations. What was interesting was not so much the argument for this transition as the process by which support grew. Those against had to ignore - or concede - that bike transit was more economical for those doing it, faster when mass transit also exists, and clearly better for the ecology. But they argued that cars exist and we don't want to be told we can't use them or that we are doing something evil by using them.

At the beginning, bike proponents kept hammering their own logic attributing car advocates' feelings to ignorance or selfishness. In reply, car advocates characterized the bikers as deviants interfering with a working system in pursuit of something that would never happen.

Progress came when bikers started to respond to what car owners were actually saying. Bikers' then less belligerently said more bikes is an option that you might actually benefit from, and that your kids and grandkids will certainly benefit from. Why not give it a limited chance to see if it has merit? And with that non-confrontational and experimental orientation, bike lanes began to spread. And then some roads were made car free for a day or two a week.

Bike dealerships spread and bikers wondered how to make production and distribution less commercial. Things got radical when bikers took on auto manufacturers seeking more electric vehicles and for bikes to be made available on a sharing, free basis to inner city users.

Conflicts grew for a time, but once bikers became open to real discussion and saw their task as addressing critics' views rather than somehow "beating" them, progress accelerated. From small groups advocating bikes in cities and larger groups using them but not fighting for their spread, more and more people got involved. Once bikers took on auto companies seeking auto workers' well being, popular support overcame defending old options.

Sometimes a contest is zero sum. One side wins and the other side loses. In a contest between those who don't own productive property and those who do, getting rid of ownership of resources and factories means one side wins and the other side loses. In contrast, a great many other oppositions are not zero sum, even though, at first, everyone may think they are. For bikes versus cars, if a well-conceived bike and mass-transit inner-city transportation pattern replaces a car-centered pattern, car folks don't lose due to costs, pollution, or even slower or less convenient transport. Make careful changes to respectfully explore implications and nearly everyone gains.

Didn't some on the car side retain their hostility and opposition, even as the evidence of benefits mounted?

Yes, but they were not fighting against the bike project itself, but against a slippery slope to systemic social change. It was a recurrent dynamic. Movements wanted involved populations to assess innovations on their own merits rather than to reject them due to fearing overall systemic change. Those who were trying to ward off broader social change sought to fight every battle on grounds that giving in was a slippery slope toward altering society's overall character.

Once movements for change understood this sub text, they realized their ability to effectively dissipate fear of RPS program writ large was critical to winning its separate components. The great bike crusades were part of that. And our opponents were partly correct. When cities allowed only bikes and mass transit in downtown areas, the number of bikers wearing RPS hats was undeniable.

Harriet, born in 2000, you have been a grassroots organizer and a trainer for other organizers. You started your activism in local communities fighting evictions and, at the same time, developing consciousness of larger scale demands and campaigns. You became active with food organizing and delivery. You were always a protector, advocate, and empowerer of the defenseless. You got involved in housing issues a bit later than Cynthia, and with a different focus, right?

Yes, I was in school. I was thinking about social change but not yet seeking it and I began to wonder about housing. First, what could improve the living situation in large apartment complexes? Everyone was fragmented. There were few shared agendas. Landlords dominated. There had to be options worth pursuing.

Second, I wondered whether some broad national policy could increase affordable housing.

What followed?

I started meeting with friends to discuss ideas. We visited housing activists and tenants' rights groups and encountered many people already in or about to join RPS, so my friends and I joined too.

So joining wasn't a major life decision to angst over?

Not remotely. We were sitting around talking, and we noted that people we liked were in RPS. and so we joined. RPS's short term benefits attracted us.

And then?

Our talks hatched two plans that were later adopted as part of RPS housing program. The first was a massive expansion of organizing in apartment complexes. We helped renters see themselves as a collective force able to control their circumstances. We would visit an apartment complex, make friends, and hear about issues and problems. Then we would make tentative suggestions and help implement modest gains. For example, sometimes elderly tenants would be on a high floor they had difficulty getting to and we would arrange an apartment swap with younger tenants from a more accessible floor. Such self-organized events displayed sympathy and a desire for overall fairness.

How did you get folks to do it?

We reached out to student tenants in places where one or more were already in RPS. Before long we approached families. We offered a bit of modesty, a bit of social engagement, and a lot of listening.

Gains that residents could themselves enact, such as making aesthetic changes in corridors, were excellent because they quickly revealed potential. Once we had some trust and excitement built up, we helped people set up tenants' food co-ops to reduce costs and time spent shopping. With the same logic, we helped set up collective approaches for handling day care and laundry. Folks with kids who worked double shifts couldn't be active, so freeing people's time became crucial. We started holding parties and hosting group events. In time, there arose the idea that maybe tenants didn't have to each individually own things that they would only rarely use but that were important to have available when the need arose. Perhaps people could share. It was like setting up a lending library - but not just for books. Such projects saved time and money, and built trust. New friendships brightened lives and foreshadowed greater gains.

Did you do this type work?

Yes, I was a tenant and organized in my complex, but the work didn't come easily for me. I wasn't a person who enters a room and immediately relates to everyone. I was shy, quiet, and not well-suited to talking with folks. Like most women I feared knocking on doors, having a man answer, and going in to talk. But I knew how much it might matter, so occasionally I did it though typically we went door to door in teams, especially for first encounters.

Once we had more trust among residents, dealing collectively with reducing drugs and sexual and spouse abuse became another focus. The idea that people could publicly talk about such horrible personal violations and collectively take steps to reduce them was at first inconceivable. Yet it didn't take long for our solutions to simpler issues to mature into giving attention to more complex ones.

As collectivism and mutual aid developed, we sought ways to adjudicate disputes, allocate resources, and win lower rents and timely repairs. We realized our apartment complex was a small society amidst others, quite like a neighborhood amidst other neighborhoods, or even a country amidst other countries.

Didn't you also get involved in broader national campaigns?

Yes, we wondered how we could build high-quality, affordable housing in non-exploitative ways featuring exemplary distribution. Who would do the work? Why would they do it? With what financing? Who would get the product?

As our group discussed these questions we thought about enlisting participation from people who had great unmet needs and under-utilized capacities. Instead of learning how to kill with blind discipline in the military, and instead of learning how to gain more advanced criminal skills to use after release from prison into a society that stigmatized their reentry, why couldn't soldiers and inmates learn useful skills, cooperate at work, and make their own decisions while generating a much-needed product? We began RPS's campaign to transform military bases and prisons to soldiers and inmates constructing low-income, high-quality housing, including giving soldiers and inmates, once they left the military or prison, first claim on houses they had helped build, with other recipients being young people, homeless people, and others in need.

Organizing began partly in communities, partly in the military and prisons. RPS members reached out to prison and military families, to people working with those constituencies, and to neighborhoods around bases and prisons. I remember hearing how setting up coffee shops around military bases was a tactic used during the Vietnam war to talk with soldiers about resisting. I also remember working with prisoners' groups, and visiting inside prisons to talk about our conversion campaign. The interactions were incredibly moving as we met and talked with young and often poor soldiers being used as war fodder, on the one hand, and with diverse people being punished sometimes for real crimes but often for trying to survive, on the other hand. They warmed not just to getting a home on release, but also to playing a powerful positive social role.

It was tumultuous, as we all knew it would be, but it had so many benefits we didn't gain a good grasp of their full scope until later.

The last major campaign focused on motels and hotels, didn't it?

We realized the number of empty rooms in hotels and motels, on average, at any moment, was roughly the same as the number of homeless people nationally, about 8 million. We decided to build a campaign around the idea that we should have housing for all before anyone could occupy dwellings that were not their own. This started by saying that all buildings that provided temporary housing for travelers should allot 20% of their rooms to permanent residents at a low income rental rate. There were lots of details, but the idea was clear enough. Luxury had to come after necessity. Of course later everything about hotels, motels, and income for housing would change as RPS progressed and more housing was built, but short of that, the partial opening of various private motels and hotels to low income residency bettered the circumstances of deserving constituencies and elevated values and practices that prepared people for winning further advances.

Finally, all these housing approaches benefitted the people doing the activity, benefitted the recipients of the products, benefitted society writ large, and strengthened various constituencies with skills, dispositions, and interconnections suited to winning still more gains.

Can you remember some pivotal moment or moments during the emergence of RPS that greatly affected you?

Here is one from my time tenant organizing. I called on an elderly couple, the Posners, to ask if they would be interested in very carefully swapping apartments with someone from the first floor so they would no longer have to walk up three flights. They looked at me after getting me some tea and cookies and the gentleman was clearly moved. The woman explained that for two years climbing the stairs had been devastating for her husband, which meant he very rarely went out, and also quite difficult for her. He had worked assembly and his legs were bad. She was, in her own words, long-lived lungs on long-lived legs.

So we talked and they told me about themselves and vice versa and it was striking to hear that they were surprised that it had never even occurred to them to see if anyone would make the switch for them and more so, that no one had ever spontaneously offered.

I took from it not just making new friends and the pleasure of having helped them, but a deep understanding of the incredible extent to which society twists us all so far from human sympathy and respect that we take callous isolation for granted. We don't question it. We don't even admit it. We quietly endure while waltzing by it. I realized that to have strong activism we had to overcome the near universal assumption of inevitable isolation and that even switching rooms could spur important consciousness raising.

Going another step back, born in 2000, when did you become radical? What caused it?

I was 19, in community college and had heard various progressive formulations, particularly about racism and global warming, but much else too. I was sympathetic, I guess you might say, but more into music, films, boys, and social media. One night I was talking with a new friend who turned out to be very radical. She was telling me about the then recent Wall Street march and arguing for doing more, including on our campus. After about an hour of describing her aims and expectations, she said, "please don't take this wrong, but I wonder why you come at every issue assuming indignity is permanent? Why don't you entertain the possibility of anything else? Why does all your thinking go into navigating current circumstances, and none into seeking change, even as you seem to pretty much accept that things are horrible"?

Her question didn't have any impact in the moment, but later I began thinking about it. Did I rule out change and take for granted horrible existing relations like I defended scientific theories against lunatic heresy? I almost settled on that being the answer, but my friend pointed out that no scientist would assume cancer was incurable at the outset of considering what to do about it, though a beneficiary of exorbitant fees for cancer treatment might. No engineer would assume a bridge couldn't span the Hudson River at the outset of trying to connect cities on either side, though someone wanting to maintain separation might. Hearing a proposed cancer cure, or a proposed bridge design, unless you had some axe to grind getting in the way of reason, you might carefully question the proposal, but you would want your doubts to be wrong. You would not hope to be right. Well, this ate at me. What was my axe to grind? Of course, radical views still had to win me over, but a big obstacle had disappeared and before long I was RPS bound.

All this made me see that everyone takes for granted that young people more easily become radical than older people. But why is that? I heard commentators point to the pressures of earning income, having family, toeing the line, but while that explained why young radicals often lose their views as they age, albeit never realizing just how profound a critique of society's roles that was, for me it didn't convincingly explain why a young person was more likely than an older person, all else equal, to become radical in the first place. What was it about being older that made one less open to becoming radical?

I decided my experience showed that young or old, to become radical requires at least implicitly recognizing that earlier you had been wrong. The older you are, the more of your life you have to admit was mistaken. If I was thirty when the conversation that began my radicalization occurred, I doubt it would have been enough. I would have been too defensive and this gave me great respect for radical longevity, and even more so for becoming radical later in life.

CHAPTER 10

ACTOR'S ACTIVISM

Celia Curie discusses Hollywood activism.

Celia Curie, born in 1994 you were an aspiring actress at the time of the first RPS convention. You became highly active in RPS while a successful actress in Hollywood. You were a Secretary of Popular Culture for the RPS shadow government, and you later became Governor of California, an office you still hold. Can you tell us how you first became radical?

I was raped by my uncle when I was fifteen. I didn't tell anyone. I was afraid, and, at first I thought it was my fault. Later I didn't want to create what would have been chaos. My father's brother did it. The fallout would be horrendous for my dad and my uncle's family, for everyone. I didn't think my uncle was violent with others and I still don't know what came over him.

Afterwards, I used the internet, in private, to learn more about rape. I went deeply into the subject and became familiar with and indebted to many feminist writers who saved my life and opened my door to radicalism.

Being raped, watching a loved one killed or jailed, being torn apart by unemployment, alcohol, or drugs, becoming malevolent, or suffering preventable illness, dominates many peoples' early memories. I had difficulty escaping my dark times not least because all around me, every year since, there were always reminders in what I saw and endured.

Just ten years later RPS was percolating, and soon thereafter, Hollywood RPS got going. Do you remember where and how it started?

The first Hollywood chapter of RPS got going when some Hollywood actors and other film people started to meet face to face to discuss how they could relate to RPS. It was shortly after the first convention and we took a few meetings to settle on joining RPS and undertaking three types of activity. We would reach out to other people in our artistic communities to join RPS. We would agitate for changes in Hollywood film practices to make our industry better reflect RPS values and aims. We would reach out to the broader population using film and our visibility as actors.

It started with just eleven Hollywood people. We got less curious about fellow actors and more curious about ideas. We assembled some RPS literature. Deciding whether to join was like deciding whether to relate to a film by collectively assessing a screenplay. As we read the material, we practiced expressing RPS views among ourselves until we were confident we not only liked RPS, but were prepared to participate in its refinement and expansion.

At that point, we began reaching out to other Hollywood people. It was tricky not just because we had to address other people's concerns, something we weren't in the habit of doing, but because one of people's foremost concerns was "Why should I bother?"

To join, required people addressing much they would rather ignore. It would cost scarce time. To what end, they asked? What would I be doing, other than talking? We thought talking, like we were doing with them, was a lot, but it quickly became clear we had to have activities beyond talking to others that new members could relate to. So we came up with some.

What was the experience like for you?

Once we committed to RPS, what we did to expand it so defined who we were becoming that it was like immersing deeply into a film role, except RPS wasn't fiction, wasn't temporary, and we weren't paid to do it.

We had been actors, but also directors and camera folks. We were men and women, Black, Latin, white, gay, straight, fathers, and mothers. All these attributes affected how we saw ourselves. Like everyone, we occupied role positions in society and our roles largely determined who we were by the requirements they imposed on us. But joining RPS changed us, often without our even knowing it was happening.

It may sound exaggerated, but it isn't. We were no longer mainly an intersection of our mainstream institutional roles. It wasn't that the mainstream roles were gone. The daily pressures of our situations, contracts, and people's expectations still pushed and pulled us. But now we were also part of RPS. We were revolutionary, and that became who we were at a more basic, defining level than the rest.

Didn't obstacles you faced intimidate you? What did you do?

We knew progress would be neither swift nor easy, but we didn't dwell on that. I don't know how to explain our reaction other than to say it was the mood of our times. No time to hesitate, time to agitate. Be the change you want.

Within a year we began three projects. The first was a school for people in the movie industry. We assembled courses about understanding current society, developing and advocating vision for a better society, and addressing the mechanics and possibilities of the film industry.

Some of us taught, but we invited some more experienced RPS folks also offer classes. We created our own curriculum, but we also borrowed materials from other RPS chapters.

Hollywood people had always been severely time stretched and we were saying to participate you need to free up ten days, and more if you wanted to teach. So we asked a lot from highly accomplished adults who were used to other people doing their bidding. Attendees not only learned a lot, they enjoyed themselves and made new friends. The schools graduated capable members.

For our second project, we uncovered and publicized the pay rates of everyone in Hollywood and then agitated for more equitable relations. You can imagine how that went over. It was a difficult sell, but the ethics were clear and with informed persistence we eventually turned the tide. Instead of our appearing crazy, those defending old ways began to appear greedy.

Our third project reached beyond Hollywood. We pressured local media producers to give space and tools to grassroots participants and we created short films and later some full length ones promoting RPS ideas and program.

I wonder if you remember when you first got together?

Eleven of us first got together at a famous actor's outrageously fancy house. We met in an enormous ornate living room. One wall was all window overlooking a massive deck with a huge pool. Beyond that floated the Pacific.

Some of us lived more or less comparably to our host. Others, including myself, had never even seen a house remotely like where we met. Those ironies and tensions played out over and over during our development.

After some chit chat, a famous actor made a tepid pitch about having held a funding event for a local candidate, saying he hoped we would do similarly in the future. Had that set the tone, we would have gone nowhere. But Matt chimed in saying that kind of involvement wasn't enough, and that the conditions most people endured overseas, as well as in the U.S., were too abysmal for band aids. He referenced global warming and war and mainly how we all knew damn well that RPS was right about society needing a new social system. His passion resonated, and we were off and running.

What opposition did you have to overcome?

Actors, directors, writers, cinematographers, singers, and artists would tell us, "Creativity is different. We are not like other workers. We should enjoy incomes commensurate to our excellence. We should do whatever we like, not having to worry about balanced job complexes sapping our focus." "It is insane" they ridiculed us, "to think that the public should have a say in planning art. Artists have to do that, and then the public likes it or not. To require artistic creators to negotiate their work with the public would extinguish all art."

We heard that over and over and continually had to disabuse artistic people of their outrageous conceit that they were uniquely special and deserved special benefits. A scientist is creative, as are doctors, designers, and builders, and, with training and balanced job complexes, we would all be creative for part of our work time. More, creativity should be its own reward. What warranted remuneration was only working hard, long, or in difficult conditions.

We pointed out that saying actors, directors, or other art workers shouldn't do balanced work implied that others who do creative work shouldn't have to either, meaning 20% of the population should dominate 80% of the population. Yes, balancing artists' circumstances for empowerment would reduce their time for creativity, but everyone doing balanced work would free the creative potentials of vast new constituencies. It would also broaden the comprehension of any artist communicating about life.

We explained that workers and consumers having self-managing say wouldn't mean the public decides what goes in a novel, play, or film, any more than it would mean the public decides what research a physicist or biologist does, or how an architect designs a building. It would mean, instead, that the public decides, in cooperation with producers, what benefits society, and, based on that, what people can usefully produce as socially valued work. If the public wanted no music - then creating music wouldn't count as socially valued work. If the public wanted little music, then the number of singers, musicians, and composers who could earn income for creating music would be accordingly low. One could still produce or create music not wanted, not least hoping to change the public's mind, but one couldn't yet call it socially valued labor.

Likewise, the same applied if the public wanted no novels, or no engineering, or no medicine. But the public doesn't have to understand or appreciate every film or painting, song or performance, every construction method or research project, to know it wants society to have art, engineering, and science. What the public settles on in light of reports from those who do the labor is what amount it wants, which in turn determines the amount producers can produce for income. But producers then decide what they create and how. The new economic logic applied just as compellingly to artistic and intellectual endeavors as to rote ones. The worth of equity, classlessness, and self management applied equally for all people, groups, and activities.

How did you understand Hollywood Stardom at the time of the first RPS convention and how did that start to change in the convention's aftermath?

When RPS first convened I had been in some commercials and gotten some minor supporting parts. I had prospects, but I certainly wasn't anything like a star. My income kept me functioning, but little more. To me, a star was a larger than life person who endured an odd loneliness, constantly threatened by out of control paparazzi and even by fans or psychopaths. My attendance at our first meeting in the actor's palatial home reinforced that view. But, before long, I started to think of Hollywood stars as people who by dint of special inborn qualities, hard work, and a lot of luck, gained access to a particular art loving audience. I started to feel we didn't deserve excessive income, yet we received excessive everything. I felt we should renounce our excessive wealth and if wealth had to be distributed unequally until we could win new social relations, we should put most of ours to social ends.

For a long time, many actors, media moguls, and other rich people, had given to various causes, some frivolous, some important to people's lives. I didn't disparage that as being only self serving, tax evading, or press priming, which it often was, but I did decide that what was more important was everyone trying to literally eliminate poverty.

What RPS activities led to new creativity in movies, theater, and all art?

Our school did so, by broadening the consciousness, skills, and confidence of workers in the industry. RPS demonstrations and policy campaigns did so as well. Less celebrated and visible, so did seeking new allies and working to solidify the commitment of existing members and especially to improve their ability and willingness to demonstrate and pursue campaigns.

The production of films about social issues where each film offered positive potentials, helped. Also important was the way those involved contributed increasing proportions of a film's revenue to projects the film advocated, as was including activists' voices, and workers and actors linking up with the associated projects and advocating them in interviews and public displays.

The major dramatic film about RPS, "Good Will Winning: The Next American Revolution," which came out in our early years and included so many famous participants, foresaw much of what later happened and elevated RPS visibility. Those who worked on it functioned collectively, with balanced responsibilities and sensible salaries. The film was a tipping point for the industry, celebrated by the many Oscars it won and our speeches on Oscar night.

You are being a bit modest. It was your Oscar and speech...

I had a great starring role and the times and the artistry of the script and film were such that I got the best female actor award. And, yes, my speech was a highpoint, but please don't exaggerate my personal role. I was in the right place at the right time. I delivered a speech many people helped write.

In any case, transcending that film and its impact, there followed the great industry strike, long nurtured by continuous agitation and organizing. It spurred change and was, I think, perhaps the first time coordinator class members in such large numbers were so outspoken for dramatically reducing coordinator class advantages. We accepted and celebrated working people's leadership. That not only turned our industry inside out, it helped spur similar activism from the sciences to architecture, law, athletics, medicine, and media.

What Hollywood resistance to RPS remains?

We now have workers councils operating throughout Hollywood and while owners and other officials still do some films the old way, well over half of today's films are done almost entirely in new, RPS ways. The new has challenged the old, gaining steadily, especially in the commitments of people first entering film work. It is the same pattern that has unfolded in schooling, health care, and most fields.

But resistance still exists, and, indeed, some people will retain their old ways until Father Time takes them offstage. One kind of opposition is honest, "I won't forego my massive income. I won't do tasks I find onerous. I like my coordinator advantages." That clarity is rare, however, because even rich people like to look in the mirror and admire themselves, not to mention retaining relations with their children, so they deny the greedy truth.

More commonly, film industry resistance to RPS asserts that "RPS would destroy artistic quality and kill aesthetic motivation. To work for RPS's 'equitable incomes,' eliminate corporate divisions of labor, and cooperatively negotiate economic allocation, would gut art."

It's the same complaint as twenty years ago, though back then the naysayers were everywhere and we had to argue with nearly everyone in the industry using analogies between racist and sexist nonsense which was at least well understood by most in Hollywood, and classist nonsense, which was foreign to most - or using some modest thought experiments to try to get our views across. Now, the naysayers are relatively few and though the beliefs and analogies are still applicable, even more compelling are the hugely successful projects undertaken in RPS style and the gigantic good will those projects generated.

How will RPS success alter future artistry for creators and audiences?

The audience for artistic work will grow due to people having more time for enjoyment and inspiration, and also new knowledge that increases "consumer" benefits. But artistic workers, like all others, will receive equitable incomes and work in balanced job complexes in industries that relate to the will of both workers and consumers. Artistic workers, like all others, will collectively self manage their involvements. Society will still admire and celebrate great art, but won't excessively enrich great artistry.

But will there be as high a level of creativity and excellence as now?

In the first decade of this century, how much high creativity and excellence was there beyond outrageous special effects and exploring the psyches of murderers? But even if we set that aside, we should see that high levels of excellent art, though important, should not be our only criteria of judgement. Think of it this way. Suppose you are looking at a workplace producing shirts. Do we have as our highest and even our only aim maximizing the quality and quantity of shirts that come out the door?

Many would initially say yes, but if we did, why not work people to death and then just dump them in the alley while calling in replacements? Why not produce way more shirts than people want? Why not produce only for the gaudy tastes of rich clientele while ignoring less expensive tastes?

Sensible output has to take into account those doing the work, those receiving the product, and those not receiving other products that could have been produced instead.

RPS's cooperative planning recognizes it is fine if we sometimes seek less output or settle for good output when seeking more or better would impose too much hardship on those involved. But that said, people in each industry will be far better able to provide more, and the public will be far better able to benefit from more, because the population will have far more of its creative potentials nurtured and supported.

Consider someone, let's call him Donald, who worries about a decline of art - or about a decline of doctoring, engineering, ecological research, or what have you. Donald bemoans lost output due to people who previously only did empowering tasks now doing balanced work. Donald believes the loss won't be offset by newly cultivated and expressed talents of the 80% of the population who were formerly silenced and subordinated. He says they lack needed talent. RPS believes Donald's view is no less classist than earlier generations thinking women and Blacks couldn't contribute creatively was sexist or racist. To claim incapacity of women and Blacks was nonsense despite that it benefitted those protecting advantages, and even seemed to explain why Blacks and women weren't doing empowered work. "It is because they can't," said the racist or sexist, "not because they are prevented." Similar, rationalizations about class seem to explain the fact that workers aren't producing art - or other creative outputs - though increasingly less so with the incredible growth of workplace councils and balanced job complexes in Hollywood.

When you attended your first Hollywood meeting, I am guessing you weren't yet revolutionary. What brought you the rest of the way?

The literature I was reading taught me a lot but working in our group was key. We become what we do, so when our group transcended aloof liberalism, I did too. For me, another big factor was thinking about kids. It wasn't, what do I want to leave them? It was, what should I say to them about right and wrong? Each good answer I had pushed me as much as them.

What was the turning point when you felt the struggle had matured from trying hard to have a chance to being assured of victory?

It was when writers, actors, directors, editors, videographers, techies, designers, drivers, dressers, stunt people, and music people, marched through Hollywood chanting and singing, and then went to neighborhood meetings for conversation and dinner at community gatherings. And especially when we did it again, and again, the same way, in New York, Chicago, Boston, Denver, Houston, Nashville, Memphis, Miami, Atlanta, Seattle, San Francisco, Portland, Minneapolis, Detroit, and Cleveland.

I hope it is okay if I ask you a personal question about acting and your experiences of it? You have been considered beautiful all your life, and I wonder what place you think this had in the past and should have in the future, in Hollywood and in society, too?

It is personal, but it is also fair. Growing up, what you look like used to have, and still has, major implications. I was, and I guess I am, by our society's standards, beautiful. None of us can see that, easily, in ourselves, but I see it in others. Sometimes a person's beauty can be mesmerizing and even addictive. But there is more to it, especially in a horribly sexist society.

At a young age I learned behavior patterns that could get me things I wanted. I didn't understand why, but I noticed how my smiles affected people, or how my being coy or flirty affected people. And these behaviors became part of who I was, with attendant gains and losses. Materially, I benefited. Psychologically, too, because I got confidence and style. But my personality warped and I got mired in feelings of entitlement and guilt.

Hollywood exaggerated the dynamics. Beauty was bankable for women, and for men too. And what was bankable was cultivated and sought, but also thrown out when it faded. So in the old days beautiful women - and men - were signed on and if you could perform reasonably well, and you weren't annoying for producers and directors, you would have a career, at least until your looks faded.

I don't know entirely how I feel about it. Being eyeballed from my preteens on, being hit on, and being sexually fantasized in many people's daily lives is horrible. Think about knowing that thousands and maybe even millions imagine doing things with or to you. Everyone undervalues everything else you are. Transcending that requires help, which is all too often absent. We should eliminate objectification and exploitation. We should also not reward riches or power to beauty.

Suppose someone is born really strong, or able to run outrageously fast, or with great reflexes, or able to think really fast. RPS says the person should not be able to turn that genetic luck into wealth, power, or unfair circumstances. So that should apply, as well, to being born looking special. But about reflexes and thinking, we don't mind that they are admired, or that having those attributes means you can do some things which, without them, you could not do. So, though it makes me nervous, shouldn't that also apply to appearance?

The odd thing is that special traits, features, qualities, or talents, in old societies, all had both benefits and debits for the person. The sex overlay gave one of those an added dimension, but if you think about it, any special quality tended to convey advantages, pressures, options, rewards, and often at least some costs. So I have a feeling all of this is going to work itself out in a new society in ways we might not be able to fully foresee yet. But I think what we can already say for sure is being lucky in the genetic lottery should not convey material advantage, greater say in society, or freedom from responsibility, nor should it impose pressures, denials, or abuse.

CHAPTER 11

HEALTH AND CLASS

Barbara Bethune and Mark Feynman discuss the emergence of the health front of RPS and its relevance for RPS views on class.

Barbara Bethune, born in 1992, you became a medical doctor and from the start questioned your profession. Your early RPS involvement solidified your purpose to revolutionize health care and you later became RPS shadow Secretary of Health. Can you tell us your path to becoming a doctor, and then into radicalism and your medical activist involvements immediately after the convention.

I became a doctor feeling I could be good at it. I developed the ambition partly from admiring doctors in the family and partly from the example of a doctor who treated me at a young age. Frustrations surfaced in college when my medical training ignored social causes and prevention. The anti-health aspects of an internship at a major Chicago hospital sealed my radicalization.

Being an intern did it?

Intern training pressured us to jump ridiculous hurdles and passively accept that we shouldn't fight the system. We could whine to friends away from the job, but we shouldn't challenge employers. Our silence let us graduate, but also prepared us to impose similar insanity on those who came after us. Our silence implied internship rituals had merit. We didn't become robots. We still cared about patients. We still had souls - most of us, anyhow. The problem was we were corralled by hospital roles that undercut our intentions.

Why would anyone put up with it?

To become a doctor we had to fulfill academic rituals and defend doctors' rights and privileges. We worked long hours for large incomes and great status, and we never thought to ourselves, this is wrong. To think such thoughts could lead to resisting our roles, which could lead us out of the profession.

Accept impositions. Respect hierarchy. Enjoy income. Bludgeon those below. Teach successors to do likewise. Then do your best for your patients.

From my family, I was familiar with dissidence, so I questioned limits. I asked why interns work for thirty or forty consecutive hours and then treat patients. It didn't provide good health care. Why accept long work hours? Why not have more doctors so each can work fewer hours?

So what was internship about?

The more I considered that, the more I felt internship mainly limited the number of doctors to keep up doctors' incomes. To join the fraternity of doctors, we had to display fealty consistent with what our future roles required. We had to comply, or quit.

I began to see interning as sophisticated hazing and to test that impression I visited a military boot camp and watched new soldiers undergo training. Clearly they weren't only learning to shoot or to work together or even to be prepared for dangerous situations. Boot camp had elements of all that, just as interning had elements of medical learning, but boot camp mainly removed residual social and moral inclinations. It produced soldiers ready, willing, and even eager to kill on command. Boot camp molded recruits to passively follow orders. It educated recruits to ask no questions. It graduated soldiers no longer able to resist orders.

Military boot camp was a cauldron of personal reconstruction designed to produce soldiers who would blindly obey orders and do extreme damage without raising the slightest question. Graduates of military boot camp would generally accept and even celebrate having no say in policies and actions.

And you felt that that was true of being an intern?

I did. After viewing the military dynamic, I looked back at interning and I saw that it sought to create doctors who would defend their huge salaries and prerogatives against any challenge regardless of the health care implications for patients and society.

Regardless? Surely that is too strong a word...

Is it? Interning created doctors who would abet pharmaceutical profit seeking at the expense of engendering opioid addictions and economic rip off. It created doctors who would denigrate nurses, keeping them excluded from decisions and blocked from activities doctors preferred to do even at the expense of patient well being. It created doctors who would defend incredibly inflated incomes by keeping down the number of doctors via exclusionary medical school practices.

Medical interning didn't mainly advance health, knowledge, or preparedness, much less compassion. It conveyed medical knowledge despite itself. I became curious about other professions so I looked and found similar dynamics for lawyers and other professions as well. Training professionals harbored a giant Catch 22. It gave diverse skills, knowledge, and confidence to a set of people even as it ensured that they wouldn't use those gains on behalf of society, but only on behalf of themselves and those above.

Becoming a doctor entailed navigating pressure, frustration, and anger, and provoked various reactions. Mostly, at least before RPS, people would try to do good and be ethical without challenging their role assignments. They believed, with good reason, that challenging their roles would change nothing and lead to personal loss. We would deliver medicine to the sick, if the sick could pay, and if tending to them wouldn't disrupt hospital or societal hierarchies, but we wouldn't take on the underlying causes of sickness and we would defend and even exploit existing relations. It wasn't just doctors bent out of shape by medicine's pliers, but also nurses, custodians, and all medical workplace employees.

Role structures in hospitals like those in law firms, political parties, churches, and other institutions, induced going along to get along. Overturning roles felt like a naive pipe dream. Complying with one's role eventually switched from something you reticently did under duress, to being who you were.

Benefiting from a monopoly on empowering work distorts one's personality, including producing blindness to one's own culpability. Someone who retains sufficient humanity to resist seems saint-like. The harm done to the personalities, values, material conditions, and social options of those below is massive.

I wanted to keep doing medicine, but I wanted to improve health for all. I felt no allegiance to a domineering class above workers, though I understood the pressures and allures of their situation.

So when I went to the convention it was mostly a "Hail Mary" gesture. I didn't know if RPS could provide a good path forward, but I would try, and I was glad I did.

Why?

At the convention, I met other doctors, nurses, and medical workers from around the country. I was less different than I had feared. At the convention, we empowered each other by sharing similar stories and desires. We talked about changes we could fight for to benefit patients and ourselves.

The ideas that gained greatest traction were seeking comprehensive single payer health care, fighting pharmaceutical companies misuse of medicines, bringing doctors to poor locales, empowering nurses, changing the income and decision-making structure of the profession, agitating for more responsible food policies, and agitating for more healthful ecological policies and work conditions.

I got active in the two aspects where I thought my contribution might be most helpful - trying to battle the pharmaceutical companies, and challenging the harsh hierarchies of income and influence inside hospitals.

How?

For combating misuse of prescriptions, we aimed direct actions at producers. We rallied and sat-in to reveal how pharmaceutical companies not only vastly over charged, but aggressively over prescribed with massive over advertising. We showed the true costs of production of drugs and the insanely high markups imposed by monopolistic pharmaceutical pricing. We shined a light on prescribing unnecessary surgery. The practices we unearthed were nauseating, but we were even more shocked to discover that most people already knew what we were revealing. It turned out we mainly needed to convince people the grotesque situation wasn't inevitable.

We brought class action suits against pharmaceutical companies. Young claimants fought misuse of mood altering medications. Elderly claimants fought companies trying to grab all their savings. Those addicted to opioids fought pharmaceutical profit seeking and drug dealing. Everyone fought the misuse of antibiotics that risked birthing super bugs and pandemics - and grotesque pricing policies. We undertook a national boycott of the worst pharmaceutical culprits.

My other focus was challenging elitist dynamics inside hospitals and health care generally. Racism and sexism had been addressed with considerable progress, but class division had never been addressed at all. First, we got people to talk at meetings. Next we sought greater income, more influence, and access to more skills for nurses. For doctors, we challenged their assumed superiority and advanced more equitable values and relations, including supporting nurses and other medical workers as well as the non medical staff. Medicine had become a rapaciously self-seeking luxury trade. We challenged its innards.

Mark Feynman, born in 1990, you became a nurse. A strong advocate for working class politics, you highlighted the interface between nurses and doctors and between workers and members of the coordinator class. I wonder if you can tell us how you first got involved and about some of your early post convention activities?

I went to the convention as a working class nurse already hostile to profit seeking and corporate hierarchy. I didn't know if the convention would sincerely address my concerns, much less respect and elevate them.

Nurses were there in force to say we hate bad health care. We should be part of providing better. We should be respected. The ridiculous allotment of power and income to doctors at the expense of nurses, technicians, and people doing other hospital work must stop. At the convention we met, talked, and shared our views. We became confident. We celebrated the emergent program and decided to form Health Care Workers United (HCWU), a movement for better health for all which later became a militant, multi-focus movement to organize medical workplaces and win broader health policy reforms. We investigated and learned about our jobs' financial logic. We learned health workers' attitudes toward their conditions. We attracted support and initiated positive campaigns.

What did you feel needed to be done regarding the interface between doctors and nurses?

A doctor discussing viruses or kidneys was typically highly informed. A doctor discussing social programs, or even the nature of the hospital he worked in, was typically incredibly ignorant. After nurses had held some sessions, we invited doctors to come and attend one. It was nurses and doctors from around the country, not nurses and nearby doctors who had direct power over them.

One nurse - me - got up and got things rolling. I said, "We respect the work you do, but we feel you are way overpaid, over protective of yourselves, and bossy toward us." Tensions rose, but I continued, "What I want to know is do you really think you are doctors and we are nurses because you are superior?" Now there was a lot of noise, not friendly. My hands were shaking, but as I proceeded, my fear morphed into anger and I got a little louder. "Do you really think you deserve more income, more status, more power? Or do you understand that you have those benefits despite there being no valid justification?"

What happened?

Emotional hell broke lose but then sensible discussion began. Do doctors have better income and more power due to some difference in ability to attain knowledge? Due to a gap in effort? Due to monopolizing empowering work?

Do the different tasks we do justify our difference in income and power? Or do our different tasks - and our different circumstances earlier in life - lead to differences and means to attain knowledge, which in turn enforce differences in income and power?

The tension was familiar. What was new was realizing how difficult it would be to overcome. We understood that we had to eliminate this class division not only in hospitals but throughout society. We had to involve current coordinator class members in RPS without their dominating RPS.

Right there, that day, that meeting, many nurses realized that should be our main contribution to RPS. Doctors and coordinator class members typically defended their advantages. They believed they were properly empowered and rewarded. They believed they helped those below. Many even believed those below are dumb, parochial, and should be grateful. They felt that while workers should join a movement for a new society, we should not have any decision making say in it. Overcoming all that was nurses' special agenda.

I sometimes forget it was that bad...

Yes, but there was more. A parallel obstacle to success was that often we nurses accepted we were incapable of empowering work and deserved less income. Or if we were not submissive, we were so furious we wanted doctors out of RPS. The sentiments were understandable, but counter productive. Even worse, we would get so angry at doctors we would sometimes get baited into rejecting training, knowledge, and skill.

I know this wasn't entirely new, but were nurses alone in addressing this when RPS was emerging, or had it arisen in other ways and realms as well?

The clash had been around for ages and even named and discussed for decades on the fringe of the left. I think nurses in this issue gained prominence in this issue because while nurses were relegated to working class subordination, our jobs weren't as successful as most working class jobs at disempowering us. We were subordinated like other workers, but we were less socialized and weakened into accepting our plight.

Nonetheless, as activists we didn't want to alienate 20% of the population who have critically important knowledge. We didn't want to antagonize them into militantly supporting the status quo and rejecting change. This meant we often put a lid on our feelings. When some of us got beyond that, our only means for gaining support was through alternative media. But back then alternative media aggressively avoided discussing these issues.

Why?

I had the same question and an analogy helped me understand.. I knew self preservation caused media owners to obstruct serious focus on the structures that elevated owners. I knew the whole ethos and culture of mainstream media vetoed private ownership being a major topic, or even a topic at all. In short, I didn't expect mainstream media to question private ownership of workplaces

I knew that within the left, even in our alternative media, worker-coordinator class relations got nearly no attention. By analogy, I realized it was like mainstream media excluding discussion of private ownership. People rarely welcomed criticisms of themselves, particularly when it challenged their wealth, power, and self image. Since left media was typically run by coordinator class members, both by position inside the media and also by prior background, they shut off attention to their situation. However, as RPS took shape, the issue surfaced into steadily greater visibility partly due to initial RPS organizers bringing it forward, but also because the issue had surfaced in the Trump/Clinton campaign a few years before.

Opposition to immigrants and blatant racism churned support for Trump but so did anger at elites for imposing collapsing services while they accumulated uncountable riches. Hypocritical lies from above confronted legitimate desires from below. Elites organized to deflect or crush opposition.

We knew that progressives had for decades won serious gains regarding race, gender, and sexuality. We hadn't won all we wanted, but we had won quite a lot. We also knew that regarding class we had addressed nothing comparable in scope and complexity to the range of issues that anti racist and anti sexist activists regularly battled over. Why not?

How could we explain substantial working class support for Trump and the ineffectiveness of progressives at enlisting widespread working class activism? What could we do about it?

> *Trump was a billionaire and didn't for a second deny it. If a large part of the anger fueling his constituency was about economic impoverishment, why were his working class supporters aggressively wedded to one of capitalism's main practitioners of impoverishing others and what did this have to do with your antipathy toward doctors?*

We needed to understand how Trump's supporters could be so angry at their personal economic plight - and they were - and at media and government - and they were - and yet be so positive about a bigoted billionaire - which many were. What happened to class consciousness? The answer was that the passionate anger coursing through a good part of Trump's supporters was, in fact, hostility to a perceived class enemy. But the class enemy was not mainly capitalists.

Most working people never personally encounter a capitalist but routinely encounter doctors, lawyers, accountants, engineers, and others who have highly empowered jobs with associated elevated status and great wealth. Workers daily serve these coordinators, obey them, and get meager but absolutely essential benefits from them, but only by accepting demeaning rules and inflated fees. Coordinators routinely treat us like children. Unsurprisingly, on average we despise coordinators even as we depend on and obey them.

You felt this way yourself?

Yes, absolutely, and I still do. I saw the advantages that coordinator class members enjoyed. I wanted our kids to become doctors, lawyers, or engineers however infrequently it could happen given the hugely different conditions people encounter growing up. We workers tended to despise doctors, lawyers, and engineers, even as we wanted our kids to become them.

When I walk around on the streets, in the mall, going to the doctor, or at work, I don't encounter capitalists, I encounter coordinator class types who dress and talk differently than I do, enjoy different movies and TV, and expect working class people to move out of their way and to follow their instructions as we go about our demeaning tasks. Workers hate being administered, bossed, rendered powerless, considered inferior and paternalized - but we acclimate to it to get by and then we become what we do.

But how does seeing all that explain Trump, or even more so, leftists' relative lack of success reaching out to working class constituencies?

Trump's voters believed Trump was personally friendly and unrelentingly forthright, even though he was a dishonest bully. For workers, Trump didn't masquerade and exude academic arrogance. He shot straight. He was not a dismissive, coordinator class type - like Clinton - who would pander to workers, talk about workers' pain, claim to support workers, but who workers could feel didn't give a damn about working people from the way she walked, the way she talked, and the very air that circulated around her, all of it so different than Trump's walk, talk, and surrounding air.

And, sad to say, while Trump's supporters' perceptions of him were horrendously misplaced, Trump's supporters' antipathy for the managers, doctors, lawyers, engineers, and accountants who earn many times what workers earn and who treat workers like children was often fully warranted.

While working class hostility to what they called political correctness, was undeniably sometimes racist or sexist, it was nearly always hostile to those who used rules, fancy manners, and obscure language to lord over us, relegate, and degrade us.

Some of us thought about the 2016 election before the vote, and decided that if Sanders ran against Trump, he would appeal directly to Trump's voters, and have answers that Trump's supporters would want to hear. When Sanders won, in that scenario, Trump's supporters would have wound up supporting or at least respecting and liking him. Their class consciousness would still be alive, but their hope would be aroused as well, and they would be moving toward opposing injustices and seeking solutions rather than scapegoating other victims.

In contrast, Clinton and a good part of the population were oil and water. Unless Clinton worked a near miracle on her substance and style, we thought that working class voters would hear nothing she said even if she tried to communicate with them. And that was the best case. We worried that if Clinton won - and in the nightmarish horror show we faced, we had to hope that she would indeed win - while her victory would have kept Trump from power and kept the right wing machine from dominating social life, and white nationalist fascism from gaining government support, Trump's supporters would feel even more angry and more ready to fight than earlier. They would have been ignored yet again. And so the phenomena of right wing populism that was trending toward fascism would not have been beaten back forever, but only stalled. The point is, our thinking was already orienting us to paying serious attention to working class / coordinator class relations.

Even more relevant to what followed, why didn't the far more accurate answers that left commentators had long given about the state of white working class lives resonate more with workers than did Trump, a billionaire owner who in fact treated workers with contempt? How could it be that decades of organizing had left so many working class men and women susceptible to this narcissistic reactionary? We knew the issue was not mainly the last six months or year. It was the last fifty years. And during that span, we realized that Democrats, and even our progressive movements, had often come across as rooted in coordinator class connections, assumptions, and values, and not as worker aligned, worker identified, or worker led. We realized our movements had often had manners, style, tone, taste, vocabulary and even policy priorities dismissive of working people. And we realized this was apparent to many workers even when some electoral candidate or anti-nuke organizer or campus radical or mindless ideologue said screw the 1% and champion workers - because their other words, phrasing, and style said I am not one of you.

We realized that leftists talked a lot about owners and profit seeking but showed no interest in changing the relation between their own class, or class to be, and the working class. We realized we didn't listen to workers with real empathy and understanding, so of course they were hostile back.

What made it even more remarkable, was that if activists had taken their ability to see the interpersonal elitism, collective cultural denigration, material inequality, and decision-making exclusion typical of race and gender hierarchies, and transferred that ability to examining the relations of coordinator/worker hierarchy, the issues would have been addressed. But activists didn't make the connection. We had the tools to see, but not the will to see.

Barbara, as a doctor, how did you feel about nurses, then, and later?

Then, I was disdainful and dismissive. I paid lip service to equity and even tried to support nurses, but ultimately thought of them as wannabe doctors who couldn't make the grade. It is embarrassing to admit, but I said I had friends who were nurses, not unlike during Jim Crow racism white folks said they had black friends. But at bottom, I thought nurses fit their position. Nurses were lucky that folks like me designed for them, administered them, and cared for them.

At the convention, I had a hard time even hearing Mark's message. It was incredible how many notions it challenged and how radicalizing the ensuing insights were. For example, seeing my relation to nurses revealed the gigantic volume of talents and skills stifled to sustain existing hierarchies. I saw the impact of my socialization and work on who I was. The way I finally understood was by seeing that with racism white people had all kinds of advantages in income, wealth, upbringing, and education. They thought they deserved their advantages. But they thought blacks and Latinos did not. Whites were worthy. Blacks and browns were not. I realized that there was very little difference between that and what nurses were saying about my attitudes toward them.

Dominant groups maintain their advantages and convince themselves those advantages are warranted by denigrating subordinate groups. I did it to nurses. That was a shocking revelation for me, and it changed me. I began to think that if society didn't squash desires, everyone could do empowering, uplifting things. I realized that most nurses could be doctors, and if being a doctor didn't appeal to some, then those could do other empowering things. I realized it was disgusting for society to have relatively few people do all the empowering tasks and use their empowerment to aggrandize themselves.

It may seem minor, but I remember that at about that time someone played, in a musical moment, John Lennon singing "Working Class Hero." I was visiting her house, and she put it on. I listened, and for me, there it was. I literally wept listening to Lennon sing, "As soon as your born they make you feel small, By giving you no time instead of it all, Till the pain is so big you feel nothing at all."

You cried?

I was overwhelmed realizing I was part of doing that to people.

How did the realization affect your views on economics more broadly?

I had heard RPS economic ideas earlier and scoffed at them as ridiculous. Balanced job complexes, income for duration, intensity, and onerousness of work, self management? Come on. Get serious. It is pie in the sky gibberish. Nonsense on stilts. Stupidity on steroids. I wanted an end to profit seeking and the economy being organized for what was then called the 1 percent, but I saw the alternative as people like me taking over. Let's remove owners, but let's leave rote workers obeying people like me because that was where they belonged.

I remember a moment in the first convention after the meeting with nurses that had so challenged me. There was a talk about RPS-type economics and after it ended, I walked up to the speaker, and said, "I am sorry." Not knowing what I was talking about, she asked, "Why?"

I answered, "For years I have dismissed your kind of economic vision as silly and impossible. I didn't think about it. I didn't evaluate it. I just dismissed it without engaging it. I now realize I did that because of my own class interests and the biases they gave me. I apologize for that."

The speaker told me she had never heard anyone acknowledge that so directly before, and thanked me for doing so. She said we are all twisted and fed by our upbringings, schooling, and social roles, and having been subjected to all that it was no sin to have imbibed elitist beliefs. It was only a sin to cling to such beliefs after we understood them. So I stopped clinging, and in time I also let the guilt go.

It is a bit of an aside but I have heard you have a kind of rare disability and I wonder if you mind if I ask what it is, and whether it has affected your political commitments?

It is a little hard to describe and people often don't believe it. You see, I have no mind's eye. I can't see anything inside my mind - nothing but black. I see with my eyes okay. But I can't put a number in my head and see it much less put two numbers there, like on a piece of paper, and add them in my mind that way. I can't see a triangle in outline, much less a blue or a green triangle, much less a scene I have experienced or a memory of a place or person, or anything I might imagine. Just black. Nothing else.

And it isn't just images I can't put in my head. I can't experience an odor in my mind. I can't hear sounds there. I look at you, I see you. I even recognize you. If you looked different than yesterday, I would know. But if I turn away, I cannot see your face in my mind, much less remember and see it tomorrow or next week or in two or five years. I can see you in person a thousand times, and the same holds true. I can't describe what you look like based on a retained image.

Similarly, I can listen to music, hear it, recognize it, love it, but I cannot play it back later in my mind. I can sing along, when a song is playing, but I cannot hear it in my mind when it isn't playing. I can recognize familiar people, but I cannot see them in my mind. This has lots of effects, crippling memory, and so on.

But the thing that was to me most striking was that I didn't know that I was different until I was about forty. I think about 1 percent are as I am, maybe less. I can't explain and I don't even know the different ways that I do things without a mind's eye that you do with your mind's eye. Once I became aware of the situation, I spent some time asking folks what they could do, to get a feel for what I couldn't do, and then I realized something amazing, at least to me.

I had deluded myself for decades. That is, if you look at TV and movies, read fiction, pay attention to sports, and so on, there are countless indicators that people use a mind's eye. Yet I was oblivious to all that. A deep desire to be normal and certainly not markedly different caused me to ignore the signals. I could ignore and still manage well, but I was clearly censoring my perceptions to maintain my self image as being like everyone else.

I learned from that the incredible power of unperceived agendas to bend thought and perception. Here was this major truth about myself that I had shut out. Seeing this made me more tolerant of the phenomenon of self delusion for reasons of self image or ideology.

I also learned, or wondered, what might be the range of attributes people have? I mean here was a really large difference among people, and it was for a very long time not even known to exist, not named, not perceived, even by those who had it. So, how many other big qualitative differences exist in the mental apparatuses that people have? It seemed to me, where there is one such difference, there are probably many more, and I don't know what to make of that observation, even now.

Barbara, I have been asking folks if they could tell us an event or campaign that particularly moved them personally, during the emergence of RPS...

You might think it would be something in the inspiring pharmaceuticals protests or the hospital occupations. And of course those, and many other health-related events and campaigns did powerfully affect me. But I have long been a fan of movies so I have to admit attending the movie Next American Revolution and then later enjoying the famous Oscar presentation and especially the wonderful Hollywood Strikes left me incredibly inspired.

I think it was partly admiration and my interest in all things films, but it was also the incredible class dimensions of it, including addressing matters of coordinator/worker division and job definition. I don't think it was a coincidence that the Hospital Renovations Movement came just a couple of years after the Hollywood Strikes. I suspect I wasn't the only medical person dramatically moved.

Mark, health care is partially about what goes on in hospitals, but it's also about the companies that provide medicine, and about how the rest of society produces health or illness. What were some of the early inclinations about each?

The class revelation, and, of course, insights about race and gender, all played a big role. You couldn't be in a hospital and daily see the horrendous denial and deprivation and not either insulate yourself from feeling anything much - which was the accepted approach as a way to try to function - or feel outraged and then move on to trying to change things.

After all, how often can you see the effects of carcinogenic pollution, monopoly-priced care, warranted hostility toward paternalistic, arrogant authorities, bullet wounds, overdoses, obesity, unemployment, escalating food costs, rampant addictions and diseases spread by profit gouging pharmaceutical policies, misuse of drugs for the mind and overuse of antibiotics, and not lose focus and plunge into depression or become activist - unless you blocked yourself from feeling.

I once went to India for a conference. I was in Mumbai traveling with a well known Indian revolutionary. We were driving and beggars were coming into the street at every stoplight seeking help. They were talented at their calling and would routinely send the worst off among them - or the one who looked worst off, at any rate - to accost the foreigner, which was me. As we travelled through the city, I got more and more distressed, but my host carried on as if nothing was wrong. I finally asked how she could stand it. She told me she had to become blind to it. She had to tune it out. And I realized she did have to do that or the pain of it all would immobilize her. But of course most who took that route developed a creeping coldness of the spirit and soul. Cultivating an ability to look away typically congealed into dispassionate anti-sociality. My activist escort was an exception, but her traveling a better path didn't negate the observation.

Another time I was talking with a prominent activist from the New Left era who talked about how in subsequent decades he was not able to retain the degree of sensitivity and openness he had felt earlier. He explained that in the Sixties and Seventies he could act, so he tuned in to the reality around him. He turned on to his full sense of human solidarity, and adopted the militant radical path of the day to express his anger. Later he could be a dissident, but to express the outrage he had allowed himself to feel earlier would not resonate or be productive. Not being able to productively express it, he couldn't let himself feel it. Like the Indian activist, he curbed his empathy.

When I thought about those examples, I realized hospitals bred a similar self censoring in our limited context. I saw that reduced empathy made perfectly good personal sense to daily function, but that writ large it buttressed the system.

Early health movements asked simple questions. Which social policies, behaviors, habits, and requirements caused people to be unhealthy? What changes could improve the situation as well as lay groundwork to go further? The health movement's growth worked wonders for allowing, admitting, and expressing our feelings.

We initiated various boycotts of unhealthy products and their manufacturers. Then we took up demands about pharmaceutical companies courting doctors to write excessive prescriptions. We took up single payer health care, and we initiated mass campaigns to provide excellent health care in rural and low income areas and in the treatment of children in schools.

The National Nurses March in 2027 was a pivotal turning point. Over 200,000 nurses marched in Chicago and no one knows how many more held strikes and marches around the country. Incredible feelings of empathy, anger, hope, and desire fueled that march. Soon after, we began campaigns in medical schools to revamp curriculum and behaviors, and in hospitals to overthrow the idea of interning as a kind of boot camp.

Can you tell us of a personally pivotal event?

What comes first to mind isn't something I talk about much, nor was it particularly pretty. It was 2023 or 2024, sometime around then. I was at work, doing my job, but also at every opportunity talking about politics and RPS, especially with nurses, but also sometimes with doctors, and even patients.

One day I went to lunch and happened to sit with a hospital psychiatrist. We had worked together, often, with no issues between us I was aware of. We got to talking, and he took great offense, feeling my views implied he was insufficiently aware or concerned about the well being of nurses, as well as being classist toward working people generally.

We hadn't been talking about him, or even such relations in general, but about attitudes to campaigns outside the hospital. I didn't intentionally push his buttons or even have it in mind, but he took it that way. And, honestly, I wouldn't be surprised if my tone or facial expressions revealed anger at things he was saying about RPS campaigns, seeing his words as classist, because I am confident I did think just those thoughts, and so it was probably apparent.

At one point he flew out of his seat, leaning on the table to hold himself up while shouting in my face. His nose wasn't more than five inches from mine. He was livid and I thought he might physically attack me. He went on for a time, making all kinds of claims about me being purely mental, uncaring, manipulative, and controlling, and also about him being a caring person.

Without belaboring, afterwards I thought a lot about it. Partly I thought about how to communicate about issues of coordinator class working class relations without so polarizing folks. But I also wondered how a trained psychiatrist who routinely had to maintain their calm in difficult situations, could get so upset over any affront at all, much less a pretty indirect one.

What I took from it was the intense power fueling our being moved to defend our views of ourselves, and the potential of that inclination to subvert our reason and even our history and connections. I also felt this friend would not have been as upset if what I had said was in his own view ridiculous, as compared to it being, as he heard it, regrettably plausible. But this meant a person closer in viewpoint than most others at the time about coordinator class and working class relations, and already at least somewhat able to see and understand the issues, could become even more polarized and hostile than a person whose views were much further away from mine. I suspect a lot of people in RPS could tell similar stories, and I hope we all learned from them. RPS history says we did.

CHAPTER 12

ATHLETICS AND RELIGION

In which Peter Cabral and Rev. Stephen Du Bois discuss athletic and religious renovation.

Peter Cabral, born in 1978, you were a militant anti racist activist focused on police violence, prison policy, and inmate organizing. You were active in ensuring that RPS program and culture nourished seeds of a racism-free intercommunalism. After a time in prison, you became a tireless speaker, organizer, and activist for legal change. You served as Secretary of the Interior in RPS shadow government and you were also a professional ballplayer for a time. Long before RPS emerged, various athletes have stood up for social justice but with RPS things took a dramatic turn. I am sure a great deal was like it was for actors and Hollywood. What was different?

I would guess that as hard as it was for actors to radicalize, athletes had greater difficulty. You see, a high proportion of us came from intensely poor circumstances. Once successful, we supported not only ourselves, but our extended families of relatives and friends. Our educational background tended to be less than that of Hollywood actors, but our sense of entitlement tended to be even higher. Hollywood actors often started as outsiders, ridiculed, without work, sharing apartments. Successful athletes, and star athletes in particular, often grew up poorer, but typically received special treatment from high school on. So athletes typically had lower income origins, less education and more responsibility for others who they know, and, by way of those ties and also their own past, a greater level of connection to criminality and oppressive culture, yet athletes also typically enjoyed a more rewarded path. We were celebrated and even worshipped much earlier in life than actors.

All that made athletes' and actors' situations different. What made athletes' and actors' situations similar was our success, whenever it came, conveyed to us feelings of immense worth and specialness. Both successful actors and successful athletes tended to think we fully deserved our incredibly inflated incomes and stature.

A few athletes took the lead when RPS emerged, just as a few athletes had related to Black Lives Matter and anti Trumpism earlier than other athletes. But, as with Hollywood, instead of relating only as individuals, athletes involvement after RPS emerged came through a range of athletes' organizations, the largest of which pursued campus organizing for college athletes and professional organizing in the large sports. But we also had neighborhood organizing focused on stadium use as well as parents organizing focused on the cultural deviance of youth athletics. We had extensive organizing around safety and for respect and income in semi pro and minor leagues.

Athletes faced severe work conditions once one took into account health risks. This began with football concussions but awareness grew dramatically with the emergence of RPS. Oscar winners and others involved in films didn't wind up crippled or dead before their time, athletes did.

For athletes to begin to renounce our wealth and status meant challenging the logic of sports itself. It led us to question why performing at a higher level got more income. Of course this was no different than questioning the link between output and income throughout the economy, but in the case of athletics it was more graphic.

How did you understand the role of athletes in society at the time of the RPS first convention, and later?

As a successful but rookie ballplayer, I knew athletes worked with intense focus to hone our abilities and perform under great pressure. I was fine with the idea that income should track our differences in achievement. Of course, in time I realized not only that it shouldn't, but that it didn't. It tracked, instead, differences in power.

I also relished all the perks that society's preoccupation with athletics conveyed, not least access to sexual favors, free goods, and endless praise. I later realized, the preoccupation revealed a society so economically skewed that it made sense for people to try to befriend or even seduce us. The whole system - and not just how we conducted ourselves when reacting to it - needed to change.

I saw the early moves by athletes to take less income in order to support their team having funds to get additional good players. On the one hand it was obscenely ludicrous. I will take 160 million instead of 210 million for five years because I support my team. On the other hand, in the perverse context these star athletes inhabited, it was a big step. It also proved to be a slippery slope. If you would take a third less to seek more wins, how about giving away half, or two thirds, or 95% to save lives and win more justice?

Like for Hollywood activists, we too had to become confident representing RPS views and to learn how to deal with our ridiculous income and the media. We began to give away large sums not only to charities, but also to RPS and other radical projects. We seriously considered the world around us. We made our first informed social judgements.

What were some of the key events for a new kind of athletics emerging?

The football player boycotts and political actions of basketball players were big, but I think the organizing among student athletes was even more important because it was so quickly rooted in organization and militance that provided a model for the pros.

A case might be made that the first step was when the quarterback, Colin Kaepernik, opposed police violence by refusing to stand for the National Anthem. That prodded so much personal soul searching. And when he started giving donations to organizations with similar agendas, his teammates heavily praised his choices. But I think the key was not one thing happening and then another, and another, with no connection among them, but when each event and project started to see itself as part of a larger process that was all of them together. This not only strengthened each individual effort, it broadened them. Collectivity made it all matter.

Soon athletes were not individually pursuing an agenda solely rooted in their own personal experience. I think that was the main RPS contribution. We went from "do the expected thing personal optics," to "take a stand for better situations for ourselves and others," to "join together to win change for all." RPS vision and practice enlarged athlete's perceptions and aspirations causing athletic activism to become more strategic, coherent, and sustained.

Do you think the Olympics battles were a factor?

Certainly. Athletes sought to bring social concerns into the Olympics starting strongly in 2020 and then overwhelmingly in 2024. Athletes began fraternizing and shunning glorification and commercialization. We began to take back sports for those doing and appreciating, and away from those commodifying and profiting.

Rio's travails, on top of those of Athens, London, and other cities became so pronounced for the bulk of their citizens, that the constant clamor by elites to get games for geopolitical and profit-seeking reasons became swamped by the correct beliefs of populations that it would happen at their expense. When athletes supported resistant communities by saying they would no longer participate if the events gutted sponsoring cities, the movement to have the games repeatedly dispersed to a bunch of cities simultaneously, with each city hosting the same single theme every four years, and with each using only venues based on existing structures or built at international expense in a manner designed to be of lasting local value, grew overwhelming.

At first pundits, athletes, and fans complained that with gymnastics in one city, track and field in another, and swimming in another, there would be no single gathering of all 10,000 or more athletes in one place. We would lose some scope of the opening and closing TV events. The complaint was correct, but it was also correct that we would gain a sane, locally beneficial and more humane set of events.

The battle for decentralizing, like almost every other battle once the proposals of RPS existed, was partly a battle for going toward RPS. But it was also beneficial in the present.

How do you think full RPS success in the future will alter athletics for athletes and fans?

I don't think the way we view an athletic contest or achievement will alter much. A beautiful shot or hit, a timely catch, a great race, will still uplift us. What will change is our view of the athletes. We will still admire great talent and focus, but we will no longer think a person should be made rich on account of it. If it is morally and economically sound for income to be for duration, intensity, and onerousness of socially valued labor at balanced jobs, then that applies not only to assembly work, farming, and doctoring, but to athletics too.

Going further, many people have been exploring the benefits of non-competitive sports and even considering what competition is and what it should become in the new society we are building. There is still plenty to resolve, but we know the basics. Excellence and accomplishment will persist even as giant material rewards for excellence and accomplishment fade and finally disappear.

Stephen Du Bois, born in 2001, you were a seminary student at the time of the first RPS convention, and you later became a priest in a progressive church in San Francisco. Famous for your hunger strikes, you became highly influential in developing RPS policies regarding religion and ecology. Do you remember how you first became radical?

When I was 16, I read a book about global warming. I was blown away. How could people allow this to happen? I then read more about ecology and economy. Before long I was trying to reverse global warming, then to combat market violations of the environment. Then I was anti capitalist. My personal and school trajectory led to becoming a priest and as an anti capitalist pastor, I became socially involved and joined RPS.

Can you remember a particular event during the rise of RPS that was especially moving or inspiring for you?

The Religious Renovations movement defined my life, but the event that first comes to mind had to do with rape and prostitution. I was a young pastor taking confession from an even younger parishioner. She was incredibly distraught confessing that, desperate for income, she had begun selling herself. She had endured rape, earlier, and now said she was "raped for a fee." She knew the degradation and endured it. She abided her grim future. She was miserable, but saw no other way. She had to choose between commercial rape and destitute hunger. Yet, she also fought to make the best of her seemingly inescapable lot. She had courage and discipline for her fatherless daughter.

Like a doctor over a dying patient, I was forbidden to let this young woman's plight affect my reasoning. But the moment stayed with me and affected how I started seeing everything. I suddenly saw pain everywhere. I saw injustice and inhumanity toward everyone who lacked means. I was furious. I don't know if it was a necessary step, but it was my step.

I learned more from the young prostitute's experience. A person trapped by circumstances often hammers out an existence which they take pride in and often come to see as natural and worthy. They may even begin to defend, protect, and celebrate their situation rather than trying to escape it. Once you understand that possibility it becomes visible everywhere, including in yourself. Robbed of well being and freedom, we learn to get by for ourselves and our families. We take justified pride in navigating deprivation and denial, but then even begin to fear its end. Organizers needed to understand that reaching people is often a more delicate task than we had earlier understood.

By the time RPS emerged, I had hope. I complained and whined less. I organized. But without that young mateless mother would I have become who I am? Perhaps, but I doubt it. I may have done my "professional" duty lockstep with religious dogma and church structure.

Religious participation in social activism has been widespread forever, but so has religious opposition to change. How would you characterize the emergence of new religious activism in the early RPS period?

Our new activism continued what had been best in earlier religious involvement, but also challenged what had been worst. To extend the best, we enlarged the efforts of many religions and churches against oppressive cultural and economic relations. To challenge the worst, we urged many religions and churches to jettison whichever of their relations, beliefs, and rituals mirrored societal injustices and prevented practitioners from challenging those injustices.

Can you give some examples of each aspect when RPS was emerging?

First, two examples of the best. When RPS was being conceived and planned, churches had become profoundly active in the Sanctuary Movements that opposed Trump's islamophobia and racism. At the same time, churches had begun expanding our efforts to address hunger and homelessness. But we didn't only open our doors to provide holiday meals or homeless shelters, or to protect folks facing deportation. Two innovations took our activism further.

First, for people using the meals and housing or seeking sanctuary, we urged participation in skills development and discussion programs based largely on RPS insights. These learning programs empowered those involved by giving them skills that could help them find a job and seek social change. The second innovation was that church members and clergy participated in those programs alongside the hungry and homeless, and then in local activist campaigns as well. The impact on people who needed to become involved in efforts at change cannot be exaggerated.

Wasn't this a bit like what right wing churches had been doing for years?

In some ways, yes, and at the time I remember thinking quite hard about that. The reactionary approach had been steal, and then bribe. Right-wing politicians would eliminate social services thereby making impoverished families desperate. Then, mega churches would offer meeting spaces, food banks, social gathering places, and job training. The condition of receiving the services was go along with the beliefs of the church by attending services. Get benefits only if you ratify and even imbibe homophobia and sexism. Destroy public services. Supply replacements. Require fealty.

But isn't what you were describing a left version of the same process?

In some ways, yes, which is why I had to think quite a lot before advocating it. The difference was when a low income or homeless person availed themselves of food, housing, or other benefits from an RPS-oriented church, joining our other efforts was optional And the content of further involvement wasn't isolating, ridiculing, and dominating others. We advanced our community and supported other communities as well.

What about inward looking innovation?

Two examples come to mind. First, building on past efforts, we opened all church roles to women. Second, beyond providing emergency food and shelter, we asked, why not also redistribute the gargantuan wealth accumulated by religions to their constituencies? Similarly, beyond including women as full participants, why not challenge the authoritarian nature of religious hierarchies and their power over those below? Why not improve religious responsibilities so they deserved female participation?

All this began not long after RPS started growing and the trends have continued ever since. There is no way to quickly communicate the personal turmoil, conflicts, and awakenings that these pursuits provoked. Religious renovation wasn't a tweak here and there. Basic beliefs were transcended. We underwent real rebirth.

Our work didn't just alter religious practices, it also addressed religious constituencies. And toward the latter, we were never dismissive and always respectful. We avoided the kind of anti-religious tone so prevalent earlier on the left. We rejected the idea that deeply religious communities, even ones who dismissed science and abided some outrageous customs were so different and so backward that communication was forever impossible. We had two reasons.

First, thinking we are two incompatible worlds was suicidal for winning real change. You can't attain a participatory society while denigrating, writing off, and making enemies of much of the population.

Second, such dismissiveness was arrogant and ignorant, really it was lazy. Of course conversation and change was possible and, however difficult, absolutely necessary.

At the time of the first RPS convention, what did you think should be the role of religions and belief in God?

I was still in school to become a pastor in a local church in a working class mixed race neighborhood in my home state of Ohio. I saw religion as a moral compass for society. I believed religion should avoid claims about how things are - such as being anti-science - and instead provide values and, when needed, insights about compatible social relations. I thought religions ought to practice what they preached. The history sexual predation within even my own religion was incredibly disconcerting to me. It almost prevented my becoming a priest.

I thought the God aspect was a matter for each person to navigate as they chose. If one person devoutly believed in God but had a value system that served him or her but no one else, and another person did not believe in God, but had a value system that served all equally, I felt the morally admirable atheist was a better model than the self serving theist. I also thought an arrogant, dismissive atheist was no model at all. You might be surprised to hear that most students I went to school with agreed, yet the church existed precisely to root such sentiments out of us..

How did religious involvements start to alter, in practice, as RPS grew? What were some important steps along the way?

It was different in different regions but, overall, rituals began to accord better with social values, which in turn also began to alter. Women becoming priests was a big milestone. Just imagine an otherwise caring priest or parishioner, much less a higher church official, who firmly believed that female priests would destroy religion. Think of him trying to relate to enlightened parishioners who would no longer attend if women weren't elevated and with aroused students who considered his views not only antiquated but immoral.

The awakening was tumultuous, and yet in Church time, it happened suddenly just as gay marriage advances had earlier been sudden, albeit subject to continuing attack. Of course the change emerged from endless earlier conflict, but the surge of recent successes was undeniably quick. The unstated overall assumptions, habits, and emblazoned beliefs of religions fractured.

When any fundamental feature of some institution is assaulted and finally replaced, a broader lesson is that change happens. The immovable moves. The insurmountable is surmounted. Conservatives feared that changes in some single horrible aspect that they too didn't even like would spread to many other aspects as well, and they had a point. Specific change can unleash general change. The task of the left was to admit the possibility and take responsibility for ensuring that all the ensuing change was good.

The massive outpouring of activism across religions in the multi-city, mass marches that simultaneously ratified both religious freedom and religious attention to social justice, was another milestone. This time the implicit message was that our sacrosanct ways really are archaic and largely habitual. Huge numbers of religious people were ready for change. When the Pope also demanded change, especially while respecting the affected base of religious participants, change quickened, but desires of the many drove it.

What was the role of your personal hunger strike? And what about controversy and opposition to change?

I held the hunger strike in 2023 to reform church practice, but the countless acts of parishioners were far more important and also more difficult to undertake. After all, I always had support, praise, and was never stepping out on a limb I couldn't step back off. Others stepped out with way less support.

As to opposition, we encountered two main kinds. On the one hand, those high in various religious communities refused to surrender their power, influence, and elite living conditions. Their virulent hostility while I was fasting shook me, as did their opposing our marches and other endeavors. These opponents never said they wanted to preserve their own circumstances. They claimed they were fighting a dissolution of faith and collapse of morality but I had a hard time hearing that because the same people who claimed such virtuous motivation displayed not the slightest concern for people in worse off communities. But if they weren't moved by concerns for denigrated people, what was left? Self interest was the obvious answer.

And yet when I actually talked to people to try to discern their thinking, I found more than self interest at work. Those who were benefitting materially from their place in religious hierarchies weren't the only ones resisting change. Huge numbers of parishioners, including poor parishioners, also resisted even innovations that would materially and socially benefit them. How could I explain when a poor parishioner would attack my hunger strike against poverty?

Consider someone who believes in some value, say she is anti war. Along comes a war. Suppose society overwhelmingly supports it. The anti-war person can support it, shut up, or oppose it. The last of these options could incur social ostracism, perhaps loss of a job, or perhaps even jail. Yet, despite the costs, such a person often chooses to oppose the war. Why?

Suppose the person had investments that would suffer from this war. Maybe his opposition was self serving and only for this case. Or suppose the person had a bunch of like-minded friends. Maybe retaining their friendship was a more powerful pressure than fearing broader social ostracism or jail. Or suppose the person had become so vested in peace beliefs that to violate them felt like psychological suicide. Or perhaps the person sincerely believed in the morality and necessity of peace, and pursued the implications of that belief.

Now return to a parishioner who resists innovative views about marriage, abortion, or obedience and initiative. Various factors analogous to those mentioned for our hypothetical opponent of war could push his or her choice, yet our culture tends to impose on us a habit of assuming that people defending old ways do so only out of narrow self interest or vile personal attitudes.

Instead, when RPS sought religious change we assumed the best of our adversaries and tried to calmly and supportively address the resistance we encountered on its own stated terms. But without compromise. As we know, the results, though still in process, have been desirable.

What do you see as the future of religion after RPS fully succeeds?

I used to watch athletes perform and then thank God. It wasn't just the incredible egotism that bothered me. I wondered why they thought God would push them higher, or faster, or whatever, than he pushed their opponent. I was pretty certain that they couldn't possibly believe what their words suggested. To my eyes, this was people playing a role to retain credibility and defend identity. But, I also knew that you are what you do, and if you play a role often enough, long enough, eventually you commit to it. Clearly, all the athletes were equally wrong in touting that their God was true and everyone else's God was false, but that didn't mean they couldn't make themselves feel that they were right about it.

I knew that what actually mattered about any religion was the worthy values it extolled and whichever rituals flexibly taught and applied those values. I felt dismissing religion had little prospect in real human interrelations and only antagonized religious communities. Humanity would never fully forego shared values and consistent rituals and celebrations, nor should it. Having various cultural codifications of moral sentiment and attitudes was a good and needed aspect of life. What I didn't have clarity about years back, was the role of ritual. Were there well conceived rituals? Should we require abiding rituals as a condition for involvement in some religion? I am still not sure about that.

Positively, rituals can provide shared experience and community, and offer a learning experience. Negatively, rituals can become inflexible impositions demanding obedience. I hope a workable conception of flexible, growth-oriented ritual emerges. I favor having a burden of proof on rejecting what has a heritage of success, but I also favor seeking improvement. Can an old version of a ritual and a different new version, or even a complete replacement, coexist simultaneously in one religion? That's a hard question.

What will full RPS success mean for religion? Surely we will still have diverse religions and many people will still identify with and celebrate religious rituals. But just as surely each religion will respect the efficacy of the rest and the heart of the matter will be the values extolled and lived. As with all cultural communities, no religion will need to circle its wagons and fight for survival. Society will collectively guarantee the rights of religions and all cultural communities to persist and will provide means to ensure it.

CHAPTER 13

COURAGEOUS COURTROOMS

Robin Kunstler and Peter Cabral, discuss legal upheaval.

Robin Kuntsler, born in 1971, you were a criminal trial lawyer and with many major crime cases for experience, you rebelled at the injustices of the criminal justice system and became active not only in aiding RPS members accosted by the state, but also in developing RPS conceptions and policies bearing on judicial affairs. You also became the first Shadow Supreme Court Justice. Do you remember how you first became radical?

I was practicing law but came to think I was practicing human herding. The legal system resembled a corrupt concoction of victim revenge plus social control through intimidation and fear. I was brokering guilt, innocence, jail terms, and fines. I was bartering, bullying, and manipulating. But even as I did the best I could within it, I got furious at the system instead of succumbing to it. I frequently went home at day's end sick over having plea bargained innocent lives into prison to avoid their receiving longer sentences from prosecutors padding resumes. I started to educate myself and I grew to want justice brought about by people, not injustice imposed by judges, prosecutors, and police.

I was revolutionized when I decided that a true practitioner of law had to be a committed agent of justice. I visited an imprisoned client who should have been free. It was typical but I left especially depressed, angry, and intent. I was awakened to my profession's unavoidable reality. Law without justice was regimentation. I rebelled at being regimented and at regimenting others.

> *Continuing with your personal journey, can you recount a particularly inspiring or moving experience you had during the period of RPS's emergence?*

While the 2024 legal workers conference centrally influenced my later agenda, my interactions as a defense attorney with clients, prosecutors, judges, and police most moved me.

On the client side, I heard about how people's stultifying lives produced drug addictions and anti sociality and about people's efforts to survive and help their children survive. For me, the illegal acts were peripheral to the real message: Society is a meat grinder and these people are its meat. Society rolls over these people, burns them, buries them. To carry on, they often follow nasty paths. Wearing their shoes, I felt I would follow those paths too.

On the court side, I heard well-off highly schooled prosecutors, erudite judges, and aggressive police officers display zero empathy for the accused. They prosecuted, judged, and restrained my clients as if eradicating diseases. They won cases, cleared dockets, punished perps, avoided embarrassment, and advanced careers. Justice played no role.

Some legal officials tried to do good but overall my profession abided horrendous outcomes and lacked legitimate values. Despite its high sounding rhetoric, my profession required complete overhaul.

> *The current advocacy model says lawyers should aid clients regardless of guilt or innocence. Can you explain that?*

If we leave people to defend themselves, skills of practitioners unrelated to the facts of some dispute would often determine outcomes. That suggests we need well-trained lawyers and prosecutors who try hard for everyone and are equally available to all disputants, which is the current rhetorical stance though it is often neglected, ignored, or violated by the different abilities and means of professional lawyers, their different fees, and the different resources of clients. At any rate, the defense tries to win regardless of any attitude about the defendant. The prosecution tries to win, but only when it believes in the guilt of the defendant. But since victories spur prosecutors' careers they work to win by any means they can muster even when they suspect innocence, and, in any event, the idea that this legalistic face-off will yield the greatest probability of truthful results strikes me as about as believable as that everyone in an economy seeking selfish private gain will best achieve sociality. But what's the alternative? Surely not that if a lawyer dislikes a client, the client gets a poor defense.

We knew judicial dangers were incredibly aggravated by lawyers and prosecutors gaining income and promotions from winning cases, regardless of justice. RPS sought to remove that factor by imposing the norms of equitable remuneration. We also knew that even beyond those involved in jurisprudence receiving incomes correlated only to effort and duration, worthy justice would require further alterations from current practices. However, how to best modify or replace the combination of courts, judges, juries, and aggressive advocacy with different mechanisms is still unclear.

So it is still pretty much an open question for RPS, even twenty years since RPS's founding and even as it is moving toward victory in society?

I am afraid so. After struggling unsuccessfully to conceive an approach to investigating and adjudicating cases that virtually guarantees truthful outcomes, my guess is there is no one right way. We may need a number of different trial methodologies where which methodology to use depends on the context.

The new technology for knowing when someone is lying is another variable. Lie detection has become so portable, accurate, and inexpensive, it introduces new complexity to all sides of life, not just jurisprudence. We are getting close to a situation where lying is virtually impossible, not only in court, but anywhere, and, as many commentators have been exploring, that is a big deal in many parts of life, both personal and social, including trials.

What judicial innovations has RPS advocated?

After the opening RPS convention, the first area we addressed was not courtroom dynamics, but policing and punishment. Policing was always problematic, particularly in the U.S., and grew steadily more perverse in the decade before the first RPS convention. On the one hand there was a major growth in police violence toward minorities, including legalized murders. As horrific as that was, looming even larger was our astronomically inflated rate of incarceration which, in virtually every case, accomplished nothing more than schooling the arrested person in becoming a more effective criminal once released since he or she typically saw no other avenue back into even modest stability and comfort than more crime.

The initial focus of judicially-related RPS work by movements of inmates, inmate's families, and members of over-policed communities, was to demand intelligent community control of police, new police training policies, demilitarization of police forces, new judicial remuneration and job roles, plus new punishment policies to emphasize rehabilitation and productive contributions to society, fellow prisoners, and self.

Peter, I think I forgot to ask earlier, do you remember your radicalization?

A friend of mine was shot and killed in a drive-by. Another friend became a gang member and was on the shooting end in some engagements before he too was shot. I grew up around needles and guns. Gangs were our means to have close allies. A gang had your back. A gang promised financial well being. We took our talents where we could best put them to use.

After my friend died I was uneasy but it didn't quite break my gang ties. But then I visited relatives and heard stories of their arrests and prosecution, and it began eating at me. I went to court a few times, and it was an incarceration parade. I got arrested, wrongly, though it wouldn't have mattered either way because it wasn't anger at the wrongful incarceration that drove me to political awareness. It was the incredible reality that prison was a school for crime that had little or nothing to do with reducing injustice.

Prison was about control and profit. My complaints went from rhetoric that I had previously ignored to reality that I lived. I had to accept and make the best, or reject. I rejected and the rest was running downhill, away from gangs and crime and toward activism.

I had a talent for explaining, hearing, and relating to others. Organizing, public speaking, and activism came naturally. I put my new talents to use where they could do most good, but I knew that but for a few random factors I'd have been a very different person.

You left the gang life but what took you into activism?

People go to their first political event for countless reasons. Maybe they already support it, they are curious, or a friend brings them. I went to a meeting in the prison yard with a friend. I found the people different, but heard talk I liked. It was interesting. I was provoked. I went to another. It took some time undoing old biases. But all told, not too long.

You were very active in early work around prisons. Do you see these matters like Robin?

Yes, but with my own tilt. When I went to prison I was arrested on trumped up charges and my incarceration was overturned after I served six years. So I was obviously familiar, firsthand, with the incarceration of innocents not only on trumped up charges, but also due to bureaucratic pressure, racism, and laws that punish victimless "crimes."

But the truth was, on entering prison I didn't have a good idea what to expect. My knowledge came from TV and a few discussions. I quickly realized plenty of inmates were innocent or over sentenced. I fought to survive. I learned how to relate and navigate. I made friends with people I could work with. Next came modest attempts to build our numbers. We shared texts from RPS. We wrote to prisoners in other prisons about our experiences and read about and discussed theirs.

By 2026, we made some serious noise. We didn't have much idea what it could achieve, but, nonetheless, we called a one day strike. The turnout was enormous. Prison labor is like this: You work at command. You anticipate violent repression. You get subsistence. Your every breath is overseen.

While our one-day strike offered demands only about prison conditions, in the week following, we thought, why not strike for a living wage, too? And why not start to work toward participating in the decisions that affect us? We should improve our current lives, but if we were supposed to eventually leave prison as citizens, we should also develop citizen-like habits. Why not implement self government?

We initiated a more sustained strike that addressed the behavior of guards, rules for visiting, availability of books, internet, and other means of communications. We demanded opportunities to conduct our own classes and challenged the status of our wages, conditions, and rights.

It wasn't easy talking with hardened inmates whose mindsets were cautious, self centered, hostile, and prone to violence. Nonetheless, our strike spread quickly from prison to prison and attracted enormous outside support. We were hard to repress. It wasn't that the guards couldn't brutalize us into temporary submission. They could, and they did, often. But we didn't fight back. And that not only won us tremendous support from outside, it also limited the violence. We would back off, seemingly lose, and within days be back on strike. Like Cool Hand Luke, a prison favorite, we got knocked down but then right back up over and over, but we took Luke one better. We weren't individually courageously escaping our hell only to be repeatedly hauled back. We were collectively replacing our hell.

Robin, how would you sum up the changes in courts and police?

We took steps we knew to be worthy and leading in the right direction. Of course, the impact of our efforts has been enormous in the huge reduction of inmates and the transformed conditions of those still incarcerated, but how much beyond these changes we still need is unclear.

A major proposal some have been exploring is that perhaps those who have committed truly violent crimes and who are legitimately deemed a danger to society ought to have, ironically, something like their own societies in which to rehabilitate and become socially responsible. It is the penal colony idea of old, but without the deprivations and fierce oversight. Perhaps small islands, instead of massive concrete towns, could host communities that mirror the best social relations we can conceive. Maybe this should become the default home for prisoners until they are ready to return to society. Maybe more stringent and less rehabilitative options should be applied only when essential for other inmates' safety. Some people are prosecuted and can rehabilitate, other people are incorrigible and will try to exploit any opportunity to take advantage of others. We don't want incarceration that produces anti social mindsets, but nor do we want incarceration that a subset of inmates violate at the expense of the rest. RPS-nurtured upheavals in prisons, in communities that have many prisoners, and in the legal profession persist right to the present and will likely continue until we settle on fully transformed relations.

I would like to ask a personal question, if you don't mind. As a criminal trial lawyer, in your younger years, did you ever defend people accused of murder in a state with the death penalty? How did you feel? And did you ever knowingly get people who were guilty entirely off from punishment and rehabilitation? How did you feel about that?

Yes, to both. On the former, I did about 15 murder trials with the death penalty possible and I was loathe to take such cases for the reasons your question anticipates.

I found it difficult to defend someone against vicious incarceration. I found it unbearable to go to court day after day, knowing that if you lose, your client - who in many cases you became friendly and even close with - would be executed. For that reason, while my stance wasn't admirable, I didn't do such cases unless I had confidence the client was innocent and we could win. Still, I lost three. Two were later freed when new evidence proved their innocence. One was nearing execution when we won an end to the death penalty. He will still be languishing in jail when we totally reform the prison system and, in my estimation, win his release.

Winning freedom for someone you know is guilty has an opposite emotional drag on the lawyer. Accomplishing that for modest crimes, I always felt nothing but good. The penalties would have achieved nothing and far exceeded anything warranted. I celebrated freeing folks from that. There were, however, other cases where I won a client freedom and he was guilty of a serious crime, in one case murder. This was severely trying for me, as I am sure it was for the families of the victim. And this is why fixing the justice system is no simple matter. I hated this, and yet, I would do it again, so long as we have the system we now endure. The closest we can come to just outcomes with this system entails lawyers always doing their best, even when our best in some sense proves to be too good.

CHAPTER 14

MEDIA MAKEOVERS

Leslie Zinn discusses media makeovers.

Leslie Zinn, born in 1978, you were an accomplished media personality on both TV and radio, famous for resisting incursions on free speech. You have advanced RPS policy and analysis not only about media, but in all matters, ably using your show for the purpose. Do you remember what got you into media and journalism, and into being radical?

In school, I was adrift and took a journalism course and had an inspiring professor, so I took another. At the same time, I enjoyed technology and got into video. I wasn't bad on camera, so I did some video commentaries, mostly for fun, and it took over my life. It wasn't like being born to sing. Had I taken a different course and met a different compelling professor, I would have likely led a different life.

My home life had been progressive, so when I started writing for the campus paper in my junior and senior years in college, I was already covering overwhelmingly progressive affairs. I was radical, even revolutionary by age 24. At 30 I was on radio with my own show, covering the economic meltdown and its aftermath.

I have been asking folks to recount a particularly moving early personal episode. Could you do that too?

Within RPS I would say the formation of Journalists for Social Responsibility, but if I have to choose one that was more personal, I'd say the massive women's demonstrations all around the U.S. and the world. It wasn't attending them that so moved me. It wasn't seeing the numbers, the slogans, the energy. It wasn't even hearing about events across the country.

Two other things had more impact. First, I got in a conversation with a couple of Trump supporters who weren't what I expected. They were caring, thinking folks, blasted by their circumstances. Taking for granted the plight of many others and seeing no end to it, they were hopeful that Trump would upend things and something good would emerge. They were wrong, but far from dumb or ignorant. They understood much about how crass and venal society was that many on the left didn't get. They listened to my words and I doubted, at that time, how many on the left would have listened to theirs. Before long Trump's racism lost them.

I knew that our gigantic resistance wouldn't immediately overthrow Trump much less transform into a movement beyond the liberalism that was preponderant at the early events. I knew achieving all that would require tremendous effort. I began to feel the need to win over citizens of our world, which meant hearing and respecting their concerns. I knew that sometimes gargantuan outpourings won gains, but other times not. I felt a pressure, responsibility, and mandate for all children. I felt intent to help the emerging resistance to Trump become a movement for positive change beyond getting liberals back in office, beyond reestablishing business as usual.

An obvious factor in social change is having our own media as well as impacting the mainstream. How did these aspects develop in RPS?

Even pre-RPS, we knew mainstream media was a cabal supporting corporate continuity. We knew it sold its audience to advertisers and constrained its content to keep its audience amenable to being commercially exploited. We knew alternative media, by contrast, existed to provide audiences information to sustain change. But then RPS solidified critical awareness and legitimated skeptical attitudes toward mainstream media and also challenged alternative media. RPS didn't say, no, don't pursue your alternative agenda. It said, wait a minute, your alternative agenda is good, but your vehicle needs a major tune-up.

RPS said that for alternative media to deliver alternative information it needed alternative structure. It wouldn't optimally provide activist information if its daily operations implicitly ratified society's guiding norms. We had long understood that that meant our roles and methods should not mimic society's racist and sexist hierarchies and that we shouldn't be owned by some person pulling strings tethering everyone. But we didn't understand the full implications of mimicking the corporate division of labor common to all mainstream institutions, or of blindly accepting market allocation. RPS pushed these two additional advisories about how alternative media ought to become better, and alternative media, though initially resistant, steadily changed.

What did the changes look like? How were they implemented? Did they affect alternative media's output?

Basically, alternative media added to our internal guidelines that we should not only reject men and women or blacks and whites doing systematically different types of work and having systematically different benefits and influence, we should also eliminate old corporate divisions of labor and in its place institute balanced job complexes. Indeed, alternative media may have been the first workplaces which systematically undertook classlessness.

It wasn't easy. In a society that has a coordinator class above a working class, people enter the workforce expecting to be in one or the other. Upbringing, schooling, living conditions, and general culture acclimate everyone to fit available roles without resisting.

Consider an alternative media institution of twenty, or two hundred, people. Odds are that before the transformations, the institution's workforce was class divided: Some employees made decisions, others carried out instructions. RPS said we should reapportion tasks so every job was comparably empowering. Only that could maintain collective self management, and only collective self management could remove class division.

But what about the complaint that if those used to making the decisions did more rote tasks the operation would collapse?

Some said we should adopt balanced jobs because it is right and once we are done, we will be better able to fulfill our media responsibilities. Others said, wait a minute, the shift will be disastrous. It may seek a worthy goal, but it will drastically reduce our current output and quality. Yes, those in the latter camp had a view that would preserve their advantages, but they said that wasn't driving them. They sought the greater good.

It wasn't easy, but change came. Training and support went a long way. The transition from most employees being ill prepared, to most becoming sufficiently competent, to most becoming powerfully excellent, didn't take long. What more highly educated folks had been doing was for the most part quite attainable by less highly educated folks. The biggest obstacle was confidence.

Some organizations transitioned by having prior empowered workers do a better mix of tasks while also training others. The temporary addition to their workload was considered fair since, for so long, they had been advantaged. Other organizations initiated a period of internal oversight of work, sort of like when you bring a new person aboard and you watch to make sure they are competent before giving them similar freedom of action as long term employees.

In any case, it wasn't long before alternative media institutions had workers who were highly knowledgable about the policies, methods, and agendas of their whole operation. Self management began to involve all workers. The switch, once we understood it's many dimensions, didn't require someone who was uninterested in, unsuited for, or who hated drawing, to draw book covers. It didn't require someone who hated doing calculations to keep financial records. Rather, people would choose a job composed of tasks that they could do well that was also comparably empowering to the jobs other people did.

One person didn't do only finances, thereby enjoying a monopoly on knowledge critical to all decisions. One person didn't do only editorial, thereby only determining substance. For each type of activity in the operation, for every area of work, various people participated. No one did overwhelmingly rote and obedient tasks. No one had insufficient connection to determining outcomes.

The impact on alternative media was to unleash the creativity of previously subordinate participants. Just as women and blacks earlier fighting against being subordinate led to improvements in alternative media coverage of gender and race, so did worker's battling for change lead to improved coverage of class.

Rejecting markets was more subtle but once alternative media began to regard market allocation with passionate hostility, we began exploring ways alternative media could collectively work together rather than each project competitively seeking donor support and audience for self, but not for all.

What about challenging mainstream media?

Before RPS, we understood mainstream media's corporate agendas but we did little more than write condemnations. RPS said, if it is right to fight against wars and global warming and to combat racist policing, shouldn't we also pressure mainstream media?

And so emerged a sustained opposition to mainstream media that went beyond analyzing it to challenging its mainstream payment procedures, salaries, and decision making methods, as well as demanding new sections of coverage that would elevate community and dissident voices. We sought accountability and we even fought for financial transfers from mainstream media to grassroots efforts.

What were some key events seeking new media?

In the first few years four steps stood out. First, we created Journalists for Social Responsibility. This took on mainstream norms and institutions with diverse campaigns noted above. It caught on in journalism schools, as well.

Second, we created Press the Press, a broad popular movement to demand changes in mainstream media. This coordinated with, supported, and sometimes pushed Journalists for Social Responsibility.

Third, we pursued workplace organizing inside alternative and mainstream media and built linkages between the two, which greatly aided each.

Fourth, we urged alternative media projects to be mutually supportive rather than destructively competitive with one another regarding everything from fundraising to coordinating news and opinion coverage.

Leslie, RPS shied away from direct ties with alternative media, but actively sought support from it and submitted content to it. RPS also helped with mainstream media battles. What guided these choices?

The thinking was, if RPS made direct connections with specific alternative media, including bringing those media under RPS auspices, ultimately, that media would lose its independence. Whatever we might prefer, the pressure to praise RPS and to repress criticism of RPS would affect choices.

Now you might think, sure, but so what? If RPS has some media that it is staffing and financially supporting, but other alternative media exist as well, won't the latter provide a counter pressure?

The answer is, yes, but as RPS grew, its media would become steadily more robust and secure, and other alternative media might fade in comparison. The former would grow. The latter would shrink. By the time RPS won, we might have a single organization dominant in the world of communications and information. So our thinking was, if we don't want that, why take a path that could potentially lead toward it?

So we sent content, sought support, and joined battles against mainstream media, and we even provided funds for all alternative media to share, but we didn't become institutionally entwined with specific alternative media.

How did alternative media fiscal security come about?

Mainstream media sells audience to advertisers. For alternative media to do that would obstruct our editorial aims. We couldn't serve fiscally poor audiences if our aim was to attract viewers with disposable income. We couldn't provide comprehensively honest information and vision if our aim required that the audience we dangled before advertisers should be ready to buy products rather than being made disgruntled, depressed, or actively hostile to commercialism by our content. We couldn't optimally insightfully criticize market driven commercialism when we were constantly commercially market driven.

But if we refused ads, how could we pay our bills? While that difficulty had existed for decades, the internet worsened the situation. The prior solution had been to seek listener, viewer, and reader donations, or sometimes foundation donations, as well as informed purchases of books, magazines, and the like. To reject ad revenue, you had to get revenue from your audience. The internet made this harder by establishing a view among users that information should be free.

People would visit sites that had ads all over and think, great, I don't have to buy the information and therefore there is no cost. They ignored that the price of what they bought throughout society included the cost of ads, and that their attention was being sold to advertisers, which should have been understood to be a major personal and social violation of worthy media motives.

Then the same people would visit alternative media sites. Before the idea that all information should be free took off, appeals for donations seemed reasonable. After free media became preferred, such appeals seemed annoying.

Why should I pay when I can get whatever information I want free from other sites? Why should I get a print subscription, or buy a book? Why should I send a donation? The change was a steady meme-like diffusion of resistance to paying. Alternative media progressively became even more perpetually fund-seeking than in its past, or ad-driven. We felt we had no other way to survive.

Alternative media at first seemed to grow with the internet, but it undeniably also suffered major losses. And the losses weren't only having to become fixated, sort of like political candidates, on fund raising. Another set of problems had to do with content and scope. The internet, and in particular Facebook, Twitter, and instant messaging, acclimated people to short content. This, in turn, wreaked havoc with people's attention spans and content expectations. When you get used to short, you seek short. Long starts to feel onerous and even oppressive. You start to assert that short is intrinsically good and long is intrinsically bad. You move from in depth, to less deep, to downright shallow. You drift toward a short is beautiful orientation, partly desperately trying to preserve audience, but in time literally extolling and advancing the ethos of short, shorter, shortest as if this trend owed to some positive logic rather than to the dictates of ad driven commercialism. We became what we did, and then we made believe we did it for reasons casting a quite false patina on ourselves.

But returning to fiscal security, the answer was RPS argued to all who would hear - both in its membership and beyond - that alternative media was a public good and should be financed by collective support from the whole community. Each item should be free to the person using it with the project as a whole funded by the community's largesse. Separate alternative media institutions shouldn't compete with each other for donor support. We should have a kind of fledgling participatory planning inside left media.

The whole progressive community should put up funds to disperse among alternative media projects in accord with sustaining their delivery of socially desirable output. Since the broader society should also contribute, RPS initiated a campaign for government support of dissident media, and for the spoils of public support to be collectively shared.

RPS brokered meetings of alternative media operations to form an alternative media industry council and urged the community of users to interactively and cooperatively negotiate the output of alternative media. The idea was that various projects would propose what they wanted to do, and what it would cost, and the sum of all that from each of its participants for each new year was what the whole alternative media industry wanted to do. This would be made known to those who use alternative media and the involved community would make known their reaction, and how much they would provide. And it would go back and forth a bit. And there would be an agreement, and thereafter, for the year, each operation would have a budget to pursue its own efforts.

All alternative media operations who subscribed to this had to forego individual fundraising, or, if they had contacts they wanted to pursue, had to report doing so and allot the donations to the collective bounty. Different projects had different budgets solely because of having different agendas that required more or less staff and resources.

It was a small instance of cooperative planning…

Yes, and while it revealed much about such planning, it wasn't a full test because it was so partial. Nonetheless, it eliminated valuable time going to endless fund raising, and it caused alternative media groups to see one another as partners rather than competitors, which led to more synergistic relations.

CHAPTER 15

ECONOMIC CAMPAIGNS

Anton Rocker discusses minimum wage and workplace organizing.

Anton Rocker, born in 1987, you were a student of linguistics and cognitive science and a prolific writer who focussed on workplace attitudes and roles and played an important part in shaping RPS workplace program and activism. You also became a Secretary of Labor for the RPS shadow government. It is hard to see how studying linguistics would have led to your workplace focus and revolutionary career. Do you remember what happened?

Sure. As you perhaps know, linguistic theory is very much beholden to Noam Chomsky's work. The guy had two lives. In one, he was this world class scientist in linguistics and cognitive science. You would read his linguistics and there would be no obscure verbiage, just clear logic and lots of evidence focussed on fundamental matters.

So one evening over a beer I was chatting with a workmate on a first date, and the fellow asked about my studies. He said he had read a lot of Chomsky, too, but he was referring to Chomsky's other incarnation as a prolific and unrelentingly radical critic of contemporary relations.

Not long thereafter I got sick and went online looking for something to read while I was bedridden. I remember I got a new Grisham legal thriller, but also decided to try one of Chomsky's political books - and that was it. I was not just impressed, but opened up so fully that in the following months my way of viewing the world transformed. By way of

Chomsky, I came across other radicals writing about economic and social life, Albert, Hahnel, Shalom, Roy, Pilger, Klein, Fletcher, Ehrenreich. Before long, I had revolutionary beliefs, book learned, but heartfelt.

I have been asking folks to recount some event from the early days of RPS that particularly inspired them. Would you please do that too?

Like most who have been in RPS all along, I was moved greatly by the first conventions. The 2024 campaign for balanced jobs was also very important for me, as was later working in the Shadow Government. But I also remember one unusual, purely personal experience. It was before the first convention, at the time of the major Wall Street March.

I took a cab to get to the march from the airport and got in a discussion with my driver. We talked about politics and the Trump fiasco and he was very angry with Trump. I asked him if he thought we would ever have a President who sincerely served the interests of working people rather than merely making believe he would do so to capture votes.

The cab driver said no, not really. We might have a president, maybe even not far off, who was sincere rather than consciously lying, but it wouldn't matter too much. Such a president would not understand the actual plight of working people. Even if she sincerely tried, she would fall short of representing workers.

So I asked, what about if we had an actual worker win as President, someone without polish, but not a rich bully like Trump? What if we elected, a real working class person with working class values and agenda?

He said it wouldn't happen. No one like that could rise into media visibility, and, in any case, such a person wouldn't win. Why, I wondered? Because workers, he said, would never vote for another worker as President. They, and he included himself, would assume a worker just wouldn't be able to do the job.

I was shook by this. So depressing, so wrong about the potential of a working person, but so right, sadly, about the history we had long endured. I knew then that for RPS to attain its goals we had to overcome this self deprecation in people's minds and hearts. Doing that molded my priorities.

What were the early workplace involvements of RPS folks?

We first tackled the minimum wage. The focus had come from an earlier range of dissent that had been called Occupy Wall Street, but had addressed many financial centers around the world. The minimum wage focus had escalated with low-income service workers in the fast food industry who fought with considerable success. Next came more general campaigns for an increased minimum wage for public service workers, and then for all workers. During the Sanders/Clinton campaign for the 2016 Democratic nomination, minimum wage efforts got national prominence. Trump's victory was a major setback, shifting focus to blocking his policies, for example blocking proposed statewide reductions of minimum wages, but by the time of our first convention, the fight for a higher minimum wage was entrenched and it was obvious RPS would support it. The only issue was could RPS bring anything new to the campaign, or would we just throw in our energies too.

The second economic impetus was about the duration of work. In the half century from 1955 to 2005, productivity per worker had soared. That meant by 2005 output per capita was almost precisely double what it had been in 1955. Yet, work duration had also gone up dramatically. After fifty years, people had less vacation time, longer work weeks, and many more people had to hold two jobs, though others suffered from having no job at all.

With the benefits of all that productivity going overwhelmingly to the wealthiest 20% - and even to the top 1% and even 0.1% - inequality horribly enlarged. Likewise, time off work was harshly reduced rather than enlarged, which further reduced quality of life. So what might RPS do about wages. And work time? The thinking at the convention went like this.

To the effort to reduce inequality by raising minimum wages, RPS should add not only our support, but also a new dimension. Why did we seek a higher minimum wage? One theory, then dominant, was the share of social product we each get will inevitably vary with property, power, and output. However, since this dynamic had gotten so exaggerated, society's lowest wages had to be raised to get us back into an acceptable pattern.

A second view was that the social product we each receive should depend only on how long we work, how hard we work, and how onerous our work is. Because those then getting the least pay also had the least power and no property, and worked longer and under worse conditions, for them to earn a higher minimum wage would move in the right direction.

This change in mindset moved the fight for a higher minimum wage from being a reformist battle that accepted current defining norms to being a fight for a somewhat better position in an ongoing battle over the entire logic of remuneration. We would fight for a higher minimum wage not to win and go home, but to win and fight on.

I remember a fight at the University of Chicago for a higher wage for groundskeepers and custodians. It adopted the RPS approach so the activists didn't argue that a correct, ethical, economically sound income was some modestly increased amount. No, they asked why are we who work longer hours, in worse conditions, and with more intensity, earning vastly less than faculty, and stupendously less than the President of the University? They fought for immediate gain, but then they fought on for more. They worked to raise basic issues and to develop lasting consciousness at every stage of their efforts. Their organizing emphasized the potentials of low paid workers, not their deprivations. It emphasized the unjust incomes of the most highly paid, not some mystical worthiness.

You said there were two RPS early priorities?

Yes, the second RPS focus was over duration of work. This had a few aspects.

First, it was about reducing the duration of work by winning more vacation time, shorter workdays, and shorter work weeks. Our main demand was to cut back to 30 hours of work per week, though we quickly realized that this wasn't enough to ensure good results.

If we cut 10 hours off all jobs, incomes that were already too low for 80% of the workforce would become 25% lower per month. Workers would have to work second jobs so that when the dust cleared, we would get back where we started in total income. The more we thought about that, the more we understood that income distribution is mainly about bargaining power, not rates of pay or hours. If we won a change in pay rates or in duration of work, but we didn't change the balance of power, then once the situation settled, some refinement would be imposed by those with power to gain back whatever they would otherwise have lost. They might raise prices so real income didn't change, though nominal wages per hour did. Or they might impose multiple jobs per person, or greatly escalate overtime so overall hours didn't change.

So we demanded 30 hours work for 40 hours pay, plus triple a worker's usual hourly rate for overtime. But then we realized that this would give a better pay rate per 30 hours not only to those who had low incomes, but also to those with higher incomes. So we modified the demand to be 30 hours work for 40 hours pay for those who were earning less than $70,000 per year, while for those earning more, it would be 30 hours at the old hourly pay rate for the reduced thirty hours or at $70,000 per year, whichever was the higher amount. In that way if you had a high income your total income could drop as much as 25%.

There was another dimension. If everyone who was working before would now work 25% less, could society get by with less product, or, if not, where would the additional product come from? The first part of making up for the lost product was to seek full employment to add labor hours back into the economy and increase worker security and bargaining power as well.

The second part was to note that some reduction of output could be ecologically good and not socially painful if we eliminated useless output. Reduction wouldn't occur, for example, in legitimate medical care, or in teaching. Cuts would center in military production, redundancy, waste, outrageous luxuries, and excessive advertising.

The point is we kept tweaking our ideas to arrive at a campaign that would win important and lasting gains that could not be whittled away, and that would also create conditions that would propel battles for still more gains.

What obstacles did RPS have to overcome to organize workers around their own workplace conditions and lack of local power?

To maintain their high profits owners must interfere with organizing efforts every way they can. To defend their profits and power they employ the straightjacket of their laws, dogma, and brute force. That, we expected. What surprised us was considerable worker resistance to RPS agendas.

For the battle for wages or conditions, the task of organizing was familiar. You had to hear the desires of people and propose demands to meet those desires. Then you had to find ways to communicate with your fellow workers to overcome their reasonable fears of being penalized for seeking to win change.

For seeking control of work, however, many workers didn't trust organizers who demanded greater power for workers, thinking it was a trick to elicit more work per hour. Another problem was many workers had imbibed the propaganda that they weren't smart enough or didn't know enough to make good decisions. Additionally, sometimes worker's felt, why should I make decisions about how to maximize profits for the owners? In fact, why should I take any initiative? Doing so will add more hassle to my life, and I won't get anything for it.

The first step to making progress was to admit that workers had good reason for their doubts. The second step was to reveal the kinds of decisions they might make and the impact it could have. The third step was deeper. We had to discuss the structure of work and why workers didn't have much knowledge or confidence in the first place, and what could change that.

This last part was the beginning of our battles to create worker assemblies to pursue worker's self management and challenge the "nothing more is possible" propaganda and the "you are too dumb to manage" propaganda workers had to some degree bought into, as well as to initiate discussions of what new relations a revamped workplace would need if it was to be really worthy and liberating. It took time, but we made steady headway less because we were right, which was true enough, and more because we were good at hearing worker's fears and carefully showing how to avoid the feared outcomes while winning immediate gains.

How was a connection made among all the efforts and what became most successful in generating support?

I think the key step was the early national campaign for a shorter work week we already talked about. For decades the duration of work by Americans had climbed. Two and three job families had declining family incomes. Workers with unpaid or even paid overtime had declining incomes. Home work entailed lost benefits and longer hours. Yet productivity per hour rose tremendously. Where did the product go? It went to the rich, war, and waste. Did people want to work their lives away to produce ever more opulence for the already opulent, more weapons for murder, and more waste for garbage dumps?

RPS began its campaign for a thirty hour work week. Firms could arrange their thirty hours however they liked, but the thirty hours was an upper limit. Firms could have someone work overtime, but for triple their usual hourly pay rate. You want more work from an individual, you pay for it.

We cut hours spent producing waste, weapons, or opulence by 25% or even more. We reduced the outlay of work 25% for all managers, lawyers, doctors and the whole coordinator class, and all workers. We refined the income aspect and added having public subsidies for on the job training to replace highly skilled work, including moving toward balanced job complexes. Our campaign didn't start with all the caveats and conditions, but when it got there, it was obvious how redistributive and radical it became.

It is a bit off topic, but I have heard you are vegan and I wondered if it has had any bearing on your RPS involvement?

Yes, my veganism is partly because a vegan diet is healthier and less expensive than a meat-heavy diet. But it is also ethical. I can't handle eating animals. I would abstain even if it hurt my own health some, or cost me more per meal.

Some people with this stance believe it is valid, unimpeachable, and unchallengeable, and see people who eat meat as immoral. Some even see eating meat as abetting murder. I don't subscribe to any of that and I also have never met anyone who I felt really believed it, their loud rhetorical flourishes aside.

On the other hand, I do think a meat-free and even a fully vegan diet is healthier for individuals and the planet. And ethically better, as well. So I do think this stance is morally worth exploring, advocating, and seeking reforms to approach. I also think our numbers are growing and I would not be surprised if a future RPS society that has been operating for some time will leave behind eating animals. But it hasn't been a core part of RPS program, and I am okay with that.

CHAPTER 16

CONCEPTS

Lydia Luxemburg discusses ideas at the heart of RPS.

Lydia Luxemburg, born in 1948, you became political in the great upheavals of the 1960s. Life-long feminist, activist, organization builder, and media worker, you were also RPS's first shadow President. I hope you won't take it as ageist, but you have been a personal inspiration for me for a long time, not least due to the longevity of your focus and effectivity.

You are very kind. Thank you.

How did you first become radicalized?

I was in college in the 1960s, caught up in the politics of the times. I became anti war due to my country's violence in Indochina. I became feminist due to sexism in society and within the left itself. I rejected that women were ornaments to be paraded or servants to do tasks men wished to avoid. I became revolutionary when my mind and heart linked in a commitment to win change.

Could you recount a personally moving or inspiring event from the past twenty years.

At Trump's inauguration the huge outpouring of women and also many men around the U.S. and the world was a timely boost for what had been my then somewhat precarious personal morale. From then on, it was one inspiring campaign after another, though of course there were also some setbacks.

One particularly moving experience came during the community control of police campaigns when I spent some time talking with people who had been jailed for crimes they did not commit, and later exonerated and released. To meet people who had been imprisoned for years, and even decades, was incredibly moving. To hear of their travail upon being released after people they had known were long gone, and due to having no home, and to see their cheer and positivity despite all the pain in their past, gave me faith in human potential. Considering all the people who accepted plea bargains to avoid worse injustice, and all the people jailed for victimless crimes, powerfully moved me.

But I also had a very different kind of experience, more personal, that had a big effect. I had decided to write a novel to get across the commitments I favored in a new way. I wrote a draft, and while I had written plenty of non fiction before, a novel was a first for me and I was unclear whether the draft had merit and quite sure I needed reactions to guide making it better.

I sent it to some friends and family members. I knew it was a lot to ask them to look at a whole book, but I asked anyway, making clear that I needed reactions to improve the book.

Five out of about twenty five people even acknowledged receiving the draft. Those five said they would get to it soon, but none did. The other twenty also didn't read it or provide comment, and didn't even acknowledge the request having occurred. Not one of the twenty five asked a single question, not even what it was like to try to write a novel, much less about its contents.

The book wasn't technical. It told about matters of society and relayed experiences key to all our lives. Yet there was no curiosity much less inclination to help.

I thought about this and at first I was hurt. It wasn't disturbing that any one person didn't reply since there could be various reasons in any individual case. What hurt was the universality of it. I was sure that had any one of these people sent me something comparable, and asked my reaction in hopes of getting help to guide improvements, I would immediately acknowledge receiving the draft, have questions about it, and then try to provide some help, or report my incapacity to do so if I tried but failed.

When I thought about that, my sadness grew, but it also changed a bit. I realized this kind of silence was emblematic of contemporary life in the U.S., especially on the left. Everyone at that time thought it showed a degree of human solidarity, civility, and sympathy to say, "have a nice day," and to otherwise appear civil and concerned. It didn't matter if you meant it or not. It was quick. It was easy. You got civility points for it. More, if you didn't do it, despite that doing it could easily have meant nothing, you were a brute. In striking contrast, to sincerely regard one another with interest about something substantive, to say caring and/or critical things and actually mean them, well, that might elicit hurt, anger, and even rebuff, and it took time. You might get negative points for your effort. So people started to avoid bothering, and before long not bothering became acceptable, then routine, then admirable.

Surface cordiality plus below the surface aloofness became the U.S. cultural norm particularly for the coordinator class - and the left. Superficial civility was familiar, understood, and accepted. Serious intent and effort, especially if it involved criticism, was unfamiliar, misunderstood, and rejected. To deem surface cordiality paternalistic was uncivil. To seek serious engagement was intrusive or selfish. Saying "hi, have a nice day," and moving on, was expected and reflexively welcomed. Wanting, or offering, more substantial interest and concern struck people as intrusive, strange, or even abusive.

We had as a people become so focused on discussing popular culture, sports, and gossip as safe ways to engage, and so removed from our abilities to evaluate and think about anything social, and from our abilities to apply ourselves beyond reflex reactions, that we tended to see acts like my timidly sending around a book draft to friends or even family for advice rather like we might see a stranger aggressively demanding we help him with something totally foreign, totally beyond us, totally lacking interest for us. An intrusion, not a sign of respect.

Ask about a ballgame, a TV show, or a new restaurant and people eagerly conversed. No risk. Auto pilot. Ask about some unquestionably horrible event, some unquestionably grotesque political enemy where there is nearly universal instant agreement, and again, people were quick to offer spontaneous opinions, which, however, in the circles where they were offered, were commonplace and accepted even before being uttered. Auto pilot.

Try to dig in and think through the cause and effect of events and views where disagreements arose. That shocked. That went too far. Offer unusual much less challenging views. That was unacceptable.

In that context, if you asked for a reaction to a new socially aimed novel or for anything that would require stretching beyond what was common and safe, and where a comment might even be thought less than ideal, the energy for engagement dissipated. You couldn't tweet a reaction to a draft of a book, so the reaction was never produced, nor even a simple acknowledgement.

The contrast to the spirited give and take of ideas and judgements I knew from my youth was glaring. Whatever the real meaning of my experience was, it impacted how I related to RPS thereafter, and affected what acts I thought could and could not reach people.

When RPS was emerging, you were around seventy and had a lifetime's worth of activism. Did it take you by surprise? Did you feel vindicated?

I felt, what took so long? Some of us knew what was needed 50 years ago. Why didn't we do a better job bringing it into being?

So RPS happening didn't surprise me but I certainly didn't feel vindicated. I was ecstatic it was happening - but I was tormented by how many lives had been lost or made less than they should have been by the fact that my generation hadn't done better in prior decades.

Even before the first convention, what ideas did you think distinguished RPS from predecessor projects that hadn't taken off? What ideas attracted you at the beginning that served as a foundation for what has emerged since?

Before I was attracted to RPS I saw the world refracted through a lens that highlighted gender so heavily that much else went largely or even completely unnoticed. I didn't explicitly think everything else was unimportant, but my attention to gender so monopolized my perceptions that I often failed to see much else.

I would go into a workplace and see how people related, what they were doing, and what they got for it - but all as men and women. Similarly when viewing church, education, sports, TV, and families, I saw men and women's different circumstances, rewards, and costs. I saw their connections and disconnections. I saw women filling roles that included mother-like and wife-like attributes and men filling roles that included father-like and husband-like attributes. I tended to miss, or at least not dwell on, the importance of other group differences.

It's odd, because I had been closer to the current RPS view back in the late sixties and early seventies, before I temporarily lost my multi-issue balance. My approach prior to RPS - but post my more balanced Sixties New Left involvements - was a bit like looking at the world through a filter that makes certain colors or shapes very intense while causing other colors or shapes to fade. I saw male and female in high definition. I saw the rest blurred.

Add to that my first hand knowledge about the situation of women, and I was highly attuned to gender and sexuality, which was good, but barely attuned to class, race, and other dynamics, which was not good. I was particularly blind to interrelations and especially to what pushed kinship so much as to alter it - as compared to how kinship pushed other facets of society, which I did see. I saw how sexist relations permeated workplaces and affected their definition, but I did not see how class relations permeated and affected family relations.

So I was initially standoffish about RPS adopting a holistic approach. At first it felt like purist badgering, even though I knew that when I was in my early twenties I had had a very similar inclination. But after awhile RPS re-convinced me we should not assume any hierarchy of importance among the different defining parts of life and society.

But why were you initially standoffish? Why didn't the insight grab you, without you resisting?

At first, I worried that if we stopped elevating kinship, sexist men would peripheralize it. I so feared that that it took considerable time for me to even hear the RPS message, much less grapple with and finally agree with it. Another aspect of it had to do with how I pursued feminism - or how other people pursued anti racism, or anti capitalism. I realized we often defensively protested ills rather than positively pursuing virtues. We had defensive mindsets and constantly called out and punished whatever we sought to ward off. Our priority was seeing ills and beating them back. We didn't advocate new positive outcomes. With our defensive mindset, we saw mainly how choices could yield men dominating and feminism yielding. We were reflexively negative.

I finally realized that my fear that kinship would be minimized was exactly what maximizing kinship did to other parts of social life - it minimized them. There had to be a better way than to pick one focus and defend it to the exclusion of attending to other focuses.

Once I realized that RPS was adding more focuses, not subtracting mine, I could see that just as pressures from gender could mold other parts of society, so could pressures arising from economy, polity, or culture mold gender. What was remarkable was as soon as I recognized such mutual interrelations, I saw them all over. RPS revealed how dynamics in one part of life could alter the features and even the defining logic of other parts. It revealed how fixating on one part could interfere with seeing interrelations. It saw class in families and schools, gender in workplaces and churches, race in government and health. It showed how economics affected politics, how race and nationality affected economics, and how gender and kinship affected culture, economy, and politics but were also affected by them. It provided a basis for a project that could unify key constituencies without submerging the concerns of any of them. It provided concepts able to overcome our biases and rejected concepts that would cause us to pursue only our most personal inclinations.

Can you give me an example or two of this?

The RPS view got me to understand that you couldn't change gender relations by focussing only on the home and upbringing. The basic structures defining sexism were certainly rooted in the home, but not only there. Sexist kinship roles have requirements for men and women. These requirements imprint people with beliefs, values, and habits producing men and women with gender-specific expectations and inclinations. These attributes didn't disappear if a man or a woman exited a living unit and entered a workplace, ballpark, or mall. Other institutions then abided or violated the family-based expectations and inclinations.

If they violated, it would cause conflict and require resolution. If they abided, there would be stability. Sometimes other institutions would begin to incorporate the same sexist logic as households. They would become not just compatible with persistent sexism, but sources of its reproduction. Feminist movements might win important changes in households, but if they ignored the sexism that had become entrenched elsewhere, emanations from those other places could push back on changed households, causing them to revert. And the same pattern holds for class and race, too.

Class and race permeate society, so sources of class and race hierarchy persist in laws and families not just in workplace and cultural venues. The incredible truth was that winning for one focus in its prime area wouldn't even win just for it, because the win would be temporary, in time wiped out by unaltered relations in other parts of society. Once one had that perspective, it was easy to see the need for broader movement connections. Before having that perspective, it was not so easy.

Can you give a less abstract example, perhaps from near the start of RPS?

The Sanders campaign, and then the rise of Donald Trump, had very profound effects. Many white men and women supported Trump, but why?

Trump was a rich, violent, egomaniacal, racist, sexist, abomination. Still, he had a lot of support that should have been for Sanders and that we would have to win over to any successful project for a truly new society.

Women and Blacks had for a long time fought hard for change precisely as women and as Blacks. Watching that and sometimes encountering it, white working class men began to assess their own situations, which were severely deteriorating due to economic losses and political marginalization.

Okay, so what is a white guy to think? If society is a battle between genders and races, and that is what the white guy thinks is being said - and if it is a personal fight at that, undertaken to a considerable degree individual by individual - then white men's worsening condition, he might deduce, must have to do with losing that battle. Along comes a thug candidate who seems ready to fight against the trend. Many identified with him.

RPS tried to understand but not blame white men. Sure, there was racism, sexism, fear, and ignorance. But what were the roots of it? RPS noticed, but didn't focus on, the Democratic Party having moved toward ignoring workers in favor of attending to professionals and addressing people only as black, female, etc. That was important. But the RPS approach was mainly about finding what we ourselves can do to win change, not about decrying what others were doing that we didn't like.

RPS asked if workers didn't see their worsening situation as a function of corporate policies and structures of which Trump was a prime emissary, where was the cause of that that we could address rather than just moan about?

Answer: it was in ourselves. We hadn't paid attention to why we weren't being heard, why our words hadn't resonated with working people. The upshot was we didn't respect, understand, relate to, hear, and learn from their concerns, so they in turn ignored, or hated, us. We didn't address the divide between workers and the professionals who RPS took to calling the coordinator class.

The second awareness to emerge was we had too often fought to improve conditions in ways that polarized others into becoming resistant to and even hostile to change. We had to learn to fight racism, sexism, and homophobia, but simultaneously support working people, and yes white male working people, not as some throwaway line, but, because doing so was right as well as a prerequisite for winning a new world.

And this was all hard for you to accept? I mean, just twenty five years later, it is second nature.

When these notions surfaced and spread, or really, for me, resurfaced and re-spread, we all had to overcome our long-held, narrow prioritizations. Some had prioritized economy and class. Some, like myself, had prioritized kinship and gender. Some had prioritized culture and race, politics and power, war and international relations, or ecology and sustainability. At the extreme, people self-consciously prioritized one area, or sometimes two or three but still a subset, above all others. Less drastically, and more often, people didn't explicitly do that, but in difficult situations would slip into that bias by way of the narrowing effect of the concepts we had forefront in our minds. I was in that camp.

To hear someone say that part of the fault for white men moving to the right was radicals doing a crappy job of communicating about coordinator class / working class relations, felt like an assault to activists who had been working hard to confront capitalism. Likewise, to hear that part of the fault rested with how blacks and women pursued their agendas, felt to many, including me, like the assertion itself was racist and sexist. So it was hard to navigate the tensions.

The more I thought about all this, the more I saw that there were two problems with over-prioritizing one focus. The first was that elevating a particular side of life to conceptual priority misled our efforts to understand society as a whole. Prioritizing a particular area under attended other areas and in so doing, missed much about critically important and mutually intersecting social relations and possibilities.

The second reason was that elevating one focus above the others pitted constituencies that needed to work together against one another. Each narrowly focused approach would pursue their own agenda largely ignoring implications for other approaches. They wouldn't say, we have to address race, class, or gender only in ways consistent with and even advancing comparably addressing the other focuses. Or they might say it, but then not act on it.

It was like we had a slippery, heavy object to move and had various teams ready to work on doing so. Each team had a part of the whole that they knew best, most wanted to move, and could tug better than they could tug any other part. Each team grabbed their part without noticing what the other teams were doing. Instead of all the teams moving all the parts in concert, with the whole object going where they intended, the teams pulled and pushed at odds with each other, so the whole object just moved a bit here and a bit there, but never far in any direction.

RPS said, hold on, each part is critical, but unless we address all of them in mutually enhancing ways, none of the parts are going to alter much. We'll get opposition and competition instead of mutual aid.

Was this basically a debate between advocates of "identity politics" and advocates of "class politics"?

Yes and no. RPS thought outside both boxes in ways that allowed each of the prior two approaches to participate without any rancor toward the other. The class focus side had its roots in pre sixties anti-capitalism that caused adherents to think class was so fundamental that analyzing events, forming agendas, and having goals had to prioritize class and economy even at the expense of all else. The class-focus idea was that the tools for being attuned to class had to be constantly in hand and utilized, but the rest, not so much. Of course there were all kinds of nuances.

The identity politics side had its roots in sixties feminist and anti racist organizing that rebelled against the class approach. It chose a new priority focus - either kinship or culture/race or sometimes both - and treated it preferentially. As the years passed, eventually race, gender, and sexuality folks began to unite, creating what some called identity politics.

An additional wrinkle was that the class-first folks always prioritized institutional dynamics. Their discussions of class and economy only rarely ventured into the day-to-day personal injuries of class. The identity politics folks instead most often prioritized the attitudes, behavior patterns, and personalities of both advocates and opponents of the focused oppressions. In some ways the debate was a complex tug of war. First one side would make headway, then the other. Every so often each side would alter a bit, as well.

The class side argued that economy is fundamental and class is paramount because economy unavoidably constrains and impacts all else. But the advocates of race, sex, gender - or all of them - made precisely the same case, with essentially the same logic. Race, sex, and or gender unavoidably constrain and impact all else. On this axis of discussion, there really was no logical reason for conflict. You could hold both stances simultaneously, and there was no reason in the underlying logic to do otherwise. You didn't have to pursue either/or. And the same was true for paying priority attention to institutions and to mindsets or behaviors. Why not do it all?

Seeing that, I never thought the objective issues of the debate had much to do with why people lined up as they did from the late 1960s on. I instead thought the operational side pushed contending stances into opposition. The class folks worried that giving priority attention to race, gender, or sexuality, much less to all three, would diminish attention to class at great cost. The race, gender, and sexuality folks worried that giving priority attention to class would diminish attention to their areas at great cost.

For unity, all that was required was for both sides to see that both claims were correct. We needed to address each focus in ways that didn't inhibit giving attention to the rest. So RPS injected a reiteration of views that had existed a long time, and been repeatedly but unsuccessfully proposed earlier. RPS said, the class folks are right about institutions being critical, and are right that class is critical. Identity folks are right mindsets and behavior patterns are critical and that gender, race, and sexuality, are critical. More, there is no contradiction between these many views as soon as each side acknowledges not only that its own views have merit, but so do the seemingly contrary but in fact completely compatible views of the other side.

RPS said, we should come at society giving forefront priority attention to institutions and to mentalities/behaviors and to race, gender, sexuality, and class and we should not try to prioritize among these focuses.

You said two RPS conceptual innovations played a major role in attracting you. What was the second?

It was something so simple that nowadays it may seem silly to mention. To be in the economy, you have to work someplace, and buy and sell. To be in a religion, you had to relate to its church or other structures. To be in a family, you had to be a mother, father, brother, or sister. More generally, to benefit from some institution, you had to comply with whatever roles you had in that institution. Your roles determined your acceptable actions.

If you were a nurse, a congressperson, a priest, a bricklayer, a short order cook, a teacher, or whatever else, to gain benefits you had to behave consistent with your role and with other roles in the institutions you navigated. There was a vernacular slogan for it, "You had to play the game."

We do what our situations require and we become what we do. It was true in a corporation, family, shopping center, church, prison, government, military, or criminal cartel. And the observation had three major implications.

First, to evaluate a workplace, family, government or whatever, we had to reveal the roles people had to relate to in that institution if they were going to get what they wanted. Having determined the roles, we had to reveal what the roles demanded of people and thus who the roles caused people to become.

Second, to move from understanding an institution to changing it, we had to decide we wanted from the institution. What roles blocked that goal? What new roles could accomplish that goal?

Third, given our circumstances and resources, we had to determine what we could fight for that would move us in our desired direction. What roles characterized our movements? Did they further or impede our aims? What changes in our ways of organizing could move us nearer our goals and also make winning further gains likely?

Can you give an example of what kind of experience made you elevate the insight about roles and institutions to a centrally guiding norm?

Early in my time with RPS I visited a worker-run glass factory in the Midwest. Workers I met there were surprisingly despondent about their new circumstances deteriorating back toward what they had known before they took over. "All the old crap is coming back," they reported, and they felt crushed by that fact because to them it said there was no alternative to the capitalist drudgery and poverty they thought they were escaping.

They had set up a workers' assembly to have democratic decision making by everyone involved. They had equalized their wages. They had created a climate of support. A year had passed since they instituted their changes yet they said in recent weeks their decision-making assembly was attended by only a few. Wage differences were returning. Work was reverting to being a debilitating, alienating chore. The workers got steadily more upset the more they described their deteriorating plight, and, most disturbingly, they attributed their worsening situation to their bosses and managers having been correct back when they had told the workers who first took over the plant, "You are naive. The inequalities and hierarchies you rebel against are part and parcel of being human. They are who we are. Your joy at taking over this workplace will evaporate into failure." And now the workers felt crushed that their predicted failure was coming true.

I had become, not long before, an RPS organizer. I knew that in taking over their workplace some people were left doing overwhelmingly rote, repetitive, and disempowering tasks while other people did mostly empowering tasks.

The workers throughout the plant had all grown up in working class homes and neighborhoods. They had little formal education. They were not elitist and they were leftist, especially at the moment of taking over. But upon occupying their factory, most of them wound up with assembly work while a few wound up with daily decision making and other empowering responsibilities.

For them that was just how things were. It was how to get work done. I pointed out that the folks with empowering tasks were, as time passed, seeing themselves as more worthy and dominating. The folks doing disempowering work were being dominated, and, as time passed, becoming more resigned to it.

We talked more, but the point of the experience that bears on your question was that it was a very graphic instance of a very particular role's implications for people's daily options overruling people's good intentions. The way the workers divided up work affected dynamics way beyond just getting the work done. It produced glass but also changed employees. It resurrected the old crap.

The analysis wasn't academic. We didn't need a whole new vocabulary and years of study to see the situation. It was simple and, oddly, for some on the left this was a kind of drawback. Some leftists mainly liked to look smart by their long sentences and big words. To speak plainly and advocate simple (but powerful) insights, upset those "scholars." To them, being clear indicated irrelevance. It may sound absurd, or perverse, but it isn't if you realize this was just another part of coordinator class habits and practices distorting left behavior.

If your status, income, and power spring from having a monopoly on empowering circumstances, then defending your status, income, and power depends on making sure your information and skills remain inaccessible to people outside your class. But regardless of academia minimizing attention to coordinator class habits, our simple ideas were not only accessible, they were intensely practical. If you don't pay close attention to choices about institutions and their roles, some seemingly innocuous choice, or a choice that seemed to you inevitable and that you took for granted, could subvert your best intentions. Retaining the old division of labor was an example. The experience of the workers taking over firms didn't just show that institutions and their roles matter, it showed that they mattered so much that we had to focus on which features were okay, on which were not okay, and on what new features would be better.

CHAPTER 17

VALUES

Bertrand Dellinger and Lydia Luxembourg discuss values at the heart of RPS.

Bertrand Dellinger, born in 1966, you were politicized by no nukes and anti war activism. You became a key advocate of RPS from its inception. You have been a renowned contributor to physics theory, as well as a social critic and militant activist. You were shadow Vice President during Lydia Luxembourg's term as president, and later you had your own term as shadow President. How did you first get involved?

Like many, I was moved by RPS's multi-dimensional aspect and it's emphasis on institutional roles but also RPS's economics, its moral approach, and the specific values it highlighted. Before I got involved in RPS, I was mainly anti war, internationalist, and worried about global warming and the possibility of nuclear catastrophe. I militantly rejected authority that wasn't absolutely essential for some specific time-bound reason. I believed in human potential and welcomed that RPS highlighted human needs.

RPS called the value that hooked me "self management," and it is, of course, the now ubiquitous idea that people should have a say in decisions in proportion as they are affected by them. RPS wasn't first to favor self management, but RPS made its commitment more precise than others had.

I liked how RPS argued against elitist notions of a few people making decisions for all. I liked how RPS found violations of self management not only in centers of corporate power, but in the dynamics of central planning, markets, electoral systems, religious institutions, and even sexual and family relations and schooling, not to mention in the dynamics of many left organizations.

Indeed, in the early days of RPS, I saw my calling as seeking self management for all people in every side of life. This got a little problematic. It wasn't that my feeling that self management was incredibly important was wrong - I was correct about that. I was wrong in having one value drive my perceptions so heavily that it overrode other values.

You said you were moved by how RPS found less obvious violations of self management. Can you give an example?

Most people fifty years ago felt they freely chose their work by applying for a job and getting it. They felt they freely chose their consumption by going to the store and purchasing it. They thought, "I didn't have to take a job or buy particular shoes. I work here or there. I buy this or that. I chose." But if the jobs we choose all have certain features we can't escape do we really choose our work? If the items to consume are tightly constrained, do we freely choose?

Imagine you are in prison and go to the commissary and purchase some items. Do you manage your choice? You certainly decided to go to the commissary and you certainly saw the available options and picked among them. However, you had no say in what was and what wasn't available - yet that largely determined what you wound up with. Outside prison, a wider selection is available, but I saw that it too was horribly constrained by market pressures.

Similarly, when I apply for a job, if my only option is to apply for jobs that are subordinate to a boss and paid a wage based on bargaining power - am I really self-managing my choice? Wasn't the main choice made before I arrived?

The period about 90 years ago was called the golden age of capitalism. Let's call the average productivity per hour at that time golden output. Roughly fifty years later, productivity per person was literally twice golden output. Another forty years to the present and it is now 3 times golden output. This means if the average duration of a job per week was 40 hours just under a century back when average productivity per person was called golden, we could have had the same golden output per person in 20 hours a week at the start of this century and in about 13 hours a week now. The reduced duration of work could produce the same wealth per person.

So who decided that instead of working a half or even a third as long as earlier, we would work longer to generate vastly more output, and, on top of that, who decided the fruits of that labor would go to a small percentage of the population or to creating weapons and other useless or harmful outputs? I didn't decide that. You didn't decide that. No one we know decided that. In fact, no person decided it. Rather, market competition required that to survive firms had to pursue a profit-seeking path. The institutional context of market allocation took away control over critically important decision making about how long we would work as well as who would get the fruits of our labors.

Consider an election. Candidates routinely lie. They compete to move news and votes where neither would otherwise go. Companies amass gargantuan databases that candidates use to clutter voters' minds with fear and anger unrelated to actual prospects. I freely pull a lever, but do I freely develop and express my views, or were my views constrained by candidate, party, and corporate machinations? From these examples, I understood more viscerally the diverse prerequisites of self management and the complexity and promise of institutions providing rather than curtailing it.

What about within the left itself? In the period from the 1960s through 2017, the idea of self management existed, but did it operate inside the left?

If you look at media organizations, organizing projects, and movement organizations like unions, ecology movements, anti war organizations, and even feminist organizations during those years, you see little self management. Instead, movement projects looked largely like mainstream institutions. Some participants made decisions. Way more participants were absent from decision making. Donors and fundraisers had incredible power, rather like owners did in mainstream society. People who were analogous to managers and engineers, or who even held the same positions such as editors and publishers in alternative media organizations, wielded great power.

When self management went from rhetoric to practice, it almost always occurred in a transitory situation where it was praised but not implanted in structure. Groups would be more or less collective, but it was a function of people's attitudes, not of adopting structures that ensured self management.

We had what was called the Occupy Movement, with vast assemblies, using hand votes to attain consensus. Yet, even there, looking more closely revealed that relatively few people called the shots. We had no lasting structures able to deal with more complex agendas and processes.

Debate between tight hierarchical decision making by only a few and incredibly loose raised-hands decision making without lasting structure and with anyone at all voting, had little to do with real self management. RPS started to pressure changes in society's election procedures, official accountability, and social relations, and also in movement organizations and projects.

I should mention that in the anarchist community, we had always rightly rejected rampant oversight, hierarchy, and authority. However, I have to admit that this had often led many of us to argue we had a right to do as we please, ignoring other people's right to be free of imposition by our choices. We proclaimed our right to riot at a demonstration, ignoring that our doing so meant others would have to stay away or endure riots. We rejected having lasting rules, laws, and even collective norms, as if every situation had to emerge anew, spontaneously, with no attention to prior agreements, whenever such a stance favored our immediate interests, but we evidenced little concern for the interests of others who were affected.

This was the worst, and certainly not all, of our anarchism, but in any event, RPS's clear enunciation of collective self management helped focus anarchist values and commitments in ways far truer to the early days of anarchism than the self-centered approaches that had become prevalent for some anarchists before RPS. Indeed, RPS actually improved and strengthened my own anarchism, and propelled much more and better anarchism from others, as well. It was remarkable that at first many anarchists, myself included, resisted the very idea that our commitments could improve, but in time we welcomed change rather than defensively rejecting it.

You said another aspect of RPS ideas that attracted you was how it approached the economy. Can you explain that?

Before RPS, I called two percent or so of the population capitalists, because those folks owned the means by which society produces and distributes goods and services. I called non-owners workers, because those folks owned only their ability to do work. I saw owners and workers clash over wages, length of the work day, pace of work, work conditions, production choices, and national economic policies, but I also missed that about a fifth of non owners have great power and influence due to their position in the economy, while four-fifths of non owners have nearly no power and influence, also due to their position in the economy. Early anarchists had observed this demarcation well over a century before RPS, but until RPS most activists didn't understand why the difference existed, or that the differences meant there were three main classes - capitalists, coordinators, and workers - not just two.

Seeing the additional class was a graphic instance of utilizing the type of institutional thinking RPS highlighted. We argued that the division of labor in corporations and throughout modern societies gave about 20 percent of non owners empowering tasks and gave about 80 percent of non owners disempowering tasks. Those with the empowering tasks accrued confidence, social connections, organizational skills, information, time, and disposition to affect affairs and define relations. Those with the disempowering tasks became habituated to obedience, fragmented from one another, and separated from information. They knew each other but they knew no one with pull. They suffered shortages of time, became exhausted, and became disposed to escape their alienated subordination as much as possible. RPS additionally explained that the coordinator class members would continue to oversee workers even with owners gone, as long as the same division of labor prevailed.

This last observation shattered my attachment to old forms of post capitalist vision. It made me ask how we might remove the features of economic institutions that gave not only the owning class but also the coordinator class both its power and its inclinations to use its power as it does. It made me ask what new institutions could deliver real classlessness.

While RPS was trying to modestly refine our understanding of race, power, and gender in light of seeing the impact of each on the rest, regarding economics it had to also show how class division arose not only from ownership but also from a corporate division of labor. At first I found it difficult and unfamiliar to understand the third class's implications in personal human terms and especially in terms of what it meant regarding vision, strategy, and people's ways of thinking, acting, talking, and writing. But as I did, it became a big part of my becoming deeply committed to RPS.

Did it impact your life choices outside RPS?

Yes, but I initially resisted.

I worked in a major university as a professor and also in a lab. In my workplace, well known scientists were paid more, had better conditions, had more influence, and were, indeed, coordinator class. So there was a real issue. Would I continue to accept the many advantages I enjoyed, which seemed like my right, or would I support efforts seeking balanced job complexes and equitable remuneration?

Powerful pressures for change came from students and newbie scientists, and also from technicians, janitors, and others who worked in traditionally powerless positions.

In contrast, at first nearly all professors resisted. We mostly found it absurd. How could it make sense for us, given all our experience and training, to do a share of cleaning up when we could be writing or doing research? We thought it would cripple science. But in time we learned that our reaction was wrong regarding productivity, much less justice.

The justice part was obvious as soon as we saw all who were involved as equally worthy human beings. The productivity part became compelling when we realized that labs with balanced job complexes were not only more humane and fulfilling, but also reduced the tensions and "office politics," that so often interfered with doing good work.

We all lived in a diseased world in which it was impossible for anyone to be fully human. One way or another, everyone who lived in our world was restrained or maladjusted. To be chained or flawed was no crime. To ignore our chains or flaws, after they became evident, was a crime.

Lydia, were you as attracted to RPS's elevation of values as Bertrand? Did RPS's new attitudes toward class play a role for you as well?

For me RPS's emphasis on diversity as a basic value had most initial impact. My coming at things as a strong feminist already disposed me toward recognizing the incredible range of options bearing on sexuality, nurturance, and bringing up children. The fact that RPS highlighted and celebrated diversity was a big plus for me. When I came to understand diversity as emanating just as logically from an ecological orientation, it helped further broaden my thinking.

Similarly, RPS wasn't the first project to urge that people ought to feel solidarity with one another. That was long since familiar. It was the way RPS coupled making values central with understanding institutions that impressed me.

For a value like solidarity, we were pushed by our institutional approach to ask what current social roles impede people feeling solidarity? What would have to happen for society's various institutions to accomplish their functions and simultaneously foster solidarity? Market competition forced buyers and sellers to fleece each other. Did that create solidarity? Of course not, and RPS's concepts pushed us to ask why not, and to consider what we could do about it.

Similarly, did families with a male operating with father duties and a female operating with mother duties foster self management or solidarity either in the adults or in their children? No? Okay, then what could we do about it? Government, hospitals, sports, media, malls, city planning, worship, everything warranted this type assessment.

In real societies, what happens in the economy affects everyone who fills economic roles because our economic roles require us to behave in certain ways and respect and implement certain norms. And this holds, albeit with different substance, for any economy, not just for the capitalism that RPS struggles to replace but for the new economy RPS favors, as well.

But RPS says the same thing holds for the institutions of kinship and the ways their roles require certain kinds of behavior from people bringing up kids and relating to one another in families. Kinship roles require that people behave in certain ways, and respect and implement a certain logic.

The economy affects our assumptions, circumstances, beliefs, and habits, and in turn we bring all these affects with us after work and beyond consumption, for example when we are at the dinner table, or in bed, or celebrating holidays, or voting. And similarly, exactly the same holds for kinship's impact on men, women, and children. Here too the effects are not confined to when we are inside families, say, or with friends, but travel with us into workplaces, places of worship, malls, and voting booths.

RPS shows how societies push and pull into a more or less stable entwined mosaic of all their key parts, as well as how this mosaic can become unstable, and can even be unraveled to become entirely transformed. Even more, it raises the question, What new mosaic should we implement?

Bertrand, what about the last key social value that RPS initially emphasized, equity? Did that resonate for you?

RPS says we should be remunerated for our effort and sacrifice. Each person should enjoy a combination of leisure and work which, overall, affords the same total benefits minus debits as every other person's mix of leisure and work. We should each get a share of the total social product in accord with the duration, intensity, and onerousness of the socially valued labor we do. If you work longer, harder, or under worse conditions, you deserve to receive more. But you do not deserve more for having special talents or for working in some more valued area, or for working with tools that increase your output, much less for owning property or for simply having sufficient power to take more.

When RPS was just getting started, this norm was completely foreign to the then current ethos of rewarding property, talent, and output. But that was society's preponderant initial negative reaction toward the innovation RPS favored. You asked about my own reaction.

Having come from an anarchist tradition, the guiding precept "from each according to ability, to each according to need" was a cornerstone of my radical identity and I vigorously defended it like I would defend a spouse or sibling. I had a nice looking banner proclaiming it on a wall in my house. I had a shirt with it printed on the front. I heard the RPS formulation as a step back and even an attack on a central component of my identity. To me, this wasn't an issue for discussion and understanding. It begged aggressive dismissal.

I later realized my anarchist norm assumed, without describing it, that an accompanying economic arrangement would allow the norm to operate. Additionally, the anarchist norm took for granted that having rules about work and consumption that limit options for each person in light of social circumstances would be intrinsically alienating and oppressive. Later, that seemed strange. After all, why shouldn't my connections with others impact my options as well as theirs? My earlier views eventually seemed to me anti social even though that was certainly not my earlier intent.

RPS caused me to ask what the norm means if we try to implement it in real relations and I began to realize that while I liked the anarchist slogan for its emotional connotations, I hadn't seriously examined its practical meaning.

Work to ability? Okay, who will say what my or your ability is? Consume to need? Okay, who will say what my or your need is? Anytime anyone went from abstract discussion to actually considering how to remunerate in some new project, these concerns arose.

If implementing the anarchist norm included someone other than me determining my ability or need it would loose its anti authoritarian impact. But if the norm meant I am free to determine my ability, how much I should work at what tasks, and how much I should get to consume, and that no one other than me should have a say in these determinations, it would let me have for consumption whatever I decided to take and to work however much or little I chose, at whatever job I chose. The norm assumed I will choose wisely, but included no structures, requirements, or mechanisms to facilitate my doing so.

I realized my anarchist "from each to each" norm had two central problems. Producing what we choose, with no attention to how well we are able to do it, would allow people to do things they cannot do well. But even if we ignore that difficulty, the maxim's first problem is if people strictly obey it and opt for the best result for themselves without assessing the effect on others, society crumbles from there being way too much demand and way too little supply.

In reply, the "from each to each" maxim's advocates would typically qualify it to accord better with their intentions. They would say their maxim really means that we should take what is fair, given our needs, and we should produce what is fair and needed, given our abilities, where the latter includes only doing work we do well enough so our product has social value. However, I was forced to recognize that with that fix I could commit to being fair, but how would I know what is fair? For that matter, what does fair even mean?

What if someone says that in their view fair is to receive income equal to what their property produces, or equal to how much society values their personal product? No anarchist would abide either view nor would any advocate of RPS. But how does the "from each to each" maxim rule out those choices? Further, whatever I decide is fair, how do I manage to make choices that implement it?

RPS convinced me that the ethically desirable and economically viable norm is that people should get income for how long they work, how hard they work, and the onerousness of the conditions under which they work, as long as their work is socially desired. We can each get that without impinging on others doing so too. RPS crucially added that none of us can make informed decisions without negotiating with one another about production and consumption to reveal both what people want and how much they want it.

This last observation convinced me the dispute wasn't only about what was ethical. It was also about what information had to be available for people to be able to be ethical. That was when I decided that the RPS norm was consistent with my anarchist desires for equitable outcomes, but that unlike "from each to each," implementing the RPS norm could reveal needed information rather than obscure it. I later realized the information was also needed for society to orient its future production sensibly in light of changing desires, but the above is what got me initially.

> *I have been asking folks to recount an event or situation during the rise of RPS that was particularly inspiring for them. Could you do so too, please*

Aside from all the major RPS campaigns and events molding me, I have to acknowledge a particular long running experience. When I was about 18, in 1984, way before RPS, I visited a girlfriend and listened to music she played from the album *Another Side of Bob Dylan*. The sound started to take over my mind. I don't know what else to say. I was not one to have a song distract me from anything else, much less 18 year-old night moves, but it started happening, and then I heard "Chimes of Freedom," and I was enthralled.

I later listened not only to that album but to a whole lot of Bob Dylan. I poured over certain lyrics until I could hear them fully. "Ah, get born, keep warm, short pants, romance, learn to dance, get dressed, get blessed, try to be a success…" I didn't just look the lyrics up. I wanted to hear them as first listeners did, decades earlier. Some songs I heard clearly right off, others I had to listen to repeatedly to get the words.

I think it was the first time something so cerebral was also so emotive for me. Dylan was the main literary engagement I ever undertook and I truly do believe that my experience of his songs contoured my life journey and especially my revolutionary desires about as much as anything else.

Many of Dylan's songs opened me to the breadth and depth of injustices in society, to the dangers its structure imposed, to the insanity, to the hypocrisy, and to social hope as well. But less known, Dylan was also an observer of critics of injustice, and as on most topics, he was both way before his time, and able to convey insights way beyond what his practical awareness of activism would seem to have permitted. He seemed to tap into wisdom that he couldn't have. I don't know where he got it. I don't know how he mined it.

Consider this passage from the song "Farewell Angelina." To my ears it is Dylan not only bidding a very gentle goodbye to Joan Baez, but a less gentle goodbye to the tumultuous movements then growing around the country which Joan wished to still relate to. Activists in those movements should have heard and acted on his words, but didn't. RPS, in some sense did, I think.

> The machine guns are roaring
> The puppets heave rocks
> The fiends nail time bombs
> To the hands of the clocks
> Call me any name you like
> I will never deny it
> Farewell Angelina
> The sky is erupting
> I must go where it's quiet

For Dylan, activists were the puppets, even the fiends, and he sought quiet. The movements of the day largely lost their best political muse, their best political troubadour, though Dylan's social brilliance went on and on.

CHAPTER 18

DEFINING OURSELVES

Dylan Cohen, Malcom King, Lydia Luxemburg, Bill Hampton, and Barbara Bethune discuss RPS's second convention and shadow government.

Dylan Cohen, born in 1981, you are a writer-activist focused on military agendas, peace movements, and campaigns aimed at military and police structure and policy. At the first RPS convention everyone agreed that decisions were temporary until there could be a second convention with greater participation. Can you tell us how the second convention came about, and what it was like?

At the first convention, participants were individuals who liked RPS ideas. Organizers had circulated materials beforehand, but most people who attended hadn't deliberated face to face in advance.

For the second convention we waited over two years and had established over 800 chapters with an average of 40 members each or 32,000 active members. 32,000 people couldn't all attend so we decided each chapter would send five people including at least two women and at least two people of color, 4,000 people in all. Chapters could choose who to send however they liked. A statewide meeting of all delegates from each state preceded the national convention, which lasted five days and included presentations, talks, discussion, debates, elections, social events, and topical meetings.

How did planning occur?

A year in advance, each chapter proposed a person to work on a planning committee and serve as convention staff. About 400 chapters proposed people. Descriptions of nominees were distributed and each chapter got five votes but had to vote for at least two women and two men, and also for at least two people of color. The 20 women and 20 men with the most votes were on the committee, as were the 20 people of color with the most votes. The committee, therefore, had to be at least 40 people and could conceivably be as many as 60. It turned out to be 49.

Those 49 became the planning committee and chose a venue, prepared advance communications, developed an agenda, invited guests, choose moderators for sessions, and arranged accommodations and food.

What from the first convention changed at the second?

The program was updated, but the most basic commitments barely changed at all. At the first convention, we worried we would blow our opportunity. At the second convention we were confident. Almost everyone felt we were building a vehicle that would take society to a new place. There was revolution in the air, but it was a quiet, calm assessment that RPS wasn't going away. We had skits that poked fun at ourselves. We were serious, but with a joyful lightness.

Even during votes on program and for the Shadow Government we stayed relaxed and emphasized diversity and respect for minority positions. Though votes were mostly lopsided, losing parties were always accommodated with means to explore their ideas further in case winning ideas proved flawed.

Tension was less than at the first convention and when we reached decisions, I sensed no bad feelings. Yet, we weren't becoming a hive mind. Since the first convention, far more people advocated richer and more varied ideas and while we had more differences about details, people had gained trust, confidence, and a sense of perspective. Activists had historically often considered only numbers of people relating and the growth of militancy as signs of movement progress. While those measures matter greatly, it was our less easily described interpersonal progress that kept growing numbers of militant RPS participants functioning well together.

> *Dylan, I forgot to ask you how you became radicalized. Do you remember?*

At war, one day I saw someone who I killed face to face. Next day, I watched a friend die. Other days, I killed and saw death but it had no face. It became just death, a nasty cousin of life, uninvited but intermittently gate crashing.

Escaping military indoctrination is hard. We learned to blindly obey orders which precluded having opinions at all. We learned we were a team, even a family. Each of us needed to regard others as a lifeline to survival. But our family had borders. To the inside, we should show respect, loyalty, and incredible solidarity. To the outside, we should show unyielding strength and, if need be, deliver horrific hostility. Battlefield connections were deep and enduring, both positive and negative. In battle, our training fostered survival and winning, but in life it bred isolation.

My radicalization began when I jettisoned false beliefs and behaviors in Iraq and deepened when I helped others do likewise. I looked at where our views came from and what alternatives existed and I saw the link between imperialism and anti sociality. I lived the link between a life-denying system and its beat up soldiers of fortune. RPS provided a natural home, it kept me sane against my PTSD, and effective in our struggle.

> *Malcolm, you ran for and won your first local election shortly after the second convention. What was the attitude toward elections that emerged from the conventions? How did RPS impact your electoral efforts?*

Yes, I won my first election back then. The RPS attitude, which hasn't changed much since, was that to run for office and to win was potentially good, but pitfalls could pervert good into bad. We liked that running could facilitate outreach to new audiences, raise consciousness, and boost morale. Winning could also gain access to resources to help win more gains in the future.

We worried that candidates might fixate on winning votes and lose track of larger aims, worrying more about vote tallies and fundraising then program. We might fall in love with holding office more than with achieving worthy aims.

RPS members helped immeasurably with my campaigns and work in office. RPS gave me a rooted sense of my role and helped me arrive at my views and practices, pushing me to be accountable. Members aided campaigns, but to avoid getting sucked into nasty electoral dynamics, RPS avoided organizational electoral participation.

Lydia, did the shadow government idea surface at that time? What did the shadow government do, and what did you do in it?

The idea was floated back when Ralph Nader had run for President as a Green. I remember wanting Nader to do it, and then, later, Sanders, feeling that without a prominent jump start, a shadow government would accomplish little. Greens actually did have a shadow government, albeit nearly invisibly, during the Obama administration. When Sanders lost the nomination in 2016 the idea surfaced again, but it didn't happen. Years later, the idea resurfaced in RPS and became part of the agenda for our second convention.

We hoped to set up a group with the same official positions as their counterparts in real government: a President, a Vice President, a cabinet, Supreme Court judges, Senators, and other posts as well.

Our idea was the shadow government would operate in parallel to the real government. We would take stands on all major issues the real government addressed, and on critical, but officially unaddressed issues as well. We would offer our views to display an alternative and to agitate for policies we favored. We would also generate and fight for our own projects and programs.

Despite the fact that I wasn't particularly prominent, I became the first President. But the key factor was the 32,000 RPS active members, and tens of thousands of other supporters who were not yet in chapters. RPS members helped generate policy and demands and agitated for them. They contributed, on average, $25 each per month, which meant nearly $10 million in the first year, and the annual amount grew dramatically due to our growing membership.

Dylan, how did the first shadow government get formed?

It was partly through an election for the President, Vice President, and Senators, and then appointments for Supreme Court Judges, Cabinet members, and others.

The shadow Senators were elected before the second national convention by State conventions. The President and Vice President were elected at the second convention. Nominations were conducted earlier, at the State conventions, and were whittled down to four for each office by a prior national online vote of all chapter members. The vote at the national convention was of the whole membership too, since each chapter got live reports from its delegates, saw speeches online, and then voted at local gatherings. In the vote at the convention, chapter tallies were reported, state by state.

Did it all go smoothly? Were their any serious problems?

There were some hiccups, of course, with people arguing about the merits of different candidates. No one knew quite what the new jobs would entail and sometimes communications got confused.

One serious problem arose, and I was involved. A group of ex-military made a collective proposal on behalf of arming so as to battle directly with police. They deemed themselves "true revolutionaries," because they were ready to shoot it out. They proclaimed that rejecting weaponry was "cowardly and phony."

They claimed that if we rejected using weapons, the status quo would inevitably win by force of arms and repression. They had a one-step argument that we could not win fundamental change unless we overcame state violence with movement violence, so anyone who said we should be non violent was conceding we could not win fundamental change.

What made this a problem wasn't that such a view was offered, but the way it was offered. These guys marched in, armed with rifles, and took the stage. This, they felt, demonstrated the power of guns. They offered their one-line logic, and from then on their only stance was you are either with us, or you are with the state.

The people present didn't want to take too strong a stance with these folks who had, after all, gone through war-time conflict — their views were a product of their history.

And your involvement?

I argued that violence would not only distort our ability to think straight and function well, but that it would play into the hands of the powers that be. Violence was terrain the state would inevitably win. Our task was to disarm state violence by making it ineffective because their use of violence against us would mean more dissent.

I was a veteran of active duty and a military organizer so I quickly gathered a group, unarmed, and we walked up on stage and said, "Now what? Are you going to shoot us? Or would shooting us do your agenda more harm than good?" We clearly weren't "cowardly and phony." We got them to leave the stage with us to talk further.

Our point was that movements thinking they can violently fight the state play into the hands of the state - which wants nothing so much as to move from politics to their terrain of military power. However, the armed guys did reveal a relevant truth. In a group, one guy with a club is a problem. Five guys with guns are an even bigger problem.

We faced two issues. On the one hand, could we handle police and military violence at local demonstrations? The answer was yes, but only by creating situations in which when the police or military used violence it would rebound to our benefit, not their's.

The second issue was trickier. Could we handle personal violence motivated by thuggery or infiltration or coming from our own people - such as these vets? It would be hard if not impossible to make internal violence counter productive for those doing it if they were beyond reason much less if they were actively trying to damage RPS. We did intervene in that way, actually, with the guys on the stage at the convention. But they weren't trying to harm RPS.

And so emerged a feeling that RPS had to have a means to deal with internal or external craziness or sabotage. Could we address this yet not corrupt the style and modes of operation of RPS and distort people's mindsets? Could we prepare for such situations without our preparedness harming us more than the situations themselves?

A first thought was, how about if we establish a few people with the training and experience for handling crazy, violent interlopers. They could be invisibly armed and prepared. But we saw that there would be problems.

First, the secrecy was disturbing. We decided the decision had to be made by the organization as a whole. We decided to elect a group who would secretly designate security folks.

Second, what if the security folks themselves became problematic? We decided we shouldn't pick the most macho and military of our members. Experienced folks should train people picked based largely on temperament.

We next decided that while our set of steps made sense, we weren't sure it was really needed. After all, we had completed two conventions and had undertaken countless demonstrations and campaigns, often running up against police and state power. So maybe paranoia about the likelihood of internal lunacy was a bigger problem for us than such lunacy itself. And it turned out that this cautiousness at undertaking the project was wise.

We had the plan ready to propose for a wide discussion and vote, but we decided to hold off until and unless practical evidence suggested it was needed. And, because of our huge growth, beyond a small scale, that time never came.

On the other hand, I and various others around the country did quietly non-violently but forcefully work with folks on how to deal with local intruders, drunks, ideologically intractable folks, infiltrators, and the like. And here we are, so I guess all was well.

Lydia, what was the hardest thing about doing the Shadow Government and what were its first successes?

Well, it was a tremendous amount of work. After all, we were generating positions on an array of issues and we needed to get the facts right, even though we lacked the giant support bureaucracy the real government had. I was constantly meeting, discussing, and then holding press conferences and giving public talks 200-250 days a year for my four-year term. It was exciting, I had a sense of accomplishment and joy in the work, but I was also exhausted.

We formed our Shadow Government mimicking the U.S. Government's structures yet everyone involved hated that set of institutions. I hated the presidency but was Shadow President. I gave speeches as Shadow President. showing the media and public the contrast between RPS and the actual government. But shadowing the government included, at least at first, a problem of accomplishing our aims using their structure.

To redress that, we decided to steadily alter our government structure, announcing organizational changes - like other polices we advocated - as things we thought should happen in the actual government. We changed election laws, funding mechanics, added and deleted various positions, and changed their mandates during my four-year term.

The hardest part, however, was keeping my head on straight. We didn't require that everyone call me Madame President and otherwise pay homage, but many did treat me that way. And I was constantly interviewed, questioned, and listened to as if I was some kind of oracle.

I had to avoid falling into elitist habits. What helped most was I appointed as my Press Secretary and Chief of Staff people who could keep me in line.

I think the first significant success was when we took on mainstream government military policies, budgets, and interventionism, with our new approach emphasizing disarmament, reallocating funding, using military forces for social good, re-tooling bases, withdrawing troops, and so on. Our proposals were so extensive, clear, and sensible and their benefits were so apparent, that the whole process - despite breaking with the entire history of U.S. militarism - gained tremendous credibility. From then on, Shadow presentations of policy were highly anticipated and taken very seriously by many.

Next, I would say our dramatically expanding social service policies, increasing minimum wages, and shortening the work week, were also effective steps. We contrasted our desired policies to the mainstream government's policies, but also invested time, energy, and funds into organizing and agitating.

Bill, the broad idea behind the RPS Shadow Government wasn't limited to government. What was the more general idea?

The "Shadow" aspect was to create models for future institutions with worthy effects in the present. Being Shadow meant these projects did functions that were done by existing institutions, but did them in parallel, and new ways.

The "worthy" aspect was that the projects should contribute to ongoing activism and people's current well being. A media or organizing project would do mostly the former, while a health clinic or day care center would do mostly the latter.

The "model" aspect was to create projects that showed how things would be different in a better future and that revealed - or discovered - new ways of operating that were suitable for future relations.

Shadow projects were initiated as you might imagine. Sometimes young people entering adult life would decide to create a media project, clinic, restaurant, law firm, or food distribution center in accord with RPS values.

Sometimes older folks who were already established in some field would transform their old institution or leave it to create a new one. We saw health clinics, day care centers, restaurants, food stores, and a few law firms transform. We also saw various teachers, health workers, day care workers, and lawyers leave existing establishments and group together to form alternatives.

So while the Shadow Government literally shadowed the real government - in contrast, health clinics, magazines, food coops, or day care centers didn't shadow some specific mainstream institution. They did similar functions but in their own alternative and separate way. It was a fuzzy distinction. For example, the shadow government was continually redefining itself to have alternative features.

Barbara, what impact did the shadow approach have? How did it interact with more direct campaigns?

Each successful shadow or alternative project educated not only those involved but also those who witnessed or interacted with it. As the efforts grew, they diversified and often experimentally tested potential features of a new society. Likewise, when a Shadow or Alternative institution worked well, it benefited its consumers and workers in the present, and its product contributed to future social change more broadly.

Why did some efforts work, where others did not?

The recurring reasons were like what plagues start-up firms more generally: lack of resources, pressure of financial shortfall, limited visibility, and lack of experience and confidence.

The miracle is that so many succeeded. It is one thing to establish equitable remuneration and balanced job complexes throughout an economy. It is quite another to do it in a tiny part of an economy that, overall, still worships personal material advance and still offers options to get such gains, albeit options whose pursuit denies other people the same gains.

If you had lots of training, skills, and knowledge, you could take a high paying job doing only empowering tasks. Or, you could instead take a job in a fragile start up where you would earn less and do considerable disempowering work. Imagine you had family and friends who perpetually warned you that the alternative endeavor was insane. Sticking with it was hard.

It was also different participating in large, classless institutions or in small ones. In the former, there were plenty of people you would like and take support from. Likewise, there were a wide range of tasks to create desirable balanced jobs from. In a small operation, you might not have any friends, and jobs would be harder to define and more likely contain elements you disliked. And any project, large or small, had to operate in the existing world where markets constantly compelled choices that impeded what you hoped to achieve.

Don't get me wrong, there were many benefits to establishing a desirable workplace even in the earliest days, but for doing so to be relatively stress free required projects becoming more prevalent and larger. Nowadays, such firms are in high demand. Even folks who might fancy themselves so worthy that they should be paid more and allowed to avoid all disempowering tasks now have considerable reason to compromise on those desires in order to enjoy a congenial workplace without class conflict.

So for all these reasons, the earliest projects were by far the hardest, most vulnerable, most demanding, and most tense. It was the pioneers, often never acknowledged, who did the most difficult work, not those who unfurled banners celebrating great victories years later. There was nothing wrong with enjoying the latter, but it would be nice if we had more respect for the unknown trailblazers.

Lydia, it seems like there was a mentality that made all this much more real and powerful than similar efforts had been earlier. Can you try to convey what that mentality was?

In slogan form, you might say we went from whining to winning. In one of my favorite quotes, all the way back in 1941, George Orwell said, "The mentality of the English left-wing intelligentsia can be studied in half a dozen weekly and monthly papers. The immediately striking thing about all these papers is their generally negative, querulous attitude, their complete lack at all times of any constructive suggestion. There is little in them except the irresponsible carping of people who have never been and never expect to be in a position of power." We got beyond that.

Can you clarify the changed mentality you are pointing to?

Think of a professional sports team. What distinguishes those that win from those that lose? Talent, training, and effort are part of it, of course. But let's assume talent, training, and effort are essentially the same for some set of teams. Then what will distinguish them? Luck will be a factor, but so will people's attitudes.

Those who think they can win and who confidently approach difficult challenges as hills to remove, go around, or climb over have a chance for a great season. Those who doubt that they can win and who despondently approach even modest hills as immovable mountains that irremediably obstruct their way have no chance for a great season.

Imagine a successful professional football or soccer coach meeting with her team. Imagine the team lost its most recent game. It's time to talk about the next game or the rest of the season. Does the coach list her team's detriments and the opponent's strengths as if they are unbridgeable impediments to success?

No, the coach respects reality, but approaches each game highlighting what her team can best affect.

Now consider the left. Just playing well at improving society isn't enough. Winning ends wars, feeds the hungry, gives dignity to the exploited, and reduces hardships. Winning creates a new world.

So does the left have a winning attitude? Can we have a good season, a good career, with our current mindset? All too often in the past the answer has been no. All too often too many of us would look at a half-full or quarter-full (movement) glass and speak only about how much was missing in tones that suggested that our glass could never be more full. Indeed, we even saw leaks in our glass where they didn't exist and imagined powers to deplete our glass's contents that our opponents did not have.

Too few activists asked, "How do we welcome more (members) to our glass and how do we retain those we have rather than watching them leak away?" Too often we went beyond sensibly analyzing the conditions that we encountered to fruitlessly whining about things we couldn't influence. Too often we paid too little attention to difficulties we could remove, go around, or climb over.

Am I exaggerating our past condition? The fact is, whether we were talking about matters of class, race, gender, political power, ecology, international relations, or whatever else, before RPS our movements weren't nearly as full of members as they needed to be for us to win even short-run reforms, much less long-run new institutions. But how many leftists wrote and spoke about what was wrong with society without accompanying their analyses with a strategic commentary, so that (even against their intent) their words had more or less the impact of moaning about the size of next week's opponent?

In contrast, how many wrote and spoke about why our movement didn't grow faster, or about why it lost the members who we did attract, and especially about what we could do to fix those failings and have better results?

How many of us wrote or spoke about the oppressiveness or power of the media, state, or corporations, as compared to writing or speaking about the attributes needed to oppose the media's, state's, and corporations' power and oppressiveness, and about the potential power of opposition and how it might be enhanced?

Did the left used to seek victory? Even as individuals, much less as a whole? Did we have shared institutional goals for the economy, the polity, families and kinship, the culture, international relations, and the ecology? Did we organize our thoughts about what to do today in light not only of our current strengths and weaknesses and of the immediate conditions we confronted and our immediate aims, but also in light of how all this related to our long-term goals?

Most of the left rightly disparaged professional sports for its commercialism, sexism, racism, and class relations. But it would have helped it we had also learned a little from them. Sports teams are the world's foremost competitors and, like it or not, we are in a competition rooted in class, gender, race, and political relations. Sports reveals that if we despondently whine, we will lose. On the other hand, if we confidently strategize, we can win. If we lack goals we will wind up somewhere we'd rather not be. If we have goals, we may attain them.

I think our cultivating a mindset to win helped the Shadow Government succeed. We weren't preening for a mirror. We weren't taking selfies to celebrate our good looks. We weren't padding resumes. We were bent on increasing our participants, infrastructure, and morale and thus our power to win immediate reforms and to lay the groundwork for further gains in the future.

We realized if participants thought that the left was not able to become a serious player in the future of our society, and that all that's really possible was tweaking existing relations this way and that, then the mood and agenda of a Shadow Government would be very different than we needed. And this applied not just to the Shadow Government, but to the whole logic of a shadow society. Establishing our underlying disposition was arguably RPS's main contribution to the whole shadow/alternative approach.

CHAPTER 19

GENDER AND RACE

Juliet Berkman, Bill Hampton, Lydia Luxemburg, Cynthia Parks, Noam Carmichael, and Peter Cabral discuss gender and race.

Juliet, feminist insights had been front and center in left activism for over fifty years before RPS, yet, RPS made dealing with gender and sexuality a core priority both for society and internally. Why was that necessary?

In 1960, even outside the home, women mostly nurtured and cleaned. Women lawyers, doctors, and engineers, were nearly as rare as red bluebirds. Women officeholders were a thought dream. Women showing initiative were all too often ostracized, confined, or beaten. By 2020 we had made huge gains but we hadn't won permanent change. As long as basic causes of male dominance persisted, even when we reduced sexist symptoms, underlying causes kept pushing for a return to old ways. High heels were rejected. But then high heels came back. Rape declined. But then rape escalated.

Feminists changed thinking, choices, habits, and laws over the decades leading to RPS, but something continued to promote sexism in each new generation. Was it genes or institutions, nature or nurture?

We saw the same pattern in our own activism. We reduced the most blatant sexism inside movements. We had diminished and at times even nearly eliminated violence against women, dismissal of women's opinions, exclusion of women from responsibility, and vile sexual objectification of women in movements - yet the ills were returning.

We said sexism was social but we weren't surprised when some people, women included, at times slipped into thinking that while we claimed to be fighting for the natural order, perhaps the natural order was sexual hierarchy and we were fighting for a situation against which "nature" kept reacting. Most feminists had such fears. I know did.

If there wasn't an answer for all the backsliding, feminism would dissipate so even on the left, even fifty years past mid twentieth century feminism, we had a gender problem. The saving grace was that RPS didn't shy away from it.

———

Bill, can you remember why a powerful feminist component was essential?

Regarding society, women still earned way less than men for the same work. Violence against women persisted and was even escalating. Women's health was still manipulated. Sexist parenting persisted.

Likewise, in the movement everyone celebrated women's leadership - but how much was there? If you looked at organizations, movement institutions, and projects, certainly way more women exerted influence than fifty years earlier, but still less than half. If you looked at what was written and published, in many instances fewer women were visible on the left than in the mainstream.

Women still feared night on the streets, suffered vicious hounding online, and lacked attentive audience. It wasn't remotely as bad as five decades earlier, but the battle wasn't fully won.

RPS felt the key problem was deep in the structure of family life as well as in many other institutions that had been pushed into conformity with sexism.

What was to be done within RPS and the movement?

Inside RPS we enacted daycare at all organizational meetings and events with a proviso that staffing should immediately be at least half male. To have daycare but reinforce the idea that it was women's work would have been one step forward but two steps back.

We also legislated that public speaking at our events, marches, teach-ins, and meetings always had to be at least fifty percent female. I remember men whining about how we were sacrificing quality for a mechanical quota system, oblivious to how we were sacrificing quality by having men who were often out of touch with the needs of half of humanity do all the talking while women wasted away their talents.

Likewise, we established that leadership for events had to be at least fifty percent female. When women were not available or were not felt to be prepared by prior experience to accomplish the tasks, we had to redress that imbalance with training and practice before the group formed. The new norm was simple. Correct gender imbalance or don't proceed.

Movement women organized themselves. They didn't care about happy smiles and promises. They weren't appeased by men saying "have a nice day." They demanded structural action or they would disrupt offending events.

I remember a meeting where there were about 60 women and 100 men. Suddenly the door opened and 20 more women came in. They told the chair to sit down, and I did. They told all those present that from then on all meetings would have at least 50% women handling organization, being chair, etc., and likewise, at least 50% women addressing topics raised. If those in the room didn't want to comply, fine, they would have to hold their meeting over unrelenting disruption.

At the same time, the rising tally of rapes on campuses spurred a sense of urgency. When a rape occurred after a radical conference in Los Angeles, and a male movement leader was the rapist, all hesitancy disappeared. Women were going to win change.

Many men still argued that to hold back events to fulfill gender norms was harmful. They didn't see dealing with gender balance as a positive part of moving events forward. Sometimes even some women agreed with not interfering. We are going too fast was their logic. We are demanding more than can be readily accomplished. Worse, if we disrupt the left we abet reaction. It was true such reforms could be ham-handed and damaging - and that we should avoid that - but most women, and many men, acknowledged that concern but no longer bought it as a reason to reject change.

We knew that to forego basic change inside the left was to consign the left to perpetual hypocrisy and weakness. We simply worked to ensure that women's militant approach carefully sought solidarity. It blamed structures, not individuals. It set standards for everyone. It said if we aren't able to do some things in a feminist manner now, then we should delay doing those things until we get ourselves ready to do them properly. Our desire to have talks or projects will have to become part of our prior desire for a proper feminist achievement. If not, nothing will proceed.

The opposition to these womens' demands always claimed to be seeking important ends now and certainly not trying to prevent feminist innovation. And while that was no doubt the sincere motive for many opponents, 50 years of postponing institutionally solidifying feminist gains had to stop sometime, and this was the time.

The main point, ultimately, was that the assault on sexism by RPS women wasn't seeking verbal commitments to feminism. It wasn't even seeking changes from male leftists in accord with feminist values. No apologies were needed or wanted. No personal blame was asserted. The women sought structural changes that would make overcoming sexism part and parcel of functioning at all.

What was most innovative was not the demands themselves, or the militance, but the tone and actions. Earlier anti-sexist efforts had typically polarized men, and even recalcitrant women, in ways that entrenched opposition. RPS anti-sexism was hostile to structures, but empathetic toward men. The goal was to organize, not antagonize. We sought informed alliance and real solidarity.

Another movement step was more subtle. RPS said that to avoid class division and classism we had to adopt job complexes balanced for empowerment effects. By similar reasoning, some RPS women suggested we had to change the kinship division of tasks to avoid a sexist gender division. We knew we all become, to a considerable degree, who our roles require us to be. We asked what changes in our roles would prevent men becoming sexist and women becoming disposed to accept sexism?

Of course, if men worked and earned more, then they would have means to dominate. So women needed higher incomes. If in dating and courting, men and women had different roles, then we would wind up with different dispositions. Women needed equal roles. But some women wondered if there was also something like empowerment that had to be balanced among men and women lest the difference in proximity to whatever that something was, produced a kinship hierarchy.

RPS members came to a broad agreement that if women do most nurturing and caring whereas men do most competing and governing, perhaps men become perverse and thuggish and women become empathetic but self denying. We concluded men needed to do a fair share of daycare and other nurturing tasks in the movement, in society, and in families.

Lydia, What was innovative in RPS's approach for society as a whole?

Much of RPS feminist program resurrected earlier feminist campaigns against violence against women and for equal pay, abortion rights, and day care, but our rationale, discussion, and the constituencies battling for the changes were new. We believed efforts in each sphere of social life should support and strengthen efforts in other spheres. We emphasized finding ways to talk about gender that went beyond ratifying feminist allies and trouncing sexist opponents. We continually addressed opponents with sympathetic understanding to reverse their allegiances.

We focused on replacing institutional structures that enforced sexism rather than on only criticizing sexist ideas or habits. One place we quickly became active was worship. Organizing women against sexist norms and requirements in nearly all religions was difficult and sometimes turned ugly, but it also inspired international attention.

But the most controversial area we addressed was in households, living units, and families. We didn't just seek equal income to change the situation of women in families - though that was very important - we sought to redefine what men and women did in their families. We couldn't impose behavior patterns on how to take care of homes or relate to children, yet, RPS sought to impact precisely those dynamics because we felt they buttressed sexist beliefs and behaviors.

We argued internally for gender-neutral parenting, calmly addressing hysterical men and women who thought it was unnatural. When we took this into the broader world, it was initially harshly attacked, but writing, speaking, and creating dramatic plays and shows about gender-neutral parenting, initiating street theatre, law suits, support groups, and having teachers bring it into classes, slowly turned the tide. At every step, two criteria guided: winning gains and not polarizing but seeking support from opponents.

Cynthia, when RPS emerged the Black Lives Matter (BLM) movement was still operating. Did RPS just take up their approach, or make some changes?

When BLM began it made no demands and overwhelmingly confined its attention to police violence against community members. A year or two passed and various members of BLM put together an impressive list of issues and demands addressing not only police violence, but all sides of life affecting Black and other non-white communities.

Not long after, RPS innovations addressed how to propose and seek changes in policing, income distribution, and cultural relations. We emphasized that victory didn't depend on winning a debate but on assembling a massive majority by presenting honest, un-compromised claims and desires, and addressing the views of opponents to create unity.

We came to realize that we each had to live our lives not only for ourselves, but as a model for others. That may seem obvious, but it really wasn't. For decades, around race and every focus of serious oppression, dissidents had too often tried to validate their agendas and justify or even celebrate their actions for themselves, then they had tried to win support for their agendas by and for others.

After all, what would winning around race mean? For RPS it meant that not only would the structural bases for racial hierarchy be gone, but everyone would see themselves firstly as members of humanity. Differentiations by community would remain important, but universal human connection would become primary. Different racial, ethnic, national, or religious allegiances would be a happenstance of birth and preference and reflect different choices that each deserved respect and room to persist. We wouldn't eliminate conflicts by eliminating differences. But nor would we exaggerate the source or implications of cultural differences, much less foster exclusivity.

This meant when an oppressed community battled against oppression, we needed to have long run success in mind. We shouldn't cater to the tastes of those in more dominant positions, but nor should we fear annoying them. We should communicate in ways seeking lasting solutions rather than momentary successes that could be later reversed by unaddressed or even needlessly provoked antagonisms.

Cynthia, thank you for your participation in these interviews. Before you go, do you think we will win? When will we have won? And, what is one lesson from this whole period that strikes you personally as most critical?

I believe we have already won. We just have to get everyone else to realize what's obvious.

Projects and campaigns are over, I guess, when people dance on the grave of past injustice, being sure by what they see and do, that it will never resurface.

Finally, a lesson I took early on, and that has always stayed with me, is that we are what we do, and we do what we are.

Noam Carmichael, born in 1995, you were active in media and public speaking, with your written work focused on popular culture and issues of political participation and race. In RPS, your work has emphasized raising consciousness, developing organizing projects, and aiding internal relations. I wonder if you remember first becoming radical?

In 2001 I was old enough to get a vague sense, with my parents' help, for the change in my situation due to my religion and appearance. I was radicalized in significant part by trying to understand Islamaphobia, and to survive and oppose it. I don't think any one incident radicalized me, but I do think one greatly influenced what kind of radical, and later revolutionary, I became. When I got to college my roommate took one look and you could feel the fear. For two weeks we worked that through, and became close friends, even to this day.

I would guess, and I think he would agree, that had we not dealt with our tensions he would have voted for Trump. I took as a lesson that we didn't navigate to a good place by becoming enemies. We did it by listening to one another and working through confusions, biases, ignorance, and worse. If you don't talk with - much less if you dismiss and denigrate - your potential enemies become your actual enemies.

I have been asking folks if they could remember a particularly inspiring or otherwise personally important event or campaign they experienced during the rise of RPS. Could you do that for us, please?

During the early period, around 2025, I had the opportunity to teach a number of times in RPS Schools for Organizers. The schools focused on movement building, organizing, and outreach, on analysis of the roots of society's ills, on vision of what society could and should be, and on insights into how to get from the current situation to the desired future one.

There were many such schools. Sometimes on a campus, sometimes in a workplace. Sometimes for people in some industry like the Hollywood schools that began in 2022 and in some ways birthed the whole extended project. Sometimes in an apartment complex. And sometimes we had schools for RPS members themselves.

At any rate, there would be intense classes, discussions, and time to socialize, as the schools typically ran for at least a week. About two thirds in, after there had emerged a level of trust and positive energy, we would have a night session to answer the question, what is responsible for your being here to learn about revolutionizing society?

Those evenings were indescribably inspiring. Some people's stories were cerebral. People would tell about first reading some new author and the eye opening effect it had on them. Or, people would tell of a first rally or march opening their views and launching them into activism. But most stories were mainly visceral with tears and trauma. I was abused as a child. I was raped. I saw a friend gunned down in the streets. I lost a parent, a friend, or a friend's parent to drugs or suicide. I lost my home and lived threadbare for years. I became addicted and escaped addiction. Sometimes it was less extreme: I was bullied in school, or I was a bully; I was cheated on, or I cheated.

People who no one expected to have such stories, told them. The mood was so cathartic that people chose to speak. The scale of the revealed pain and suffering and the scope of the revealed courage cemented my commitments and made me more of a listener than I had been before.

What was your view of the implication of race for issues of leadership inside RPS?

The direct implication had been well known for a long time. An organization seeking a better society would have to welcome and benefit from society's racial communities. It would have to elevate members of diverse communities to leadership. It would have to convey to communities predominant say over their own affairs.

How?

We asked should we accomplish these aims in a way that creates even greater antagonisms, or should we do it in a way that reduces antagonisms? We realized we needed to always seek a new society rather than merely be right about short term issues.

Of course a major cultural issue was minority communities suffering low income, little influence, and escalating danger. But even while tackling all that, we knew we might focus so centrally on that that we would become blind to other matters, or downplay them, or even use a short term view about race to supersede other concerns. So we saw we had to add to a race focus, a gender, class, and authority focus, just like vice versa.

There was another issue, very controversial, in which if I remember right you played a role. It was about who should organize whom?

I attended an early RPS-sponsored meeting about working on an anti racist campaign. There was a seeming understanding among the experienced blacks present, and more widely too - and an analogous view held among women about sexism - that it was not their responsibility to organize among white people, or, in the case of women, among men. It was only another burden to expect blacks to explain racism or otherwise combat racism among white folks by talking with them, or women to explain or combat sexism among men by talking with them. White folks and men had do the talking to other white folks and men.

This formulation had been repeated so often, so forcefully, so emotively, for so many years, that it had become an axiom. To doubt the view was itself taken as racist or sexist, which was in part why so few challenged the view, at least out loud. But I doubted the view, and I was forthright about challenging it, out loud.

I remember when the controversy specifically erupted for RPS. A prominent black activist conveyed this view to some young white kid just getting going in RPS with a tone that said, "Newbie, you are backward, you have to clean up your thinking that I have some responsibility for telling you about racism as compared to your educating yourself and other whites."

This upset me. It brought my doubt to a head. So I said, "Wait a minute. I am an activist, I am anti racist, I am black, I am experienced, and I get that in a wonderful world I wouldn't have to worry about educating anyone about racism, much less about spending time educating racist white folks. I get that. For sure. And I get that it is annoying and time consuming and even disturbing to have to do all that. But I don't see how my agreeing on that much implies that I literally shouldn't now sometimes talk to whites, educate whites, and organize whites about racism. Why does that follow?"

If I shouldn't do anything that compared to being burden-free in a better world is an imposition, then I also shouldn't organize blacks. That is a burden too, compared to not having racism. But I do it, not every minute, but often, when I think it can contribute to overcoming racism. So isn't the right question about my talking to white people about the nature of, the impact of, and the ways to overcome racism? Isn't it, will my talking to white folks about racism help the anti racist cause? And if that is the wise guiding question, then when I am in a better position to successfully communicate or organize with other whites than are whites who are present, shouldn't I do it? I think I should."

I got shouted down, but I didn't fade away. And I knew that a great many folks agreed with what I had said, because they told me so after the meeting. Sadly, they were intimidated from saying they agreed by fear of being of being called racist and ostracized. So I kept at it and discussions began. Before long the old viewpoint started to come unravelled.

As all can see now, this should have been easy to achieve but it wasn't for reasons of identity, habit, and protecting prior views.

The main issue, which was hard to surface, was the same as in many other cases. Were we trying to win? Did we believe we could win, or were we just hammering out a stance that felt okay and made some modest gains without seeking long term goals?

My point wasn't that blacks - or women in the parallel case - should spend all their time talking fruitlessly with totally intractable white racists or male sexists. No, my point was that there were many situations in which blacks and women knew more and could better convey and motivate what they knew to whites and men than could other whites or men, and have consciousness raised by our efforts to do so.

I should probably add that the same applied to talking to people of our own backgrounds, who held contrary and even hostile views. There, too, the right calculus wasn't how much of a burden was it to respectfully suffer hearing their confusions and anger, but how necessary was overcoming their confusions and anger to winning change?

There was another related view of the times RPS jettisoned, yes?

I assume you mean the idea of "white skin privilege." Yes, we felt the word privilege connoted something one ought not have. You should renounce your privileges. The trouble was when folks spoke and wrote about what the white skin privileges were, it turned out that for a great many the problem wasn't that whites had them, but rather that others did not. Safety from denigration, confidence in access and representation, fair treatment, and so on.

Talking about renouncing white skin privilege, particularly to poor and dismissed whites, made whites think the aim was to take minimal basic things from them, rather than to guarantee everyone those things and much more.

It occurs to me that the changes from earlier that you mention, and others in these interviews mentioned, are mostly about outreach, do you think that's true?

To a large extent, yes. Earlier activists looking back and seeing no revolutionary gains would deduce a need for something new and would come up with some more complex, obscure, arcane formulation, as if past failings had to do with some missing hugely difficult idea that needed to be discovered and elevated by way of very nearly unreadable texts. This was, I think, nonsense. The big problems weren't missing ideas but ideas not reaching and involving large audiences. RPS mostly took existing insights, and even vision, and found far better ways to popularly communicate them and involve ever more people in refining and employing and seeking to implement them. I would even say we went from activism that was ruled by academia to academia that was renovated by activism. And we went from seeing self expression as activism to seeing activism as selves communicating.

Peter, can you remember an event or campaign or anything else, during the period of RPS growth, that was particularly meaningful for your own history?

Oh, there were many, mainly involving sports organizing, like the Olympic Campaigns and especially the athletes' boycotts for Community Safety. There was also the prison and legal organizing, like the Community Control of Police Campaign and the Legal Workers Conference - because I was so much closer to the sports and legal work than to other RPS efforts.

But for something a bit less public, I remember being in college, over a decade before RPS. I was an athlete but also a fan. I heard a talk by Noam Chomsky in which he discussed sports and its role.

Chomsky described viewing his classmates rooting passionately for a sports team in high school, and his not being able to understand. They don't know anyone involved, he thought. They have no close connections with any of the players on either team, yet they become invested as if their lives are at stake. How could that happen? Why did that happen?

I realized it was true for me. I could watch a college sports event, or a pro sports event, and know nothing about anyone on the field beyond their talent level, and yet be incredibly vested in "my team's" fortunes. I would even say we - as in "we got such and such a new player, we looked good," or "the refs screwed us" (never them), despite my having zero actual connection to the team.

Was there a healthy aspect? What were the unhealthy aspects? Thinking about it had a major long term effect on my relations to sports and also my understanding of how people formed and defended stances sometimes based on logic and evidence, but sometimes based on other things entirely.

Can you talk about the situation around the initial RPS race focus, the police repression of Blacks and other minorities?

People were being killed on the streets, sometimes for minor violations, often for no offense at all. Shot, point blank, even in the back. We knew lynching disciplined the entire slave community, induced fear in all slaves, and simultaneously induced a kind of bloodlust in the public - also, ironically, rooted in fear. How different was the police execution of young Blacks in the streets?

Fear put residents of black neighborhoods constantly on guard to avoid upsetting police. Life was conducted by carefully navigating even your own streets to avoid repression. And it wasn't just killings that induced fear. Drones flying over communities had a similar impact. So did getting stopped, frisked, and arrested for being Black. U.S. incarceration rates were unique in the developed world, and still worse for minorities.

How do you deal with a community that has a quarter of its population in jail or on parole? Imagine parents having to prepare their kids to navigate that. Imagine kids having to view parents behind bars, or vice versa.

Communities were incredibly impoverished with unemployment at depression levels. Yet everyone knew how to get by reasonably well, albeit with incredible risk. Deal drugs. For decades drugs flowed into poor communities, particularly black communities. And with drugs came guns. So when police expressed fear, that wasn't entirely make believe. There was real danger that society fed, not only with stereotypes, but with gun policies that armed drug dealers and anyone who wanted to fire away. It got so that every little dispute held the danger of a gun emerging. Laws began to allow guns in public places, even in schools.

The only sustainable solution was to raise incomes and opportunities, and eliminate the guns and drug dealing by eliminating their sources throughout society. But it wouldn't happen overnight and meanwhile the constant tension, fear, and violence from the police and incarcerations were creating an environment that seemed a hellish spiral of no return.

Eventually, lots of notable blacks, particularly popular athletes, started to protest the situation. Remember the sit downs during the national anthem? But of course lone acts weren't going to achieve much without huge participation.

Then, after the Trump-induced diversions, there was a press conference of various athletes. Their relatives were getting shot, becoming addicted, living in fear of police, and getting sick. The athletes calmly said we will not play in any city until there is an all-day meeting, organized by us, in that city, between police and community residents and leaders, with ourselves chairing, to discuss new norms and procedures for community safety - and until that kind of negotiation establishes a program which is being implemented. Even then, we will only play in the city when minority community members say they want us to. Either engineer a solution for your city, or your city will suffer bedlam as a public pariah.

Impressively, the demand was delivered without anger or recrimination. Blame wasn't the point. The athletes not only delivered their call - rapidly supported by steadily more players in diverse sports - they also went to the cities and literally marched on city halls with huge numbers of people, first mostly black, but then more and more diverse.

Of course at first there was a giant outcry against the athletes. You are rich jocks. Who are you to dictate to us? Who are you to - withhold your own labor? Protest injustice? Call for cooperation and discussion leading to a plan good for community and also police safety? The athletes were so prominent and our visibility was so high that our real agendas became visible and hysteria was muted.

How do you think it started? After all, this could have been done any time for decades?

I think that often we don't understand how hard it is to march to the beat of a different drummer, to risk hostility and isolation, and, for people like these, to withstand pressures from family, neighbors, and workmates and risk potential loss of jobs and income. Pressures against becoming active were not only will I be ridiculed by media or punished by owners, but if I do this will it matter and will I get pressured into doing even more? Am I embarking on a slippery slope I should avoid? But as to how it got going, I think the earliest cause, looking back, and thinking over the prior period, was quite ironic. When the quarterback of the San Francisco football team, Colin Kapaernik, had before RPS, refused to stand for the national anthem, the local police department threatened to not send cops to games as security.

Hold on, a few people thought. If the police can refuse to protect events because they don't like being criticized, why can't we refuse to play at events, because we don't like our families, friends, and ourselves having to live and sometimes die in fear? You think that thought for a while, you get angry enough, and, well…you may take a big step, collectively.

What did they win?

Three things relatively quickly in city after city, and then nationally. New gun control laws shut down distribution points and constrained production. Prosecution shifted from incarceration toward rehabilitation, including rapid release for non violent offenders. Regular events for whole police forces, communities, and local sports teams that included setting up sports leagues and holding picnics and then, as musicians got involved, concerts, with affordable prices and surplus revenues donated back to communities.

It was largely a bottom-up series of actions and choices that avoided politicians' oversight and control but put enormous pressure on them. And of course, it created new implications for sharing the costs of athletic events and for making social use of revenues. And then came community control of police, and new training.

And it all fed into the parallel issues of income distribution, job definition, and the like. Not to mention leading to athletes becoming huge financial supporters of activism and also reevaluating their whole approach to sports - something that the athletes certainly didn't initially have in mind, including questioning the level of remuneration, the health aspects, and so on. It turned out you could be a great athlete and be pretty damn smart, and socially effective, too. Ali's army, we started calling ourselves.

CHAPTER 20

CLASS

Mark Feynman, Lydia Luxemburg, and Juliet Berkman discuss issues of class in RPS and beyond.

Mark, what impact did new understandings of class have on RPS internally. What was the problem to address?

The uncontroversial commitment we all shared was to remove the basis of capitalist domination, their ownership of the means by which production occurs - land, equipment, factories, resources - the means of production. That much we all knew with zero reservations. Cooperating workers had to take all that property for self managed administration. The question we weren't so sure about was how to eliminate capitalist owners ruling without enshrining a new boss in place of the old one?

How could we attract, retain, and elevate working class members to control economic life, but not lose too many coordinator class members? Railing at capitalism wasn't sufficient to ensure we arrived where we desired.

Our project would entail that current doctors, lawyers, engineers, scientists and all who benefitted from holding a monopoly on empowering work, do a fair share of disempowering work for a fair income. But not all coordinator class members were quick to see the upside or discount the downside. Unless they developed solidarity with others, coordinator class members would cling to the idea they are special and deserve better conditions and income.

It was one thing to envision future institutions sustaining classlessness. It was another thing to find a path to implementing those institutions that maximized workers' rise but didn't unnecessarily polarize coordinator opposition.

We knew that once workers became attuned to the reason for their plight being not only that owners buy and sell their labor, but also that coordinator class members monopolize empowering circumstances to gain great power and income, their intuitive dislike for the dismissiveness they so often encountered from coordinator class members would escalate into profound class anger.

So that anger is on one side and on the other side, you have some coordinator class folks agreeing with the need for classlessness but still harboring a whole lot of habits and assumptions degrading workers who had suffered worse schooling and conditions, and you also have other coordinator class members - a large majority at first - who don't accept the aim at all, but instead persist in believing that their dominance is simply a fact of life due to their intrinsic talents and capacities and not anything unjust, and that trying to overcome the difference would actually hurt everyone.

This is actually not so different than navigating race and gender divides in ways that undo the oppressions but do not jettison those who had benefitted from them, but it had been so much less discussed before RPS that for all intents and purposes RPS was first traversing this class terrain and encountering these class difficulties.

With owners it was simple. Get out of our way, period. With the coordinator class, it was more complex. Yes, the goal was to end their dominance. But their work had to be spread and refined, not eliminated.

Our RPS task was to have self management inside the organization, just as we sought it outside. We needed a consistent way of dispersing organizational tasks and responsibilities to make up for prior differences in training and confidence. We needed daily participation to elevate working class members and hold coordinator class members in check, even if we sometimes had to lose some people's talents. And just like racism and sexism have structural institutional bases that must be challenged but also have long term effects on behavior and culture which if left to fester can easily bring back the old role relations, so too for coordinator classism.

Many types of movements, sometimes even labor movements (due to their bureaucracies) and certainly ecology movements, anti war movements, and more local movements, had for many decades embodied coordinator class preferences. It would appear in almost every facet - not just who made the decisions but also what TV shows people would extoll or denigrate, what sports, what foods and diets. A leftist would read the *New York Times,* even while proclaiming it was a monstrous hotbed of manipulation and lies. A worker would read the sports page of a local tabloid. Who was foolish?

Indeed, often self proclaimed progressives and radicals had classist attitudes - as in negative gun control overtones castigating workers favoring guns, or the anti McDonalds franchise campaigns that were often about keeping low income people out of neighborhoods. Even ecological movements often embodied such values and assumptions. I remember once asking an anti nuke power plant activist (and I opposed nukes too) what he thought about the clear and present damage of coal mining in generating black lung disease and other ailments for the miners, as compared to the quite healthy circumstances, for the most part, of nuclear power plant workers, and he had not only not thought about it, he couldn't even hear it.

For him the plight of miners didn't exist. His focus was plant failure that could kill people like him. He had the right position about nukes, but his tone and manner put off working people from supporting the no nukes cause, and understandably so. The same would occur in the utter unconcern from some - not all - ecological activists for people's jobs. Instead of emphasizing getting miners new jobs, coordinatorist climate fighters emphasized only shutting mines, rather than shutting them and ensuring improved life conditions for all who previously worked in them or depended on their proximity.

So what steps were taken to deal with class in RPS?

First, we adopted balanced job complexes and self management as goals for our own chapters and organization, including making up for deficits in learning and confidence on one side, and for excesses of arrogance and entitled expectation on the other side.

Second, we recruited heavily among people with working class backgrounds and instituted changes to make their participation manageable despite other pressures they faced.

Third, we self consciously had working people take the lead regarding the internal culture and forms of celebration and socializing within RPS.

Okay, but in your local RPS chapter, what did all this translate into and what difficulties had to be overcome even once you were doing the above?

Everyone in the chapter had responsibilities such as scheduling meetings, preparing snacks, cleaning up after meetings, preparing an agenda, preparing materials, recruiting, researching for possible campaigns, and, later, developing views and preparing materials for current and future campaigns. We assigned tasks in a balanced way, or even sometimes we would have those with the most experience and confidence actually do more of the less empowering tasks, to redress the prior imbalance. And self management, wasn't just about democratic votes, it also focused on the process leading up to voting. We insured that those with greater confidence and prior knowledge did not dominate discussions and that those with less confidence and prior knowledge became steadily more vocal and involved. We had an unusual rule, for example, that votes could not be taken until working class members were collectively satisfied they had fully voiced their views and been sincerely heard. In the beginning this created tension, but the emphasis on attaining real solidarity overrode backsliding.

Part of participating was people becoming knowledgable about social change and specifically about RPS views and vision. People also had to become skilled in public speaking and in making compelling arguments. So we soon realized we needed internal training and practice.

Then something remarkable became evident. The gap between a coordinator doctor, engineer, or accountant and a worker driver, assembler, or short order cook obviously included a huge difference in particular specific knowledge and to bridge that difference would require conveying knowledge of particular disciplines. But, the gap between a coordinator RPS member and a worker RPS member regarding issues of social change involved quite modest differences in knowledge, and was overwhelmingly, instead, a matter of using different terms and having more or fewer references to book learning.

We did have a big language gap as worker and coordinator members used different words. There was also a big confidence gap and also a big public speaking gap - especially if the speaking had to adhere to coordinator class norms. But it turned out that as far as actual understanding and insight, there was no large, one way gap. And as far as communicating with non members, worker members were quickly better at it than coordinator class members.

When we asked a worker to explain, challenge, or support RPS views, he or she typically had a hard time, at first, either not yet knowing the specifics or being too nervous. But when we asked a coordinator class member to do it, the presentation was mostly mechanical. The coordinator class person could reel off a bunch of words but couldn't explain their meaning for daily life situations in a convincing fashion. It was often rote, with little relevant meaning.

When working people saw and felt that, they saw a reason to chime in. And as they got more confident, they realized that they brought a level of understanding and experience that the coordinator folks lacked but covered over with fancy words. These steps therefore proved beneficial not only for worker participation, but for the substance of discussions and understanding. First hand knowledge had to be shared. Obscure words had to be jettisoned.

We also had a really demanding recruiting norm. At the outset we had fourteen people in my chapter, nine of coordinator background and aspirations, and five who were working class. So, we talked it through and agreed that RPS would ultimately need to much more closely reflect societal conditions - roughly 80% working class and 20% coordinator class. We did not want to not recruit people, yet we agreed for every new coordinator class member we would need to recruit at least two new working class members. We then also assigned recruiting disproportionately to working class members so that in time the ratio would get still better. Like everything else, this was difficult for everyone. For the coordinator class members it meant they could not just go out and recruit friends, family members, and the like, even if those individuals were strongly pro RPS. Recruiting more coordinators often had to wait. And for the working class members, it also imposed a burden. They had to do great recruiting, and they had to push their coordinator class fellow members to do so as well, but among working class people. Otherwise everything would stall.

RPS was about winning new institutions but along the way, with old institutions in place, we needed new movement focus, style, and composition. When someone would say, "But we could be bigger quicker if we ditched these silly requirements," we had to not just reject the view, but also to understand their feelings and convince them that being bigger quicker, without classlessness, was not better. Slower the right way was better.

Getting working people to join, attend meetings, and energetically relate was difficult even for those who were eager to do it. How did we provide ways for people with incredibly demanding work and home lives to participate?

The answer was that joining the organization had to reduce people's life difficulties. For example, a chapter, much less an organization, had people with diverse skills and talents. These could be directed at reducing the time working class members had to spend dealing with bureaucracies. We could collectivize and reduce the costs of certain life tasks, not least food shopping and day care. We knew scale was critical for all this, and so we proposed to RPS that when chapters grew and divided in two, the assembly of chapters take as a key priority utilizing energies and talents across all member chapters on behalf of all the members being able to better participate.

Lydia, what about class writ larger, in society?

Larger scale meant more ways to address issues, and more resources to bring to bear, but the impersonality of dealing with people you didn't know made some things harder.

Of course we fought owners for changes weakening them and challenging their control and profit making, but that was familiar and obvious. What was new was that we applied the same kinds of anti classist thinking, and even program, to society and its components as we did to RPS. We undertook campaigns for accountability in a great many workplaces but, even more important, we undertook campaigns for job redefinition to spread empowering tasks in workplaces and later in industries. This meant battling for worker power in day-to-day decision making as well as broad social policies - sometimes via union battles, sometimes via workplace councils. It also meant applying the same participation and leadership norms to national RPS campaigns and events as we were opting for in chapter-based campaigns and events.

Perhaps the largest example was the massive campaign RPS undertook for a shorter work day and work week. We knew we had to fight for working class, not coordinator class, needs. So the campaign began around minimum wage increases. Workers in particular industries - in this case it was at Walmart and Amazon and a few other mass suppliers - began to agitate for more time off. This was initially partly about vacation and partly about forced overtime, but relatively quickly matured into more general demands for a thirty hour work week.

Seeking a shorter work week had to mean hourly wages had to go up so total income didn't drop, which meant an hourly wage increase by one third. If you were earning $15 an hour earlier, then after a switch to a 30 hour work week you would be earning $20 an hour so your total income of $600 a week would not change.

But what if you were earning $60 an hour before or $150 an hour or more before. Should you now earn $80 an hour, after, or $200 an hour or more after? Workers decided if your income was over $70,000 per year, why not have the battle for a shorter work week bring things more into line?

So now the demand was that everyone would work 30 instead of 40 hours a week. Everyone would then receive an hourly pay increase of at most one third up to their earning $70,000 a year but would get no increase beyond that.

The next question was how would owners pay more to their lower income employees for fewer hours? By earning less profit, of course. But what if, to avoid losses, owners imposed overtime to raise output to try to make up for new costs? Okay, let's allow overtime, but make it always optional, not forced, and have overtime pay being not time and a half, but triple time.

There was another aspect. Consider doctors in a hospital. After the change the owners would have them working thirty hour weeks and would have to pay triple time to get more labor from them. Hospitals needed labor, as did society. What would happen?

The answer was either the owners would pay the higher rate, or they would have to redefine work to get more doctor-like contributions out of other employees, mainly nurses - and even start to pressure the school system to produce more doctors. These trends all positively impacted class relations. And this wasn't just about hospitals, it affected the whole economy.

Juliet, did challenging class division succeed? What was the turning point?

I think it all worked incredibly well when you consider it was challenging hundreds of years of uninterrupted class division and regimentation, and it was doing so not in a comparable number of centuries but in just a few decades while also confronting and winning gains against owners. I doubt there was only one turning point - but I will offer up a possibility, or two, actually.

The first was when almost all Amazon workers sat down at their posts and declared that they would not move and would not allow anyone else to take their places, and would not cease their sit down strike until

Amazon changed its policies in accord with their demands. That was monumental. I can still remember hearing reports of it, seeing videos on the news, and going there and lending my support. It was my most exciting moment up to that time.

How did people react?

At first, people throughout the country were flabbergasted. These workers, after all, were effectively invisible beyond Amazon's doors. How many were there? It turns out there were almost 300,000. We had bought our books and goods of all kinds from Amazon by simply clicking a link. There appeared to be no humans involved. We had no awareness of 300,000 people working in harsh conditions for long hours at low pay.

After just a few days it became clear this was a massive escalation of militance and innovation in labor activism. Families and friends brought food and tents so the Amazon workers could make good on their threat to stay until victory. Students from nearby campuses turned out in force to bring needed supplies and stand outside, providing a buffer against police intervention. Everyone was watching, and then came the turning point.

The owners said clean this up to the police. And first attempts to do so were made, but the workers said no. You come in these warehouses you won't go back out again with any of us. We will die first. The warehouses will be ravaged, and you will suffer in the chaos, as well. That was a hell of a message.

At the same time, tens of thousands of supporters rallied outside. We pledged to ward off attempts at violent suppression. The spirit was incredible. Here we were, in the streets, ready to be bashed mercilessly, but hellbent on staying. Like the workers inside, we were set to remain.

With such an atmosphere of resistance and solidarity emanating from Amazon workers, what could the owners and the police do? It became clear to Amazon, to the police, and to everyone else, that force would breed more resistance. And right there a lot of people learned that the way to prevent the state, or scabs, or private police, or anyone else from using force to suppress dissent was to create a situation where the use of force would do more damage to the interests of those employing it than would not using force. And it became clear, as well, that what could accomplish that, was having so much support and so much willingness to not give in, that forceful intervention would totally backfire.

We learned not only about warding off repression, but also about the ins and outs of collectivity and struggle. Mutual aid was essential. It came from people surrounding the sit ins, from families, and then even from local restaurants providing food, and from farmers. Young lawyers and doctors volunteered. Off duty cops surreptitiously visited, talked, and learned, and then started visiting openly.

Support took countless forms including support strikes spreading outward in unity. Every day people were learning all across the country from what they were seeing and hearing about the events. And after just a week, UPS workers stopped delivering, and then Fed Ex workers did too, and by that point, society was reeling, and the companies had to give in. Bam. New work hours. Bam. New payment schemes. And then, as the campaign spread and workers in other firms raised similar demands, everyone knew what came next.

Say no to our demands, and we will sit in our workplaces, and you will lose. Bring on the cops, smash us, and we will come right back. Lie about us all you want, the days of people believing you are over. Issue court orders and injunctions, and we will rip them up and add to our demands that there be no prosecutions. Get even tougher, and watch chaos collapse your workplaces while causing our support to grow greater.

Owners were hog tied. Police felt officially responsible to follow orders, but police wanted normalized work hours, too. And in response to that, another lesson emerged. Instead of regarding police as spawns from hell, we should save that category for their bosses and the owners above. We should see rank and file police as citizens, as workers. We should realize how they are like us. And as we managed to do that - even in the face of their often bludgeoning us - we undertook to reach out and talk with them, meet with them, and even rally them.

Do you remember when children of the workers plus their friends started pushing for local schools to visit the sites and provide support. That was another image unbearable to the authorities they could not suppress. For owners, capitulation became the only solution.

A second but related turning point in class conflict, I think, was a change in underlying ideas, assumptions, and habits bearing on coordinator/worker relations. This was most evident in a campaign at Harvard medical school, of all places. There had been a campaign on campus to raise the wages of Harvard's low income kitchen and custodial workers. Initially this was undertaken by workers with some undergraduate student allies, but then became a broader movement. The students were, in many cases, RPS-influenced or RPS members, and they joined the campaign to improve the conditions of workers while also trying to educate the whole campus about what incomes and class relations really ought to be.

While demands sought specific wage increases, as they had a few years earlier in a similar struggle, this time the rhetoric altered and began asking why those who clean classrooms should earn less than those who stand in front of them comfortably talking to students. And sure enough, after who knows how many dorm and classroom discussions plus work stoppages, teach ins, and repressive administration threats and actions, a group of med students, some in RPS, started to raise a ruckus about admissions policies, training methods, and the culture of the profession they were supposed to enter.

From its start among medical students at Harvard and a few other sites there exploded into visibility groups like Doctors for the People, Lawyers for the People, Accountants for the People, Engineers, Architects, and Faculty for the People, and so on. Every case had some operational flaws and many residual bad habits operating obstructively, and every case encountered intense resistance from folks not wanting such radical change, but the mood was sincerely about redefining the relations between each profession and the population, and even about redefining the responsibility of the profession, including its tasks, remuneration, and social responsibilities. For many in the coordinator class service and not self rose from rhetoric to reality.

So I think these two examples, both fighting owners but the latter also addressing the distribution of empowering work, including within their own ranks, were "turning points." We would not only attenuate class rule, we would eliminate all forms of class division.

CHAPTER 21

LEADERSHIP, PACE, SOLIDARITY

Robin Kunstler, Celia Curie, and Noam Carmichael, leadership, pace, and solidarity.

Robin, one of the contentious issues in RPS has been the question of leadership. As RPS's first Shadow Supreme Court Justice, you likely have views on this. Why was it contentious?

In most complex and especially new endeavors someone must go first. Others see their example, hear it, assess it, and if they follow suit, there has been an act of leadership. No one thinks that is bad per se.

Rosa Parks not going to the back of the bus was not bad. Bernie Sanders initiating a campaign for President was not bad. Your neighbor being first in the community to call a meeting about a dangerous intersection needing a new stoplight is not bad.

Indeed, everyone agrees that that aspect of leadership is a good and inevitable fact of life. We are not a hive species that has one mind which always operates in unison. It is good when someone provides exemplary behavior or ideas which resonate with others.

What is bad is when someone who goes first and provides leadership accrues excessive power and wealth and becomes personally distorted.

Consider the becoming perverse problem first. You provide leadership, how do you view your own act? Let's say you often have ideas or undertake steps that others later emulate. Do you consider yourself superior and more important? Do you ignore other people's views? Do you think only your views matter?

This is ego inflation. It distorts personality and choices. It slides into elitism. It evidences the oft repeated but rarely understood claim that power corrupts and absolute power corrupts absolutely.

Next, consider the wealth and power problem. That leadership garners praise and respect is appropriate, but if the praise and respect get parlayed into control over positions of influence, and then that increased influence yields power and wealth, that is inappropriate. Arriving at a worthy idea or practice before others shouldn't convey increased income or a greater say in outcomes. Even worse, it should not create conditions for a repeat performance, and another, leading to entrenched power and wealth.

What were views emerged as the best solution to avoid the pitfalls of leadership?

The RPS solution on the personal side was to try to change the self perception that goes with leadership. In everyone's mind the definition of providing leadership had to become to step out first in ideas or behavior in ways that welcomed others to do the same. We realized the best leader causes others to lead too. Positive leadership precedes others but elevates them. Positive leadership recognizes, reiterates, and never forgets that to lead means to provide without taking, to give without receiving.

We wanted self management. We wanted social roles that did not aggrandize anyone on the basis of his or her having had good ideas or having done something admirable. But we had to escape a vicious circle. Until new institutions were firmly in place, acts of leadership tended to reinstall past relations. But attaining new institutions required acts of leadership.

One answer to that seeming Catch-22 was to curtail leadership recurring. In other words, if someone had some combination of attributes that caused that person to repeatedly arrive at good ideas or good choices earlier than others, to avoid the person's inexorable elevation we could temporarily prevent him or her being able to continually exert leadership. We would lose some good contributions from that person, but we would prevent that person's personal trajectory from interfering with still more important gains.

The second answer was to get all the benefits such a person can provide, but remain diligent about preventing the person from becoming elitist and entrenching their influence.

Where did you come down in this dispute?

I thought both sides were right and we needed a judicious mix. We should not let one person's creativity, innovation, courage, or whatever it might be, crowd out the possibility of others rising in their creativity but we should also try to find ways to get as much good as possible from everyone.

I once worked with a group of twenty people. Three of them continually jumped ahead toward seeing good solutions for each issue that arose. Everyone else was crowded out from contributing that kind of leadership by the three people's speed. Each time the three people excelled, they became more confident and more practiced at it. Others became acclimated to hearing answers and not providing them. Entrenchment occurred.

As we began to understand the dynamic we knew we would have to reign in the folks who were recurrently leading so that others might fill the space. Of course those early leaders, if they had adopted the mindset that true leadership firstly elevates others, would not mind and would even welcome the restraint - but even if they did not, the steps would need to be taken.

I should say, this is of course delicate. It had to be done sensitively to increase both overall creativity and initiative and at the same time approach classlessness. But we did notice one thing relevant to how to proceed.

Take that twenty person group, again. Suppose mainly two are leading, let's say it is Joe and Jill. We suggest that they hang back, be quiet, wait on others to arrive at the leading insight. An argument ensues and Joe and Jill protest that they would be hampered, even oppressed, by this choice.

This happened often and similarities appeared. First, it was for those other than Joe and Jill to assess the value of Joe and Jill's contributions, not for Joe and Jill to do so. Perhaps they weren't as excellent as they thought. Second, Joe and Jill were not being hampered, restrained, or even repressed. They were being told, hold on, use your insight, creativity, and courage, to mentor, train, and spur on others. Lead by creating more leadership. Once people became good at this, many of the dangers associated with diversifying leadership dissipated.

Celia, another issue that recurs often is what is the appropriate pace of change. How have you understood that?

In some ways it is the same issue. Do we want to advance as much as possible, as fast as possible, and then bring along as many other people as possible? Or do we want to elicit the broadest possible advance, and move forward together as much as possible?

Let me give you an example that perhaps highlights the issues. When there was a growing labor movement in Cleveland seeking a higher minimum wage, better conditions, and a shorter work week well before efforts attained similar strength elsewhere in the country, Cleveland's workers came up against this issue. Some said, "Let's just go all out. Let's occupy factories, disrupt downtown. Fight to win. We won't have enough support to prevent national guard repression, nor to sustain ourselves, and we will have to back down. But the rest of the country will see our uprising. Our aggressiveness will inspire others. It will spread. We won't win now, but by moving fast we will contribute greatly to winning later."

Others said, "Wait a minute. First, others in the country will see us losing. Is that going to inspire them to emulate us? If we follow that path, after we get repressed and lose, what will we have achieved? We will have taken our growing movement and trashed it. Instead, why not keep building and send out emissaries to other towns and cities to explain how we have proceeded and how they can do likewise, and how, if we all do, we will all together win?

"Instead of now occupying factories and causing repression and losing, why not keep on building our chapters in the factories, and propose how we would operate the factories, and support counter institutions until we have sufficient support here in Cleveland to take them over? Faster pace that leads backward is not better than slower pace that leads forward."

RPS emphasized trying different approaches and keeping them all operational, which often allowed mutual compromise. Sometimes you could partly try fast pace, partly try slower pace, test each, and then put more effort into whatever worked better. This was ideal when people did not want to be able to brag about being right or to win an argument, but wanted to follow the best path whatever it turned out to be.

Can you give some instances of all these possibilities?

Cleveland took the patient approach. Boston had a similar choice, but it was earlier and more about campus activism. There are lots of schools around Boston and the student movement grew there earlier than in most of the rest of the country. Should the students go as quick as they could, escalating and getting repressed before there was mass support, to spur others on? Or should they go slower, develop more of a base, less visibly to others, but more sustained? And in fact they did find a way to try both approaches, at least to a degree.

Most of the campuses embarked on a slower approach of building organizations and reaching out to local communities but at the same time, MIT and Boston University had massive occupations and confrontations. The mix turned out well. Students on other campuses supported the militant events, but simultaneously urged those involved to relate to the longer-term efforts. The militant events caught the eyes of the nation, as intended, but the parallel endeavors also got visibility and were the lasting legacy.

Another example was the way many demonstrations adopted a multi-tactic approach. A massive march would be followed by a big civil disobedience event. Each would give strength and add meaning to the other. But, one could participate however one preferred, rather than either be involved or not. Strikes and boycotts developed diverse ways of relating, as did big teach-ins and accompanying demonstrations or sit-ins.

Could you recount an event or situation during the rise of RPS that was particularly important or inspiring for you?

I was moved beyond measure by two events in particular, the hotel and motel occupations of 2030 and the national prisoners strike of 2034.

You know, one feeling about prisoners is, well, they are captured. There is not much point organizing folks who have already been taken away. But another feeling - more humane, but also more strategic - is that these are victims of injustice. They are part of why we revolt. They are part of who revolts. It takes effort and clarity to see it, and the prisoners' campaign brought that.

It was an accident of circumstance that I happened to be visiting one of the prisons with an artistic show while it was occupied. There was no way to leave, and I like to think I would not have left even if I could have, but I don't know. The fear of a re-run of Attica - a long past site of prison struggle and massacre - was palpable, and I was certainly scared. But the scale of external support, and the wavering by the guards, precluded anything like that. Still, it felt imminent, and yet the prisoners carried on. Their courage was incredible.

And the housing battles, they were just so out of the box, and at the same time so perfect at revealing the inane priorities of profit seeking and market competition that they touched me very deeply.

Noam, another area of potentially serious differences had to do with issues of solidarity and their implications for being true to one's views. Can you tell us the form of this issue?

Showing solidarity means acting in accord with the interests of others, and supporting others in their pursuits. Enjoying autonomy means functioning without intrusion from without. Clearly you shouldn't always support but nor should you always ignore others' wishes. So the question was, what mindset and choices have the best chance of coming up with a desirable mix.

Consider a movement against racism or sexism. It certainly doesn't want to be subject to the will of racists/sexists, nor even to the will of well-meaning people in the dominant community who are, however, insufficiently aware of the dynamics of racism/sexism. It wants to be more autonomous than that. It wants to explore its own views, pursue its own agenda, learn from its own mistakes, and benefit from its own insights.

Over fifty years before RPS was born this wisdom was encapsulated in the idea of what was called the autonomous women's movement, including efforts like Bread and Roses in Massachusetts and various anti racist efforts beginning with what was called Black Power and including groups like the Black Panthers and the Latin Young Lords.

Women and Blacks were tired of men or whites determining their agendas. They were even tired of having to constantly argue with men or whites, rather than developing as they saw fit without having to continually expend excessive time and energy dealing with male or white complaints. And for those reasons the idea of autonomy arose for the women's movement and the Black power movement, meaning they operated under their own control and pretty much unconnected to other aggregations of non female, non black people.

That was fine, in theory, but it had a potential operational problem. Such a movement could lose a lot of solidarity from others. So, some would say, why diminish our overall power with this autonomy stuff? And others would say, why subject ourselves to endless hassle with folks who are trying to keep us down, or even with sincere folks who don't understand our situation?

So, what was the RPS solution?

The thinking went like this: we often. need autonomy but also need solidarity. How can we have both? We clearly needed to develop cross constituency ties of a new form.

One familiar kind of cross constituency tie was called a coalition. We could have a massive coalition containing women's organizations, anti racist organizations, and so on, which all align about some particular concern, for example ending a war. Back in the height of Sixties, two huge anti war coalitions organized around slightly different approaches to ending the war in Vietnam. Each had unity only regarding the war.

A coalition wouldn't prevent a women's organization from operating autonomously, and it would allow a degree of solidarity around whatever was the unifying issue of the coalition. The problem was that the solidarity was too limited. Typically, it was about one thing, such as ending a war. The component organizations and movements didn't enjoy the benefits of solidarity from other coalition members for their own agendas, nor did they offer solidarity to other members for anything beyond the unifying coalition focus. A coalition accomplished something, but not enough. This was true over and over, including with climate activism coalitions around the time RPS first developed.

RPS did not want to replicate the Sixties or any other period so we greatly extended the logic of autonomy plus solidarity. What if we worked together on what we might call our greatest common sum agenda? This was different, and initially even seemed outlandish.

The idea was that various groups and projects should join into a "bloc." Each group and project would retain its autonomy to pursue its own specific program as it decided. But, each group and project would also pledge to support the programs the other bloc members proposed.

The agenda of the bloc would be the sum of all the agendas of its component organizations, movements, and projects. Each part of the agenda would come from the autonomous leadership of one or another partner in the bloc, but everyone would adopt it all. Everyone would receive and give solidarity, even while everyone retained autonomy regarding its agenda.

Did it work?

It was more subtle than it may sound. Suppose we take the women's movement discussed earlier. It has a program, agenda, and style of operations oriented primarily around feminist activism against sexism. If it joins a bloc with others, then its program becomes one part of the program of the whole bloc. It will receive support from the other members. Reciprocally, as a member, it will support others regarding their programs. Two complexities made this hard. First, to join an organization that was in a bloc, I had to decide not only that I liked the organization, but that I liked the bloc, as well. Organizations worried this would reduce their membership.

Second, if a bloc included two organizations with contradictory programs, the overall bloc program would have to contain both aspects, even though contradictory, and the members would have to support each other. At first that seemed ludicrous, yet it wasn't.

If the overall purpose of the bloc was shared - and in the case of RPS, the purpose was winning a new society with various agreed features - then the contradictory program components could each be seen as a possibility that should be explored to see what works. If one proved better, then, in time, it would be chosen. While the choice was uncertain and unresolved, having the two contrary aspects both in play would elevate diversity, a key RPS value.

As soon as groups with a particular agenda began reaping the benefits of solidarity from others and, in turn, began celebrating helping others, the confusion began to dissipate. So in practice, it has worked really well.

The idea for having a bloc resulted first from trying to improve on coalitions, and second from trying to embody in the movement what should become approaches of society writ large, once society was transformed.

> *Noam, before moving on, could you tell us, do you think we will win? When will we have won? And, in just a few last words, what is one lesson from this whole period that strikes you as particularly critical?*

I think we won when we completed our second convention. There was still plenty to do, but since then, the wind is now at our back, pushing us forward. I suppose our project will end when we no longer need to imagine victory. Finally, a lesson that was critical for me has been recognizing that solidarity requires and breeds security and confidence but security and confidence permit and sustain solidarity.

CHAPTER 22

REFORMS, REVOLUTION, VIOLENCE

Lydia Luxemburg, Andrej Goldman, Peter Cabral, and Juliet Berkman discuss reforms, revolution, and violence.

Lydia, the question of seeking reform or revolution has been contentious among leftists as long as there has been a left, including at the outset of RPS. First, what was the debate?

The debate was, are seeking reforms and seeking revolution mutually exclusive, or are they mutually beneficial?

One side said, since RPS is committed to fundamentally transforming society's defining institutions it should reject seeking reforms such as increasing the minimum wage, affirmative action, or taxing fossil fuel use because reforms improve some conditions but don't alter the underlying institutions. For example, winning a higher minimum wage leaves the market and corporate power in place to reverse our gains as soon as they can. Even beneficial reforms are unstable, because pressures from existing institutions, in time, either reverse them or rearrange circumstances so that while the formal changes persist, the benefits they were meant to convey are reduced or eliminated by offsetting deficits. For instance, winning a wage increase is offset by rising prices. Fines for pollution are offset by increasing other pollution or passing on the fees to others.

Those opposing reforms argued that anything short of revolution wins gains that disappear and enforces the status quo by assuming its continuation.

Proponents of reforms argued that the benefits from reforms, like a higher minimum wage or pollution limits, are real and can be substantial for the people involved. Dismissing people's efforts to win such changes for being less than seeking revolution and to not support, or even denigrate such efforts, is callous.

Proponents of reforms added that while many people dismiss fighting for reforms in the abstract, no one would tell workers seeking a higher minimum wage, or activists trying to end a war, that they are nothing but system supporters and should stop their misguided endeavors. Likewise, people do not typically move from uninvolved to revolutionary in one giant leap. It is the experience of fighting for reforms that raises consciousness, confidence, and skills to sustain longer-term commitments.

Andrej, what has been the RPS solution?

The RPS attitude was, "why not fight for reforms in non-reformist ways?" We should fight for reforms using language that explains our ultimate motives, aims, and methods and in ways that build lasting organization. We should ensure that upon winning a reform as many people as possible desire further gains and are in better position to win them.

In sum, RPS said we should fight for winnable gains now in ways that enhance people's desire to win greater gains later, that improve people's organizational means to win greater gains later, and that create lasting structures to contribute to a trajectory of change leading toward new institutions.

And the key to this view becoming predominant was for people who favored transforming society to recognize that wanting immediate modest changes didn't negate seeking long-run fundamental change.

Can you provide an example of people following this logic?

The national campaign for a higher minimum wage as well as local industry campaigns for wage innovations each sought to win an immediate demand, but also argued for full equitable income for duration, intensity, and onerousness of socially valued labor. They explained their ethics, logic, and implications. They emphasized that their immediate goal was not an end but a step toward larger gains. And it was the same for all kinds of pollution-related efforts to get cleaner and safer industrial practices, while also addressing long-term issues of structure, and even, of markets and preferred participatory planning.

Peter, another issue was whether or not to use violence in seeking change. Can you explain the contending views?

On one side people said overcoming our existing system will encounter elites defending their advantages so unless we are prepared to overcome violent repression with greater violence in reply, we will ultimately be crushed. Therefore, we have to become both psychologically and materially capable of deploying violence. Since that won't happen overnight or automatically, preparedness requires our possessing the tools that violence needs and becoming adept and confident using them.

We have to pursue our organizing and winning of reforms and our building of institutions in ways that make us better able to violently beat back repression, since otherwise we will ultimately succumb to repression no matter how good we are at our other activities. I should admit, this was my view at the outset.

On the other side, people replied that the existing system could not be overcome through violence. The left could not beat the military. It could not match the training, mindset, and tools of state repression. Futile attempts to do so would make military agencies more aggressive even while distorting our own values. Breaking people out of jail wasn't a solution for draconian jailing but a sure way to enlarge it. Bombing media outlets or mimicking their manipulativeness wasn't a solution to their manipulations, but a sure way to enhance them.

If we escalated from warding off blows at rallies with our arms to using sticks or shields, they would hit us with weapons that break sticks and shields. If we escalated to throwing rocks or molotov cocktails, they would use guns. If we picked up guns, they would use tanks. Violence was and always would be their terrain. Unless we could find a way to win that did not rely on violence, we would lose. We had to organize, win reforms, and build alternative institutions in ways that made us steadily better able to deploy non violent struggle.

Our solution to state violence was to create contexts where using violence against dissent only produced more dissent. The solution to jailing protestors was to create a context where jailing protestors produced more protest, including inside jails and among jail keepers. The solution to media machinations was our own growing media and our movements within mainstream media, as well as an enlightened public that elite lies couldn't lead astray.

The debate wasn't about a distant crunch time battle. If the path to a new society ultimately required sufficient violence to overcome the police and military, then getting ready for that was essential and there was no time like the present. But if the path to a new society had to avoid violence, then developing non violent discipline and methods as well as contexts in which repressive violence only intensified dissent was essential and there was no time like the present.

What was the RPS outcome that permitted people to operate well together?

This dispute could not end in a simple compromise. For one side violence was necessary, and because they deemed it necessary, they also typically deemed it positive - even virtuous. For the other side violence was immoral and destructive of effective left mindsets and prospects.

That violence was terrain the state dominated and would inexorably win was, I came to agree, irrefutable unless one felt, wait, if we let that view prevail then we will not prepare to be violent, and we will without question lose, so we must reject that observation despite its likely validity. I realized eventually that that was my own initial inconsistent mindset. I was focused on police violence. I took it for granted as inevitable. I took fighting back for granted as well. It seemed cowardly to say it was suicidal. Pointing at police preparedness, arms, and mindset in contrast to ours didn't convince me otherwise, though it should have. And there were a lot of folks like me. Our reaction to violence, coercion, and lies was to think we must fight back on the same terms or lose.

For those arguing against a positive place for violence to reach those favoring violence, like myself, they had to convince us non violence could win. And that was the RPS approach when it claimed that while fighting with the state on the field of violence was suicidal, creating conditions in which the state could not deploy violence without suffering more than if they did not employ violence, could win. And that became RPS logic.

The task regarding violence was to reduce the state's ability to deploy it, either directly by measures won against the state that limited its options - such as demilitarizing police and winning civilian community control over police or even gaining support by organizing among the police - or indirectly by creating conditions wherein violent repression would do more to aid and enlarge activism than it would do to repress and diminish activism.

You mention exceptions - what was that about?

Consider a strike. Suppose strike breakers prepare to bully their way through your picket line. Locking arms against that, and swinging back at assaults, would be an example of violence that RPS felt was warranted and potentially effective. Similarly, suppose we occupied some building and created a blockade of supporters to keep cops or others from entering. Or at times we might even burn down some hated target, if conditions were right for it. But these kinds of acts weren't undertaken chaotically but methodically. They required clear rationales and careful steps. Events, projects, and actions had to continually enlarge support for dissent, and not diminish it. This meant attracting and holding allies and also developing and preserving effective, sustainable mindsets and methods.

Was there a turning point where you felt this battle was won?

It was official policy starting with the second convention, so I guess you might say it was won then. But, in fact, well after that there were plenty of RPS folks who felt great internal pressure to fight violence with violence and who kept making the case to do so, with some even breaking ranks at times to do it, though this always yielded predicted losses. I think the perspective finally fully collapsed when street gangs in various communities began to undertake political commitments and adopted two surprising policies.

First, they turned in their guns and began to support civilian control of police. These weren't kids with clubs or bricks. They were street-schooled fighters renouncing gun violence they had long lived with. It was powerful.

And, second, and perhaps even more critical, the same gangs began urging their members to apply for jobs within the police, and not long after, RPS acknowledged that choice as a highly respected activist "career path". The idea was simple. Those fit to do so would join the police and the military and begin transforming them from within. We had all heard about the incredible success of anti war activists doing this with the army so many decades earlier during the Vietnam war, and in that light it was surprising how long it took to see the obvious relevance to our own time.

Of course, not just anyone could join the police and maintain a steadfast commitment to social activism, but for those who could - emotionally and physically - it was clearly a far more effective and courageous choice than going to a sports shop, buying a shotgun, and practicing shooting tin cans to prepare for confrontations which would, if they ever came, end in sad defeat.

Another key turning point was earlier when football in the U.S. became embroiled in controversy about the damage the sport did to the athletes, particularly via concussions. When the anthem protests began, largely about police violence, a new dimension was added. And then there was controversy about violence against women by players. Pile on Trump's misogyny and the situation intensified.

Suddenly you had very mainstream people all over society discussing violence, and particularly violence against women. Some sports shows on radio even had commentators blasting the NFL not only for its hypocrisies and violence, but even for its connection to the military and police, and for its fostering an alcohol-permeated culture with its ads.

It isn't always easy to calculate the impact of a reform struggle. Did it win anything at all? What lasting impact did it have on people's views? And mostly did it establish grounds upon which to win more. But the turmoil around sports related violence is perhaps a good example, though likely largely inadvertent, of the positive possibilities.

The percolating impact on the future of sport and national attitudes against misogyny went deep and broad. When a sport show suggests, as some did, that fans should perhaps boycott watching football until there were changes, or that teams should be forced to stop their alcohol commercials, seeds are being laid regarding what is possible and worthy regarding violence. I think such seeds contributed to RPS emerging. In contrast, demands to abolish football with threats of violence or made disdainfully of more limited reforms to protect the health of players or to reduce and eliminate sexist violations off field, would have had no broader ramifications, and would have won nothing. But more limited calls coming from players, fans, sports writers, and on air announcers, sparked sports audiences and participants toward new awareness, won some gains that mattered, and laid seeds to win more. I think the emerging anti violence mentality was a significant factor influencing RPS attitudes and choices and the continuing sports related activism by participants and fans alike. And of course subsequent rejection of thee Trump-inspired fascistic white supremacist violence followed and further matured the insights.

Couple all that with the observation, borne out too often to ignore, that movements adopting violent methods would feed residual macho misogyny and authoritarian inclinations in themselves so much as to distort their own culture and exclude major constituencies from participating, and the case against movement violence was complete. The prominent role of military veterans was also critical. After all, they experienced what others were only guessing at.

Juliet, as a pacifist, I wonder if you have felt fully satisfied by the RPS approach to violence.

I believe in non violence as a principle, with no caveats. But I also understand that there is a gargantuan difference between violence to enforce domination and extract advantage, and violence in self defense to ward off oppression. That is why I have no trouble respecting and working with people who have far more violence-imbued beliefs than RPS.

I feel zero hostility toward strikers blocking scabs, even though I wouldn't do it or recommend it. And I would extend that to a population violently defending against invasion, even though, again, I think such choices are ultimately counter productive.

Living in a world bequeathed by the past that has much that is human and beautiful, but also much that is vile and ugly is not easy. I think RPS has hammered out a politically, socially, strategically, and tactically wise stance. In fact, being honest, given the world we live in, I think it is probably a wiser stance than if RPS were to say no violence, period.

Is there a contradiction between my personal credo and my organizational credo? Perhaps, but sometimes in horrible circumstances what would be both ethical and sound in more desirable circumstances simply no longer works - at least until desirable circumstances are achieved.

I have taken as a model in these matters David Dellinger, who was a pacifist but very militant and open-minded activist in the 1960s. His example of being a pacifist and yet supporting the Black Panther Party, of being a pacifist and yet supporting the Vietnamese fighting against the

U.S. invasion, inspired me greatly especially as I understood it steadily more over the years. I wish more people knew of his courageous acts and views. Indeed, it is a very sad commentary that Dillinger isn't a celebrated figure of American history. But I imagine he will be, as RPS unfolds in the years ahead and resurrects the best of our past.

RPS is not pacifist in the full ethical sense that I favor. Its anti-violence owes overwhelmingly to believing violence is suicidal for trying to win a better society. I think RPS is right about that but I also have this overarching moral pressure that I feel, though I admit that for history and for humanity it is probably just as well that RPS doesn't feel that overarching pressure quite as strongly as I do.

Juliet, I have one last last question, please. Do you think we will win? When will we have won? And, in just a few last words, what is one lesson from this whole period that strikes you as particularly critical?

Twenty years ago I hoped we would win. Now, I know we will. Don't you? Just yesterday, my niece asked me when it will be over. We happened to be in my kitchen and looking around I said when top and bottom refer only to shelves, not to people. She understood, and smiled.

Finally, I think the lesson I have perhaps learned most profoundly is that all places and all. times have this much in common, until humans share dignity and justice, struggle will continue.

CHAPTER 23

ELECTIONS

Mayor Bill Hampton, Celia Curie, Lydia Luxemburg, Bertrand Dellinger, and Malcolm King discuss electoral participation.

Bill, what have your various electoral campaigns and holding office as a Mayor in New York taught you about the pitfalls and benefits of elections and even electoral office?

Personal desires aside, someone seeking to renovate society runs for office for one or more of three reasons:

1. To win and use the power of the office for change.
2. To educate in order to improve prospects for winning change.
3. To pressure other candidates and officials in positive ways.

Running for office can provide massive public access for communications and also open many paths for instituting changes. Malcolm's Senate campaigns in Ohio, for example, Celia's Governor Campaigns in California, and also my Mayoral campaigns in New York, among many others, did quite a lot to help RPS gain visibility and to help its ideas gain acceptance.

In the case of a Senator, unlike an executive position, Malcolm couldn't enact changes himself, but he could sponsor bills and use his visibility to support and aid movements. Celia and I could do similar work but also implement programs.

What about the debits?

These are more subtle, but very important. And there are many.

For example, it is easy to get caught up in the tallying aspect of elections and to lose track of larger organizing issues and possibilities. This can even happen to excellent left candidates who start with an overarching agenda they see the election as but a part of, if, later, under the pressure of campaigning, they start to have eyes only for winning votes. It can happen to people even while they are decrying the same tendency as it has affected other people.

A second deadly dynamic is for a candidate to become too self-enamored and, again, lose track of larger forces at play. This can cause a candidate to feel everyone should bow to his or her will and advisors and campaign workers must bend their words to suit what the candidate wants to hear rather than to convey accurate assessments. As the candidate starts to feel more self important, aides start to feel a junior version of the same thing. They then function more to further their own brand, or the candidate's, than to pursue broader agendas. Sometimes this dynamic can have more benign causes, as when people around a candidate try to maintain access only to be in position to have a good effect - yet the sought good effects are sacrificed, in practice, to maintaining the access.

Suppose you are in a group of ten who have the ear of a candidate who is personally reeling a bit, morally and politically, under all the pressures and getting very pushy in the group of ten, chairing every session, scowling at unwanted news, praising preferred news, and finally kicking someone out of the inner circle for bearing bad news or being critical.

You are in the circle. You feel you should try to reverse the trend, but you know you will lose your inner circle access if you go too far so you curb your inclinations out of a perfectly sensible desire to be in position to have a positive effect at all. Your motivations are sincere, yet the result is the same as if they were self serving. The candidate drifts toward elitism and the inner circle slides into abetting the candidate's dissolution.

The fixation causing such trends need not be about vote tallying or expanding the candidate's authority, it could be about money. Elections in the U.S. are expensive and an incredible percentage of the effort expended in any election turns out to be pursuing donations. You can imagine what that can lead to when those delivering the bigger dollars have their own agendas. Candidates or officials wind up bought off. Indeed, even when the fundraising is from a base of supporters making small donations, the perpetual need to write letters and make effective appeals for money is overwhelming and can lead to devolution of the benefits of running.

All in all I think RPS has approached elections wisely. We have celebrated excellent candidates running, educating, winning, and using office. Our members have assisted, but as an organization we have avoided taking any formal part in the electoral process. We have organizationally focused on grassroots organizing, movement building, and pressuring elites, including elected politicians, including from RPS, to make desired changes.

Often many RPS members worked hard on a campaign, including mine, but the organization never collectively and officially engaged and thus never got caught up in the dynamics. Soon, I think we will be in position to have an RPS member as President, where everyone knows just exactly what they are getting. But even in that case, while I would imagine virtually every RPS member will substantially aid the campaign with incredible outlays of time and effort, I think the organization as a collective entity will steer clear.

But what about the problem of focusing on electing one person, and missing that a single person is effectively powerless?

I think we should recognize that an electoral approach, like any other approach, requires numbers to be most effective, but that doesn't imply that a lone victory is worthless. Rather, it says that the more folks we have in office and the more those folks have grass roots connections, the better.

Suppose we go back to the time of Sanders' attempt to become President. What if he had gotten the Democratic Party nomination and beaten Trump? Some suggested that it would make no difference because Sanders was dishonest and insincere. Some said his agenda wasn't maximal and nothing short of maximal matters. But many had more sensible and subtle concerns that echoed what Sanders himself warned.

If Sanders had won, he would have been President, yes, but nearly all the governors, Senators, Congresspeople, police chiefs and officers, and military command would still have been wedded to existing social relations. So, said these analysts, Sanders could have done nothing fundamental. Now, if, like Sanders, they had said that to accomplish much he would need massive popular support, that would have been true. With such support, even if he built lots of it while in office, of course he could have improved the life conditions of diverse constituencies in the present while also warding off continuing slides toward hell by combatting global warming. He could have worked to create more grassroots support, awareness, and commitment and to galvanize that into campaigns for critical reforms immediately helping people and paving the way for further gains. He could have sped up RPS.

Consider Hugo Chavez years earlier winning the Presidency in Venezuela. It is not an exact analogy, but not too far off for the point we are discussing. He had Miraflores, Venezuela's White House, but he had no governors, a few mayors out of hundreds, and few legislators and nearly no local police. And yet he did a ton, which could have gone much further but for various mistakes, I believe, not least failing to organize among opposition constituencies, as well as due to outside factors.

The point is, a sensible approach to electoral work should focus on a wide array of offices: many local, fewer statewide, and fewer still national - just as we have been doing for the past twenty years. But if you manage to win the more encompassing positions and you don't succumb to the various pitfalls of the process, then holding office can be very helpful indeed.

Bill, can I ask, please, do you think we will win? When will we have won? And, in just a few last words, what is one lesson from this whole period that strikes you as particularly critical?

Of course we will win. And I would say our revolution will be over when there is no meaning to the phrase poor country or even poor person. What will be next? I look forward to seeing.

One personal lesson? Here's one I often emphasized when running for Mayor. My home is my home. Your home is your home. But my castle is your castle is our society.

Celia, tell us a bit about running for and becoming Governor of California. What did you take from the electoral experience?

We traversed the state repeatedly talking directly to many people through public gatherings, speeches, and TV addresses. The debates reached millions more. Throughout, we extolled RPS program and urged RPS involvement. We constantly indicated not only the programs and policies we would try to rapidly institute, but also where we hoped these changes would lead.

When we started, we didn't anticipate winning. We ran to organize widely, to pressure whoever would win, and to develop organization for future campaigns and especially for grassroots organizing. We thought we could broaden understanding and support for RPS ideas and build new organization and membership to advance movements at every step. We swore to one another that we wouldn't compromise any of that to win more votes.

Our definition of winning the election was to do all that we intended without compromise, and then, if by some chance we actually got most votes, terrific. Yet even with that commitment, the pressure to compromise came not just from the media, potential donors, and endorsers, but from inside the campaign as well. The prospect of victory was like a drug.

It often diverted us from seeking broader real success. You are about to give a speech to some large crowd, constituency, or organization. What do you do?

Approach one: You describe your intentions, beliefs, values, and agenda, making your strongest case for them.

Approach two: You examine polling results to determine what your audience is thinking and then you tailor your words to try to win them over.

I think what kept us on the first approach was good people delivering criticism without fearing I would dismiss them, plus our shared mindset that an electoral victory would be counter productive if we took an elitist path.

We maintained our priorities after winning, too. I was in office only a week when we began implementing our full program. We didn't at any point think, okay, let's get that important gain, short of our full aim, by way of this or that compromise of our other aims. No. We said let's get everything we laid out, and more, let's do it by way of popular power, not by back room compromises.

This wasn't as hard as it might have been due to the scale and commitment of public support we had for the full program. Without so much support and its tendency to steadily increase, we would have always been afraid that not compromising would win nothing, rather than always feeling that not compromising was the way to win everything.

Celia, to close, I would like to ask, do you think we will win? When will we have won? And, in just a few last words, what is one lesson from this whole period that strikes you as particularly critical?

The arc of history says we will win and so do I. I guess the RPS project will be over when we no longer need to ask, when is it over? And as a lesson I have learned, realizing that I owe to you and vice versa, or our dream is deferred.

Lydia, you were RPS Shadow Government President. Did it give you an understanding of the benefits of holding office?

Even in shadow office you quickly learn that the main determinants of policies and directions are institutional features. The structure of the governing bodies is critical, but so are the concentrations of power in various other places - mainly corporations. So you learn that short of transforming all those institutions - which is the ultimate goal - you have to have sources of power, pressure, and creative innovation beyond your office, or what you win will be nothing remotely like what you desired to win.

So right off we sought institutional changes in our own version of the government, partly as a model for things to seek in the world and partly so we could do more good in our own work.

Do you look forward to RPS actually fielding a President in the near future?

Left activists understand that existing institutions structurally serve the rich and powerful. They often take from that insight one correct conclusion and one incorrect conclusion, at least in my view.

The correct conclusion is that we need new institutions. The incorrect conclusion, is that we should have nothing to do with flawed institutions.

The error is saying we want a new society for the whole population, but we don't want to relate to the population. We want a new society spanning all defining institutions, but we don't want to battle within those institutions. We want to criticize institutions and rail at them from without or replace them by building from scratch, but we don't want to engage them from within.

My reply has always been, railing at institutions from without is certainly essential and so is creating alternatives from scratch that can serve as models to raise consciousness. But, in addition, suppose someone said to radical working people, "We want a new economy, so stop operating in this one." It would be absurd. First, it would mean ceding that terrain to those who are not radical. Second, it would entail giving up one's job. Third, it would jettison access to all the lessons we can learn from operating within existing institutions, not only what's wrong with them, but what's needed in their place. Finally, it would forego victories inside those institutions that would make people's lives better now.

It may be hard to see, I would add, but the government is similar to the economy in all those regards, with added aspects. Corporations are entirely profit-seeking. In government too, the deck is heavily stacked, and the structural pressures to compromise and become what you don't want to be are enormous. But it is also true that there is some room to maneuver. We can win policy gains by winning elections and using levers of power to influence outcomes.

At any rate, my feeling is that elections certainly involve serious pitfalls, but refusing to operate inside the government would forego large gains we could win. So, yes, I think we have gotten to the point where our support is so broad, and even more important, so deep, that we can and should now win at the highest level.

Lydia, to close, I would like to ask, do you think we will win? When will we have won? And, in just a few last words, what is one lesson from this whole period that strikes you as particularly critical?

Winning requires truth, justice, and momentum. We have had the first two as long as I can remember, which is all the way back to the 1960s. We now have momentum as well, and I believe that makes victory certain.

On when we will have won, I will quote my favorite poet. We will have won when the sun respects every face on the deck.

Finally, as one lesson, I guess I would pick that informed reason needs true sympathy and true sympathy needs informed reason.

Bertrand, you too were an RPS shadow President, after serving as Vice President with Lydia. Do you see the situation similarly?

Yes, very much so but if I had to suggest a difference I think I may be somewhat more sympathetic to those who are so caught up in rejecting reformism that they go overboard and avoid all reforms and mainstream institutions. I get the sentiment. Hell, in my bones, I even share it as a kind of feeling, but only a feeling.

The levels of hypocrisy rooted in conforming to injustice are so intrinsic to mainstream structures that it is hard - though not impossible - to avoid getting sucked in and corrupted. A trick, however, can help. We don't think it is inevitable that if you get a job on an assembly line you will become an advocate of wage slavery. Why not? Aspects of such a job certainly push people toward bad views and habits, namely, becoming subservient and misinformed. But since your role in the corporation is that of a victim, you may retain integrity and operate in its bounds without becoming its advocate.

Suppose, in contrast, you win an elected office in national or local government. Or, for that matter, suppose you take a job as a manager in a workplace. This is different. You are, or at least you can be, recipient of the benefits and purveyor of the ills.

So the trick is even as you take office, you must define yourself to be an opponent of your position and your role. You have to literally see yourself as a fifth column operating inside to pursue interests defined outside.

In the years I served in Lydia's administration, we made great headway but it was quite hard. Instead of mainly working on change, much and sometimes even most of our energy had to go to developing our shadow methods and procedures and filling our posts. By the time I became Shadow Potus, our structures and procedures were stable and effective, so we could give more time to birthing and battling for new policies.

Building campaigns to transform from the elitist electoral college approach to direct voting with multi party preferential balloting was a massive victory we celebrated. And yes, I think that advances in popular awareness and desire have gotten us to a place where an RPS-identified candidate can not just become president, but can take office with a huge mandate and with fellow RPS advocates occupying positions all over the country.

Malcolm, do you anticipate an RPS candidate, perhaps yourself, winning the 2044 election?

It is still nearly four years off so we are on thin ground predicting anything, but, yes, I think this time we will win outright with at least 60% support. We have had a number of progressive administrations that negotiated with us in good faith and sided with many of our efforts and had to give in on much of the rest of what we sought. The population is now ready for a transformation.

When New York, California, Ohio, and surprisingly Texas and then others too elected not only progressive but RPS governors by large margins, and when those governors proceeded to aid RPS efforts at the state and local level, the result was incredibly positive for nearly everyone. The die was cast. The momentum became undeniable.

I think the biggest consciousness shift was back in 2024 when working class support for right wing reaction finally collapsed. Fear of immigrants and minorities polarizing millions into casting conservative votes, collapsed. People understood that the real source of pain and suffering for working people was profit seeking and people were enjoying steadily growing racial solidarity.

By 2028, and then especially 2032, the class antagonism toward coordinator elitism and their material advantages had also largely transformed. It didn't disappear, but it became highly informed and switched from opposing liberalism or progressivism to opposing coordinator obscurantism and elitism aimed at maintaining coordinator dominance. It had grown to understand the division of labor and the need for excellent education for all.

In 2036 and 2040, those trends continued, and the old style two party habits overwhelmingly died, but I think the final tipping point was the growing popular belief in a viable alternative system.

We moved from people siding with RPS views and values in their hearts but not believing that RPS could actually deliver, and therefore not actively supporting RPS program for the country, to people having faith that a new society is possible and worth winning, and that supporting a candidate offering RPS program would be a real step forward.

I think in 2044 there will be one pivotal issue. If I vote for revolution, am I voting for an idea I like but which will mean unlimited chaos and civil strife because opposition to a new society will be too strong to overcome - or am I voting for a careful, unrelenting struggle that will culminate in implementing a new society at every level? And I think the answer will now finally come down as the latter for an overwhelming majority of our population.

Winning the presidency, even if we don't also win Congress and the Senate - though I think we will, by considerable margins - will greatly speed up our long march through the institutions, both changing them from within and replacing them with complete alternatives. It will be far easier and quicker to finish workers and consumers collectively taking over workplaces and services with the government overwhelmingly abetting every step.

Just think of a new president using executive orders to support workers taking over companies, even beyond the massive takeovers we have already witnessed. Or of a new President transitioning military production and bases to social uses as a matter of positive desire and principle across the world. Or of a new president helping create the infrastructure of a new society, not simply from above, but responding to pressure from movements even while welcoming that pressure and aiding its development. Envision the new president legitimating, empowering, and welcoming police defense of the public seeking to self manage their lives and expropriate their workplaces.

Malcolm, do you think we will win? When will we have won? And, in just a few last words, what is one lesson from this whole period that strikes you as particularly critical?

A few decades ago, to believe we would win took a huge leap of faith. Now the path is evident. So yes, I believe we will win. But I think winning comes well before our related tasks are over. There is, after all, a whole new world to construct. It will all be over, I guess, when children don't know what war is. And what will come after that - I have no idea. Finally, what has been a lesson special for me? Perhaps this simple and well known one. Ends inform means. Means win ends.

CHAPTER 24

POLITICAL AND KINSHIP VISION

*Bertrand Dellinger and Lydia Luxemburg
discuss Political and Kinship Vision.*

Bertrand, in seeking an overview of values and ideas that formed and still form the foundation of RPS, we have come to vision, and though of course it has been written about, discussed, reviled, advocated, shared, and pursued for a quarter century and is now very well known, maybe you can briefly describe key elements of the political vision of RPS.

When asked what's your vision, past activists would list societal virtues or accomplishments like equity, justice, and so on.

For RPS, what is your vision means what institutions does RPS favor to attain accomplishments like equity, justice, and self management? Asked what's your vision, we always describe preferred institutions and their roles, because ignoring that aspect would undercut whatever we might propose regarding values.

So, for politics, RPS recognized that political activity includes legislation of laws, adjudication of disputes, and collective implementation of shared programs. A new political system should of course accomplish these functions, but also produce solidarity and diversity.

We asked, if we are part of a community, state, or country, how must we organize ourselves to attain such results? How must we interact so our decision making will advance each citizen via the advance of all citizens? How might we respect multiple paths forward and not enshrine one right mind or one right path?

We knew polity should have internal structure and role relations that generate fair outcomes, redress past imbalances, prevent future ones, and produce collective self management for all. But how might we organizationally accomplish those diverse aims compatibly with one another?

We knew we needed to respect past experiences and lessons but also to try new ideas. We took the grassroots mechanisms activists tended to spontaneously form as our starting place by seeking nested councils with primary-level councils including every adult in the society in local councils, and some folks elected to higher level councils, and another layer, and another.

Through practical experience we learned that the number of members in each council should be low enough to guarantee that people could be involved in face-to-face discussions, yet high enough to allow an adequate diversity of opinion and ensure that the number of levels of councils accommodating all society was manageable. Twenty five members per council proved a good choice. With twenty five, seven layers would cover even the largest country.

Within each council we had to decide the mandates of representatives and associated responsibilities, procedures of debate and evaluation, and rules of voting and tallying. How should we arrive at a preference for using one approach over another at particular levels and for particular types of decisions?

The RPS answer was that we should in every case seek self-management by methods that would also reliably arrive at wise choices. Likewise, we should protect and pursue diversity. We should maintain solidaritous feelings and practices. We should get things done without debilitating delays.

Reasonable people, we realized, would often disagree about some issue or other. Some people might see the facts of a matter, say abortion or a more local issue of land development, differently than others. Some might calculate incorrectly, say about the merits of some judicial mechanism, while others are accurate. Some might have different priorities, values, or intuitions than others about complex implications of a new law about space travel or pollution, or just putting a new pool in a neighborhood.

We realized that the trick to attaining successful legislative structure would be to have a system that allows collectively and collaboratively self-managed choices in which everyone agrees that outcomes are reached fairly for all and subject to review even while alternative options are still explored. This is what we felt a nested council system, emphasizing participatory deliberations and guided by commitments to self-management, solidarity, and diversity could achieve.

Beyond legislation, however we also knew that judicial systems often address judicial review (are our laws themselves just?), criminal justice (have specific individuals violated laws?), and civil adjudication (how do we resolve disputes?).

We undertook many experiments in how to hold legislation and people accountable and arrived at favoring a court system that would operate with hierarchical levels adjudicating disputed council choices.

Is ours the best approach possible? Can we refine it to better implement self-management? Experimentation, much of which is under way or still to come, will tell.

For criminal matters and also civil adjudication, diverse lawyers and legal advocates proposed and tested various options until we settled on a court system modestly different from what we had had earlier, plus community controlled police with balanced job complexes and remuneration for effort and sacrifice. About police, in particular, there was a great deal of struggle.

Back when RPS was forming police departments were still being militarized, not humanized. Incarceration was soaring and was almost totally punitive. Police still frequently engaged in racist, sexist, and classist violations ranging from harassment all the way through unjust arrest and murder. We had mass struggles over all that, building on the earlier Black Lives Matter movement, featuring demonstrations, rallies, marches, occupations, and strikes. Indeed, prisoner strikes began shortly before RPS got moving and then accelerated greatly. So did actions by families of prisoners and by community members seeking lawfulness instead of repression for their neighborhoods.

The upshot was to reduce the punitive aspect of law enforcement and emphasize rehabilitation. Police function, methods, and control have ever since been challenged with demonstrations, internal organizing, new laws, and community oversight, and by all that substantially transformed - which has been critical, I should say, not only to developing clarity about a new polity, but also about movement relations in the period we have gone through.

Why did RPS's view of police inspire outrage in many leftists who desired a better society?

Until we have a new society police often act in ways that hurt rather than help all but narrow elites. RPS and other activists had long encountered that, not least when police repressed us. Many concluded that in a new society we must entirely do away with police. Indeed, that was the most prevalent view among our most energetic members in the earliest days of RPS. But going from rejecting aspects of policing to rejecting all possible institutional means of accomplishing worthy police functions was highly controversial.

Can you explain that point a bit more?

This broad type of dispute has come up repeatedly in the history of RPS and prior radicalism as well. For example, governments often hurt rather than help all but narrow elites. Just look at history. They spy, regulate, incarcerate, rob, torture, and murder. Must we, therefore, get rid of all political/government functions?

Workplaces often spew pollution, violate labor, and manipulate consumers, and, in doing so, hurt rather than help all but narrow elites. Must we get rid of all structured workplace institutions?

Families, cultures, schools, journalists, and doctors even today often pursue horribly restrictive and destructive habits and beliefs. Must we get rid of all institutional structures for addressing nurturance, socialization, education, celebration, and communication?

My point is, a person urging rejection of workplaces, police, polity, or families typically claims doing so will liberate the virtues of humanity. Yet, the person is simultaneously saying humanity is too flawed to create institutions to collectively accomplish various social functions without unleashing debilitating effects. While holding up a banner proclaiming human perfection, the critic of having workplace, police, political, or familial institutions ironically assumes human failings preclude institutions having desirable attributes.

Such disputes were surprisingly hard to resolve. Imagine saying we need an improved version of policing to people who had routinely had their heads smashed by a cop or had witnessed a family member gunned down by one. Enormous passions arose. Resolutions weren't quick. At times people even left RPS, at least for a time, over such matters. Even RPS willingness to retain exploration of ways of dealing with disputes and criminality that did not involve retaining a police function - in case the majority view that that function had to remain, albeit redefined drastically, was wrong - weren't enough to keep some anti police members involved.

To understand what by now is a virtually non-existent view, imagine you were an RPS member and you had been raped and RPS was saying there is a place for rape, suitably redefined, in the new society we seek. You would be horrified. You would fight the insanity, and if you lost, justifiably decide the new organization was not worth your support and involvement. I think some members who left over RPS retaining policing as part of a new society left with a similar level of disgust and anger. What was admirable about RPS is that even in their absence we kept the exploration of alternatives going. That didn't lead to eliminating policing per se, but it did lead to many improvements in our understanding of what police training and functions ought to include including our realizing that it is not policing, but adjudication, legal advocacy, and legal decision making that are most difficult to dramatically improve in a better society. That is where issues remain most vague and experimental.

Wasn't there a strategic aspect to this, too?

Yes, how do we relate to the police now? To put it very starkly, do we treat them as enemies beyond reason or as potential allies to be organized? This discussion had the same passions as the visionary one, but added dimension of immediacy and strategy. Did we better aid prospects for winning changes now, and more later, by treating police like aliens or vicious animals, or by being realistic about their situations and views, but trying to communicate with and even organize them?

There was a barely remembered face-off of sorts about this not long before RPS emerged. A socialist organization that was growing dramatically with an influx of people motivated by fighting Trump had a convention and elected a steering committee.

One candidate, who won, had a long and very impressive history of labor organizing. After the ballot it came out...though anyone looking at his record could have easily known earlier, that he had organized with a police union. Considerable bedlam ensued due to various people feeling that should disqualify him. There was considerable friction. One chapter issued a statement about opposing police violence as if organizing police was incompatible with the view. So, even then, even in a socialist organization, a great many took police organizing not as serious and wise, even essential, activism, but as sell out. That was sad, but it wasn't long before the ensuing discussion spread new views. The simple truth was that demonizing opponents did nothing to reduce or reverse their opposition, and, as well, made us far less personally admirable.

Lydia, what does RPS say about kinship? How did its views on how to accomplish procreation, nurturance, and socialization emerge?

RPS values implied that kinship roles should enhance solidarity, preserve diversity, apportion benefits and responsibilities fairly, and convey self-managing influence - all as makes sense in every sphere of life. So with that set of desires, many questions arose for us. Should families continue as we now know them? Whatever families we will have, what else should exist? Should upbringing diverge greatly from what we now know? What about courting and sexual coupling? How should the old and young interact with adults and how should adults interact with the elderly and the young?

To fulfill our values, we knew that new kinship relations would have to liberate women and men rather than causing the former to be subordinate to the latter. But how? The truth is, we are still answering.

We knew the gain from transforming kinship would be removing the features that produce sexism, homophobia, and ageism, plus establishing an array of positive improvements that we could only guess at until we had more fully experimented with more complete proposals. But we also knew that not all gender related suffering would entirely disappear. Even in a wonderful society, I might love someone who did not love me. Previously strong ties could wither. Rape and other violent acts might still occur, albeit vastly less often. Social change wouldn't remove the pain of losing friends and relatives to premature death. All adults would not suddenly be equally adept at relating positively with children or with the elderly, or vice versa.

We thought new relations would eliminate the systematic violation of women, gays, lesbians, bisexuals, transgenders, children, and the elderly, but we also knew that new relations would not eliminate all individual violations. We thought changes would eliminate the structural coercion of men and women, of hetero and homosexuals, and of adults and children into patterns that systematically violate solidarity, diversity, equity, and self-management, but also knew they would not eliminate all individual violations.

What would institutions defining better kinship look like?

RPS knew contemporary societies consign women to less empowering and fulfilling options than men. We had to determine the defining social structures we needed to alter to remove that systematic ordering.

Feminism had long taught that sexism takes overt form in men having dominant and wealthier conditions than women and that it takes more subtle form via longstanding habits of communication and behavior. Feminists had also shown how sexism is produced and reproduced by institutions that differentiate men and women, coercively as in rape and battering, but also more subtly via mutually accepted role differences in home life, work, and celebration. And feminists had shown the cumulative impact of past sexist experiences on what people think, desire, and feel, and on what people habitually or consciously do.

If we wanted to find the source of gender injustice, it stood to reason we had to determine which social institutions - and which roles within those institutions - give men and women responsibilities, conditions, and circumstances that elevate men above women. One structure that had been discussed decades earlier was that men father but women mother. That is, men and women fulfill two quite dissimilar roles vis a vis the next generation and pass on different expectations via those different roles.

Feminists from that earlier time had asked, "What if instead of women mothering and men fathering, women and men each related to children with the same mix of responsibilities called parenting? What if instead of one gender doing the nurturing, tending, cleaning, and other maintenance tasks called mothering, and the other gender doing the decision-based tasks called fathering, both genders did a mix of all the roles called parenting?"

The argument for this said that mothering and fathering are socially and not biologically defined roles. As mothers, women produce daughters who, in turn, not only have mothering capacities but want to mother and not father, while as fathers, men produce sons who not only have fathering capacities but want to father and not mother. We thought about those formulations and decided that perhaps one feature of a vastly improved society would be that men and women both parent. There would be no mothering versus fathering, just parenting.

Before long many young parents, and some older ones too, decided to test this out. You can imagine the intensity of feelings this aroused. Through history, including in your own upbringing, everyone practiced mothering and fathering. Your child's life is at stake. There are no take backs, no do overs. Nonetheless, you decide to break the mold. We will each parent. That is no small step but had actually begun, piecemeal, for many, without explicit clarity, just trying to make home life more fair, years earlier. But it was in RPS and by its efforts that the practice accelerated and became self conscious. Much of it was simply changing one's own personal choices, but not all. For example, to have parenting and not mothering and fathering required parental leave for newborn care, not leave for women only, so that battle had to be waged as well.

Another typical structure that had come into question long before RPS for many feminists was the isolated and insular character of the nuclear family. Should child care and familial involvement rest on only one or two biological parents, or should it instead involve many more people - perhaps an extended family, friends, and community members?

It seemed highly unlikely a good society should or even could have rules that required a few typical household organizations and family structures such that everyone would enact only those. We wouldn't expect adults would, by law, have to live alone, in pairs, or in groups in any one or even in any few preferred patterns. The key point would likely be diversity but also that whatever multiple and diverse patterns existed, each option should embody features that call forth gender equity rather than gender hierarchy. So people have experimented with home life patterns aimed at broadening the care taking and interaction children enjoy, and at enlarging their participation in judgements, as well.

We have been guided by hope that people brought up this way will not only be full, capable, and confident, but also lack differentiations that limit and confine the personality and life trajectories of children to some kind of narrow feminine or narrow masculine mold.

And we have been guided by similar hopes about sexuality and intergenerational relations. We still don't know what fully liberated sexuality will be like - in all its multitude of preferences and practices - or all the diverse forms of intergenerational relations adults and their children and elders will enter into. But we do believe no one approach will be elevated above all others and that all admired options will preclude purposely producing in people a proclivity to dominate, rule, be subordinate, or obey based on biological sex, sexual orientation, age, or any other social or biological characteristic.

Even 20 years into RPS, we have only rough ideas what sex-gender patterns will emerge in a better future - for example, monogamous and not, hetero, homo, or bi-sexual, and involving transformed caregiving institutions, families, schools, and other spaces for children as well as for adults and the elderly - but we are confident that actors of all ages, genders, and preferences will engage in non-oppressive consensual sexual relations, free from stigma.

Of course there has been much internal dispute about aspects of this. A key thing, however, has been our flexibility and continued study of implications and options right to the present. It was hard to avoid being polarized into aggressive defensiveness when people would accuse us of trying to eliminate families or to wipe out love or childhood. But as with so many other issues, we learned to put a premium on being patient and respectful in such interchanges.

I hope you won't mind if I ask a question here that stands separate from the above, and is also a bit personal. I know you just turned 75 and I wonder if you would be willing to tell us your feelings about aging?

My father would sometimes repeat this old line to me by a famous poet named Robert Browning. It went "Grow old along with me, the best is yet to be." Nice rhyme, I guess meaningful to some, and uplifting for them. I didn't begrudge my father his pleasure at the words, but to me the sentiment was a giant fudge, or even a delusional lie. My father died of Alzheimer's. In the end he didn't know who anyone was. Was that best?

For my elderliness, and this is, I think, a bit rare, the couplet carries some truth because the RPS project has been the core of my aims and hopes and is now nearing full success. There is incredible joy and serenity in that. But that welcome companion to my aging - an aspect that brightens each new year - has nothing to do with aging per se, only with when I happen to be lucky enough to be elderly and growing even more elderly.

Aging itself is, let's be honest, the ultimate scourge of life. Save for rare exceptions, and supposing we avoid other worse ends, aging diminishes, demolishes, and as its climax totally eliminates our mobility. Aging dims, darkens, and finally switches off our conceptual power and even our perception itself. Aging murders our friends, family, and ourself.

I can't celebrate that. I don't see a positive point in telling the young to look forward to growing old and I won't do it. By all means, look forward to learning more and study to make it happen. Look forward to gaining wisdom, and investigate widely to make it so. But look forward to the flip side of late life's passing years, which is declining capacities? I don't think so.

RPS is bringing institutions that won't curb but will instead elevate our human potentials. That's good. Aging curbs our potentials. That's bad. Health matters, solidarity matters, and we are causing society to supply each in greater abundance than ever in history, but aging shatters health.

Respect for the achievement and wisdom that duration allows matters, and the new values that are increasingly guiding life choices daily enrich respect. That's good. Aging adds experiences but dims memories. That's a mixed bag.

Aging isn't as devastating for us as it was for our forebears and it will become less devastating still for our children. Celebrate that. The best for society, for humanity, is yet to be and coming on strong. Celebrate that. But for each of us the devolution that is aging remains. Can I offer any positive advice about that now that stairs and even getting up out of a chair, loom as daily obstacles.

Don't welcome funerals but don't bemoan age. Stay young of mind and soul as best you can. Even shut age out. Deny its impact, if that works for you. Keep feeling 18 or 30 or whatever age works for you but as athletes used to say, there is no point in denying that Father Time never loses. Here is my own trick. Don't revel in glory days. Even more don't measure current accomplishment by yesterday's criteria. Use what you can muster to do what you desire. Not doing late in life what you could do early in life is not failing. It is inevitable. Not doing late in life what you can do late in life, that is a different story.

CHAPTER 25

ECONOMIC AND CULTURAL VISION

Andrej Goldman, Peter Cabral, Lydia Luxemburg and Bertrand Dellinger discuss economic and cultural vision.

Andrej, what about RPS economic vision? What does it seek?

RPS economics proposes to carry out production, consumption, and allocation in a classless, equitable manner. It seeks to deliver to each person self-managing say. It seeks to produce not only desired goods and services, but also desirable solidarity and diversity.

To accomplish these ideals we of course needed venues where people could determine their actions in accord with other people doing likewise. We found such venues in workplace and community councils often seen in historical risings in the past. The idea we added was that each actor should have a say in council decisions proportionate to the impact of the decided issue on them.

To use a workplace example, sometimes just a few workers would be the most affected constituency and would decide their own actions in context of overarching decisions by the whole workplace council. Sometimes the whole workplace council would be directly involved and decide, for example, work hours for all. The point would be to best approximate people having a say proportionate to the effect on them while respecting that others should enjoy that same right. We tested all these patterns in our own projects, of course, but also, as much as possible, in workplaces via reforms that moved toward RPS vision.

In the usual corporate pattern, about 20% does overwhelmingly empowering tasks while 80% does overwhelmingly disempowering tasks. The former do work that conveys to them confidence, social and conceptual skills, knowledge of the workplace and its possibilities, and effective decision making habits. The latter do work that diminishes confidence, reduces social and conceptual skills, reduces knowledge of the workplace and its possibilities, instills habits of obedience, and bores and exhausts them.

RPS members, like everyone in society, have extensive personal experience that some jobs have better conditions and involve more enjoyable and engaging work than others. We knew this differential could be offset by income considerations but we knew it would be harder to improve a second aspect.

Some who work within a corporate arrangement become ready to govern, others become ready to be governed where the difference derives from people's position in the division of labor. RPS saw and focused on this because our concepts highlighted role structures and their implications and our values highlighted impact on people's ability to participate. Seeing their different situations, RPS called the the dominant 20% the coordinator class and called the subordinate 80% the working class.

RPS members saw that in past experience eliminating owners' relative monopoly on property could succeed at that essential step but not significantly alter the coordinator/worker hierarchy. We saw that 20th century socialism, despite that it's ownership change had eliminated capitalists, had not ended class rule. We realized we had to not only change ownership to eliminate the core of capitalism but also break the coordinator class's monopoly on empowering circumstances. Rather than segregate empowering tasks into a relatively few jobs that a relatively few people would hold, we had to spread empowering tasks through all jobs by establishing what RPS called balanced job complexes.

In this line of thought, beyond escaping the rule of owners, each person should do a mix of tasks they are capable of and comfortable at. The mix you would do and the mix I would do and the mix everyone else would do, should be balanced from one person to the next for the empowering effect of work on the worker doing it. This balancing should occur not only inside each workplace, but across workplaces as well. As a result, we would each have responsibility for an array of tasks that summed to a comparably empowering overall situation and we would each be comparably prepared by our daily work life to confidently participate in workers and consumers councils. We would eliminate not only the capital worker relation, but also the coordinator worker relation.

> So at this point you had briefly outlined a new approach to making decisions and a new division of labor. What about income? What became RPS's view of each person's rightful claim on the social product? How much should we get? What is responsible and fair? What works?

RPS said people who are too young or too old - or who are otherwise unable to work gainfully - should get a full income anyhow, but people who could work should have an income reflecting the duration, intensity, and onerousness of their socially valuable labor.

I shouldn't be remunerated as an athlete, a singer, or anything else for which my abilities don't allow me to produce outputs others want to have. But I should be remunerated for anything I do well enough for my efforts to be socially valuable.

Similarly, if I want to consume more out of the total social product than average, I should be able to do so by virtue of working more hours, or more intensely, or perhaps doing some more onerous tasks.

RPS initially settled on this as fair but before long we also realized it was needed to facilitate consumption matching production, to convey sensible incentives, and to convey essential indicators of people's preferences for leisure and for different kinds of work and different products.

What about allocation?

RPS members knew we also needed to replace markets and central planning. For that, we settled on advocating cooperative negotiation among workers and consumers councils. Each council would announce their desires and then update their offers in light of what others offered. Various structures would help with assessing costs, benefits, and preferences. There would be no center or periphery, no top or bottom. People would self-manage their production and consumption in light of emergent measures of personal, social, and environmental costs and benefits. Personal motives and behaviors would mesh with those of self-managed councils and fit with balanced job complexes and remuneration for duration, intensity, and onerousness of socially valued labor.

RPS claimed this overall economic vision could accomplish production, consumption, and allocation without class division and in accord with people's needs and desires as well as with ecological sustainability and social harmony.

RPS members in workplaces and communities began to agitate for changes in accord. In some cases this has already taken us to partial cooperative planning, where federations of worker self managed workplaces in industries mutually negotiate their interconnections and where communities and surrounding providers communally negotiate their production and consumption.

If RPS claims for the benefits of full-scale participatory planning prove true, then the overall RPS economic vision will be a worthy alternative to capitalism and also to what has been called market or centrally planned socialism - which RPS members call coordinatorism.

Of course, beyond the broad aspects of RPS economic vision, there are countless details, some of which are pretty settled after the past twenty years of experiences in RPS workplaces, occupied corporate firms, and via exploring the implications of reforms. But much else, indeed far more at the most practical level, will emerge from further experience and, in particular, only once participatory planning occurs for a time throughout the whole economy so its implications for behaviors and habits are more evident. This is true not least because there is undoubtedly no one right answer to every aspect. Rather different populations, industries, technologies, heritages, and preferences will lead to an endless variety of details for RPS economies and firms, even as the core elements of self managing councils, equitable remuneration, balanced job complexes, and participatory planning form the backbone of it all.

It can't be that this vision arose and won support without dissent from outside and even inside RPS. What was that like?

Outside RPS, critics said equitable remuneration would not elicit creativity and productivity. Balanced job complexes and self management would sacrifice quality for false justice. Participatory planning would sacrifice efficiency, and even viability, for false solidarity.

RPS responses appeared in countless exchanges, debates, and presentations. Equitable remuneration would not only be morally sound and socially positive, it would deliver needed information and desirable levels of both work and creativity. Balanced job complexes and self management would not only be morally sound and socially positive, it would unleash huge swaths of human creativity and capacity while eliminating waste associated with class division. Participatory planning would not only eliminate the built-in motivational and informational ills of markets, the authoritarianism of central planning, and the ecological irrationality of both, it would positively unearth the information needed for sound choices and would mesh compatibly with equitable remuneration, self management, and classlessness.

Both critics and advocates could not be right. Resolution came when we could point at ever more successful experiments.

Within RPS, however, the debate was more about the implications of different visionary commitments for strategic success. Those who opposed the emerging vision felt that it risked alienating too many people - mainly of the coordinator class - to the detriment of RPS advancing. Dissidents said why not offer a less controversial economic vision closer to our current immediate potentials? When and if consciousness and conditions permit, we can promote our full desires in accord with new possibilities.

So within RPS, one side was saying we have to be very careful not to alienate coordinator class identified people. We cannot afford their absence from activism both for reasons of numbers, and also for reasons of needing various skills they can bring. The other side, and I was on it, agreed that welcoming coordinator class involvement was necessary, but argued that to welcome coordinator involvement without being clear about our ultimate aims would interfere with attaining what was sought on two counts.

First, the duplicity would itself repel many and be internally corrosive. Second, to seek coordinator involvement without simultaneously addressing the dangers of coordinator co-option of the entire project invited disaster. To advance without coordinator class folks would be difficult, and likely even impossible, we agreed, so we should certainly avoid that. However, to advance with coordinator class involvement but without attention to the potential for it to subvert other aims risked suicide. If we advocated anti capitalist but not anti coordinatorist vision, we would wind up with no project due to not attracting workers or with a project subordinate to coordinator class interests and aims.

The second position won overwhelmingly and in this case it was hard to maintain the minority position at the same time as pursuing the majority one. The best we could do was to establish a standing committee to continually reevaluate visionary commitments and their strategic implications in light of learning more about each from developments more generally. But I must admit it wasn't long before the emphasis moved toward discerning further essential aspects of the favored vision, with the minority positions to drop balanced job complexes and to drop self management dipping into complete inattention. What remained at all times a flexible focus, however, was how best to grow and develop RPS in accord with attaining its ultimate goals.

I should add that some members left RPS over this. But I think it is fair to note that few if any who left were working class. And while each person who left over this difference operated for a time in progressive political ways, as they fell back into daily life coordinator involvements they typically fell away from dissent, or when they decided to persist in dissent, in time they rejoined RPS.

Fears that the full vision would cause some coordinator class people to not relate positively to RPS were therefore correct - particularly for the folks arguing it. But for many other coordinator class members, and for more as each month and year passed, the predication was wrong.

Indeed, one of the most celebratory dynamics that occurred during all these years of RPS growth, was not just coordinator class members signing up to RPS, but their happily teaching their skills to worker's while progressively dispensing with their non worthy practices and attitudes. It paralleled, for example, whites fighting against their prior racism and men fighting against their prior sexism, but often with larger personal material losses and fewer historical precedents.

Andrej, I want to finally ask, do you think we will win? When will we have won? And, in just a few last words, what is one lesson from this whole period that strikes you as particularly critical?

Yes, I am confident we will win. Short of a comet-level interruption, there is no turning back from how far we have come. I think it is hard to define a moment of victory, but perhaps RPS will have won when revolutionary aspirations beyond RPS drive activism. For me, I think maybe the key lesson is that truth is the only authority worth allegiance.

Peter, what about issues of culture? How did RPS thinking proceed about vision for that?

We knew we would not be magically reborn in a future desirable society, free of our past and unaware of our historical roots. On the contrary, we knew our historical memory, continuing sensitivity to past and present social process, and persistent understanding of our own and of our society's history would all be enhanced during the process of reaching a desirable society. Rather than our diverse cultural roots becoming submerged on the road to a better world, we believed they would persist and instead of homogenizing cultures, the transition to a better world would need to appreciate the historical contributions of different communities more than ever before, including guaranteeing them greater rather than lesser means for their further development. We felt our task was to respect and celebrate cultural communities, but also avoid their having destructive mutual hostilities.

We saw that trying to erase the horrors of genocide, imperialism, racism, jingoism, ethnocentrism, and religious persecution by attempting to integrate distinct historical communities into one cultural niche had earlier proved about as destructive as the nightmares this approach sought to expunge.

We knew from history and our own life lessons that "cultural homogenization" - whether racist, fundamentalist, or even leftist - ignored the positive aspects of cultural differences that give people a sense of who they are and where they come from. We knew cultural homogenization offered few opportunities for variety and cultural self-management. We knew it would heighten exactly the community antagonisms it said it wanted to overcome.

We also knew that in a competitive and mutually hostile environment, religious, racial, ethnic, and national communities often developed into sectarian camps, each concerned first and foremost with defending itself from real and imagined threats, including even waging war on others to do so. Even so, we knew the presence of racial and other cultural hierarchies throughout society and history no more meant we should eliminate cultural diversity than the existence of gender, sexual, economic, or political hierarchies meant we should eliminate diversity in those realms. We had to remove cultural oppression while we respected and preserved diversity.

Dominant community groups have always rationalized their positions of privilege with myths about their own superiority and the presumed inferiority of those they oppress. Such materially-motivated myths in time have typically attained a life of their own transcending material relations with brutal effects.

Some within oppressed communities internalized myths of their inferiority and attempted to imitate, or at least accommodate, dominant cultures while others in oppressed communities defended the integrity of their own cultural traditions while combating racist ideologies used to justify their oppression.

RPS concluded that cultural salvation does not lie in trying to remove the distinctions between communities but in eliminating racist institutions, dispelling racist ideologies, and changing the environments within which historical communities interrelate to allow communities to maintain and celebrate difference without fear of subjugation. We called the RPS alternative "intercommunalism," to pay homage to the Black resistance movements of the late 1960s. Intercommunalism emphasizes respecting and preserving cultures by guaranteeing each community sufficient material and social resources to confidently reproduce itself.

We sought to replace negative intercommunity relations with positive ones. We wanted to eliminate any threat of cultural extinction by guaranteeing that every community has the means to carry on their traditions, languages, and self definitions. Not only would each community possess the particular wisdoms of its own historical experience, but the intercommunalist interaction of different cultures would enhance the characteristics of each and provide a richness that no single approach could ever attain.

In accord with self-management, RPS realized that individuals should be free to choose the cultural communities they prefer rather than elders or others defining their choices, particularly on the basis of prejudice.

We also realized that while those outside a community should be free to criticize cultural practices that violate humane norms, external intervention beyond criticism should be disallowed except to guarantee that all members of every community have the right of dissent and freedom to leave without incurring any material or broader social loss.

Most important, RPS realized that until a lengthy history of autonomy and solidarity overcomes suspicion and fear between communities. Intercommunalism would make it incumbent on the more powerful community with less reason to fear domination to unilaterally begin the process of de-escalating disputes. When need be, oversight and enforcement could occur by way of an intercommunal legal apparatus specializing in conflict resolution.

The RPS intercommunalist goal is therefore to create an environment in which no community feels threatened so each community feels free to learn from and share with others. But given the historical legacy of negative intercommunity relations, RPS knew it would be delusional to believe this could be achieved overnight. Perhaps even more so than in other areas, intercommunalist relations would have to be constructed, step by step, until a different historical legacy and set of behavioral expectations prevails. Nor would it always be easy to decide what constitutes the "necessary means" that communities should be guaranteed for cultural reproduction, or exactly what development free from "unwarranted outside interference" means in particular situations.

But it seemed and it still seems certain that every community should be guaranteed sufficient material and communication means to self-define and self-develop its own cultural traditions, and to represent its culture to all other communities in the context of limited aggregate means and equal rights to those means for all - just as all of its members, by virtue of participatory economic, political, and kin relations, should be equitably remunerated and comparably self-managing.

Was there a minority or dissenting view in RPS?

Yes, or perhaps I should say, sort of. The concern was, and it still exists, couldn't this all become mere rhetoric? Couldn't it become co-optive without really dealing with the full dynamics of racism, religious bigotry, and the like?

People who worried about this said, look, with economics we are proposing specific institutions whose character is such that operating within them guarantees attaining the preferred values they are chosen to reach. If we win the institutions, we are going to reach the conditions we seek. But with community and race, the situation is less clear. We support nothing comparable to balanced job complexes or participatory planning producing the cultural outcomes we seek. We have only the injunction that folks should abide certain rules and norms, and that communities should be protected and provided means to persist. It sounds fine, but some claimed that on paper we had already had that much, and it hadn't worked.

The reply was, okay, what more is needed? Surely you don't want to ghettoize different communities, and, other than that, what specific features do you think we should add to the intercommunalist vision?

The upshot has been to agree on the vision, but also to continually reassess it for effectivity, and that if it seemed to fall short, we would refine it to do better.

Peter, do you think we will win? When will we have won? And, in just a few last words, what is one lesson from this whole period that strikes you as particularly critical?

There is an old sports expression that sometimes applies, the game is ours to lose. It means if we carry on well, we will win. That is where I think we are at. When will it be done? I guess I would say when prehistory, which is ultimately what we are battling to transcend, announces, okay, I have had enough, you win. Finally, I think a hard lesson for me, and an essential one, was that self management subverts violence and violence subverts self management.

Lydia, would you like to add any final comment about the ideas and values of RPS vision before we shift back to examining historical events and program?

RPS vision has always been rooted in a clear statement of values we desire for humanity and then trying our best to conceive institutions consistent with those values. Most other visionary approaches look at the present and find instance after instance of undesirable attributes, and then try to find replacements, one after another.

Our visionary approach is that we ask what we want. If it is unreal or impossible, okay, we try again. But once we settle on what we really want, we don't let what we see all around us keep us from conceiving what is needed to meet our full desires.

I guess it sounds a little academic but it is the difference between vision that tinkers with the present and fails to get much beyond it, and vision that desires a very different future and avoids being stopped by the chains of today.

Another virtue of the values-first approach is that it speaks to people by celebrating their humanity rather than rejecting history's inhumanities. It celebrates aims rather than excoriating shackles. Positive aspirations drive the process.

The second thing I would like to say is that concepts, values, and vision are free creations of human thought and discussion. They are not products of the will of a king, a priest, a god, or even a wise sage. Only collective assessment, testing, and advocacy can establish them. But their being human creations nonetheless means they can be flawed, time-bound, and need frequent renovation.

Values may embody misconceptions that render one or more things we favor contrary to our intents. Concepts may have insufficient scope or diverge from accuracy. Vision may be unattainable or internally contradictory, or it could have unforeseen negative implications. RPS recognizes all these possibilities and therefore its own fallibility. It constantly tests and upgrades its commitments.

Here is how I think of it. Scientists are people just like all the rest of us. They sometimes have biases that distort their perceptions. They sometimes develop self serving ways of seeing or psychological commitments to pet ideas or even to ideas on which their reputation or income depends. But science is supposed to serve truth. It is supposed to always seek to alter itself by finding and correcting flaws and developing new understanding. To continually self renovate, science doesn't merely say to scientists, be good, innovate, don't perpetuate. No, science incorporates diverse arrangements, roles, and incentives meant to create an enquiring, flexible, and always forward reaching mindset. These don't always work perfectly, to be sure. But they create a truth-seeking dynamic that doesn't exist, say, in religious studies or in old style politics of the past.

My point is that RPS very self consciously sees its concepts, values, and vision the way science sees its hypotheses. We try to make our views as optimal as we can, but we try not to become so wed to our views that we then try to ward off improvement just to preserve the past and our connections with it.

Not all of us do this well, and no individual does it perfectly, but because RPS prioritizes this flexible, growth-oriented approach, and sets aside resources and time explicitly for the purpose, it most often attains flexibility. This RPS approach is opposite to the usual talmudic approach to ideology. It is a key RPS virtue, and certainly one that has motivated my becoming and remaining a member.

Bertrand, you are a physicist. Does what Lydia has offered here resonate for you, too? Does your science background impact your political work?

I think Lydia has it exactly right.

In my life as a scientist I conceive ideas, figure ways to test them, induce people to help do the tests, examine the results, and either rejoice in the merit the ideas display, or move on to other ideas.

Revolutionary politics should work similarly but we need to realize there are difficulties. In social situations the number of variables is often too high to get clear results. Sometimes you can't arrange experiments to give definitive information about what works and what doesn't. Even in physics it typically pays to keep respectable ideas around after they seem to fail in case new information makes them important again, or in case examining them reveals a new angle on information that yields valuable insights. And this is even more true in political activism where definitive results are much harder to achieve. We should test ideas and constantly try to improve them. We should not ward off criticism as if finding fault would be harmful.

I don't think my physics itself has any lessons for people conducting their daily affairs. The life and times of elementary particles and cosmological models is way too distant from the life and times of activists and social visions to have relevance for that. But I do think the approach of scientists to both new and old ideas, and to evidence and logic, and, at our best, to each other as well, does have lessons for people conducting their daily affairs and particularly for people trying to improve society.

CHAPTER 26

MEDIA SEEDS

*Bertrand Dellinger, Mark Feynman,
and Leslie Zinn discuss media future.*

Bertrand, what was the origin of the phrase "planting the seeds of the future in the present," and what does it mean?

I think it was originally an anarchist slogan but whatever its source, it certainly means that the attitudes, social relations, and structures we plant determine our harvest. If you want daisies, plant daisies. If you want roses, plant roses. If you plant weeds, you won't harvest daisies or roses no matter how well you water your weeds. We should not plant seeds today which will become other than what we want tomorrow.

Suppose an RPS project needs funds. Why not sell opioids to get the revenue? Partly it is because it would be immoral but the more instructive reason is because the mindsets and practices associated with selling opioids would breed tendencies contrary to our aims.

Suppose a media project needs funds. Why not sell ads? Selling ads means selling an audience they want to reach to commercial outfits which means attracting an audience that has disposable income and making sure that your content doesn't keep them from buying what advertisers offer. Selling ads will subvert your project, even if you intended to save it.

This type of calculation comes up often in electoral campaigns, grassroots tactical choices, and even deciding how to make decisions. To intelligently navigate such matters requires clarity about the basic features of the society we seek. Without that clarity, we can't think wisely about the seeds we are planting.

Mark, what was the RPS attitude toward the internet and social media? How did planting seeds of the future play out in that realm?

When RPS was forming, the internet was a mixed bag for creating a better society. Positively, the internet facilitated popular participation in disseminating information, aided in announcing actions and conveying instructions, and facilitated spreading analysis and vision. These benefits were significantly compromised, however, by the tremendous volume of junk news and nonsense that complicated finding valuable content. A premium on attracting eyes to ads led to clickbait headlines that diverged ever more from honest communication.

Also negatively, the internet rewarded extreme brevity. Users acclimated to short, shorter, shortest. Declining attention spans produced more brevity, fueling a downward spiral. It was incredibly jarring to hear very sensible people, highly informed and radical, putting forth ideas for improving society with 140 character limits on supporting argument offered for each point.

Additionally, corporate surveillance tracked people's internet use to amass gigantic databases which were sold to advertisers and for spying by the state. Privacy was extinguished. Finally, though many thought internet browsing and YouTube viewing were fundamentally decentralizing and de-commercializing, very quickly they instead conveyed more ads than TV and magazines had, and the ads were far more intrusive. Centralization accelerated as a huge majority of traffic went through few sites until with a nearly infinite selection of little venues to visit, traffic was nonetheless overwhelmingly about ten or fifteen sites - not to mention Facebook trying to replace the whole of the World Wide Web with Facebook housed versions.

At the same time, the internet plus smart phones and social media also elevated nastiness, escalated bullying, and produced narcissistic vapidity. People might disagree about how to weigh the relative debits and virtues, but whatever the balance, why not try to remove the debits while enlarging the virtues? Why not provide services that would elevate substance and solidarity while retaining ease of use and scope?

Of course RPS put up web sites and produced podcasts. And of course we tried to ensure that commenting and forums were civil, and that click bait and ads were absent. Nonetheless, many of us worried that even as we were trying to thwart bad habits, on balance we might be having more negative than positive effect. The number of left sites that began to employ click bait and short pieces and to have endless links for jumping about at the expense of maintaining focus, kept growing. Sites did it in pursuit of greater outreach, which was certainly understandable, but was having more readers for shorter durations a real gain other than for advertisers?

We decided to create our own People's Social Media, where we would facilitate inexpensive networking, flexible outreach, and insightful debate without ads, data mining, spying, bullying, manipulation, or the constraints and pressures that generated an inclination toward short and thin. But how could we do that?

The answer that various tech-oriented folks proposed rehashed some earlier attempts. We would create our own version of Facebook and Twitter, but combined in one system and with transparent features and revenues going to progressive sponsoring projects.

Each sponsor would become a source for cross constituency connections. We would have no length limitations, no ads, and no spying. Our system would be international since there were no national borders to internet connectivity. RPS first created a system that went into use in the U.S. about fifteen years ago, and immediately welcomed people, social movements, and organizations in other countries to join.

The process was what you might anticipate from RPS. We got together, wrote software, got some people who would do the work, and offered it up. The system operates with balanced job complexes and keeps things inexpensive for users while pledging that beyond its workers' receiving equitable wages and allotting funds sufficient to cover costs, all revenues from the low monthly fees would go to the many sponsoring organizations.

At first the effort had to overcome old habits and biases. Perhaps hardest of all, at first we lacked the benefits of scale which existing systems had but which our new project could not gain until it had time to grow. This was a familiar Catch 22. You couldn't attract people based on the system's value without already having attracted people to give the system value.

In this sense, the success of new social media was like the success of RPS or any political organization, or even of a new book, for that matter. It depended on first participants taking a leap of faith to join or use or read it before sufficient scale made participating by others obviously beneficial.

What allowed success was a steadily escalating desire for something new. A subset of potential participants perceived in the RPS project a nearly full social media glass even while our new system was operationally nearly empty. This optimistic audience provided a base that foreshadowed real value for all users which in turn ensured a steady march of new users.

There must have been other difficulties in actually creating the system?

I wasn't involved with the programming details, but I had friends who were and they would tell me about endless hassling over all kinds of issues from database design, to features, to fonts, colors, layout, and so on.

When a group is creating something valuable, often each participant sees his or her differences with other participants as monumentally important because they are all so focussed on details. They tend to lose the forest for the trees. They think anything less than perfect will slide into disaster, and that their own favored notions are critical to perfection.

I would bet the process took twice as long, maybe even three times as long as it would have taken had all those working on it been seeking what they wound up with from the start. Still, they did finally get it done. And thereafter, if my friends are to be believed, by the time they unveiled their creation, they had already pretty much forgot about their earlier disputes, save for a few modest aesthetic and ease of navigation differences that were still being explored for possible inclusion later.

People are diverse. When creating a new social media system, or, for that matter, RPS itself, countless differences arise and it is often hard to distinguish nitpicking from more serious differences that have major implications. Seeking a new world doesn't free one from this kind of complexity or from sometimes needless hassle. Nonetheless, we can minimize waste by becoming less egocentric and more willing to test rather than dispute possibilities.

Leslie, what about media more generally, beyond the internet?

Two big trends began in the early days of RPS that continue to this day. We renovated many existing media projects by instituting equitable remuneration and balanced job complexes, and we created some new, larger scale projects.

Adding the new features couldn't have been easy...

True. The leaders of various projects were often their founders or at least people who had worked tirelessly for years. Imagine telling them they could no longer have sole control or enjoy what they thought were totally justified higher incomes than others got. For staffs, and sometimes for users too, confronting such leaders' dominance was no picnic. The leaders were not enemies and had a ton of accumulated skills. When we told such a leader to cede control to attain self-managed decision making, or to accept disempowering tasks to eliminate class difference, or to receive equitable income to promote equity and solidarity, the leaders typically felt their compliance would hurt their institution. They believed themselves indispensable and wanted to keep their familiar situation. We argued that for a media institution to have good editorial content regarding coordinator class/working class interactions and to be an instructive model able to fulfill everyone involved, change had to come. It should be done in ways that would not sacrifice the institution, of course, but it should be done.

Partly changes were about race and gender, which had been percolating for decades so that resistance to that was already tenuous and progress considerable. More controversial change addressed class division, and on that issue the battle was intense. More, the changes sought for remuneration and especially division of labor and decision making weren't only controversial for media leaders. They also put pressure on staff members who would have to become newly involved in decisions, do empowering tasks, and generally bear more responsibility.

Did you go through it personally?

Yes, very much so. Early on, in my workplace, I was the main decision maker. When these sentiments arose I said to their advocates, "What the hell are you talking about? I have given my life to this project. Some of you have been here a few years, or a year, or even just a few months. You want to displace me? You think that is fair? You think it would benefit our work to jettison my ability, knowledge, contacts, and experience?"

My reasoning seemed to me morally and logically unimpeachable and it took me awhile to realize it wasn't. What first won me over was realizing that before the change our publishing had said zero - not a single thing - about the dynamics of working class/coordinator class relations. In fact, it said nearly nothing about workplace self management, division of labor, or even markets.

That shouldn't have been surprising but I had been oblivious to it. When an institution has an attribute - in this case a corporate division of labor - that serves those with authority and also parallels ills present in society, then that attribute will tend to be off limits for internal discussion. So I realized that we needed the change, even if only on behalf of improving the quality of our editorial product, which, ironically, is what I had thought I was defending when I opposed change.

Oh, there was certainly some truth in my initial reservations. Sometimes an organization changed so precipitously, and even callously, that the organization lost its prior leaders. But, on balance, the main problem was the obstinacy of prior leaders counter productively defending class-stratified relations instead of lending their support and experience to establishing classlessness.

Was the situation similar for newly emerging media efforts?

A typical new media project would start with folks from different backgrounds. Some had more knowledge, skill, confidence, and contacts than others and would naturally become dominant unless there were structures that elevated everyone's participation. This is why when projects began and believed in solidarity and collectivity, but didn't adopt balanced job complexes, old ways resurfaced. The lesson was, don't ignore institutional features.

One powerful positive example was when folks got together and decided to generate a national network of local talk podcast shows. It was done from the start in a way embodying the values of RPS. The participants were highly engaged and positive, the product was rich and diverse, and the growth rate was incredible.

Did you ever personally feel strange devoting so much of your air time to promoting RPS views? Did you ever feel like you were an agent of RPS in media, rather than a media person doing her job?

No, though I considered the possibility, I did not feel that way. However, how I felt probably owed a lot to the rate of growth of RPS. My self definition and mandate was to provide news and analysis bearing on achieving social change. I was a member of RPS from its origin and because RPS grew so fast, my media task included covering it, addressing its views, and hearing from its participants. Even if I wasn't a member, simply on news grounds, RPS would have been a main focus. Addressing it, interviewing its members, and reporting its campaigns followed naturally because RPS was developing so fast and was so relevant and important. So my personal desires matched up with my media responsibilities.

But suppose RPS's growth had been much slower. Would you have emphasized RPS as much as you did, and if so, would you have felt like an agent of RPS more than a capable media person?

I am not sure. Is a right wing or a left wing columnist by reason of their political allegiance not a media person but only an ideologue? Or is the person both? Or is she even just a media person?

My feeling is everyone who does media - indeed everyone who communicates - has views and those views rightly impact what they choose to communicate. We should all strive for honesty and accuracy in what we offer. For our desires to cause us to be dishonest or inaccurate is wrong, whoever does it. But way short of that kind of violation of communicative ethics, what we highlight, our tone, and certainly the lessons we draw and aims we propose, all inevitably reflect not only seeking to be honest and accurate, but also to advance what we personally find important, and even what we personally favor. Our values and aims inevitably inform what we do. As worthy media people, we should admit and explain that, not deny it.

So I think my answer is had RPS grown more slowly and been less influential, I would nonetheless have pushed it hard, but I would always have made clear that I was doing so not based on an assessment that as news it was already that influential, but because I felt its intelligence and values, and what I hoped it would become, already made it news worthy.

Leslie, to close, could you tell us, do you think we will win? When will we have won? And, in just a few last words, what is one lesson from this whole period that strikes you as particularly critical?

Yes, I think war and prehistory are our past and that peace and history are our future. I guess as a media person I might say that our project will be over when our message is our medium and vice versa. A personal guiding lesson I took was act the way you'd like to be and soon you'll be the way you chose to act.

CHAPTER 27

HEALTH AND JUSTICE SEEDS

Barbara Bethune, Mark Feynman, and Robin Kunstler, discuss health and justice future.

Barbara, what seeds did you plant in hospitals?

There were two main sites of direct medical struggle: clinics and hospitals. When creating new clinics it was possible to incorporate RPS values and norms right from the start. The main issue was finding employees who desired that type of workplace. The benefits were in the quality of relations employees and patients enjoyed, and the insights for other clinics to emulate.

With already established clinics, a subset of employees would want to transition but others - typically the doctors and administrators who enjoyed higher pay, better conditions, and greater say - would not want to. The dominant dynamic was that once there were many successful newly designed clinics, resistance to change in old clinics grew much more difficult to justify. Since the new clinics worked better for patients, opponents couldn't argue that the huge disparities in income and influence they wanted to preserve were morally warranted.

Changing existing hospitals was more complex. Hospital struggle had people on both sides. Nurses typically wanted more say, more training, and better medical care, and typically welcomed doing a fair share of disempowering work. They were eager to be the kind of collectively self managing worker a new RPS style hospital required. Doctors typically argued against such changes, and owners and boards of directors did so as well. Most staff sided with nurses, but often hesitated for fear of repercussions and due to sometimes buying doctors' claims of superiority.

It took major struggle to win modest steps on a new path, but we won open budgets, new pay rates, review boards composed of employees and the right of employee assemblies to make many decisions, steadily enhanced on the job training programs, and reapportioning tasks into new job definitions. We held consciousness raising activities. We invited advisors from transformed clinics. We organized patients and communities, too. We held strikes and sit ins.

Mark, what were the biggest health industry problems to overcome?

In the private hospitals, when employees fought for costly changes at the expense of profits, owners battled. When employees fought for open books, owners battled. When employees fought for higher wages, owners battled. The second opponent of change was the hospital administration, accountants, lawyers, and many doctors.

The owners had property as the basis for their advantage. After a point it was almost impossible for them to convincingly claim that their property-based profits were warranted at all, much less at the expense of patients. It was clearly self serving and immoral.

The coordinators, however, could claim they were essential to the hospital because they had indispensable talents and knowledge. They could argue that for them to do fewer empowering tasks or receive less pay would diminish the quality of care for patients. If the surgeons in some hospital were doing 100 surgeries a week but cut back to 50, what the hell would happen to the patients?

We had two counter arguments. First, over time we could make the change by having more people trained to do the needed work, and second, the amount of newly trained doctors needed could be reduced if hospitals were not delivering inessential surgeries to generate extra income and profit - a very common practice - and if far more attention was given to preventive medicine.

Due to the above considerations, a campaign aimed at the owners could responsibly demand everything it wanted, right off. But if a project aimed at the coordinator class / working class division demanded all it wanted, its immediate gains would have been offset by immediate damage to patients. Therefore, the second project had to win a trajectory of changes, including training programs, changes in medical schools and hospitals, and changes in diverse policies.

What were some turning point victories along the way?

Where I was employed, the turning point was when tasks were reapportioned. At first we asked, what doctor tasks could nurses immediately take on? What tasks could we reduce or jettison? What might doctors do that would involve them more in the rote and less fulfilling parts of hospital work?

The initial changes were modest, but nonetheless established the need to evaluate and make decisions about the division of tasks in hospital work. After establishing that, I felt it was all downhill to a really healthy hospital.

I remember the first meeting I was at where the agenda was to argue for or against evaluating the division of labor. There were raucous fights about every suggestion that came from the nurses and other employees. Some of what the doctors had to say was incredibly classist and degrading. And yet, I was elated. I knew the key step had been taken. Once it was legitimate to look at job roles and reapportion tasks to create a better hospital, in my mind it was inevitable we would win all the way to balanced job complexes and self management.

It wasn't just that we had won recognition of the legitimacy of carefully and patiently altering job definitions. It was that we had won that and we workers now knew the score. Our victory was non-reformist. Its meaning and value resided precisely in its future.

Mark, do you think we will win? When will we have won? And what is one lesson from this whole period that you found particularly critical?

When I realized classlessness was possible, I knew we had to win. When I saw awareness spread, I knew we would win, and I think we will have won when classism is no more. A lesson I took was respect requires reciprocity, reciprocity produces respect.

Barbara, what about social policies, insurance, and pharmaceutical policies?

In this, the public, as consumer recipients of health care, played a much greater role. The first step was winning single payer health care for all. Then came a number of related victories around medical pricing and funding. But the really profound confrontation - because it was with some of the most powerful corporations in society and provoked much broader debate and conflict - was to gain control of pharmaceutical production and distribution.

You might think, when we got free medical care and single payer coverage what difference did the prices of the medicines make? The answer was, just because the individual patient was no longer paying for medicines, the government was still paying with funds that should have been spent on valuable projects rather than funneled to pharmaceutical owners.

But what could we do? Tell people to boycott medicine? Not a very appealing stance. Have workers in medicine manufacturing workplaces cut off the flow of medicines? That would destroy the sick to save them. The owners legitimately claimed we couldn't survive without what they provided. People would suffer immeasurably without medicine. If we were going to win the battle, we needed an approach that would steadily build support, win gains, and eventually fully win. What could that be?

We started "medicine for health not profit." We demanded that the government impose price controls on pharmaceutical companies and that it take over any company that violated those controls. Corporate fear of this, well before the left had gotten anywhere near calling for it, had been at the heart of elite rejection of single payer health care all along, and their image of impending loss had been correct.

Our problem was how do we mount sufficient pressure on the government for it to impose enforceable requirements on pharmaceutical companies, without our boycotting the companies or calling for work stoppages at them?

The answer was widespread public campaigns that pinpointed company heads, owners, and other decision makers, revealing their hypocrisy and calling on them to change. We did this to raise consciousness, win gains, and force the government not just to adopt health care for all, but to use its bargaining power to continually force lower medicine prices at threat of nationalization if the companies did not comply. But what pressure could get the government to act in such a way? Partly risk at the polling booths. Partly realizing that to ignore the growing struggle against the pharmaceutical companies would not only cause the movement to grow even stronger, it would also cause it to enlarge its focus beyond health care.

> *Barbara, to conclude, do you think we will win? When will we have won? And what is one lesson from this whole period that strikes you as particularly critical?*

Injustice will persist as residue and exception for a long time, but institutions that enshrine it will not, and I guess we will have gotten to that point when social health is normal and social illness is deviant.

As to a personal lesson, as a doctor I think it is something more or less like what Che Guevara, also a doctor, decided as he was determining his path through life. He felt that to sincerely do medicine he had to forgo carrying a medical bag and instead carry a rifle. His country had to escape subordination to Cuban elites and U.S. neocolonialism.

My situation, country, and times, were obviously very different than his. I didn't need a rifle, I needed marching shoes. Still, I think the shared lesson is healthy institutions means healthy people so delivering healthy people has to mean winning healthy institutions.

Robin, what about the legal system?

The main focus had to be revising our approach to prosecution. As with other situations, this could occur by changing the court system or by creating alternatives parallel to the current courts.

For the former, part of it was changing laws and punishments, but also renovating the approach to prosecution and adjudication. Winning changes in penalties, particularly for victimless and non violent crimes, hugely altered the life of the court and dramatically reduced the incredible price to individuals and society of incarcerations. But then came need for a deeper renovation of the whole process to bring it into line with civilized values - including stronger guarantees for the accused, collectivizing criminal procedures, and having the state pay bills on all sides. The main change in mentality was to shift from a tone of retribution against violators and narrow material and organizational self advancement on the part of practitioners, to rehabilitation in sentencing and incarceration and equitable remuneration for practitioners so they could reclaim sensible motivations.

Much was underway before RPS surfaced, but the breadth of RPS membership and its cross discipline focus added greatly by enlarging the battle lines from families trying to help the accused and inmates, to mass movements of prisoners and families, and then to student movements among prospective practitioners in criminal justice programs and law schools, plus solidarity from other movements, all fighting to change the system.

What about prisons and jails?

The problems were well known. More people in prison than in colleges was an incredible blot on society. Half to two thirds of those in U.S. prisons would not be in prison in Europe, even if they were guilty of what they were arrested for. Horrible poverty and subordination alongside cultural exhortations to become rich led to perpetual depression followed by desperate acts. Stupendous hypocrisy and rip off on all sides regularized the mindset of "me first and screw you." Markets rewarded and regimented that sentiment.

Incredible abuse and over crowding made prisons schools for future crime. Being a more effective criminal was something you could learn in prison, and future crime was many inmate's only available avenue toward survival after release. The horrors went on and on.

Inmates were virtual slaves. They worked for the state for nearly nothing. They had every moment of their days supervised by authorities free to punish them pretty much however they wished and whenever they wanted. Courts were assembly lines that produced prisoners who filled cells to keep the whole complex churning.

I think the biggest turning point was when prisoner activism inspired prison guards, who were typically notoriously hardened and made callous by their own less than ideal conditions, to nonetheless mount solidarity strikes supporting prisoner actions against overcrowding and slave labor. Of course, some guards were made so brutal and dismissive by their experiences they defended the grossly confrontational prison system, but others somehow retained or rediscovered their humanity and that, plus knowing firsthand the horror of incarceration, caused them to dissent. They began to reject their own circumstances and the circumstances of prisoners, like the police began to have misgivings about repressing rallies, marches, strikes, and demonstrations. Sympathy from those the state paid to keep order for those rising up against the state was a sure sign fundamental change was coming.

Would there be crime in future society? Would there be police and courts?

Back before RPS many on the left answered that there would be no crime, no police, no courts. For them, this had to be true because otherwise their whole orientation was at risk. Others of us were always confused by that. Why did astute people feel that to admit there would still be crime, police, and need to adjudicate disputes would be a slippery slope toward admitting that there is no alternative to class, race, and gender injustice?

You certainly have to believe people are capable of good will, solidarity, and self management to believe in the RPS vision for society. But it isn't necessary to believe that complex circumstances would never generate anti social actions or sentiments. Not only is it not necessary, it is pretty much absurd.

We know from history that people can do vile things. When you switch from institutions that make behaving in vile ways the best or only route to well being or even survival, to institutions that oppose vile behavior, you get much less vile behavior. You might even say that the only vile behavior you get in the new situation is overt pathology, drunken violence, jealous violence, and so on. But, even if that proves true, that is not nothing.

We don't fully know, even with all the considerable experiments we already have, what the maturation of a just and peaceful society will mean for many aspects of human relations, including crime. But I don't see any reason to think that all crime will disappear, that there will never be tense standoffs, criminal violence, or anger at unfair behavior. I see no reason to think we won't need people trained to handle difficult conflictual situations, to discover the perpetrators of crimes, and to adjudicate disputes.

I believe there will be massively less crime for many reasons. People won't do it out of desperation for livable conditions. Nor will people be able to criminally amass great wealth since having such wealth would make evident having stolen it since in a good society there would no legal avenue to amassing great wealth. But that doesn't mean there will be no crime and no dangerous situations. And just as with flying an airplane, or doing a kidney transplant, there is no reason to say that everyone should be ready to deal with it.

The argument before RPS said that police have means to exploit their situation at the expense of others so we need to get rid of police. Well, pilots could exploit their situation, so could doctors, builders, and a whole host of different folks. The issue isn't some abstract possibility of wrong-doing, but whether a pursuit is organized in such a way as to propel its practitioners into paranoid, hyper aggressive, anti social viewpoints and give them, as well, incentives to exploit their circumstances. Getting rid of ill conceptions, eliminating exploitable circumstances, and eliminating inessential functions are sensible steps. Eliminating "policing" is not sensible.

> *Robin, do you think we will win? When will we have won? And what is one lesson from this whole period that strikes you as particularly critical?*

In history's court the past is past and the future is ours. I think a sign we will have won will be when law of conscience trumps law of government. And as a lawyer and judge, a lesson I took early on and that has guided me since is that justice, not law, is a worthy partner, a powerful ally, a transcendent guide.

CHAPTER 28

EDUCATION AND ECONOMY SEEDS

Bertrand Dellinger, Anton Rocker, and Harriet Lennon discuss education and economy future.

Bertrand, universities and schooling more generally were also subject to renovation, weren't they?

Yes, as RPS was being born, universities and schools had all the problems they had had for decades past. As earlier, they were repositories of dull drill, extinguished feeling, narrowed vision, and destroyed character, and there was one new problem as well. The attention span and motivation of students had seriously deteriorated.

I and many friends who were teaching back then found that we couldn't usefully give lectures any longer. The problem was that the students would sit in the large lecture halls and have on their laps phones, tablets, or even laptops, and they would give far more attention to those than to the lecture. Lectures required sustained attention. The electronic doo-dads fostered flitting from thing to thing. Students sat there texting, emailing, watching short videos, listening to music, browsing. Click, click, click, they jumped from brief focus to brief focus. It was so habitual they became driven to avoid the operational dissonance of trying to maintain a serious, sustained, focus. They weren't good at multitasking. They were good at flitting. And they gravitated toward doing what they were good at doing. So they would quickly flit from focus to focus and it even seeped downward from colleges to become the norm in high schools too. Kids would have ear buds in, listening to music, during class.

As faculty, to teach we felt we had to find ways to nuggetize our messages so as to accommodate the short focus of our students. But nuggetizing our messages only cemented the dynamic...

It must have been incredibly frustrating...

It was. People are born ignorant, no doubt about that. But we are made stupid by faulty education. To see students drift away was like being pummeled, daily, by failure. It was hard not to get hostile toward the students. They were killing their own curiosity. They preferred to mentally die than think. But, in truth, the trend was not confined to young people.

At a family holiday gathering, for example, whereas when I was young, there would be joking around, and TV, too, there would also be serious talk about matters of intellectual interest and issues of the day. In particular, the young would be curious. They would want to hear reasons for what was going on around them. Likewise for adults.

But in the immediate pre RPS period, kids would sit on a couch with a tablet, laptop, and phone, and with the TV on. They would flit from one to the other. They couldn't even focus on something they still were interested in much less have sustained interest in something substantial. They were almost proud of social ignorance. Party and play. Shop till we drop. Flit from Facebook to Twitter to TV to web site, and back. Do it again. Hold views based on their repetition on those venues. Screw evidence. Know little. Investigate nothing. Of course, this wasn't all young people but it was way too many. And it wasn't just them. It really was a sad state of affairs. And it virally spread to adults as well, not least because they accepted it in their kids. In time, like kids like parents. So while parents weren't so enmeshed in screens, they were more into gossip and consumption/TV talk than anything more lasting.

What was new about the situation was we had ever present social media, selfies, and news as entertainment. Serious ideas annoyed short attention spans. Imagine that. And that doesn't even include the incredible dishonesty, judgementalism, and bullying that social media inspired.

Returning to schooling, all this greatly aggravated what had already been long present and which was ultimately even more critical, which was that the prevalent education process wasn't primarily about education. Schools socialized and sometimes transferred (highly constrained) lessons and skills but mainly they delivered students, like any other product, suitably packaged for their consumers, their future employers. And what was suitable to the future employers of course depended on the role the student would fill.

This meant roughly 80% of people coming out of public schools should be prepared to endure boredom and take orders, the two main prerequisites to being a desirable hire for an employer trying to fill working class jobs. The other 20% should have particular knowledge suited to accounting, medicine, engineering, or whatever - but also a disposition suitable to maintaining dominance over workers below while obeying owners above.

When schools delivered folks ready for those two futures, they were by the old society's standards succeeding. Their graduates would comfortably fill the slots they were destined for. Their graduates weren't underprepared for their tasks, or, even worse, disinclined to accept their tasks or over prepared for them.

So RPS educational transformation, like for other domains, had to be comprehensive. One path was to create new schools from scratch. Many RPS folks set up neighborhood schools, did group home schooling, or initiated summer schools and other such innovations for children and also for workmates and townsfolk. A few even created new institutions for higher learning.

But transforming education was also about battling inside existing schools. Public school teachers, community college teachers, and especially grad students at many colleges and universities, were a bit like nurses in hospitals. Many were themselves eager to be productive workers of a new self managing kind. And they were ready to fight for it with strikes and other actions. But educational transformation was also, even more than many other transformations, about society overall.

In any society, education has to prepare people to participate. Having education generate confident, capable adults requires having a society that needs confident, capable adults. So educational transformation had two powerful advocates. Students, teachers, and families battled for better results in their current or new schools and people all over society battled for society's future.

In RPS both factors influenced movements seeking to develop new educational institutions or to steadily alter existing ones while demanding broad educational policy changes. We sought to fulfill students and teachers by seeking new social relations that would require from schools new citizens. That was a long term revolutionary aspect of our non reformist approach to education.

Where has it led?

Changes are still happening, but some big gains have been vastly increased involvement of communities and parents in schooling and learning. You probably remember not just the demand to open schools but the occupational and community programs that were then enacted, at night, fait accompli, all over the country. Early on, these campaigns demanded opening thousands of schools in the afternoons and evenings for all kinds of activities and learning, not only by students, but by adults too. But then we realized, what the hell, why are we asking anyone. The schools are there, we should just go in and use them. And we did. Not least inviting police to have courses too, to enjoy classes too, which did wonders for dimming their ardor for repressing school takeovers.

The reduction of class size with the steady increase in number of teachers has been another huge gain. But the main thing, I think, has been the infusion into schools of the mindset that education should uncover and nurture people's curiosity and talents in whatever directions people desire, and the infusion of a critical mindset into classroom pursuits, replacing old patterns of discipline, topics, drill, memorization, competitiveness, and the like with self directed learning and cooperative exploration and with the broader society gaining from that, rather than the broader society restricting schools to providing fodder for business.

Higher education, like public education, also had to become relevant to people's fulfillment rather than to people passively fitting unfulfilling slots waiting in society. Partly this was a matter of the approach of faculty. Should we hammer in facts to no intellectual benefit, as in the past, or should we foster comprehension and critical thinking, to huge intellectual benefit, in the future?

You might think this would have been trivial to attain. What teacher would want to regiment rather than facilitate? But it wasn't trivial because many existing teachers had become habituated to old ways, adept at them, and scared of failing at new tasks. Still, it had to happen and it did.

Another big change was a matter of what students pursued, what they had available to read, who they had available to talk with, what they could attain. The whole notion of learning as a mutual project, and of caring for the place of learning as a collective pursuit, and especially the idea that society should bend its roles to the outcomes of enlightened learning, rather than schools curtailing enlightened learning to accommodate a restrictive society, totally changed the relations among all the actors, just as with other institutions.

What do you think was the turning point after which you felt that you were no longer battling against the odds, the odds were now on your side?

I think there were quite a few. For example, the first occupation of a public school - it was in Chicago - with the ensuing mass meeting to determine what uses the school could be put to at night, was one. You saw that happen, you saw people experience that their surroundings should benefit them rather than their restraining themselves to fit harsh surroundings, and you knew right away that it would spread and the ramifications would be profound and irreversible. And what an immense change in terms of people's involvement and in the attitudes people had to schools and education that and other school occupations led to.

Similarly, I think the campaign by RPS to provide alternative online curricula that challenged the prevalent social science and history texts had a huge effect, too. It is ironic that right wing fundamentalist types had a campaign of this sort early in Trump's era, trying to send kids to school carrying the incredibly warped anti science myths and lies they favored. That failed. But when lots of kids came into classes highly knowledgeable about flaws in the old lessons, confident, and able to think through evidence and logical connections, it succeeded, not least because while a bit scared over the changes, many teachers quickly saw the students' preparedness as supportive rather than challenging. This began in San Francisco and Boston, but then spread very rapidly. It put immense pressure on faculty to do better, and many faculty quickly not only saw the potential of real learning, but overcame their fear of repercussions from above and began to work to help provide it.

For me, another key happening was when students on the campus where I was teaching at the time, NYU, called a strike, shut down the place, and then reopened it for a full week of nothing but faculty student discussion of faculty student relations and the purpose of education and implications for how it should be conducted. The students didn't just call for discussion. They came to the sessions profoundly prepared. They chaired. They had ideas. They won respect at an entirely new level, and convinced faculty of their aims. The feeling of community that emerged, which was helped along by all kinds of social events the students conducted each night and sometimes during the day, too, was itself incredibly powerful. Commitment to what was called student faculty power, in place of administrative power, became ubiquitous.

Perhaps most surprising were campaigns by students in elite professional schools demanding preparation for balanced job complexes and for solidarity in place of elite control and classist separatism. It wasn't all elite school students, of course, but those efforts were stunning instances of human solidarity. They accelerated emerging participatory mentalities and policies throughout society.

Also critical, but more familiar and rooted in activism that preceded RPS, was the upheaval of student and academic life regarding the role of women and cultural communities. But that too changed somewhat. Earlier the campus focus was largely on the tone of daily life, on personal affronts, or what were called, I think, micro aggressions. Of course all that was real even if sometimes handled imperfectly, but as RPS agendas began to have influence a second focus became underlying campus social relations, the composition of faculty, the course curriculum, and particularly, and most innovatively, what had earlier been called the town gown interface. This mirrored public school's opening to the community. Now it was universities providing programs for local residents and research and resources for local activism.

All in all, instead of education being a bulwark of system maintenance, education became a propellant of system change. Elites had always feared this possibility, and fought as best they could to prevent it, but our day came and once the trend was sufficiently developed it became self fueling and unstoppable.

All the way back in the 1960s/1970s, shortly after the upheavals of those times, elites evaluating the situation decided that a big part of the cause was that public schools had, due to the space race with Russia and emphasis on enriched education that it had spurred, become a very serious social problem. Public schools were graduating way too many students who expected to creatively utilize their intelligence and initiative in society. When these students encountered the regimentation and subordination characteristic of typical daily life pre RPS, they were round pegs headed for square holes. And many said no, not with my life you don't, spurring the cultural and political rebellions of the time.

Elites looked at that and said, we can't ever have that again. We have to change things. We have to reapportion school funds, change curriculum, and impose rules on teachers, all to ensure that the next generation and the one after that accept and even welcome their limited lot in life rather than questioning and rejecting it. And elites acted on that self serving insight and for decades it worked as they wanted, leading to poorly educated graduates who felt lucky to get work at all - and to the hypocritical and ignorant mess that was the U.S. educational system by about 2010, say, much less under Trump.

RPS pursued an opposite approach. Instead of squashing most students into passive conformity and making the rest elitist, we sought to conduct education based on the real needs and potentials of all students. We sought to nurture desires and insights wherever they led and that is precisely what RPS-inspired educational activism and movements have been doing.

———

Anton, where do we stand regarding new workplaces?

I don't have a full accounting and I doubt anyone does but just before RPS began I read there were 300 large, effective worker coops in the U.S., though maybe there were more, I don't know. Other than a very few, however, these weren't remotely RPS style workplaces but were instead dominated by coordinator class officials. Though they typically had considerably more worker participation and more equitable remuneration schemes than mainstream corporations, they had no clear redefinition of job roles and had barely any awareness of issues regarding markets. The latter two absences restricted and distorted the aspirations of workers across virtually all these fledgling efforts.

As RPS emerged, nonetheless, co-ops were the quickest workplace converts. Not having owners - something that was true of all non profits which were similar in various respects to the coops and often overlapped completely - the owner-aspect of opposition to an RPS trajectory was absent and the anti-owner aspect of program was already implemented. Likewise, co-op workers already had a rhetoric of workplace participation and democracy, if not the full reality of it, which meant they were at least part way to an RPS stance. The additional step was to embrace self management, including transforming the division of labor and becoming aware of the pressures of markets and of ways to ward off and eventually transcend those pressures.

So, RPS workplace progress had three paths: take worker co-ops another step; organize inside corporations for a trajectory of RPS oriented changes; and set up new fully RPS identified and structured workplaces.

One of the largest factors affecting the speed of such developments was each effort's willingness to see itself as deserving society-wide emulation and its participants agitating not only for their own individual project, but for others to become as involved as they were, as well. But this was hard to elicit.

I remember an early trip to a workplace in Columbus Ohio. I arrived and got a tour from a few employees. The firm had been in grave trouble and the owners had decided to sell off its assets. The workers felt they could salvage the firm for themselves. The firm could have then become a worker co-op of the limited sort but partly because of the advanced awareness of some of the workers, and partly because many of the coordinator class staff decided they wanted to leave due to thinking that without the owners the firm would collapse, the new firm moved pretty quickly in more radical directions.

This was pretty common to the period of the 2020s. Sometimes involved workers would make incomes equitable and institute workplace democracy in councils but ignore job definitions and operate with little change regarding market competition. Other times the transformation of a firm would be more complete, including implementing balanced job complexes and full worker self management.

In the former case, the struggle in the workplace would persist largely as a contest between coordinators and workers who were still structurally at odds. In the latter case, the struggle was instead workers against old habits and the pressures of the market and banks.

But what I want to note, and what I encountered in my Columbus trip visiting one of the more developed efforts, is different. Talking to them about their redefinition of their work and social relations was exciting and joyful, to be sure. But there came a moment when I asked how their relatives and friends outside who still worked at typical capitalist corporate workplaces regarded their efforts. Were they having success organizing such folks to follow the new path?

And now came a shock. The workers who were so proud of their achievements in seeking new job definitions and collective self management and so happy about the redefinition of their workplaces unanimously said they didn't talk about their project even with family and friends much less with larger audiences. They said folks at other firms would do something similar to what they were doing only if their firms met hard times and the owners decided to cash out so they were left with no choice but to take over or become unemployed.

I asked directly, would you take a job in a corporation, if I offered it, giving up your project, no longer having any say, no longer having new type jobs, but in return receiving much higher pay from me? They all said don't be ridiculous. Life depends on income, sure, but fulfillment, pleasure, dignity, and justice are not measured by wages alone.

I said, okay, if you feel that way, why can't you explain the benefits of transforming workplaces to your relatives and friends so that they would begin to pursue such aims even in their profitable firms, rather than only when their owners abdicate? They shrugged and said that just like they didn't do that, other folks wouldn't do it until they became desperate.

I am still not sure what was at work in this mindset, but it was obviously poison for change. Perhaps it was a variant on hopelessness but it was coming from people who, oddly, had great hope, at least for themselves. Maybe it was a way to avoid the discomfort of clashing with relatives and friends, even if doing so could open a path to greater well being and unity for all. Or maybe they literally believed what they were telling me - that as long as there were profit seeking capitalist firms to employ folks, folks would not seek something different and better. I don't know, but if the view persisted it would mean that each transformed workplace would remain an isolated phenomenon, without wider impact, because those involved would not take their insights to others.

RPS realized that this worker reticence to reach out had to be overcome. A coop transforming, a corporation undergoing internal struggles, and a new firm getting up and running, would each have to report their efforts and experiences. They would each have to see their task as not simply establishing their own firm, but also enlisting others to do likewise. Isolated firms with increased equity and justice were positive, of course, but what really mattered was having each such beachhead become a prod for attaining more.

Some implications were that RPS emphasized creating workers councils and then federations of all workplaces that had such councils, where the federation would take responsibility for mutual aid, mutual defense, and even mutual insurance. Also, RPS sponsored events bringing workers from advanced projects to speak at other venues, including helping with preparations. It also made films and reports. When these things happened - the whole picture altered.

So, before RPS there were roughly 30 million small businesses in the U.S. About 20,000 of those, which sounds like a whole lot but is less than a tenth of a percent, had more than 500 employees, though I think this didn't count schools, churches, universities, most hospitals, public service industries, etc. Today I would guess there are perhaps 2 million well established RPS small businesses, and another 5 million that are struggling with transforming and that could join the RPS count without much more change. RPS ideas battle for influence in nearly all the rest, too. And there are about 3,000 500 person or more RPS oriented workplaces, and another 2,000 with very substantial struggles going on, and all 20,000 include RPS style campaigns and in most cases already have growing degrees of council organization. And the situation is considerably more advanced in educational, health, and other public service domains.

In short, RPS economics are spreading in the form of actual new RPS institutions, advanced face offs inside old non RPS institutions over becoming new, and less advanced but still quite serious organizing efforts in the rest. And the momentum is now all ours.

> *Anton, do you think we will win? When will we have won? And, in just a few last words, what is one lesson from this whole period that struck you as particularly critical?*

A few years back I stared at police arrayed at a mass event, and watched them transform from enemies into allies. I knew then that it was only a matter of time until we would win. I think that time will have arrived when peace and justice are synonyms. Finally, a lesson I learned pretty early on, and that has only been ratified and enlarged for me since, is that diversity produces continuity and continuity permits diversity.

> *Harriet, what about arriving at connections among all these efforts, and also, in particular, at new ways to allocate in the economy?*

Our allocation question was how should we connect RPS-ish or fully RPS workplaces to one another? How could we go from competitive market allocation to cooperative collectively negotiated participatory planning? What steps would advance that process?

We realized not far into the development of RPS that we had to discover how to make changes in the economy that generate not only more just outcomes now, but also a mindset and structures that could melt into the future we desire. We knew every great dream begins with a dreamer. But we also knew a dream you dream alone remains only a dream, whereas a dream you dream with others can become reality.

Various reforms like price controls, constraints on competitive behavior, pollution controls and other ecological requirements, minimum wage laws, open book requirements, progressive taxes, and shortened duration of work, could all constrain market operations and could simultaneously, if proposed and discussed with the purpose firmly evidenced and emphasized, point toward non market possibilities. So all those were typically part of RPS efforts. But I think you are asking more about the initial emergence of participatory planning structures.

We began, necessarily, with small scale projects. For example, in a neighborhood, consumers - and typically this would be renters in large apartment complexes - would start to use their collective power to win better circumstances but would also begin to cooperatively apportion their assets to everyone's advantage, while they undertook all manner of struggles.

So in these cases there would emerge food coops where large groups pooled their buying capacity to extract better rates from suppliers. But then, something even more interesting and progressive would happen. After all, using bargaining power to get better prices helped folks in need and even established a new balance of power by overcoming disempowering fragmentation, but it didn't establish a fundamentally new way of operating.

The more fundamental change came when workers and nearby communities began to negotiate outcomes with one another. Of course sometimes this was pretty easy since the workers in the RPS workplaces were also consumers in the vicinity and also lived in the apartments that were organizing. But not always. Sometimes, instead, the apartment councils and the worker councils, often but not only food producers, were some distance apart and didn't have overlapping memberships. Still new practices spread from neighbors trusting workers they knew, to trusting people with whom they had no prior contact. And these new practices were not to compete in a zero sum exchange based on power, but, instead, to negotiate exchanges taking into account the relative circumstances and impacts on all involved. This was a huge step.

At first it happened only quite locally, but nonetheless, the associated practices and mindsets had more general relevance. If it could happen for a locale, why not for a city, state, or country? Why not for the world?

RPS's broad and skeletal vision of cooperative, collaborative negotiation of economic inputs and outputs began to develop practical substance. People started to have personal experiences of what it could look like and achieve. People began to realize the incredible restrictions built into their familiar seemingly unavoidable market defined realities.

At the same time, popular movements for oversight of broader economic sectors - for example, what was called participatory budgeting to oversee government expenditures - had a similar dynamic. Again, those involved consciously decided their preferences based on discussion and negotiation rather than succumbing to competitive bargaining power. Coops and consumer councils networked together to build grassroots dimensions of participatory planning. Simultaneously, industry- and even society-wide restraints on prices and salaries as well as new ecological practices won by broad movement campaigns foreshadowed national federations of worker and consumer councils planning public goods investments.

So where are we now? We still have mostly private ownership. Markets are still in place and operating. But the most dynamic and exciting parts of economic life, the parts that people admire and wish to be part of, are largely RPS oriented. There is, you might say, a proud and hopeful RPS economy operating in the midst of a moribund holdover capitalist economy. We are no longer odd upstarts considered weird and hopeless compared to apparently permanent and sensible corporate actors. No, we are the future and everyone knows it. Everyone is more or less patiently and eagerly carrying through with transforming lives and relations. The change is clearly coming for all.

Of course there is still fierce opposition. But it has the character of an aging athlete trying to hold off father time. We don't want to kill off the adherents of the old. We simply want to keep diminishing their sway, reducing their holdings, and when we can, updating their mentalities, even while we also welcome them, whenever they see clear to realizing that it is their only dignified and workable path, to join our endeavors by entering jobs, positions, and roles of the RPS sort.

But I should say that this approach of building the new alongside the old, is not without risk. While there are still owners, they conspire as their natural pursuit to block and reverse our advances. That we know this threat persists guides us to unrelentingly restrict their options, and to continually win new perches from which to fight, leaving them no viable means to blunt our progress.

This explains, as well, why RPS has given so much attention and energy to growing our own media and contesting old media, and to enlisting our supporters into police forces and the military, and to forthrightly addressing the views of opponent citizens - not owners, but average folks - with continual respectful attention, constantly taking our progress with them as our measure of success, not the stridency or brilliance of our repeating our own virtues, while our opponents stay hostile.

Harriet, do you think we will win? When will we have won? And, in just a few last words, what is one lesson from this whole period that has struck you personally as particularly critical for you?

Yes, I think we will win. Life prevails and so will we. I guess we will have unalterably and fully won when history records that prehistory is no more. For me a personal lesson I took, and retained, was that violence breeds injustice whereas non violence breeds mutual aid.

CHAPTER 29

WORLD AND PLANET

In which Bertrand Dellinger, Dylan Cohen, and Stephen Du Bois address war and peace and ecology.

Bertrand, what do you think a full RPS victory in the U.S. will mean for world affairs?

Back during the U.S. war on Vietnam and Indochina the government used as a pretext what they called the Domino Theory. The idea was that if a country fell into the hands of the Soviets, more countries would fall too. If Vietnam went, Thailand, Indonesia, and Japan, would follow. It was idiocy, of course, as it was stated, but a variant of the same refrain was called by Noam Chomsky, the threat of a good example.

His idea was if Vietnam could show that it was possible to escape U.S. domination and create a desirable society, why not other countries, not only in Indochina, but all over the world?

Of course, in this interpretation of the dynamic, what elites feared was actually a good thing, and trying to prevent it was a horrible thing. The U.S. reply was to make the carpet-bombed human cost of extrication from our dominance too high to contemplate.

There are many conceivable dimensions of a full RPS victory in the U.S. for world affairs. First, with the U.S. no longer pursuing imperial ambitions and instead solidarity and internationalism, a main cause of international violations will be removed. A main obstacle - though not the only obstacle to peaceful world affairs - will be gone.

Another impact is the threat of a good example. If the population of the U.S. can escape tutelage to old structural institutional forms to create a new society, why can't others? Of course, we already see this happening all around the world, and a case can be made, for that matter, that the early Vietnamese example, though not initially fully successful for Vietnam, and though not adopting RPS style content until quite recently, did spread lessons and aspirations worldwide that later fueled RPS itself.

At any rate, I think full RPS victory in the U.S. will shortly follow, or precede, comparable victories for new social forms in most if not all of the world. Once many major countries are on the side of justice, how long can injustice prevail? It loses its material defenders and its aura of invincible inevitability.

What's RPS's take on international relations?

The aim remains self management, classlessness, inter communalism, and feminism. RPS realizes centuries of distorted economic and social development can't be eliminated in minutes across the globe, any more than we can do that overnight in the U.S., but it also asserts that there is no worthy reason why some countries should endlessly retain giant advantages from the past and others endlessly retain giant deficits.

So the main international point is to find a way to redress inequalities so that we live in a world where there is justice not only within some countries, but within all countries and across borders as well.

So how do we do that?

One aspect will be engaging in international trade in a new way. Trade occurs when one party enters an agreement to provide another party an item where overall benefits outweigh overall costs. But how should the benefits accrue to the two parties?

In market transactions and geopolitical relations, the benefits of trade accrue in accord with bargaining power, not justice. The more powerful trader grabs most benefits and the gap between more powerful and weaker actors widens. If I start with more, I get more benefit, so even though you get some gain, my advantage grows larger. The RPS approach is the bulk of the benefits of trade should always go to the poorer country. That plus direct aid from wealthier to poorer countries, would be the essence of international agreements among RPS style countries operating in a better future.

> Bertrand, to close, I would like to ask, do you think we will win? When will we have won? And, in just a few last words, what is one lesson from this whole period that strikes you as particularly critical?

If we do not try, we cannot win. If we do try, we can. And I think winning will be in our past when reason and sympathy compatibly guide human choices. The main thing I learned was that perfection blocks excellence, but excellence propels perfection.

> Dylan, did you believe when you joined RPS that it would usher in an end to war? Do you think it will?

Suppose I asked, Miguel, did you believe when becoming involved with RPS that it would usher in an end to crime? Do you now think it will?

I bet you would answer, as I would, no, I did not believe that though I thought RPS would hugely diminish crime because social lives of citizens would engender far greater mutual aid, or perhaps better put, would not stifle such sentiments. But, still, all manner of pathologies could cause violations, or honest disagreements, or fierce anger, so we wouldn't have no crime, but would have vastly less crime.

By analogy you might think I would answer that with RPS success the odds of wars between countries will diminish hugely, but war will not disappear. But I actually think, and I hope, that a couple of additional factors bearing on war between countries, as compared to crime between individuals, will change the calculus.

War involves vast numbers of people. What's more, war depends on prior arms production, military organization, and training. The collective scale of war means, I think, that reduced motivations for it, reduced mentalities willing to accommodate it, and reduced preparedness for it, will literally end it. We could still have lone advocates of war, like we would have lone criminals, but once social relations are transformed, I don't believe we will have whole countries eager, willing, or even able to wage war.

What have you felt to be our most important steps on the road to no more war?

In a general sense, I think the steady emergence of RPS-like movements and organizations in countries all over the world has mattered even more than single-issue efforts on behalf of peace. But if I had to pick one thing that has turned the corner toward eliminating war it would probably be the massive campaigns to transform military bases around the world into vehicles for social programs of reconstruction and protection against natural disasters. Those campaigns not only overtly oppose war and injustice, they also offer positive paths and make clear that arguments against peace are not about what's possible, but only about what benefits the rich and powerful.

I have been privileged to attend numerous demonstrations and participate in many campaigns around the world, around demobilizing or retooling bases. For me, seeing not just the anti war sentiment these transformations nourish, but the sense of possibility and optimism they convey has been profoundly moving. Connecting desires for ecological sanity and equitable reconstruction to internationalist anti war desires keeps gaining support. I now think peace for all time is within our grasp. The next big peace dance will be on the graves of the world's last masters of war.

Dylan, to close, could you tell us, do you think we will win? When will we have won? And, in just a few last words, what is one lesson from this whole period that strikes you as particularly critical?

Of course we will win. I just wish many more could have lived long enough to enjoy the days to follow. An indicator of when the victory will be ours - perhaps when we are American, Russian, Jewish, Muslim, or anything else, only to further our humanity. A lesson I have taken is that unity of will is powerful. Diversity of mind is essential. And passive obedience destroys both.

Stephen, how did you become deeply involved in ecological activism?

I happened to be in Haiti during a massive hurricane in 2016. I saw high water wipe out homes and take lives. It was frightening, depressing, and then, in short order, infuriating. The local poverty and lack of serious international help made the damage even more devastating than the winds entailed, and I realized that the storm, and so many others like it, owed significantly to corporate elites making earth-eviscerating decisions.

I was only 15 years old for that hurricane, but I had already heard a bit about global warming and climate change in school and from my parents. Still, I was a kid, and everything seemed possible, and nothing seemed so bad that I should be deterred from my daily desires. I had personal world's to conquer. Global warming was beyond my reach. But the hurricane changed me.

I was there. I felt its fury. I felt like saying, okay, I have had enough, stop already, but it had no ears to hear me. The experience made personal what I had read about global warming. Climate change was no longer abstract. It was horrendous disasters crushing humans and places. It was hard rain falling. And you couldn't pray or beg its end.

I was shattered, but before long I gained back some equilibrium and started to read voraciously about the interconnections of living things and their environments, and about the effects of human choices on each.

If being in the storm was frightening, then reading and thinking about global warming was even more frightening. Calls for action weren't alarmist. If we didn't change our ways, devastation would rain down from the sky and rise up from the sea. Everything was broken. I became Green, and then radical.

Did you feel there was a turning point from just witnessing ecological decline to being on a path toward ecological success?

The more I read the more I felt that most people were either delusionally denying the obvious, or that they admitted it, at least somewhat, but just went on about their lives in the belief that whatever will be will be. Working to affect the possibilities was beyond them. It was the alienation of our times. A harsh formulation was that we were trying to be happy idiots.

People often knew the situation, and even its utility for elites, but so what? They felt powerless. I soon realized that to alter our deadly trajectory people would have to see a clear path to a better situation. They would have to see how they could lend their energies so their contribution would matter.

That's why I think the turning point was when significant sectors of the population not only believed in the immense danger of global warming, but also realized there was a route to survival they could meaningfully contribute to.

Of course, some people honestly thought getting a long-lasting light bulb, keeping the thermostat down, taking short showers, or segmenting their trash, was all they should concern themselves with. But most people knew the economy had to jettison fossil fuels for renewable energy - among other changes. And they knew such transformations would require massive public pressure.

So the issue for each person was: Can I contribute to generating that pressure worth my time, given my impact? And this possibility, even this inevitability of their own personal efficacy, is what RPS had to get people to see if people were going to join broad movements and RPS itself.

And when that message got through to millions of people - not reams of documentation about climate disasters and prospects, but a believable message about the changes that could correct present failings and especially about the behaviors that could win those changes, we passed the turning point.

> *Reverend, could you tell us, do you think we will win? When will we have won? And, in just a few last words, what is one lesson from this whole period that strikes you as particularly critical?*

I wouldn't tell anyone to stop praying for victory, but regardless of who does that, yes, people will continue to struggle and we will win. I think victory will be ours when we see belief and evidence lock arms. And the key lesson for me? How about history is a powerful container but courageous people transcend its bounds.

CHAPTER 30

SHIP AHOY

Miguel Guevara has a few final words.

Interviewing for RPS/2044, meeting the people, hearing their history, considering their insights, feeling their motivations, and sharing their confidence, has been incredibly instructive. I hope the lessons and inspiration I took will translate to whoever reads RPS/2044.

Many pages discuss consciousness raising because it dominated the initial RPS agenda. Many more pages discuss contesting for power because doing so became RPS's central focus as more people joined the struggle. Some have been about constructing new relations, and with an RPS national victory in 2044, I expect that construction will become the heart, soul, and spine of our living project as we, all together, build a new society and world.

In 2017, no one thought we could be where we are in 2042, but isn't that normal for massive fundamental change? Had the project taken longer - as it might in some different setting - I believe the upside would be that even delayed, even with more hurdles to overcome and more setbacks, the arc of history would nonetheless get essentially to where we are about to be.

In other cases the struggle might have different features, but wherever and whenever modern revolution happens, I expect it will achieve the same underlying liberation from all the old ties that bind. That is why my questions to the interviewees largely ignored details contingent on time and place and highlighted general and even near universal insights and lessons.

I thank, again, all the interviewees. And I thank you, dear reader, for getting to this point. I hope you will now take a little time to visit our book site at rps2044.org, to participate in furthering the prospects intimated in RPS/2044. You can use tools at the site to engage with one another and with the interviewees about whatever thoughts and ideas may strike you as needed. I hope to see you there!

At the start of this book I placed two verses of a favorite song. I think they fit well here at the end, too.

> Oh, the fishes will laugh
> As they swim out of the path
> And the seagulls they'll be smiling
> And the rocks on the sand
> Will proudly stand
> The hour that the ship comes in
>
> And the words that are used
> For to get the ship confused
> Will not be understood as they're spoken
> For the chains of the sea
> Will have busted in the night
> And will be buried at the bottom of the ocean

- Bob Dylan

AFTERWORD

Dear Reader,

We consider RPS/2044 a work in progress. As insights grow and time passes, it could improve as an indicative oral history. With greater creativity, it could also be improved by spawning a screenplay or novel portraying the same interviews, or, more ambitiously, one presenting RPS history, conveying many of the same events and characters in a more dramatic format.

The real measure of any work is what it motivates. With that in mind, we offer a website for this book's readers and contributors at rps2044.org. You can comment on any part of the book. You can offer reactions, criticisms, or even propose different wording for us to consider including in updates of the online version and for any new ebook version or new print edition. You can even post your own efforts to write a "story" or a screenplay version of any part, or of the whole of *RPS/2044*, or perhaps in parallel to it, or for a different country, altered as you might like. We have even thought about a possible movie title, *Good Will Winning*.

Finally, you can also ask questions for us, or for any of the interviewees using email sent to sysop@zmag.org, or using links at the *RPS/2044* site. Answers will appear publicly on the site.

Michael Albert, 2017
Miguel Guevara, 2042

POSTSCRIPT

In November 2044, Senator Malcolm King was elected President of the U.S. with his running mate, Governor Celia Curie. The following interview occurred on December 1, 2044.

> *Mr. President, what an incredible pleasure it must be for you to celebrate your victory and settle on invitations for joining your new Administration.*

Miguel, first, call me Malcolm…

> *I can't do that, it would be presumptuous.*

You can do it. And it would be sensible. Really, why should anyone call me Mr. President? If you call me Malcolm, officials tell us, you will slide toward rampaging disobedience. I see the situation differently. Deification denies respect. Calling me Mr. President would push you toward subservience. It would push me toward egomania. My name is Malcolm. Please use it.

> *Okay, Malcolm, a few weeks have passed since the election, how do you feel?*

Elated. Eager. Cautious. Enervated. But I know we won by a multi-year tsunami of energy and involvement. Ideas won. Program won. Vision won. Millions of volunteers and 100 million voters won.

> *Were you surprised?*

Thirty years ago, I would have said nothing like this was possible in my lifetime. Yet, here we are. We could discuss countless factors. We could consider the importance of the new portable lie detectors. How could justice lose when no candidate could lie without everyone knowing? But our election's primary dynamic was that hope overcame despair. Activism overcame passivity. Vision propelled hope. Sustained outreach created courage.

New ideas spread joy in barrooms and despair in backrooms. Soul searching bent minds. Radical activism established models and built organization oriented to continually win more. An unyielding, diminution of despair accelerated an avalanche of desire. From town to town, city to city, and state to state, that is what I saw.

When you first entered the Oval Office, what were your thoughts and feelings?

I didn't go into that oddly oriented room and feel awe at its celebrity. I didn't feel connected to a great governmental heritage. I didn't feel humbled being where so many past presidents had been. Their history is not mine. For me, being in the Oval Office was like being in a hall of horrors, not in a museum of good deeds.

I looked at the presidential portraits and saw an abyss. I looked at them and felt, how can I remove these pictures without being misunderstood? How can I put in their place pictures of those who resisted the machinations of past presidents? In the past two weeks I found beautiful art with just those attributes, and as soon I can remodel, I will go on TV and channel the late great Howard Zinn to explain my distaste at the past presidential portraits and my pleasure at the prospect of daily seeing the dissident people's art I will put up instead.

That may cause a ruckus, don't you think?

It may traumatize some citizens, I don't know. If it does, I will sympathize and explain, but, nonetheless, as we remake our future, while we need not beat ourselves up over our past, we should certainly come to grips with it.

It has been three weeks. What have you done, beyond planning to remodel?

Mostly, we have been finding people to fill posts and also considering which posts to eliminate or redefine. We have our program. We know our agenda. But we also know we can't do it all at once, much as we would like to, so we have also been assessing which aspects we should pursue first.

Should we quickly enlarge the Supreme Court by appointing a few new additional members since it makes zero sense to have anything less than a court of diversity to help usher in our new society?

Should we call for a constitutional convention so we can get right to the heart of redefining how our government works? RPS shadow governments have already blazed a path. Should we follow it immediately?

Should we not only re-name the Defense Department, the State Department, and various others, but immediately reconcile their roles with our revolutionary aspirations and appoint new Secretaries in accord?

Should we accelerate the ongoing transformation of our armed forces to socially worthy agendas?

Should we engage in massive prison pardons even as we renovate all aspects of the legal process into wise civility and redemption?

Should we immediately enlarge government programs seeking climate redemption, ecological balance, equitable allocation, and all the rest that our movement has focussed on?

Should we legalize all on-going workplace occupations and urge, aid, and defend new ones, also enforcing tax and other policy trends leading toward equitable, cooperative economics?

At the same time, should I get it firmly into my head and never forget that it isn't me doing any of that. It isn't he, she, them, or it. It is a vast social movement?

So when you ask about what we have done in the last three weeks, a good part has been finding folks to appoint to work in this government, who will not only admirably fulfill their responsibilities but who will also curb my tendency to ego-inflate and who will keep themselves and me in touch with popular energies and desires.

You have spent the whole campaign indicating your public intentions, but can you tell me your purely personal goals for the next four years?

To keep my head on straight, to honor the activists who went before us, to do my part in constructing our new society, and to help others in other parts of the world re-mold their societies as they decide.

Less personally, you and RPS members all over the country speak of this as a time of construction compared to recent years that you have called times of consciousness raising and contestation. Can you explain this?

When RPS first formed its relatively few members had beliefs seriously different from those of their neighbors, schoolmates, workmates, and often even from their relatives. Our emphasis had to be reaching out, discussing those differences, and raising consciousness.

That aspect of seeking change will never end, but as steadily more people became aroused and involved it became possible to mount struggles for immediate albeit limited changes. We increasingly contested authorities for gains. As our struggles became larger and more effective, they became the defining aspect of our work. We were still raising consciousness, but our deeds started to be more instrumental to our growth.

As we kept growing, and kept contesting, in time we became able to create and maintain innovative new structures both for immediate benefit and also as models and seeds of a better future. That aspect then steadily grew in importance, even as the other two persisted. We constructed, and now construction has become preponderant.

Seen this way, there are three aspects or moments, to our revolutionary process - and probably to any revolutionary process - and while all three always operate, the weight of focus and accomplishment tends to shift. We started mainly consciousness raising. We moved to mainly contesting. Finally, we will mainly construct. Revolution advances from chronicling nightmares that defer desirable dreams, to winning elements of desirable dreams, to making desirable dreams reality.

Returning to now, do you have special plans for Inauguration Day?

It should be joyful but it won't be if ten million folks come to DC for the day. That many people, no matter how mutually supportively they act, would overwhelm facilities. Yet we know even more than ten million want to attend events to share their joy. Why so many?

The revolution's joyous want to come. And that's not just activists but rebels and rakes. It's outcasts, the gentle, the kind. It's poets and painters, bricklayers and truck drivers. It's saints and sinners too. Indeed, which un-harmful, gentle soul won't want to come? Our chimes are going to toll loud and long. Who won't want to hear them up close?

History has till now been so harsh and unkind that too many people will want to dance in the streets of our little town, which is why we are having events in all states, and in fact in all counties in the U.S. And I suspect there will be celebrations around the world as well, partly because other countries are on their own roads to their own transformations, and partly in the celebratory knowledge that the U.S. is going to do its share to reset the international table by setting aside our missiles. How does it go: We shall beat our swords into plowshares, and our spears into pruning hooks. We shall not lift up sword against nation, neither shall we learn war any more.

In 2000, to mark the changing of the century, there were events around the world. Each celebrant country and population partied in its own way. I envision something like that happening. Why not? We aren't celebrating an abstract, arbitrary date. We are celebrating a decades-long struggle, a centuries long struggle, that is now embarked on creating new history. We are riding the arc of history, at last. We are not embarking on year 2045, but on year 1.

We will have people from government positions at as many of the celebrations as we can manage, and people deeply involved in RPS will attend all of them, of course. There won't be one jet bomber in the air. Not one drone. It won't be self congratulatory pomp and circumstance.

But you are perhaps asking only about the Washington event. And here, while it will be up to those doing the planning and those attending, and I imagine it will be raucous but also determined, and I hope we can have one part of it left for me to handle. The music playlist. I want to choose that! And I want it to play loud and long with entries going way back in our history and stretching to the present. I want it to remember suffering, honor struggles, and foreshadow liberation. Music matters, and I would like the honor and responsibility of settling on the inauguration playlist.

> *So I get that you are redesigning your office walls, resetting the chimes, selecting guardians of your program and your public connection and service, and researching songs. But once you take office, what is your highest priority for your first hundred days?*

Pursuing the campaigns I mentioned earlier, plus ensuring that the second hundred and the tenth hundred days, and the years after, also come off as they ought to.

> *Thank you, Malcolm. I know you have to rush off now but I would like to say I think you will have no trouble earning the informed respect you favor and contributing to creating the positive new relations we all desire.*

I am glad to hear you feel that way, because I would like to respectfully request that you join me in the endeavor as my Press Secretary. After all, you have interviewed me and many others, asking questions we have had to answer. Now it is your turn to do the answering. You can start fielding questions the day after inauguration from your compatriots in media who I hope will be as insightful in what they wish to know as you have been.

> *I am at a loss for words. I had no idea. I don't know what to say... I haven't been interviewed, vetted, nothing...*

Consider this your interview. Consider your past public involvement your vetting. Say yes. You will do great.

Alright, okay, how could I possibly not try to help. I am humbled and I will strive to do my best for a better future, but there is just one thing. Don't expect me to ever say I serve at the pleasure of the President. I can only be Press Secretary if I serve the interests of the people, the revolution, and the future. Your personal pleasure, or even permission, has to have nothing to do with my daily choices. Is that acceptable?

It is not only acceptable. It is my preference. Welcome to the administration.

ADDENDUM

Excerpt from Miguel Guevara's
Press Briefing, April 9, 2045

Good morning. As usual we have a lot of ground to cover so let's begin.

If you will bear with me a minute, I would like to offer a few words before taking your questions.

Yesterday President Malcolm King spoke to the UN General Assembly and the world. His speech was simple, emotional, and even blunt. It reflected unfolding events and aspirations.

In the first part he apologized. In the second part he promised. In the third part he celebrated. In the conclusion he embraced.

The apologies were for our country's military and fiscal role in international mayhem and injustice from World War II and before to the present, from Latin America to Asia and from Europe to Africa. He apologized for Korea, the Philippines, Indonesia, Guyana, Vietnam, Cambodia, Laos, the Congo/Zaire, Brazil, the Dominican Republic, Cuba, Chile, Greece, East Timor, Nicaragua, Grenada, El Salvador, Libya, Panama, Iraq, Afghanistan, Haiti, Yugoslavia, Iran, Venezuela, Somalia, Syria, and more. He apologized for our support of dictators, exploitative extractions, arms shipments and arms use, threats, boycotts, and destruction, for our massacring native Americans, our slavery and racism, our sexism and sexual predation, and for Hiroshima, Nagasaki, and more.

He promised to reverse our history of exploitation and violence toward others and in its place enact a new agenda of sharing and respect. He promised we would study war no more and instead foster solidarity and mutual aid with the same energy and effort that we previously put to war making and profit seeking. He promised and evidenced an entirely new and compassionate, internationalist mindset.

He celebrated transforming our defining institutions of polity, economy, culture, and kinship, and our relation to the natural environment to remove hierarchies of wealth and power and to attain a sustainable new historical beginning.

He embraced all those who have already or who will now take up similar aims, as they deem suitable, worldwide. Amidst our tremendous, sustaining, and enriching diversity, Malcolm urged that we also need to embrace our shared universal humanity. We need to celebrate and apply our shared values of human liberation - solidarity, diversity, equity, self management, international peace, and environmental balance - to our own countries, each in mutual aid with the rest.

He urged that we let go of greed and profit seeking, self aggrandizement and power wielding, and together usher in a new time of joyous exploration of our capacities. Malcolm embraced all who will do so, and the UN itself as a valuable tool for the task.

Now, if you have questions…yes, Leslie, why don't you begin…

THE INTERVIEWEES

Below are brief biographies of our many interviewees. My gratitude goes to these revolutionaries for sharing their insights. To get to know them has been an incredible honor. In case you haven't already noticed, their names pay homage to some admirable figures from history: Alexander Berkman, Emma Goldman, Malcolm X, Martin Luther King Jr., Fred Hampton, Rosa Parks, Norman Bethune, Richard Feynman, Harriet Tubman, John Lennon, Anton Pannekoek, Rudolf Rocker, Rosa Luxembourg, Bertrand Russell, David Dellinger, Celia Sanchez, Madame Curie, Amilcar Cabral, W.E.B. Dubois, William Kuntsler, Howard Zinn, Stokely Carmichael, and Leonard Cohen.

RPS/2044 also pays tribute, again merely by way of names, to some people from our time: Juliet Schor, Andrej Grubacic, Bill Fletcher, Cynthia Peters, Barbara Ehrenreich, Mark Evans, Lydia Sargent, Peter Bohmer, Stephen Shalom, Robin Hahnel, Leslie Cagan, Noam Chomsky, and Bob Dylan.

Beyond paying respects, none of the characters in *RPS/2044* are modeled on, or even at all reflective of, much less do they speak for or try to represent anyone listed above.

First Appearing in Chapter 1: First Steps

Juliet Berkman, a militant feminist born in 1993, became politically engaged roughly in parallel with the emergence of RPS. A workplace and union organizer known for her effective advocacy of non violent tactics and her ability to talk with understanding and sympathy to people holding seriously contrary views, Juliet has been centrally involved with RPS from its earliest days and a shadow Secretary of Labor.

Andrej Goldman, an economist and activist born in 1987, was radicalized some years before RPS's emergence and has been closely involved for its duration. He has held various movement jobs, staff positions, and other odd jobs for income while writing numerous books and articles and teaching in various institutions. Deeply involved in the process of arriving at and continually revising RPS program and vision, Andrej is well placed to talk about the history of each.

First Appearing in Chapter 2: Overcoming Cynicism

Senator Malcolm King born in 1985, was an avid student of history by schooling, an assembly worker and cook by early employment. He became a political candidate and ultimately a U.S. Senator. Malcolm was attracted to RPS and became a member, then a prominent activist, and thereafter ran for office within the Democratic Party in Ohio. Later, he became the first highly placed national office holder to use his position and abilities to propel RPS platform.

First Appearing in Chapter 3: Getting Started

Mayor Bill Hampton, born in 1997, became highly active in immigration and anti racist politics and then became involved in RPS, not least focusing on issues of city life, transportation, and urban planning which he was active in conceiving and organizing for. In time, he became a prominent inner city activist and local candidate, and then Mayoral candidate, and finally Mayor of New York City.

First Appearing in Chapter 6: The First Convention

Cynthia Parks, born in 1992, watched her family lose their modest home in 1998 due to the housing crash of the time. Years later she became an advocate for inexpensive quality public housing. She became, as well, a staunch proponent of what was then called rights for the city and has worked within RPS ever since on related programs and organizing and staffing diverse campaigns. A militant activist, a tireless staff contributor to project after project, Cynthia was the secretary of housing in the second RPS shadow government.

First Appearing in Chapter 9: Housing & Rights to the City

Harriet Lennon, born in 2000, has been a grassroots organizer of extreme effectivity to the point of also being a trainer for other organizers. Harriet started her activism in local communities fighting evictions and, at the same time, developing consciousness of housing issues that later merged into larger scale demands and campaigns, without ever losing track, however, of the local dimension. Harriet became very active, in particular, with food organizing and delivery, a protector and advocate of the defenseless.

First Appearing in Chapter 10: Actor's Activism

Governor Celia Curie, born in 1994 and an aspiring actress at the time of the first RPS convention, became highly active in RPS while a successful actress in Hollywood, not least in politically inspired films, including her famous Oscar acceptance speech. She became, in time, and for a time, Secretary of Popular Culture for the RPS shadow government, a Cabinet position created specifically for RPS purposes, after which she also became actual Governor of California.

First Appearing in Chapter 11: Health and Class

Barbara Bethune, born in 1992, became a medical doctor and researcher questioning from the very start her profession. Barbara's early involvement in RPS solidified her purpose as revolutionizing health care, a focus she has retained since, not least as an RPS shadow government Secretary of Health.

Mark Feynman, born in 1990, became a nurse by trade. Mark has been a strong advocate for working class politics, highlighting the interface between nurses and doctors and between workers and members of the coordinator class. Mark has been in RPS from its inception and a pivotal figure in both its class commitments and its workplace and worker constituency organizing.

First Appearing in Chapter 12: Athletics and Religion

Peter Cabral, born in 1978, has long been a militant anti racist activist. Peter focused in the years before RPS on police violence and prison policy, including inmate organizing. He was active in RPS from its inception and focused much energy on ensuring RPS program and internal culture provided seeds of a racism free inter communalism. After a time in prison himself, and not least due to his activism while inside and continuing activism after his release, Peter became a tireless speaker, organizer, and activist for community affairs and prison and legal change. He served as Secretary of the Interior in RPS shadow government, as well. And with all that, Peter was also a professional ballplayer for a time.

Reverend Stephen Du Bois, born in 2001, was a seminary student at the time of the first RPS convention. Stephen became a priest in a progressive church in San Francisco. Famous for his hunger strike efforts, he became highly influential and active in the development of RPS policies regarding religion and also ecology.

First Appearing in Chapter 13: Courageous Courtrooms

Robin Kunstler, born in 1971, was a criminal trial lawyer with many major crime cases for experience. Robin rebelled at the injustices of the criminal justice system and became active not only in aiding RPS members accosted by the state, but also in developing RPS conceptions and policies bearing on judicial affairs, including becoming the first Shadow Supreme Court Justice.

First Appearing in Chapter 14: Media Makeovers

Leslie Zinn, born in 1978, has been an accomplished media personality on both TV and radio, famous for resisting incursions on free speech, Leslie advanced RPS policies and analysis not only about media, but in all matters, ably using her shows for the purpose.

First Appearing in Chapter 15: Early Economic Campaigns

Anton Rocker, born in 1987, was a student of linguistics and cognitive science and a prolific writer, before joining RPS, Anton's focus on workplace attitudes and roles played an important role in shaping the emergence of RPS workplace program and activism. Anton became, in time, and for a time, Secretary of Labor for the RPS shadow government.

First Appearing in Chapter 16: Concepts

Lydia Luxemburg, 93 when I interviewed her, was born in 1946 and became political in the great upheavals of the 1960s. Lydia has held many jobs over the course of her life but in just a few minutes of our time together it was clear that only one was permanent and basic to her motivations and perceptions, that of revolutionary. Life-long feminist, activist, organization builder, and media worker, she is one of the best RPS participants for addressing its past and future contours, including having been its first shadow government President.

First Appearing in Chapter 17: Values

Bertrand Dellinger, born in 1966, was politicized by his no nukes and anti war activism. He became a key advocate of RPS from its inception, and like Lydia is exceptionally well placed to discuss virtually every aspect of its development. Bertrand has been a university professor of physics and world renowned contributor to physics theory, as well as a social critic and militant activist his entire adult life. He was shadow Vice President during Lydia Luxembourg's term as president, and later had his own term as shadow President, as well.

First Appearing in Chapter 18: Defining Ourselves

Dylan Cohen, born in 1981, ex military, became a writer activist focused on understanding and relating constructively to working class and particularly military service-related agendas. Relating strongly to other ex military, Dylan became involved with peace movements but also with campaigns aimed at military and police structure and policy.

First Appearing in Chapter 19: Gender and Race

Noam Carmichael, born in 1995, was active in media and public speaking before joining RPS. Noam's written work focuses on popular culture and broad social trends, especially issues of political participation and race. In RPS, his work has emphasized raising consciousness, developing organizing projects, media, and aiding RPS internal relations.

Made in the USA
San Bernardino, CA
21 April 2018